LONESOME ROAD

One Among the Indians

The Strange House at Newburyport

Darkness Over the Land

Dougal Looks for Birds

James the Vine Puller

Tana and the Useless Monkey

The Star in the Forest

Sarah the Dragon Lady

Kate of Still Waters

LONESOME ROAD

Martha Bennett Stiles

GNOMON

The characters in this novel are fictional.
Any resemblance to actual people
is a coincidence.

FIRST EDITION

ISBN 0-917788-69-9
LCCC 98-70542

Published by
GNOMON PRESS
P.O. BOX 475
FRANKFORT
KENTUCKY
40602-0475

For Alfred and Martha Armstrong,
J. T. Baldwin and Bernice Speese,
of the College of William and Mary—
their generosity to students like me
can never be surpassed or repaid.

LONESOME ROAD

"And I look down the road, and the road look narrow.
 And I look down the road, and the road look long.
 And I look down the road, and the road look lonesome.
 Ain't nobody here can go there with me."

April frost glitters where the shadow of the mailbox and its post paints a gallows on the hard earth. A boy stands where the shadow almost touches his toes. He is considering climbing the fence that separates him from the field where a gray mare quietly grazes. She is due to foal soon; he would give his baseball not to be leaving her. Suddenly his head turns.

From the field a killdeer cries out. The boy's mother loves these boomerang-winged birds who, like her, were once creatures of the shore. The boy scarcely hears them; he is listening for danger.

The boy imagines that the mailbox is a tree which he has planted, and that at any moment men with axes may drive their Jeep into view over the rise where the big yellow Bourbon County bus appears at that hour every school day. The men will want to chop down the tree. He hears them shout first orders, then threats. He knows what they want, though they speak only Korean. When he stands resolute between them and the tree, they try to kill him. There are five of them. With his book bag he knocks their axes aside, one after another. When he gets his hands on one of these axes, the men scramble back into their Jeep.

The car that slows to a stop beside the boy is a 1980 Chevrolet with the battle flag of the Confederacy—the flag of half his great-great-grandfathers—fluttering from its antenna. The boy has stopped signaling base camp with his walkie-talkie.

The Chevrolet's idling engine is even louder than its radio. Born to lose, *the radio whines with belligerent self-pity. Despite the chill, the driver has rolled down his front windows. His car sits out at night, and he doesn't fool with wiping off the damn condensation.*

The driver is in his twenties. His jaw is lean and winter reddened; it has a sullen slackness. He wears a blue shirt faded from many launderings, none recent. His sleeves are rolled up, revealing muscular forearms, their hair too light to obscure the work of the Panama City tattoo artist who was probably the only person in that country who gave him his money's worth, though he spent all that

3

he had. He eyes the boy through kinky bangs. "Hey Lang," he asks, "you talking to the mailbox?"

Lang's best friend Breck's bus stop is just around the corner. Lang chafes at his parents' rule that he may not walk there unescorted. Offered a lift, he barely hesitates.

Breck is still inside. He is telling his mother that he doesn't need his jacket and she is zipping it up on him when the rusty Chevrolet drives by without stopping.

Ten years ago at Saratoga the mockingbird sang in the moon-blanched roses all night long. Grove and I, newly wed, were already too well-advised to imagine that our future lay before us like a land of dreams, but it seems now that we did spend the next nine and a half years sleepwalking. Not even sirens shrieking through the night woke me. I heard them, but my trance went on, almost three more days.

The night I heard the sirens scream by our farm, the April moon was rather like my life, not perfectly full, but so nearly, that a casual observer would have thought it so. A few hours earlier I had walked to our barn under that fair moon, with Grove safely home for the night, with our son and daughter asleep in their beds, our three mares, all pregnant, in their stalls. Surely it would have been difficult then not to feel that Grove and I had been granted a divine dispensation.

Now it is June, and our mares stay out at night with their foals. Now the barn's big doors stand open to catch as much as possible of the wind that was an enemy in April. Now the enemy is something else.

The night I heard the sirens, I was sitting up with our youngest mare, "Thankless," because she was due to foal in nine days. I customarily take the first shift, and Grove, who gets home tired from his veterinary rounds, takes the second. We can observe the foaling stall without leaving the warm tack room, through a window in their joint wall, and I had brought a book and a coffee thermos, and a letter from our son's godmother, Eva von Strehlenau, that I meant to answer before I permitted myself to open either. Katisha, our elder barn cat, had darted into the tack room between my feet, settling herself lovingly in my lap the minute I sat down. My lap is warmer than a concrete floor.

Eva von Strehlenau was my favorite roommate at the University of Kentucky. When my parents gave me a trip to Europe for graduation, I flew to Munich, where Eva had promised not to begin her "pencil-sharpening job" until she and her handsome brother had introduced me to the seats of Western culture. Four years later, about the time I married Grove Brough (it rhymes with tough), Eva was promoted to editor. I sent her the little rectangular Bigelow carpet sample from our new house, along with one of Bigelow's cartoon ads. In our letters to each other, I dilate on Eva's "title on the door" and she dilates on my beautiful horses and children, but the truth is that each of us chose what she most wanted.

Is it not ironic, that letter I was answering mused, *that the girl from the USA with its Equality for Women, Careers for Women, Power for Women, turns out all* Kinder und Küche *while Mr. G. B. Shaw's "worthy, respectable, dutiful German" is picking up men at the races at 34? And dropping them as fast as hot rivets, never fear, and scurrying back to her "title on the door."*

A rhetorical question, but I laid down Eva's letter and contemplated Thankless, phlegmatically chomping her hay. With a son, a daughter, five thoroughbreds and two cats, I had supposed that my letters were lively.

My local contemporaries, too many of them, give me free advice and ask questions beginning "But don't you—"

Women of my mother's generation approve of my choice of professions. In February, when Grove and both children had been down with rotten colds, I had suggested to Eva that such approval came from vixens with bloody brush-stumps, gratified to see a fresh tail in the trap. "Never try to be funny in a letter," my mother counselled my brother and me when we were growing up. "The person who gets the letter can't see your expression or hear your tone of voice, and may not know that you're joking." Eva always knows. Page one of the letter I had just laid down was an ink sketch of a tail-less vixen smugly knitting four booties.

As a schoolgirl, I planned on having all the children my husband could afford. Beyond pre-teen thoughts about how nice it would be when I was discovered to have a peerless soprano voice, I never envisioned any other job for myself than bringing up children. I savored the picture of myself in beautiful gowns on the stages of the major cities of the world, but I never took singing lessons. I read every column on child-rearing that passed before my eyes.

My voice is and has always been very ordinary.

In college, I became "aware" and "responsible" and lowered my demands on the earth's resources to what just three children would consume, no matter how rich a man I married. I would have one of each sex. For the third I was graciously prepared to accept whichever side of the coin faced up. Grove's enthusiasm let me give myself permission for a fourth, possibly one of the things that had made me love him.

Page two of Eva's letter was encouraging me about my plans for my daughter, who will be old enough to go to kindergarten come September. Already friends had been asking if I would go back to my old desk at *The Blood-Horse*. I preferred, as I had told Eva, to teach Joanna to read myself and have that one more year with her.

We didn't send Lang to kindergarten.

The most rewarding work, I told Kat silently, *is the work for which one is uniquely suited. You are uniquely suited to killing mice. I am uniquely suited to being Lang Brough's mother, Grove Brough's wife, Joanna Brough's mother. Because I love them more than anyone else can love them. Because I care intensely about every snarl in their hair, every inflection in their voices, every smile, more than I care about anything else in the world. They are my* "without which nothing."

Around ten the wind began to rise, rattling the barn's end doors. For the sake of diversion, I leaned over to dial the local weather recording. I tried not to jiggle the sleeping Kat, but she abandoned me in disgust.

For a second I thought the line was dead. Then I heard Grove's low laughter and reflexively hung up. I remember the laugh well — half delighted, half bemused. My deserted lap felt cold. Time to replenish everybody's hay, I decided. By the time I reclaimed my chair from Kat, the wind had quieted. There was no reason to pick up the telephone again.

When sirens screamed by at quarter of two, I supposed there

had been another wreck on Russell Cave Road. The last one killed a teenager coming home from too much party, coming home in his first car, his birthday present. He was sixteen and had had his license three days. I thanked God Lang was in his bunk, safe, from that, for eight more years.

We were all four safe that night.

~❧2❧~

Horse vets are pre-dawn risers. At 5:35 the morning after the sirens, I was caroling "Sun's up" at Lang's door.

"Son's up!" Lang called back. This ritual joke, his own, marked him as my child. Jokes and Grove repel each other before breakfast (and Joanna is going to be just like him).

In April I have to draw a whole gallon of water before the water begins to run warm enough to wash my hands. I know, because I catch and use it in the humidifier. When we used to laugh a lot, this was one of the things Grove laughed at.

How could someone so compulsively careful about details as I—one gallon of water!—be so careless about things of infinite importance?

As Grove and Lang took off their barn boots that April morning, I could tell by their faces that Grove didn't think any of the mares was about to bless us early. Officially, our best mare had sixteen days to go before foaling; her dam, twenty-three, and Thankless, eight. "Stuffed their guts all night," Grove announced, and set the empty coffee thermos on the counter. "Is there more?"

He had drunk a quart since relieving me at two o'clock, and his eyes were bloodshot.

"That Thankless is so dumb," Lang followed Grove into the kitchen to tell me. "When I go to feed her she gets in between me and her feed tub. I'm only trying to help her and she makes me hit her every day."

"Just like a woman," said his father.

Lang cut his eye at me. I made my best tigress face. He smirked, wrinkling the little scar that he picked up last summer. "I wish

8

Thankless would hurry up and foal. I promised Breck he can come see it when she does. Is that OK?"

"Promise first, ask later," observed his father.

"Breck is welcome." I sidestepped the issue of sequence. "But remember: you wait for that bus by your own mailbox. No running down that public road at rush hour to wait at Breck's."

"Honey, you've been telling him that every day for a week. Just tell him once and if he forgets, land on him. Let him do the worrying. He's younger than you."

Lang put on one of his own standard repertoire, the *100% unjustly attacked* face. He had never disobeyed our order since we realized we needed to give it. "Hey, I forgot that," I answered Grove, "he's getting so tall."

"Tall!" Grove laid his hand flat on top of Lang's head. "He's a midget. He just combs his hair straight up to fool you."

In fact, his crown is nearly level with my shoulders. Less than a foot and he won't have to look up when he gives me backchat. "Two minutes of seven, giraffe," I warned him. "Time to shave off that mustache and go."

He dropped his napkin on the floor, wiped the cocoa off his upper lip with the back of his hand, and ran for his book bag and baseball cap.

At 7:10 I took the binoculars off the sideboard, where they live for quick appraisals of the front field (dubious horse behavior; trespassing dogs; seldom-seen birds) and focused them on our mailbox. I had done this daily for the past ten school days—ever since Grove, driving back from a dawn C-section, had seen that red baseball cap at the Smith mailbox, a quarter of a mile from home.

Yes, he had gone to play there before. Whenever the bus was late. No, it had not occurred to him that this might not be OK. "I don't walk *on* the road, I walk *beside* the road."

I remember how the backs of my knees felt light, how my mind's eye saw his body flying through the air, his blood. I wanted to grab him by both shoulders—to keep him safe, to shake him. Such visions are a legacy of my brother's violent death, I guess. I kept my voice reasonable. "You can't walk any further from the road than David Trimble's fence, and you saw what somebody's truck did to that last summer. You think you'd be harder to bust up than a stone fence?"

Focusing my binoculars through our dining room window on a red cap, I admonished myself that Grove was right: telling Lang once was enough. The boy under the red cap was standing straight as the mailbox post beside him. "Is he there?" Grove asked quietly.

"Like a soldier."

We smiled at each other, the immemorial helpless smile of parents, in which pain, joy, pride, and astonishment intermingle like the colors of sunrise.

The long yellow school bus groaned to a halt. In my mind's ear I heard the cheerful frog-chorus of the children already aboard, the wheezing open and slamming shut of the door. The bus shuddered on. Grove and I verified that Joanna still slept, then we went to the barn.

When we could joke, Grove liked to predict that Joanna will sleep through the Second Coming, if He comes before 8 a.m.

"Wash the pregnant mare's udder daily," says the book Grove gave me our first Christmas. "This massage accustoms her to the treatment she will get from her foal, and...."

Anyone can groom our old mare and her valuable daughter unassisted, but the gray mare is a horse of a different choler. We call her Thankless because her registered name is "La Dame Sans Merci." We assume the breeder omitted the "Belle" only because the Jockey Club rejects names that fill over eighteen spaces — there's nothing wrong with Thankless's looks. Grove bought her, in foal for the first time, last November. In April, she was still tossing her head at the glimpse of a washcloth. Eight days before she was due to be surprised by joy, her evasive leaps were as breathtaking as any gazelle's, or Giselle's. "She'll never nurse," Grove kept assuring me.

"Thankless will be a fine mother once she sees the foal," I kept assuring *him*. I remember weeping the first time I was pregnant because various ambivalences made me dread that I would not love our child properly, that it would somehow sense my reservations from the way I held it as it nursed, and so would grow up criminal.

"There are more things in heaven and earth," I told Grove, "than are dreamt of at Ohio State University vet school."

I led Thankless to join the other two mares in the front field, and Grove put out the colts.

Already last fall Grove had warned me off attempting to lead Ten. "Ten is too dangerous," he said.

"Ten is too *valuable*," I amended. Whether Ten is nicknamed for Tennessee Williams or Bo Derek depends on who asks. He is the best colt we have ever bred — handsome enough, Grove had assured me, for August's select Saratoga auction. We've never before raised a yearling good enough for that sale. This was going to be our most joyful summer since the one when Lang was born. If Ten had jerked free of me and taken off, he wouldn't have had to break a leg or collide with the front end of a truck on Clay Pike to devastate our hopes. Just a little scrape keeps a yearling out of the summer sales. It's no accident that the colts' spring pasture is behind the house where they're inaccessible to the kind of driver who pulls over and fires his shotgun for the joy of making big animals run. Such an idiot paused long enough on Holcomb Road one day to put a plastic bag over a Secretariat yearling's head and presumably stood there laughing (or salivating) while it ran itself to death. A yearling will walk up to the fence to see what the stranger with the bag has, but a mare will keep her foal the field's width away.

Why have I not been as good a mother as the stupidest mare alive?

A stream cuts our front field in two, and from our bedroom, on the east end of the house, we can see where it continues across our eastern neighbor's road and drains into a succession of little ponds that catch the moonlight like an opal necklace. In the South Carolina Low Country where I was born, such ponds would nurture egrets, white and sharp as ecstasy. Here in Central Kentucky they host blackbirds by summer and herons all year round and, of course, horses. During foaling season we pasture our mares in our front field because, except for a bit that curves around the east end of the house, it is visible from our dining room and kitchen windows.

Grove left for his rounds Tuesday morning at quarter of eight as usual. Ervil Knecht, our farm hand, was just turning in the driveway.

Ervil, we have since found out, has an honorable discharge from the United States Army, and no record at the National Crime Information Center. Ervil, we think, we all think, is clean.

Joanna has never been afraid of him.

My sewing room, at the west end of our house, is where we shelve the children's books. Its view is of a vegetable garden beside a dozen fruit trees, and beyond them, our barn. Once Lang started school Joanna became avid to learn to read; every weekday after breakfast she comes to the sewing room for a half hour lesson. I sit at the machine my mother gave me for an engagement present, because if I proposed to marry a *horse* doctor (instead of an ambassador), I had certainly better learn to make my own clothes. Joanna sits in front of the little portable blackboard on which I chalk her texts.

When I began to teach Lang his letters, our doctor warned me that the print in school primers can be too small for preschoolers. Primers bored Lang, so I began making up my own lessons. I add only one sound per lesson, whether a new letter sound or a new diphthong. Otherwise, anything goes. "A charming rich French charioteer" isn't your standard primer hero, but Joanna races right along with mine.

I didn't teach Lang to read until his fifth birthday. Joanna has always walked faster in the trail he has broken for her. I remind myself of this whenever I'm tempted to think her precocious.

On Tuesdays, Joanna reads into our tape recorder, so she can hear how well she's doing. In late April, she was working on f. "A foolish fop," she was reading when the oven timer commenced its implacable signal: 8:45, time to check the mares.

The mares were out of sight from the dining room and kitchen; I walked unworried toward the bedroom, brisk only because Joanna was waiting. Then I heard a horse scream.

What I saw as I entered the bedroom sent me diving for the intercom.

The mares were milling like an assaulted ants' nest close by their fence. Opposite them, in the colts' field across the safety lane, the bay colt reared and plunged, screaming and striking with his forelegs at a thick and powerfully built white horse confronting him across his fence, answering him scream for scream and lunge for lunge. Behind the bay, the chestnut colt raced in frenzied circles. As I reached for the intercom call button, the bay colt's hoofs struck wood and slid to earth, spared only by chance from going between the fence planks and snapping a cannon bone.

I pressed an SOS, but knew that if Ervil had the tractor going, he would never hear. "Loose horse!" I called to Joanna as I ran for the front door. "You *stay in that room!*" I threw open the door just in time to see Ervil running out of the barn, chain shank in one hand, feed bucket in the other. By the time I got to them, the horse had his head in the bucket and the shank on his halter. I knew the horse—Luke. It belonged to Zad Thacker, our neighbor a couple of miles down the road. "Shove him in a stall," I gasped, "and come help me check for wounds."

The mares were dark with sweat and their distended veins were like mountain ranges on a bas-relief map, but only the mare who is number one in the pecking order and confronts threats first was injured—Ten's dam, naturally, our most valuable mare. Kicking at the stallion through the boards, she had scraped one shin and gashed a hind leg. I smeared both wounds with salve and we turned to the colts. "Uncle first," I directed. Uncle wasn't the one whom a simple scrape could keep out of that summer sale and cost us thousands of dollars, but he was the one I had seen strike the fence.

Both of us felt both forelegs, and I thanked God reflexively in silent childish language that dear Uncle had been spared one of those bone-breaks which, for all man's care, is the horse's death. Through some marvel, there was no fracture, through some marvel we simply accept—as we must accept our equally inexplicable tragedies.

Ten didn't have a mark on him.

I believe that for a scared second Ervil thought I was going to embrace him.

Ervil got back to his stall cleaning, and I returned to the house to spring Joanna. Woe if my literal-minded daughter needs to go to the bathroom while under orders to stay exactly where she is.

The voice that answered the telephone at Hereward Stud, Grove's first daily stop, wasn't Farm Secretary Fran Warren's, but that of her new assistant.

Even before I left my job at *The Blood-Horse,* I knew Fran as a voice that called to ask current advertising rates four times a year, and now that I've been married to Hereward's vet for ten years, Fran and I are as near to old friends as I can ever come in Kentucky. We are comrades in two enterprises, which are inseparable, for us—shaking a living out of the thoroughbred industry, and cosseting Grove Brough—and there isn't much difference between what we say and what we mean when we talk to each other.

The new assistant's voice reacted as to a call from the Chairman of the Board's wife, begged for the privilege of getting on the other line and checking with all the barns for Grove's location if I didn't mind holding, please, just for a minute, Mrs. Brough.

"Want Himself?" Fran would have said. "Hang onto your pants while I track him down." That respectful new voice made me feel matronly.

"Will you be passing this way for lunch?" I asked Grove.

Silence. Then: "Barn 8 had a filly this morning that can't stay up to nurse, plus they've got six mares for me to check for breeding. As soon as I'm through here, I've got to go to Blue Hill; one of their studs fell off a mare and—"

Much later I tried to decide if there'd been a particular reason that spring day for this song and dance about where he meant to lunch. All I'd expected was a yes or no. "I'm asking because we've got a couple of minor casualties here that you might want Ervil to give shots if you aren't—"

"*Ten?*"

"Untouched." All the way to my inner ear I could feel his relief like sunshine from the earphone. "Uncle took some bites, and the pride of the farm gashed her left stifle. Nothing to curdle her colostrum."

"I hate like hell to give a mare an antibiotic so close to foaling, but go ahead and have Ervil give Uncle a shot. How'd they get hurt?"

"Zad Thacker's Luke came to call. We've got him in the barn."

Grove's response was unprintable, or would have been a generation ago, and I didn't blame him. Letting a stallion loose on a breeding farm like ours could put it out of business in an hour.

Zad answered his telephone himself. "Thank the Lord, Ruth; we didn't know where he'd got to. His gate got knocked down while we were puttin' out the far. You know we had a far last night?"

I winced at the tightening that is always my gut's response to word of fire on a horse farm. "No! *Wait*—was it right before two?"

"Sumpn like that. You hear the sireens?"

A horse is so beautiful and large, it's hard even for someone who has examined an equine skull to believe that his brain isn't much bigger than an opossum's, but when fire frightens a horse, he has one of two responses. In his stall, his response is *No one shall prize me out of my sanctuary.* Out of it, his response is *Get back in it,* and he will run through flames to do that. Sometimes, at the risk of being trampled to death, you can blindfold a horse and lead him to safety (for all he knows, you're leading him round and round within his magic circle), but once his eyes are uncovered, he will almost always find some way to break free and run back to his stall. It is almost impossible to save horses from a stable fire. And they scream.

"It was that storage shed back 'ere behind the barn," said Zad, "where I keep straw. Did keep."

"What about the barn, Zad?"

"Never did catch. Far company hosed that side that faced the shed, you know, so wouldn't no sparks—"

"Horses all OK, then?"

"Them old sireens gottem upset is all."

Now I just wanted Zad to hang up, so I could call Grove back. I'd never forgive myself if Grove groused to somebody about his irresponsible neighbor and the grouse got back to Zad.

Fortunately, Grove is the most discreet man I know, both by nature and because his work takes him back and forth between farms whose owners are related and connected in all manner of ways which Grove's mere twelve years in Central Kentucky couldn't possibly enable him to master. Questions like who is financing what, who is sleeping with what, who has hated whom for two months or two generations, make a minefield of Grove's practice. Therefore he is discreet.

At least about his professional life.

"And all them people come to watch the shed burn didn't quiet 'em none. You wouldn't believe how many people's on the road at two a.m. till you have you a far. That's how Luke come to get loose; somebody backed a car right through that gate, and we didn't see it till daylight. I was so worried about the foaling mares, I never even thought about him. Listen, Ruth, he didn't do you no damage, did he? I'll pay for it. He didn't hurt none of your horses, did he?"

"No, no, no; everything's under control. Listen, how did that shed come to catch fire?"

Zad didn't answer at once. "Farchief said a lots of times it'll be faulty warrin'."

"I didn't know you had lights in that shed."

"Didn't."

I felt sick. Either an arsonist hates his victim and will do something else to him shortly — sand in the gas tanks, broached fences, poisoned dog — or he's insane and there's no knowing where the next fire will be set or when, only that it is sure to flame.

There is an oak tree three-quarters of the way from our barn to the pike. Joanna began meeting Lang every afternoon in late March, and she gloried in setting off by herself. "You may meet Lang at that oak," we told her. "Not one step beyond." We thought, we both thought, we should strive to allow Joanna as much independence as was safe to give her. We thought letting her meet Lang in good weather was reasonable. We actually thought that.

At three o'clock Tuesday afternoon I helped Joanna get into her wraps, and she trudged off. I made cocoa. The children arrived for it together, which never failed to move me. My own beloved brother

Langdon was patient and loving with me too, but not when I was four. Somebody called him "nursie," and he was embarrassed to be seen on the street with me. Had I been content to walk a dissociating distance behind, he would have tolerated me, but I didn't know that. All one hot Charleston summer we weekly set off together to spend our allowance on Eskimo pies. All summer mine fell off its stick as I ran to try to catch up with him. Never did my wailing move him. "I didn't tell you to run."

Lang's red cap bent to listen to Joanna's prattle as they came up the drive, together, was a sight to sting my eyes. While they consumed cocoa and Sally Lunn muffins, Joanna detailed to Lang every leaf that had stirred during his absence. Lang concentrated on his fodder and I studied my son.

He's tall for his age, bony and knock-kneed, his weight at present not keeping up with his height. Big front teeth already, but no bridge to his nose. He has Grove's straight eyebrows, my transparent skin, flushing like a camellia when he's brought in a run or hooked a keeper—or when he's angry. (Fortunately he is more sweet-tempered than not, usually going along with what his friend Breck suggests, even more accommodating to his Cousin Tad, who is five years older.) The eyes he blinks at me over his cocoa mug are most often blue; but unlike Joanna's they change with the weather, and may be almost slate or nearly green, given the right sky. His hair is consistently the color of fresh wheat straw, except when he darkens it with a wet comb, trying to make it look as straight as Breck's. (He has a widow's peak as stubborn as a mane that wants to hang on the off side.) His musical enthusiasms are painful to me, coinciding as they do with whatever Tad or Breck endorses at the moment (hard rock and Johnny Cash, respectively), but otherwise an altogether satisfactory boy, good in school, good about helping Ervil or his father around the barn. A son to rejoice in.

After fifteen minutes, I interrupted Joanna's account to Lang of every leaf that had stirred in his absence, to remind him that it was time to put on barn clothes and tackle his homework so as to be ready to help with chores as soon as his father got home.

I gave him this reminder, and this explanation, five days a week. *What is he forgetting now, that might help him?*

Then I went to count mares through the east window. As I silently blessed each, I heard the children shouting, Joanna first. "Well, it's my room, too!"

"Will you just get out of here? Mo-ther!"

Joanna, taken by surprise, was near tears.

"How can I change clothes with her in here?"

"You and Snoopy come help me mend," I told Joanna.

"Snoopy wants to stay in his own room."

"Breck has a room by himself," Lang said.

I took Joanna firmly by the hand. "We don't have another room to give you," I told Lang. We shortly heard his books thump on the dining room table all the way in the sewing room.

Ten minutes later I sidled out on Joanna's reinterpretation of *Goldilocks* to go count mares again. Joanna and her narrative followed me closely. Lang slammed his palm on the table. "Oh, Joanna! Now I've got to add this whole column all over!"

"The same words at half the volume make twice the effect, my friend," I said, remembering just in time not to let my own voice rise.

"Well, why can't I have a desk in my room? Breck has a desk in his room."

"There isn't space for a desk in your room."

"There could be. There could be space."

"Come show me where."

"You could put Joanna's bureau somewhere else. I could do it for you."

"One kick and splat, huh?—no more rival nestling!" I didn't even try to keep a straight face. "What you can do right now is finish your homework, *at* the dining room table, *with* no more complaining. What you cannot do, ducky, is have all the worms."

Joanna and I saw Grove turn in and stop at the barn to check his yearlings. Suddenly I remembered leaving the wheelbarrow in his garage space. Joanna pounded after me, downstairs, through the basement and into the garage to clear Grove's way.

The first boot Grove took off poured a pint of something onto the garage floor. He stood looking at it, almost as surprised as we. "What's that?" Joanna demanded.

"Blood, I guess. Just from foaling," he reassured me. Joanna was coolly watching it run toward her feet.

I sent her upstairs to throw Grove down a towel, and the moment she was gone asked, "Did you get my message about the fire?"

"Mmmhmm. I remember, two or three cars went by this morning just in the time I was walking from the house to the barn, and I was surprised at so much traffic at two a.m. Thought maybe spring was coming early this year...." He trailed off, smiling to himself.

Later I tried to remember just how he sounded when he said that, just how he looked.

"What became of the guy Zad fired last fall?" I asked. "Does he still live around here?"

The farm hand in question had been slow, sullen, and dirty—so dirty that as I'd driven home one day with the back seat completely taken up with groceries and dry cleaning and had come upon him trudging along beside the pike, I'd looked straight ahead and hoped he wouldn't guess that I recognized him. Eventually Zad had fired him for stealing tack. "If he'd just wanted to use it himself," Zad had told us apologetically, "but he was fencing it in Lexington."

"You put that boy out of your mind," Grove answered me. "The more people talk about that fire, the more chance somebody'll get interested in setting another. Zad probably lost his shed because Milly's decided to smoke."

Zad's daughter, a fourteen-year-old with the look of a tallow sculpture that hot weather has settled into curves and bulges, had recently taken to wearing orange lipstick and laughing a good deal at things not intentionally or often even discernibly funny. I myself thought that Milly would have been asleep long before that straw blazed up, but I kept still. Going from farm to farm, vets can spread the plague quicker than flies. I respect Grove for setting his face against gossip, even though it means he tells me less than I'd like and discourages me from telling him as much as I'd like.

When I asked Grove what he thought of our best mare's gash, he answered, "It's a long way from her heart."

"You didn't find anything on Ten?"

"Sweat. *Dried sweat.*" He shook his head, his expression somewhere between awe at the abyss into which we had almost plunged, and joy. "We must lead charmed lives."

And I guess we indeed had led charmed lives. I guess that was the watershed.

That night, with a cat asleep in my lap and my feet in front of the purring tack room space heater, I rearranged our house. First, Joanna's consent. Not hard. She would consider the change a promotion.

Then a cot for Joanna in my sewing room. We had promised Grove's sister-in-law to keep his nephew, Tad, again this summer while she went to summer school again, so Joanna was about to be dislodged for a long spell anyway. She hadn't minded the cot arrangement last year, any more than she's ever minded it for Breck Smith's overnights. (And that was just as important to me, because half what Lang has to offer Breck is a double decker bunk, horses being the other half.)

Breck has a battery operated baseball game, a remote controlled airplane with a four-foot wingspan, and his own color TV, but Norma Lee bought his bed at an *Antique Shoppe,* and flounced the mattress.

So: Joanna's cot in my sewing room, and then if Ten made the summer sale, we should add that room we'd talked about for six years. Buying another mare could wait.

I didn't tell Lang my plans at breakfast Wednesday morning because I didn't want to seem to be rewarding his bad manners. I was going to wait for his next report card; they were always good. That's why I didn't tell him.

～❧3❧～ {Ruth

Maybe if we didn't do our own foal-watching—if we'd hired somebody. It's crazy for Grove to take over from me at the barn at two a.m. and then work straight through till supper. He came in Wednesday, the twenty-first morning of April, looking sodden, his eyes at half mast, his chin stippled blue, and of course, I'd had less than four hours in bed myself.

Lang's cheeks were deep pink. Grove had kept himself awake at night's end by feeding early, so when Lang had arrived as usual at six, he had been allowed to lead the quieter two mares out to pasture.

"They don't need grooming the way I need sleep," Grove told me. After breakfast he went straight from the table to our bedroom, admonishing me over his shoulder not to let him lie there past seven-thirty. I don't remember whether he roughed Lang's hair, or patted his shoulder, or even spoke to him as he left. He says he did not.

Lang put on his coat at seven just as always. "Have you ever noticed," he stopped at the door to inquire, "that Thankless likes to walk on the path, but Lagoon likes to walk beside the path?" The artful way he reminded me of his rare responsibility one more time reminded me also how fearfully important it was to him to be grown up. Just in time, I stopped myself from hugging him. I saw him through the door with his schoolbag over his shoulder, my elbows hugged close to my sides so that they also wouldn't forget. I didn't hug him goodbye. Since Grove and I weren't going to groom the mares, I poured myself another cup of coffee.

I hadn't half-finished my coffee when I realized that I was nodding off and that the mares had drifted east to where I couldn't see them. I tiptoed down the hall to have a look through our bedroom window.

Grove had passed out on top of the bedspread. I would close the curtains once I'd checked the mares, I thought, but before I got as far as the window, I saw that Thankless had separated herself from the other two and was lying down beyond the creek.

Usually the mares browse like a squadron, the space between each two equal, constant, and minimal. I tiptoed down the deck's broad steps and hurried across the yard to where I could see the gray mare's tail. Peeping out from under it was a white balloon. Even awake, Grove wouldn't hear if I called. I slid under the fence and ran, wading in my sneakers right through the icy creek.

Thankless heaved herself up when she saw me. Given somebody to keep the other mares away, the field is a better place for delivery than the barn, where a foal can get killed slamming straight from the womb into a concrete wall. This was Thankless's first foal, however, and after Grove's angry prediction that she wouldn't know it from a coyote, I knew he'd want her where he could catch her after she delivered. I led her into the foaling stall and hurried to the tack room intercom.

I watched Thankless through the window while I waited for Grove's response. My chest felt as if I'd come up from a dive almost too late. Hers was steaming like a frosted lawn in sunshine. She ranged the stall; the foal's feet stuck out stiff and fragile as wineglass stems, coming every several seconds within inches of shattering against a wall. As I jammed the call key a third time, she lay down.

On Clay Pike, somebody blew his horn three or four blasts, and Thankless got up again. Grove answered the intercom, then I raced to steer Thankless to stall center.

People rushing past our farm to work are always getting stuck behind a hay wagon or a horse-trailer, I prayerfully reminded myself, because what I dreaded was that the honking meant that Zad Thacker's stallion was abroad again, and I couldn't go look because now Thankless was fixing to lie down with her butt aimed straight at a corner.

An hour later Grove was more than pleased to admit that I had been right about Thankless's hormones or instincts or whatever it is that makes an exhausted mare lift her sweat-drenched neck and stretch it out toward the new creature behind her, like Michelangelo's God reaching out his hand toward Adam. At the colt's first snuffle, Thankless began to talk to him, to try to get where she could lick him.

I rejected the idea of dashing back to the house and getting on dry shoes and laying out Joanna's breakfast so she wouldn't waken bewildered in an empty house. Joanna never wakens from a warm bed until she's hosed out of it, and I didn't want to miss the colt's next discovery.

As Grove helped the wobbling colt stand up, Thankless turned to face him, whickering encouragement. Though he gazed about in wild surmise, he didn't fall. Thankless nuzzled his face and Grove and I grinned at each other with the elation and relief that always follow a live birth, no matter how many you've seen. The colt took his first few amazing steps toward his mother, while she continued to lick him, talk to him, and back away from him as fast as he advanced. When he went off balance and lurched toward her udder, she squealed and kicked and sidled away, leaving the poor fellow sprawled on the straw.

The colt struggled to his feet again, unaided this time. Thankless sniffed him warily. Once he renewed his search, not even Grove could hold her still. "Get the twitch," he said.

I ran for the twitch, a stick with a small loop of rope on one end. Grove twisted the loop of rope around a piece of the mare's upper lip and held on while I steadied the colt and tried to guide him toward where everybody except Thankless wanted him.

He nosed her flank; he prodded her belly. He made sucking noises with his tongue, but he never once opened his mouth. I remembered tickling the corners of my own first-born's mouth those first few days when all he seemed to want was sleep. I managed to squirt a little milk on the colt's lips and his searching grew more urgent. I squirted milk on my forefinger, squirmed it in between the colt's hard, toothless gums and popped a teat in beside it. Thankless stood still as a setter on point. I saw Grove slowly relaxing the tension on the twitch. We both edged away.

Thankless squealed, kicked at the colt, and shoved her rump into the nearest corner.

The confused colt stood teetering alone in the middle of the stall, not seeming to know whether he should stumble after his mother or to me. "Call Hereward," Grove said wearily, "and tell 'em I'll be a while yet."

Hereward Stud is one of the biggest thoroughbred farms in the Bluegrass and is Grove's number one client. Lucille Harper, the new assistant secretary, answered. A thoroughbred breeder's wife who isn't polite to stud farm secretaries deserves to have her marriage annulled; I took time to ask Lucille how she was liking the job. ("Thank you, Mrs. Brough, you're so kind to ask. I like it very much, Mrs. Brough.") I knew that Lucille was a vet's daughter, so I told her a little about the scene in the foaling stall. ("Well, Mrs.

Brough, I'm sure he'll know just what to do, he's so experienced. He's so—"). Grove began motioning me to come *on*.

A foaling was inevitably a reminder that I myself would never give birth, nurse, again. To stand in sodden icy socks being called Mrs. Brough for punctuation would have depressed me even without my anxiety over the bewildered foal.

I got back just in time to see Thankless land a hoof on the colt's neck and send him staggering halfway across the stall to collapse on the straw. Grove snatched up the rope shank and whacked and went on whacking her startled nose. "You Goddamned bitch, now you *cut that out!*" I didn't realize I'd been counting until he threw down the shank at twelve. The colt was making no attempt to rise. I ran my hands over his neck and worked each of his legs, dreading a broken spine. He made no effort to look at me. Grove knelt beside me and I moved out of his way.

The one danger shared by every animal born to a living mother has been death at her hands. No wonder maternal rejection is ranked least forgivable in humanity's catalogue of sins. For millennia, if she did not suckle, we starved. Every one of us has been delivered without warning into the terrifying power of a monster twenty times our size, her hungry jaws capable of ripping off our hands at one snatch, her own hands capable of hurling our thin-shelled brains against the wall at any moment, her feet of stamping our bellies to juice. Her hot breath closes our eyes. In her lap we lie, helpless and vulnerable as jellyfish on the sand. Only her love keeps us alive unharmed long enough to escape her. As I watched *La Dame Sans Merci* position herself at bay while Grove examined her foal for fatal injury, I told myself that I was a good mother; Lang had been lucky to be born to me.

"He's all right," Grove said. "Just worn out. Come on away and let her smell him some more." He went across the aisle for a flake of straw to cover the bare spot the colt had scraped as he skidded, and I stood watching Thankless through the stall bars, scared every time I had to blink. When the colt began to stir and try to rise, I had to grip the bars to keep from rushing to him.

The colt wobbled hopefully toward his mother, whose heartbeat had been his music for eleven months. Her tail swished nervously.

Tentatively his nose nudged her foreleg. I heard Grove behind me. As the colt bumped along her ribs, Thankless stood rigid, one white-rimmed glittering eye fixed on Grove. At last the small tongue made contact with her udder; her belly rose as she gasped like a child plunging into cold water. Then the colt was nursing and Thankless was licking his haunches.

"All you need to be brave is the knowledge that it's more dangerous to retreat than to stand," Grove quoted grimly. "Then maybe *God will save you."* I felt one of those floods of affection that water the roots of marriage long after fruition. I suppose a doctor would say they are glandular, would say that my nervous system was just going off Red Alert, but doctors used to say that babies' smiles are just gas.

Like her father, Joanna has little to say at breakfast, and though at supper she'll pack in a mouthful that would disgrace a center fielder, she eats her morning oatmeal at the rate of a closet vampire. I bring my mending basket to the table and sit with my daughter. Some day something will be confided at breakfast that wouldn't have been told but for this daily communion, and all the years of being there will pay off.

Wednesday morning, word of a new foal in the barn got Joanna through breakfast in record time. I didn't have to caution her that our Thankless child was not a teddy bear because Thankless, paying no attention to us, munching steadily at her hay, always drifted between us and him wherever he and we maneuvered ourselves.

Mares do not trust their young to God, not for a second.

"What's his name? I think we should call him Curly, for his tail." I was thinking of Serpent's Tooth, myself, but foresaw myself outvoted. "Lang will be *so mad,* when he finds out I saw Curly first!"

"Lang likes you to have pleasure," I demurred mildly. Joanna took no notice.

At 3:15 as usual, she set off to meet Lang. I took some milk over to the barn cats, so as to be there when she showed him the colt, lest her yearning to embrace it should overcome her. So I *was* thinking of the children's safety. I thought of it constantly.

25

I was topping off Thankless's water bucket when I heard Joanna weeping up the drive. She sounded too furious, too betrayed, for a simple skinned knee. She had made, I suspected, too much of having seen the colt first. I went out to comfort her. Sure enough, Lang was already out of sight.

At my appearance, Joanna stopped in her tracks so as to put all her strength into howling. "Mr. Radford wouldn't let Lang off the bus!" she got out between gasps. "The bus wouldn't stop!"

I sent Joanna to the house to wash her face, and I strode to the tack room telephone. "Did that son of mine come home with yours?" I asked Norma Lee Smith, knowing very well that he had, reviewing my disciplinary options as I spoke.

"Breck says Lang didn't come to school today," Norma Lee said. "I was going to call and ask you if he was sick."

A pitcher of hot water emptied over my head, the back of my head—hot water was running down my back, my legs. The next moment I was blue-cold. I began to dial.

Later I would ask Lang's teacher if he had been inattentive lately? Had he seemed unhappy? Had there been any kind of unusual incident, any stranger on the playground? Had she noticed Lang forming some new attachment, to someone other than the Smith boy? *Why hadn't she called me?* That afternoon I asked only whether Breck Smith was correct. Breck was correct.

Weaver Radford has been driving a Bourbon County school bus ever since his sons got big enough to cut his tobacco for him. He knows the name not just of every child who rides his bus, but of every child's older brothers and sisters. Weaver was just pulling in, "Be careful how you kick my heart around!" her radio warned in the background, then Weaver's cheerful voice.

"My son's teacher says he wasn't at school today, Weaver; what can you tell me?" *Be careful how you kick my heart around!* "I can't tell you anything, Miz Brough. He wasn't at the box and I couldn't see him on your road or nothing. I blew real good on the horn. If I'd of seen him pop out the front door, I'd of waited on him. I figured he was sick."

"I always call Mrs. Radford when Lang isn't going to be on the bus!"

"Yes, ma'am." I could see him swallow and shift his feet. "Where do you reckon he's at?"

"I have no idea!" I hung up before he could say anything more. Later I worried that a heart attack might have toppled him then and there. Later still, I wished one had.

It would be impossible for Lang's body to lie on or beside Clay Pike for as much as twenty minutes in the daytime without being seen. I was two furlongs from the Pike. What I needed most was to get hold of Grove.

Grove answered in his car between farms. "He's probably playin' hooky and fell asleep somewhere. You say Breck's home? Well, don't worry. Did you look by the pond?"

A two-acre pond lies behind the field behind our house, its sparkle enticing as a witch's mirror. One soul-stealing sliver is just visible from our deck, but the rest nestles in a hollow where grown-ups can't oversee it from the house. From the barn, even the hollow is invisible.

"I haven't looked anywhere. Norma Lee's checking the roadside between us and them. Her yard man's helping. I haven't looked anywhere."

"Well, go look by the pond, and I'll be there in twenty minutes and give him a good talkin' to."

He was dropping his g's just the way he does around nervous clients he thinks may relax if he seems relaxed. "All right," I said. A cold dead eel lay coiled and heavy in my gut.

I ran all the way from the barn to the house. Joanna met me at the front door. "Did Lang go home with Mr. Radford?"

"No, and you don't have to wait for him, either. There are some fresh raisin muffins—"

"Mama—"

"—on the table. Hop up on your chair and—"

"Mama?"

"—I'll give you some milk."

"Is Lang—"

"Put your napkin in your lap. Little girls require better manners than horses." I talked my way through the basement stairway door.

Lang's fly rod was in its place.

Joanna emptied her mouth the second I reappeared, and Grove's line was busy. "Mama, where did Mr. Radford take Lang?"

"Mr. Radford didn't take Lang anywhere; do you want some jam on your muffins?"

"Yes, please. Where did Lang go?"

"Strawberry or plum?"

"Strawberry. When is Lang going to see the colt?"

"Lang is going to see the colt just as soon as his father gets through with him. Now drink your milk; I have to do one quick errand outside."

I closed the door and strode off, knowing Lang would not be at the pond, expecting to find him there, glad Grove wasn't so alarmed as I. If Grove wasn't scared, I was probably just silly. Halfway to the pond, I began to run. I ran to take my son in my arms. I ran to dispose of this hopeless errand and get on to one that made some sense. The pond was a natural place for Lang to spend a hot summer afternoon with his Cousin Tad, with his friend Breck, with turtles and dragonflies, but not to go alone in this buzz-less April that was chilling me to my marrow even as I ran.

There was nothing at the pond that didn't belong there but the usual beer cans. Coming back, I ran all the way.

We keep the sheriff's number posted beside the kitchen phone. I managed to get the receiver to my ear before Joanna could swallow enough to speak.

Grove had already notified the sheriff. I leaned against the refrigerator as the eel in my gut shuddered to life and coiled tighter.

I'm familiar with Sheriff Maggard, a native of this county, grizzled, weathered, with the eyes of a man who knows where the grapes of wrath are stored. "I'm glad you called, Miz Brough. Could you give us a description of exactly what your son was wearing when you last saw him? Dr. Brough was only certain of the cap."

"Go wash your face, Joanna," I responded. "You've got milk all the way to your nose."

Sheriff Maggard waited patiently till the child was out of earshot, patiently wrote what I told him. "Thank you, Miz Brough.

Now what about the color of socks and make of underwear? Miz Brough? Could you tell us those things? Miz Brough?"

They thought they might find Lang in his underwear?

They thought they might find Lang's underwear and not Lang.

Joanna came back into the room and I slid down till I was sitting on the floor so I could put my arm around her while I answered Vernon Maggard.

"Thank you, Miz Brough. Now, I'm sending a man out there; he's a state detective, Albert Blount. Albert's had a lot of experience; he knows his business. I hope you'll give him all the hep you can. We want that little boy home for supper."

Could he imagine I needed to be admonished to cooperate with someone trying to find my child?

I stood up to put the receiver back in its cradle and saw a blue car turn in our driveway. My heart leapt and I opened my mouth to tell the sheriff never mind, someone's bringing my son this minute, but the receiver was already humming.

"Mama, someone's coming up our road! Who's coming up our road? Mama? Mama—"

There was nothing tentative about the way the car swung toward our house. It came as if someone instructing its driver knew exactly where he was, someone like a child coming home.

"Mama, is that Lang?"

Of course, of course it was. "Put your dishes in the sink, please, Joanna." I stepped outside in time to watch a lean black man in a gray seersucker suit park the otherwise empty car and get out.

Now I understood why the sheriff had stressed the competence of the man he was sending, and why his voice had had the same elaborate casualness as Grove's when Grove is dropping his g's.

After his race, what I noticed about State Detective Albert Blount was his youth. He looked younger than Grove (and in fact, Albert is a year or two younger than I). Grove, I reminded Grove that night, not only is as competent as any older vet in Central Kentucky, he is probably more aware of the latest technology. Half of police work, I suggested, might be knowing what equipment has been developed and how to use it. (In April, I was rationalizing. Now, in June, I know I spoke the truth.)

29

The hand I shook was brown and pink like certain orchids. The human mind is no more manageable than a puppy. Oblivious to sharp commands to sit at attention, it darts and rummages. Even as I was congratulating myself that State Detective Albert Blount's race gave me no pause, I was seeing that hand extended at other houses, and trying to calculate how its reception would affect his effectiveness, searching for my son.

"I don't know if you've talked to your husband since he talked to me? We'd like a recent photograph of Langdon."

Not Langdon; Langdon is my brother, who is dead. *Lang is alive.*

"Dr. Brough thought you could find us one taken in natural light. That would be best."

Not his school picture then. "Come in." My mind darted ahead of us, rummaged through stacks of snapshots—Lang and Tad Brough pitching horseshoes; Lang the day he lost both front teeth; Lang and Joanna hanging wooden horses on the Christmas tree. No; for that one, I'd used a flash. I hurried us into the house, anxious to find the right picture instantly, anxious to show Detective Blount that our floors weren't littered with broken pieces of things thrown at an eight-year-old who had then run away, that our other child was not bruised or scarred or filthy or thin; anxious to show that I would not keep a black detective standing in the yard.

Country child Joanna is glad of any visitor. She met us at the door and followed us into the dining room, to which I flew to bring the big *This Year's* envelope of loose snapshots and empty it onto the table. Detective Blount squatted on his heels like a whittler to talk to Joanna from her own height, while I feverishly sorted pictures.

"We have a colt. Lang hasn't seen it, but I have."

"Does Lang like the horses?" I hadn't corrected him, but I never heard him call Lang *Langdon* again, after Joanna called him Lang.

"Umhmmm." Joanna had discovered something absorbing about her left sneaker.

"Who likes the horses better, you or Lang?"

"We both do. Lang likes the horses and the cats. He likes the black cat better and I like—"

One of Albert Blount's consistent inconsistencies, I have observed, is the sympathy on his face when he talks to children. To the rest of us, his expression divulges next to nothing. Like the eyes of an old priest who's heard everything, they just wait. They do not turn what he is hearing into a dialogue to which they contribute half. They do not alarm his informant with their own alarm, or with revulsion, or with quickened interest. However heinous the narrative may be, or trivial it may seem, he hears it all. Though I'd been studying his face and tones of voice from the moment of his arrival, I had no idea how much or little of my dread he shared.

The arrival in front of our house of three marked police cars in rapid succession answered that question. Very politely Detective Blount introduced me to three uniformed state troopers and formally requested my permission for them to search our premises. Joanna, who never clings, placed herself so close to my legs we were touching as three armed men commenced an inspection of her home from room to room, from garage to basement, from barn and pond where I told them I had been, to hay shed, where I had not dreamt of looking. They were searching for a body, and they were perfectly prepared to learn that Grove or I or both of us knew exactly where it was.

I expected this inspection to leave us with a nightmare of disarray, but the troopers were as neat as they were quiet. Their search disturbed our order no more than it disturbed Detective Blount's inspection of the dozen pictures I had spread out for him on the dining room table. Joanna, at least, began to relax.

Among the pictures I had thought might do were a pair taken at Cave Run the day Lang caught his first fish, and with little pause, Detective Blount picked up the one snapped by Grove of Lang, his fish, and his grinning godfather, Ken Staunton. Then he put it down and chose the second, the one taken by Ken of Lang, fish and Grove. In that one, Lang has mastered his self-conscious smirk and is gravely looking square into the camera. And I had to sit down, because I knew this detective was choosing that picture instead of the other to help identify Lang because he believed that wherever Lang was, he was not smiling.

"Has Lang ever broken a bone, Mrs. Brough?"

"What?"

"Does your doctor have any x-rays of him?"

The eyes above the mouth that rephrased the question remained the same, but I felt my own widen as I realized why the question was asked. "No," I said, as firmly as if their absence would rule out their need.

Joanna isn't one to relinquish attention indefinitely. "I have a Snoopy," she announced. "Want to see him?"

"Sure I want to see him," Detective Blount said.

She turned at once to go for Snoopy.

"Comb your hair before you come back, Joanna," I said quickly, forcing myself to wait until she was out of the room to begin asking questions, forcing myself not to grab this man by the sleeve as I asked them. "Have you thought some hit-and-run hophead maybe threw his body into the trunk in a panic and roared off? How could you—What—"

"Every body shop for six hundred miles has been alerted, Mrs. Brough. And every hospital."

I felt faint, but I steadied myself on the table, hoping he didn't notice. I didn't want to be a distraction; I wanted answers. But the moment cost me the lead. While seeming unhurried, Detective Blount got his next question in ahead of mine. "Did Lang leave any of his school books behind this morning, Mrs. Brough?"

My mouth was quicker than my startled mind. "His book bag was full," it said.

Detective Blount waited without visible reaction for the couple of seconds it took me to see what a non-answer this was. "You might check his room to see if there's anything he would ordinarily have taken with him. Are you missing anything from your food cupboards?"

"What do you mean?" I asked—fiercely, because I knew.

"Sometimes a kid who's got an idea to cut a few classes will stick a little food in his book bag, instead of his homework. Do you have a cookie jar? A fruit bowl? Do you know how much bread you had?"

Something about his scrupulous enunciation, even tone of voice, and unchanging neutral expression told me that it would be quicker to inventory every shelf in the kitchen than to argue with this man, and the quicker he abandoned the idea that Lang had missed the bus on purpose, the sooner I too could breathe evenly.

He followed me from cupboard to cupboard. I realized that he knew nothing was going to be missing quite as well as I did when he told me what he needed from me next. His first step after Sheriff Maggard had hung up on Grove and turned to him had been to call Lexington for bloodhounds. They were on the way.

"Pajamas would be good," Albert suggested, managing not to seem to stop short as Joanna reappeared.

Snoopy was brought to Joanna last summer by her Cousin Tad. Now his plush is less than lush, nap-worn in both senses of the word. Gravely, Albert accepted him. "That's a special dog. I think that dog is a hound; what do you think?"

"He's a Snoopy."

"A Snoopy. I have a friend with some very snoopy hounds; their noses are snoopy and their ears are droopy, and they're as big as your colt." Joanna looked at him appraisingly. "Do you believe me?" She giggled, not wanting to be made a fool of, but neither wanting to rebuff this charming man. "Would you like to see them?"

Joanna looked to me. We have taught them not to accept the invitations of strangers—we have taught them that!

"You can go stand right there by that window and watch," I told her, backing out of the room as I spoke. "Mr. Blount's hounds will be here in five minutes." Under Lang's pillow, I found his pajamas. There wasn't a schoolbook in the room.

The handler was a Lexington policeman. His two dogs stood panting where Lang had stepped off the stoop nine and one half hours before. When they lowered their muzzles, their skin fell over their eyes.

Nothing seemed real. I kept seeing myself the victim in a television drama, kept waiting for a signal that no more performance was required of me, waiting for the cameras to be rolled away and Lang to come around the corner.

In a TV production, the handler would be the boy-hero's father, and before the second frame, we would love him for his devotion to his dogs. The man to whom Detective Blount now introduced me maneuvered his animals like a driver manipulating a gear shift. I took Lang's pajama shirt out of the bag in which I had smuggled it out of the house, and gave it to him. I was obliged to take the chance that Joanna would recognize it through the dining room window.

As I stepped back, the handler began to switch the long heavy lead from each dog's collar to its harness. On Clay Pike I saw Grove's car turn in our driveway. I pointed. The two men looked, nodded, and turned back to the dogs. The car hurrying toward us could have been one more cloud moving over the pasture. The handler gave each dog a couple of tugs. The dogs became very still. He gave them our child's rumpled shirt and said, "Find 'im."

The dogs took two deep breaths, lifted their heads high in the air and tossed them from side to side. As Grove stepped out of his car, they dropped their noses to the path and ran off like a couple of moles in cinematic fast-motion, straight for the mailbox.

I didn't know whether to run from Grove because I had broken our lives or run to him because godlike, he would fix them. His face was grim, but he gave me one swift, hard embrace and a searching look—was *I* all right—before turning to Detective Blount. Before I could choke out introductions they had exchanged names, shaken hands, and turned their attention to the dogs.

The dogs stopped at the mailbox. My eyes flew to Grove and met his. The look on his face terrified me.

The handler led the dogs up and down both sides of Clay Pike, but they were adamant: Lang's smell ceased abruptly where he had waited for Weaver Radford. Had I really thought those dogs would lead me to my child? Incredulous, betrayed, I stood watching them mill and snuffle, blind as fate.

Lunging for the ringing telephone, I tripped over Joanna and Snoopy. *Lang! After he told me where he was, I wouldn't even ask him "Why?" before I told him corned beef hash for supper, the kind you love.* "Yes?" I answered. *Hello takes twice as long as yes.*

"Ruth, is it really Lang who's gone?"

Sunset through the kitchen windows was iodine dripping into pale red water.

"Ruth?"

The major occupation of the horror victim is comforting everyone who knows her. I began to offer Caroline Averoyne the list of hopes and reassurances I was reciting to all my shaken friends who needed to be told that their children were safe—nothing could have happened to mine; that they were safe—nothing had happened that I couldn't bear. Joanna was bending over her shin. "Just a second, Caroline; Joanna needs me."

"Snoopy's feelings are hurt."

She had not once let go of Snoopy since she'd fetched him to show to Detective Blount. "Let me kiss Snoopy and make him well." As I spoke these words, I felt a wave of sickness that almost made me forget the receiver lying on the counter. The sunset was turning to dried blood and Joanna, Caroline, everyone, was waiting for me to kiss and make well, to get Lang in from under that awful sky before it went totally black.

I soothed Caroline back to her own nestling and opened the cupboard. Canned hash and—*and because this ring was Lang, all the ice cream in the freezer!* "Yes?"

"The police were here," Norma Lee Smith informed me.

I leaned my forehead against the cupboard door and closed my eyes.

"They asked all about you and Grove. They wanted to know how you get along and how much you drink and how you treat Lang and whether—" I could imagine. Grove and I had undergone our own grilling. "And they asked Breck if Lang complained about you, or talked about going on a trip. Have you had your radio on?"

"No, Norma Lee, Grove and I have been too busy to turn on our radio."

Four feet from my mouth, the state's gadgetry, left us by Albert Blount, registered my angry tone of voice. Maybe if she played it twice, I thought, Norma Lee would register it too.

"It's been on WCDR twice."

I said nothing.

"Did they drain the pond?"

"No, Norma Lee, they did not drain the pond."

"Well, that's the first—"

"An eight-year-old does not go swimming in April in Kentucky. Anyway, I looked all around the pond and I did not find one thing." Too much later I would remember that this was not so.

"You wouldn't, if he just fell in."

"*What?*"

"If he just tried to gig a frog and fell in."

I felt my throat closing up.

Rainfall has flooded that pond three times since I came to this farm, drowning trees and gullying the nearby road, but I always looked vague and drifted off when Grove talked of filling the whole thing in, because herons feed there, and Lang— Neither of us can speak of it now, but Lang's proudest moment last year came when he and Tad Brough brought in two bluegills, and Tad volunteered that Lang had caught the larger.

"You've heard of the Holliday case, haven't you?" Norma Lee was asking.

"What holiday case?" My blood told me not to ask. I slid down to the floor and beckoned Joanna to come scrunch beside me.

"Keith Holliday, the little boy they found in his parents' pool. He disappeared around Christmas one year, and the police searched the pool, but it was so covered with that green allergy stuff they didn't see him, and then it froze over that night and he lay there all winter, twenty feet from their house. What?"

"I said, I need this line for Lang." I could have told Norma Lee that as a hiding place for Lang, police bloodhounds had rejected our pond, our woods, our fencerows, and every building on the place in favor of a one-foot-by-two-foot mailbox. I could hear her voice the length of my arm as I rose. I reached over and gently placed the receiver in its cradle.

But the line of a popular vet doesn't stay free for ten minutes when the radio is broadcasting that his son is lost. "Why," I demanded sobbing in Grove's arms that night, "do people say such stupid things to us?"

"Because they have no alternative. We are not in a position to be pleased."

Grove is so often fair that I used to think he always was.

That was April. Now, in June, the telephone's silence is a vise tightening on my skull.

Lang was born nine years ago this month, on our first wedding anniversary. This thrilled us as an omen so good it almost shook our faith in Unbelief. Never outside the reigning houses of the Middle Ages was a child more desired. *Never* was a child more adored. Every day Grove came home for lunch bringing flowers, wine, a shining face. By the time Lang was a month old, his internal clock wakened him each evening just at the time Grove usually got home, and as he heard his father's voice, he began laughing.

I felt justified. I was ready to face anyone, indeed anxious to encounter everyone I ever had encountered. Nothing in twenty-six years of gaucherie, muffed opportunities, disappointing intellect, and unimpressive character amounted to a hill of beans beside the man who had chosen me and the astonishing child we had produced, a child whose marvelous qualities no praise could have overstated. I am not surprised that Mary took the Eastern Star in stride.

We named him Langdon Courtonne Brough for my brother, who was murdered while I was in college. Grove, really Alan Grove, has been called by his middle name from the day of his birth to distinguish him from his uncle, who lived with his six daughters just down the street. Grove is always telling me how this messes up his mail or his records. He insisted that he did not want a namesake.

My mother was almost happier than I that Grove and I were expecting a child and might name it for my brother. My brother's death had sandbagged her; my pregnancy restored her to a kind of feverish life. It was as if she thought I had a chance to give Langdon life again.

As for me, once Lang was born, I asked nothing more from life but a daughter, and even told myself that if I could produce nothing but sons, I could content myself with daughters-in-law and granddaughters. That was when I first realized how many deaths my brother's was to my mother. Not just her son was snatched from her arms, but her grandchildren.

Grove has also lost his only sibling, and we seem to have reacted in much the same way. The first time he and I talked about children, he vowed he wanted a baseball team. Our serious goal when we married was four. Lang came like fruit out of a vending machine —ask and it shall be given. Four seemed a reasonable number. There was no hint of the anguish we would go through trying to produce Joanna. I promised myself a year to nurse, six months to rest, and a year to present Lang his first brother or sister, which we would name either for Grove's mother, or for Grove himself. I would insist.

Grove was besotted with his son. From clients' wives I heard how each professional visit now began with an update on Lang. "Central Kentucky hears about it every time that baby farts," Fran Warren told me. Seeing that Grove's happiness equalled mine, multiplied mine, I had tried to prepare myself for the jealousy I would undoubtedly feel sometimes when Grove divided his affections. I was amazed to realize that there was no division. For the first time I could ponder the supposed unity of the holy trinity without the mental equivalent of raucous laughter. We three were one. Any love Grove expressed for the baby, he felt for me. This was the perfection of that time: every thing I did for Lang, I did for Grove, and every light-ray of affection he radiated toward that child, warmed me.

At Grove's insistence, I called my parents. Mercifully, my mother was out. My father did what he could for me, then said, "Now let me speak to Grove." I went to the bedroom and noiselessly picked up the extension. "I'll give them the picture Ruth sent us at

38

Christmas," my father was saying. "Picked up on the roadside, no telling where he might wind up. Might be the nearest warehouse, might be South Carolina. I know our station manager. It'll be on tonight."

"Picked up on the roadside." There it was. I had let our little son stand all alone beside the public road. Roadside. All this spring and summer that word has continued its drumbeat in my head. Last month, after Grove had to come to Kroger's and get me, to give me a sedative and put me to bed, he suggested gently that maybe I would find a counselor helpful, somebody just to talk to about things. "Maybe she could talk you out of this idea you've got that every damned thing that happens is your fault."

Of course I didn't take Grove's suggestion. The only counsel I needed was where to find Lang. Though Grove was right to this extent: day in, day out, what has occupied my thoughts since April is tracing how, starting with my earliest memories, my faults and failures have led inexorably to Lang's unimaginable fate.

Unimaginable not because I can't picture it, but because I cannot bear to. "The police are checking every motel within six hundred miles for anybody who checked in with a child like Lang after seven a.m. on April twenty-first," Albert Blount had told me in that kind voice I have come to recognize, that wants me to believe something is being done and something will come of it. And I had struggled not to throw up on his shoes at the sudden picture of Lang in a motel.

My father wanted me to have the stimulation of going out of South Carolina for college. My grades weren't good enough for William and Mary, my parents' first choice, but I was accepted at the University of Kentucky.

Langdon graduated tenth in his class at West Point. After his death, my sophomore year at UK, I started for the first time to study. I hated that my parents had lost their brilliant child and been left only one so ordinary. My grades, however I toiled, continued about what they'd been at Ashley Hall, my prep school. "Nobody wants to marry a bluestocking," Mother tried to comfort us both.

My first Christmas after college, I went home, and Eva von Strehlenau's dashing brother Peter, who was in this country on a trade mission, flew down to Charleston to see me. Mother forgave me everything.

But I didn't marry Peter.

My father is a highly successful architect in Charleston, a city that considers itself the most beautiful and architecturally enlightened in the United States. My brother's grades would have made him Phi Beta Kappa, in a civilian college. My husband did so well at Ohio State that their vet school accepted him after only three years of pre-vet courses, instead of the standard four. I know that I am intellectually inferior to those three. As Grove is quick to remind me, whenever he imagines I'm needling him for what he believes I consider his provincialism, English was the least challenging, most self-indulgent choice of majors I could have made.

I graduated from UK just as I was when I arrived a freshman: unintellectual, unambitious. After graduation, I took a job at *The Blood-Horse,* a Lexington-based magazine, doing work I encouraged my parents to infer was editorial. I was relieved, not frustrated, when pregnancy caused me to resign a couple of months short of my first wedding anniversary. I never wrote to either of my alumnae bulletins about this job. My first letter to either was to announce Lang's birth.

Am I expected to write them now?

Eight o'clock came and Lang had not called. There was a draft on the back of Joanna's neck. The covers had to be tucked exactly under her chin and under Snoopy's chin. Her father as well as I had to hug her good night. Then the covers had to be arranged again. Zad Thacker's eldest was foal-watching for us. Were we poor peasants, we could all three have slept close together on our straw-strewn floor, and that would have suited me as well as Joanna best that night. "Where do the dogs live?" Joanna asked us, me with my hand on the night-light switch, Grove already at her door. She lay on her back. Through her eyes, I, too, stared up at the absence of that accustomed bulge in the overhead mattress.

"The dogs live in Lexington."

"What are their names?"

"Their names are Banahan and Lisle," I improvised.

"How old are they?"

"You go to sleep now, honey," Grove said.

All the way to our room Grove's hand was on my back, ready, I felt, to push if I faltered. As he closed our door, I drew a sharp breath, not knowing yet what I was going to say, and his words cut me off. "Ruth, we are not going to lose our son."

"Where is he?" I cried, but I don't think Grove heard me.

"I will tear this Goddamned state apart!"

"Yes," I whispered into his chest.

"We'll get him back, Ruth. We'll get him back."

"Yes," I whispered again.

But we couldn't stand in each other's arms lying to each other all night.

As soon as Grove stepped under the shower, I stole back down the hall to turn on the front lights, for anyone who should try to find us in the night. Grove had already turned them on.

Joanna heard me. "Mama?"

"I'm going to use your shower, OK?" If I stood under the water long enough, she would be asleep before I had to abandon her.

I turned the nozzle to massage.

I had not checked Lang at the mailbox that morning because I was preoccupied with Thankless. Possibly at the very moment I was tiptoeing to our bedroom window to locate the mares, Lang was being hurtled into hell. If Thankless had not begun to foal just when she did, I would have looked out when the school bus arrived and Weaver Radford blew its horn. That must have been the horn I heard as I was trying to get Thankless down again in the foaling stall. But for Thankless, I would have known eight hours sooner. *Eight hours.* I wished if I were going to throw up I would do it here, where the shower would drown out the noise and wash away the mess. I rested my head on my hands against the wall and let the hot water pummel my back.

Grove asleep on our bed, I looking with the kitchen binoculars at Lang, standing solemn as a drummer boy beside his post. The car pulls over. The driver leans almost horizontal and opens the passenger door. Is it a man? I can't tell. It has to be someone Lang knows; Lang would never get in a stranger's car. Do I recognize the car? I try to picture the car of anyone I know, and fail.

I watch Lang get into the car. Do I cry out at once to Grove? Do I run for our car, chase the kidnapper down, demand my child, recover Lang before he realizes his danger? I see my car forcing the other off the road, both of the other car's front doors opening, both Lang and the driver spilling out—just as Grove arrives in our truck and pins the kidnapper against his car. I embrace Lang. I hustle him into our car.

Once, as Grove and I worked into dusk in our garden, we saw a pickup truck pull off the road beside our grazing mares, heard a terrific blast (Grove went down next morning and recovered a twenty-gauge shotgun shell), watched our whole herd gallop off without, this time, breaking any leg, heard the truck's occupants let out a few drugstore cowboy whoops, and helplessly watched them zoom off down Clay Pike. In less time than it would have taken Grove to run for our truck, theirs was out of sight, and side roads off Clay Pike are numerous as mole tunnels.

I wouldn't have wasted vital time trying to pursue Lang; I would have reached for the kitchen phone and dialed 911. Every road in Bourbon County would have been blocked in minutes.

But I had not done any of these things. *And I had not hugged him goodbye.*

When I stepped out of the shower, Grove was leaning against the basin with my towel hung over his folded arms, waiting for me.

Our lovemaking was desperate, abrupt, uncharacteristically silent. Therapy was what we were about, not pleasure. I, to my surprise, passed in a short time from numb cooperation (*anything* I could do for poor Grove!) to co-beneficiary. Though my never-ceasing thoughts were abstracted, my body was not. I have since learned to count on this.

Afterwards Grove slept, and I lay awake thinking about Keith Holliday, and Chinese Lagoon.

The second (not the first) night that Grove and I were married, I declared, "Ah feel like a w-a-w-tah lily on a Chahnese lagoon."

Two years later, when the registration papers came back for our mare Blithe Spirit's filly, I discovered that Grove had named her for that Tennessee Williams line.

Blithe was nursing Lagoon the spring I was nursing Lang. Lang got weaned first. He was just learning to toddle when Lagoon was abruptly taken from her dam. There was no way to prepare either of them, and no way to tell Blithe Spirit afterward that her baby had not been dragged off by lions, no way to assure the filly that she would not be. Blithe was our only mare then; there was no consoling company for dam or weanling. The one ran frantically up and down her fence, calling. The other we put in a stall where she couldn't see her mother and kill herself trying to get to her. Grove hung a transistor radio near the stall to keep the pair from hearing each other's cries, and if the filly was capable of acknowledging any species but her own, to lessen her terror that she was alone on the dark side of the moon. Later Lang and I went to check on her and to my encouragement, didn't hear her as we approached the barn.

The filly lay on the straw, her sides heaving and dark with sweat. When she saw me, her piteous eyes grew even wider and her pink gums parted in a bleat whose hoarseness told me why we hadn't heard her from outside. The straw was all piles and bare spots where she'd been pawing. I set Lang on a bale in the safe aisle while I took a pitchfork to Lagoon's bedding.

The filly seemed to take some comfort from my presence. I knelt stroking her as long as Lang would tolerate it. When I went back to him, my embrace was a tacit promise that he would never lie on the floor of a strange locked room, streaked with tears and hoarse with pain and terror.

Thursday morning there was no use pretending either of us was asleep, and Grove went very early to the barn. The third time I checked through the kitchen window whether he was, please Oh God, coming back yet, the scene had changed and my heart kicked like a jackrabbit. A car was parked beside our mailbox. At 6 A.M.

Grove didn't answer the intercom. I tore out the front door, and collided with him. "Car!"

He didn't even look where I pointed. "It's Blount, honey. He'll be stoppin' everybody that goes by this time of day." Even as Grove spoke, the blue car by our mailbox was joined by a police car and the two drivers got out to confer. Did they expect to find Lang in someone's back seat? Again I saw a crumpled body in a locked trunk and my bowels tried to empty. "He told me he'd be there. Somebody who goes to work the same time every mornin' gets to recognize everybody he always sees, even if he never knows who they are. He might notice a stranger walkin' down the road, or a car not usually there. Or one missin' that usually *is* there."

Dropping his g's again. What else had Detective Blount told him?

"I'm taking the car," Grove said. His partner and their intern were somehow sharing his rounds between them. I didn't ask where he was going to look. I sensed that he didn't know. "I'll call you every two hours." *Don't leave me,* I wanted to wail, and *Go, go, **hurry**.* I nodded dumbly.

I waited to call Joanna until the police car and Detective Blount's Chevrolet were gone. She got up without a word. She didn't ask to see the colt. She didn't ask about Lang. Each time I left the room, she followed me. Mostly we sat in my bedroom, where there's a telephone—on the floor, where I could hold her.

I could have told Lang he could have a room of his own. "Now that you're reading, Joanna, I think you're old enough to move into the grown-up women's room, where the books are, where I do grown-up women's work. Sharing a room with a brother is for little girls." She couldn't wait.

44

We could have had her cot all set up by the time Lang got home.
At the telephone's ring, I felt Joanna go rigid.

"Mrs. Brough? This is Bill Loomer."

I came as close as I ever have come to fainting. "All right," I said.

Loomer & Barlow is Paris's biggest funeral home. I closed my eyes and waited. *I will not make an upset in front of Joanna.* I seized on that thought, concentrated on it as one focuses on a stain on the labor room ceiling.

But Loomer & Barlow did not have Lang's body.

Middle-aged boy scouts is what Grove calls React, the Paris organization of which Bill Loomer is president. "We're going to look for your boy," Bill told me. "We'd like to park our vehicles at your place and fan out from there."

React members, Grove says, are the kind who direct parking at band concerts as importantly as if they were assigning lifeboat seats. They're the kind who dream of putting on hard hats and telling the rest of us to pull down our blackout shades. At every opportunity they stow their ladders and brushes or lock their tool kits or hang their aprons in their diner kitchens and drive around listening on their CB radios for chances to be the kind of civil defenders we all whooped at in "The Russians Are Coming, The Russians Are Coming." *I was glad they were coming.*

React, the state police, the Paris police, the sheriff's department and the Paris and Bourbon County fire departments had divided an aerial map of Bourbon County among themselves and each group was going to search its allotted section. Albert Blount was responsible; he called to tell me about it seconds after I hung up on Bill Loomer. I closed the draperies. "The sunlight," I told Joanna, "is fading the bedspread."

I fetched Joanna stacks of picture books. "I'm going outside to supervise some workmen, and I promised your father one of us would be here when he calls. Would you *sit right here* and answer the telephone, so he won't be disappointed?"

"We'll cover every square yard for two miles," Bill Loomer had told me. That would include the barn, where Thankless was ready to kick any stranger in the head who ventured into the stall with her colt. I hurried to beat the men to the barn, then waited for them

45

in the aisle beside the tack room door—opened, so I could snatch up the telephone on its first ring. I leaned against the cold wall, thinking of Keith Holliday and of that other little boy in the Fayette County subdivision who disappeared from his own yard in mid-winter, and whose mother found him when the March thaws uncovered his body where the snow had slid off the back porch roof and buried him in his tracks. House-to-house searchers had walked close enough to that child to hear the crystals forming in his blood.

The men who filled our barnyard and parking lot with their Fords and camper-topped pickup trucks had the beefy faces of Dickensian tavern keepers, the gaunt faces of the Virginians who walked through the Cumberland Gap with their squirrel rifles on their shoulders. We made a primal scene. A child of the community is missing. Grove and I will never be Kentuckians, but Lang, I felt tears start as I reflected, Lang is one. Without a second thought, every man there had left his work, that no one was going to do for him. Women who had lost a child to Indians, to bears, to forest confusion, had seen groups assemble that looked just like this, that stood quietly, communicated with each other all that was necessary in very few words. The men in my yard were gravely deferential to me: a little embarrassed, braced for hysterics, anxious to start. I told Bill Loomer what Lang had been wearing and what schoolbooks I definitely could remember he'd been carrying. To the sheriff and Albert Blount I had only thought to say, "olive drab book bag," but perhaps one book had been dropped. Lang's name was in each, but perhaps someone tore those pages out.

Perhaps even Grove would have welcomed Bill Loomer's help. I know a UK faculty couple with three Ph.D.s between them, in physics and biochemistry. When their son failed to call them on schedule after a canoe trip, they did every possible sensible thing. Then they consulted a medium. I loved these men who set off quick and serious as bird dogs to find our child, theirs and mine.

The man assigned the barn, who scoured it for any rag of Lang's clothing, was a cook at Red's Burgerburg, he told me—Roszell Randall. "I know your little boy, Miz Brough. He's a real good kid. He comes in sometimes with his friend. We had us some real good talks. Told me all about his horses, how his daddy's a vet. Thought the world of his daddy. He never would have run away, Miz Brough."

We are not in a position to be pleased. Do I want to be reassured that my child is a captive?

Burgerburg is walking distance from Lang's school, but I'd had no idea that Lang and Breck ever went there. How often? Murder rose in my heart. Which careless teacher let them off the school grounds? How often? Lang's allowance would have paid for precious few such visits, but Breck's.... Who else may have heard Lang telling Red's cook about his father, the rich horse doctor?

Questioned along these lines, Roszell Randall looked disturbed, then, quickly, unaffectedly sincere. He assured me of all the safest things. Then he changed the subject. "Some of the places we look may seem funny to you" (no one was laughing), "but we're not just searching for a person, we're searching for where one might have *been*. Somebody might have spent the night on your place the day before—" He let the "before" hang. "He might have left something—a match cover, anything."

He didn't need to spell this out for me. Those two empty beer cans by our pond that I had dismissed from my mind on sight had been inspected, I had learned from Grove, by one of Albert Blount's troopers for brand (was it a kind sold locally?), type of can, and possible contents — cigarette butt, any kind of paper, anything.

The cans had been old, local, and empty, and when Roszell Randall finished with our barn and moved on, his hands were equally empty.

Thankless was striding back and forth between her two windows, though their view was the same—the embattled house, the clot of vehicles, the men scurrying over the farm like ants on a dead body. I leaned against her stall door and fought to keep a rising wave of nausea under control. The cans had been clueless, but they might not have been, and I had not spared them a thought. What else had I seen and dismissed that might have led us to Lang?

Officially, Albert Blount's post is Dry Ridge, but he is responsible for five counties, and he has a desk in the courthouse of each. Until yesterday, this has been a convenience.

In the eleven years since Albert's mother framed his law enforcement degree and Albert put on Kentucky's uniform, Albert has found two children: a small boy who had fallen into an abandoned well on his neighbors' farm, and a fourteen-year-old Mayfield girl who had tried to hitch a ride to the Derby. The well she had fallen into was deeper still; Albert knows he saved her life. The drowned child, pathology told him, drowned before the police were called, before his family missed him. Albert wants to believe that, but today it is no comfort. The Broughs' son had been gone eight hours before Sheriff Maggard came to Albert with the case and asked Albert to take it himself, not to assign it to one of the men he commands. The Dry Ridge Post is an hour's drive away. "You live here; you grew up here," the sheriff said. "You know every road and every no-good in the county. And you're already here."

"It's not where you've spent your time, it's how you spent it," Albert wanted to tell Vernon Maggard. Missing children are an urban problem. Lexington's police have found many times more than any Kentucky state trooper has ever even looked for. Lang Brough would be better off if his case lay within Lexington's jurisdiction, Albert feels, and if his parents don't suspect this, they will come to know it, should the search for their son drag on, and everything Albert has learned points to its dragging on. So far the father has been businesslike. Albert is not deceived by this; he is too self-controlled himself to mistake such control in others for effortless. The mother is ready to shatter at a tone of voice.

The first step Albert and his troopers took on leaving the Broughs Wednesday was to divide Clay Pike among themselves and visit every dwelling on it. "Do you have any help?" is one of the first questions put to each householder. "Have you had any in the past year? Has anyone left you lately? Within the past year?" Nobody in Bourbon County is hiring tobacco help in April, but most hire choppers for a couple of weeks every fall. "Do you have the names and addresses of last fall's workers?" Albert and his troopers asked each farmer.

Mostly the answer was no. "You know how it is," one said. "They come down out of the hills, work two or three days, go home. When they feel like working again, they come back, but by that time, my crop's in. They work for somebody else, two or three days. I rarely ever know the names of most of 'em. I have this one boy, been coming to me five years; he'll get up a crew. I work who he brings."

"Did you have trouble with anybody working for you?" Albert asked everywhere. The Broughs in the course of their interview had told him about the hand Zad Thacker had fired. Zad had added little. Zad hasn't seen the thieving bastard since he ordered him off the place last September.

"I don't know where he went to. Don't know and don't care. Straight to hell, most like! If he's dead, anyway. Hope he is."

The summer Albert turned fifteen, he followed his father onto the payroll at Lochlann Farm. He considers that what he learned watching his father with horses has been as useful to him in detective work as anything he learned at Eastern Kentucky University.

On the side, the late Tom Blount was one of the ring handlers who showed the million-dollar horses at the Lexington thoroughbred auctions, but his regular work for forty-four years was with the training of young horses at Lochlann. Long before the summer that Albert became a groom there, he had been going to the farm with his father to open gates and hand tools. Tom Blount's hands were more interesting to watch than his face. "A horse ain't a monkey," he told Albert. "Don't do a piece of good to make faces at him. But he listens. He hears every breath you draw." Talking to the frantic, the recalcitrant, the suspicious, Albert breathes evenly. His tone is always measured, his face impassive.

"Did the guy give you any address while he was working for you?" he had asked Zad. "Do you know where he lived then?"

The angry lines had deepened between Zad's eyebrows. "He didn't only work for me but a few months."

Zad had not paid Social Security for the man, Albert had deduced, and has never had any address for him. Albert had moved on before Zad's defensiveness shut him up. "Did he say where he worked before he came to you? Did he give any references?"

"Said he'd done farm work. I don't ask my help for no references. If a boy looks strong and wants to work and can work, I let him work!"

Albert had recorded everything Zad told him in his notebook and driven to the next farm.

~⊰ 7 ⊱~   {Ruth

One September a *Blood-Horse* photographer, Jim Winnall, took me to the Thoroughbred Club's annual Yearling Sale cocktail party. These buffets are held outside, a short walk from where the yearlings are stabled. Jim steered us to a table where he saw a vet he knew.

The vet, who had a pleasant, sensible-seeming voice and manner, introduced Jim and me to the young woman he'd brought. Her name didn't register because from the start I privately called her Overflowed. She had that ready-for-pleasure look a little extra weight gives a complacent young woman; clearly she doesn't deny herself what she savors. She acknowledged her introduction to me with barely a nod, and at once got out a cigarette for Jim to light for her.

The sky was all scudding clouds, and table conversation was about how soon they were going to empty on us. "If I have to show that colt in the mud, it'll cost me $3000," one breeder fretted.

"It's not going to rain today," the vet said. His accent was out-of-state; nobody even glanced at him. The sky was slowly turning that combination of black and yellow that makes Kentuckians talk about last summer's tornadoes.

"Made a path through my tobacco you could drive a—"

"She had just broke water when the power went off. I set up that battery—"

Grit peppered our faces and a twig from the maple lashing above us plopped stem-down into my bourbon, jaunty as a mint sprig. "Well, what do you say, honey," the breeder beside me asked: "Are we about to get soaked?"

Ashley Hall girls don't take sides in social conversations. I smiled at my neighbor. "Where I grew up, we always knew when it was going to rain, because we'd see the seagulls flying in ahead of it from the ocean." I smiled at the vet.

"Where did you grow up, Ruth?"

As he spoke my name, I felt a little sting. "Charleston."

"South Carolina."

"Yes, I meant to say —"

"No, you didn't. People from Charleston, West Virginia say they're from Charleston, West Virginia. People from Charleston, South Carolina say they're from Charleston."

Of course I blushed; I always blush.

Overflowed tapped the ash from her cigarette like a cow stamping her warning. Her voice was languid. "Where I grew up, we always knew when rain was coming because we saw the niggers flying in ahead of it from the fields."

I glanced anxiously at the butler-types behind the nearby serving table. Jim, mistaking my glance, jumped up. "Here, let me get you a clean glass."

I tossed the twig on the ground. "This is fine," I said.

Overflowed emptied her glass in two swallows and held it up. I appraised her nails, speculating on just how long blood could be exposed to oxygen and remain that red.

Someone asked if anyone had seen the Pope on TV. The CIA had admitted mining Nicaragua's harbors, and the Pope was warning against escalating warfare, "God save us!"

"It'll be 'God save us!' if the Russians get Nicaragua," my neighbor promised.

I didn't have any more brothers for ignorant armies to kill, whatever the divine response. "Oh, God will save you," I muttered, "fear you not."

"Be you the men you've been," the vet finished Housman's line, and we looked at each other.

Grove was twenty-seven that fall. Emily Dickinson claimed that her eyes were the color of the sherry the guest leaves in the glass. Grove's were more like the marsala Mother's cook pours on veal. His hair, also brown, was cut a little shorter than modish. I feel about modish male haircuts as I feel about pencil moustaches: both betray an inordinate amount of time spent in front of a mirror. A style that requires meticulous primping always makes me wonder *Why aren't you out playing in the sunshine?* The men all wore jackets that hot afternoon, but I deduced from looking at Grove's hands that he was muscular. (Grove's hands are ideal for his work —not too big to reach far up a mare's rectum and render judgment on the softness of her follicles, but strong enough to turn her foal over and get it out of there if she has bad luck.) He held his shoulders back and his neck straighter than any other man at the table.

My reaction to good masculine posture has always been atavistic, which is to say, pure selfish. The man who sits and stands erect seems readier to react—to me, or to any danger to me. I tried this theory on Eva once, years before I met Grove, but the conversation deteriorated at once into erection *double-entendres,* and I always wind up retreating from such matches because of the way my face colors.

The University of Kentucky was staging "Summer and Smoke" the week I met Grove, and two days after that party, he called me at *The Blood-Horse* and invited me. I was thrilled. I had not told him where I worked.

After the play we talked about how God saved A. E. Housman's queen, about my only brother hacked to pieces by North Korean axes in a demilitarized zone. Grove had read of it. "You're the only American who has!" I told him passionately. "I was at UK when it happened. Nobody on campus even seemed to know we had men *in* Korea! Nobody knows it now! Everybody knows exactly how many men we lost in Beirut last year."

"Two hundred and nineteen. One of them was my brother."

My throat always tightened anyway when I talked about Langdon; now I could hardly speak. "I'm sorry."

He gripped my hand once and let it go as he nodded. "Ted was luckier than your brother. He left a wife and son."

I couldn't immediately see the luck in leaving a shattered widow and a fatherless infant, but I realized that men have their own ways of thinking. "My brother was brilliant. Nobody doubted he would make general. Now there's only me, and I'm not doing much."

"You're doing fine. Just don't let your parents pressure you into marriage. They're probably frantic."

I stared at him, and I knew by the tingle that my face was a traffic light. We'd just been arguing about Tennessee Williams women, who are all, I had objected, just like "Summer and Smoke's" Alma —"frenzied driven victims, compulsively, feverishly, helplessly, obsessed with sex!"

"Not sex, reproduction."

I'd had to laugh with him. "No wonder Tennessee Williams is afraid of women, if that's what he thinks we're like."

As to A. E. Housman, the joke was on me. Grove was not the poetry lover I thought him that day he capped my "Shropshire Lad." The girl he was interested in at Ohio State had goaded him for the narrowness of his pre-vet curriculum, so he had sat in on the English Literature course she was taking—"until she came to class with another guy's pin on her sweater!" I try to be grateful to this siren, not jealous of her. Jim Winnall never talked to me about anything except our mutual employer or UK's Wildcats, and he was typical. I waited for Grove's second call.

I would not have described Grove as handsome then—which surprises me, because now I think he is conspicuously handsome — but I never mistook his voice for anyone else's on the telephone.

As I would know Lang's.

~❧8❧~   {Ruth

I had no nightmares Wednesday night, because I didn't sleep. Thursday I called Jake Averoyne, our family doctor, Caroline's husband, and asked him for valium, seconal, anything. Jake talked to me at some length, kindly, reasonably, uselessly.

"I can't believe you won't help me," I protested. Jake has been my best friend here almost as long as he's been my doctor, and that's been ten years.

"I am helping you," Jake said. I hung up on him.

Jake's office is on Ephraim McDowell Street, an appropriate address for a physician. Ephraim McDowell was the Kentucky doctor who performed the first abdominal surgery. "This street would bear *my* name," Jake told me early on, "if Great-great-great-grandfather had been willing to cut open a bible-quoting female without morphine, penicillin, malpractice insurance or earplugs."

"It ought to have been named Crawford Street," I replied. Jane Crawford is the one who insisted on the surgery that made McDowell famous. Bolstered only by scriptures recited by herself, Jane Crawford endured his removal of her twenty-two pound abdominal tumor.

If the conditions for getting Lang back were that I had to bear him all over again, had to deliver him by C-section with no anesthetic, could I do it? Oh, how gratefully!

"I don't want you gaining more than twenty pounds," Jake admonished when Lang was about three months in the making. "No more fudge cake."

"I thought when I came to *Paris,* I'd be *exhorted* to eat cake," I protested. "But I can see you're no Marie Antoinette, Doctor."

That's when I learned that Jake had majored in history, that if Jake's father hadn't been the fifth James Averoyne to practice medicine in Paris, Jake would probably be a history professor. "How can you live in Bourbon County and subscribe to such a slander?" he berated me. According to Jake, Marie Antoinette deserves our pity.

"She was a frivolous spendthrift," I said. "Headstrong—"

"Headstrong until they cut it off," Jake allowed.

"—shallow—"

"She *was* shallow," Jake agreed sadly, "until she was in too deep to get out. But she never said *Let them eat cake.*" When I came for my next checkup, Jake handed me a paperback biography of Marie Antoinette. "Read it while you're waiting in poor, overworked doctors' offices," he suggested.

Memories of banter, of any and all happiness before we dreamt we would lose Lang, are intolerable now. I still have the paperback.

I am now almost exactly the age of Marie Antoinette when her little boy was snatched from her and starved to death. He was one year younger than Lang.

⤳9↩

{Ruth

We all slept as poorly the second night Lang was gone as the first. We're told that nightmares play at magical speed, so probably the same scream Thursday night made me dream of the hideous place Lang was, and almost simultaneously woke me. I ran to Joanna's bedside and held her sweaty, struggling body. "Don't let them catch Lang!" At first I couldn't make out what else she was babbling, but as I held and rocked her, she grew more coherent and I understood that "them" meant the bloodhounds. The dogs must be stopped before they ate Lang, as she had seen them eat his pajamas.

Friday morning, heavy frost browned every quince blossom. I was glad to see them ruined. With Joanna and *The Book of Puppies,* I sat on the floor beside the bedroom telephone table. "This funny pup can almost turn around inside his skin," I read aloud. Ruefully, I pondered the generation gap, that robs us of language as if we were immigrants. The shores of four are so far behind me, my own child can understand me only if I pick words out of books, rejecting those which come first and naturally to me. Pointing out that no one can be afraid of a dog that looks like Charles de Gaulle, doesn't work with someone born in this decade.

I have not sailed anywhere. I know the three simple words Joanna wants to hear: Lang is home. We are marooned on the same island.

Good Friday's mail brought an expensively stiff white card with butterflies embossed on its face. Inside were the printed words *butterflies...because...* and the signature of one of Grove's clients. I shoved it back in its envelope. A good enough customer that I feel obliged to put up with her, she is the kind who asks me "Don't you" questions. "Don't you ever think you might go back for your

Master's?" "Don't you want to *grow*?" She has a sweet daughter Joanna's age who has been in nursery school since the age of two, and she apparently feels the time I spend on Joanna as a reproach to her law practice. Thinking of her now is a kick in my gut, brought up as I was on mean-spirited stories like *The Monkey's Paw,* in which every wish is hideously granted. More than once I have entreated the gods of love not to give her to my son for a mother-in-law.

Turning that thick card over and again over in my hand, I knew it was only the first, and I felt a heaviness in all my limbs. Years ago I sat day after desolate day helping my mother acknowledge such cards. The tears began to roll down my cheeks.

Fortunately Joanna was in bed. ("Naptime," I had commanded, and held her hand until she slept.) As I stood not even wiping my face, I felt myself begin to rock on my heels. Suddenly I slung the mail against the wall, jammed my fist against my mouth, and ran down the basement steps. I made it into the garage, but I'd hardly slammed the truck's door on myself before my tears became sobs and I was half lying down with my face mashed into the seat, beating the cushion with my fist.

At last I was exhausted. I could have slept there and then, but I forced myself upstairs to my bed. All Grove needed was to find me slumped over in the front of our truck in a closed garage.

The chances of that were small, but the chances of everything that was happening to us were so small, I had lost any feeling for odds.

In any case, I couldn't hear the telephone in the truck.

As I opened the door at the head of the basement stairs, the doorbell was ringing.

Through the dining room window, I saw my friend Margot's red Mustang convertible in the driveway. Margot never parks in our lot; the gravel is a threat to her beautiful leather high heels.

"Ruth!" Margot thrust a bottle of Jim Beam at me as I opened the door. "It makes me com-*mode*-hugging sick! The world's full of bastards."

"Joanna's asleep," I whispered.

"Poor little beast!" Margot cried. She followed me into the living

56

room, catching herself with one flat hand against the wall when she stumbled on the entryway rug. "Listen, Ruth: if you and Grove run dry any time the stores are closed, call me." Margot sat down and began stirring in her handbag for her cigarettes.

I set the Jim Beam on the kitchen counter and took Margot an ash tray while my mind hustled around our shelves for something I might be able to get her to eat.

Margot Dag was my classmate at UK, until she dropped out to marry Chuck Callet. Margot's parents own Hereward Stud; the wedding took place in their antebellum mansion. The sheriff's department sent three cars to Hereward for the morning. The caterer assigned a dozen uniformed youths to park the guests' cars, and the society photographers outnumbered them and the deputy sheriffs together. The wedding cake shimmered in tiers like the dogwood cut from Hereward's woods that morning to decorate the house. The bride was drunk.

Last winter Margot brought her two children home to Hereward from Morehead, Kentucky, population roughly 8000, counting the students at MSU, where Chuck is one of the football coaches. She had made Chuck's life hell for twelve years and could not take it anymore. "I would worry," Norma Lee advised me. Grove is at Hereward daily.

"I think it would be a kindness if Grove did flirt with Margot a little," I answered. Had I taken the trouble to answer Norma Lee seriously, I would have told her that Grove, Lang, Joanna and I were a closed circle, proof against all witchcraft.

That is what will drive me insane if I let myself think about it. How, with Grove and me loving Lang as intensely, as deeply, as unceasingly as we did, as we do, could anything have penetrated our magic?

"I feel so sorry for you. I know it's just like a death in the family," friends say, but they're wrong. They are desperately wrong.

In the first weeks after Langdon was killed, I slept more than at any other time of my life, and though I did dream of him, he was always dead in those dreams. I never had to waken from Langdon living to reconfront his death. This spring was different. As soon as I lay down, I felt as if my senses were doubled, watching, listening for Lang, as if my eyes were trying to be ears and my ears were trying to be eyes. I couldn't sleep for turning over in my mind where Lang could be, what was happening to him—replaying, as if I could rewrite the script, every decision I ever had made. If I had walked him to the bus. If we had sent him to Sayre School, so that Grove was driving him door to door—no waiting on a public road for a bus driven by a dolt. If I had worked harder at Ashley Hall and William and Mary had accepted me and I never had set foot in Kentucky, never married Grove Brough, never created Lang to betray him. When after hours of *ifs* I did slide into sleep, my mental projector immediately put on a film of Lang safe at home so vivid that I woke in the dark feeling intense relief, so intense it would have had me sobbing, if it had endured another second, but of course it did not endure, not even a second. I wondered how long *I* could endure?

∼❧10❧∼   {Ruth

We met Fred and Norma Lee Smith through Lang. Already in first grade, Breckinridge Worthington Beall Smith was his best friend. ("I thought with a name like Smith, he'd better have plenty of initials," Norma Lee confided.) The Smiths overindulge Breck materially, which has made things sticky for Grove and me now and then. That used to worry me.

After Norma Lee called to tell me about Albert Blount's visit to the Smith household, she stewed for a couple of days and on Good Friday, called me again. "Are you sure the police have the best man they could get on the job?" she wanted to know. I felt the stirring of the kind of anger a woman feels when her obstetrician's divinity is questioned. If there was any doubt I couldn't afford, it was the doubt that the very best was being done for Lang that conceivably could be done. "I mean, it seems to me things have just *boggled* down. I mean, you know, maybe a black isn't the best one for the job. I'm not saying they can't be a detective, but just, well—if it was me, I'd wonder. Daddy says police work is so technical anymore."

I reproached myself for not having warned Norma Lee that in

addition to the discretionary equipment Albert had left with us, the telephone company had put a trap on our telephone which was recording the numbers and words of all our callers. "Lieutenant Blount wants us to keep our line clear," I said. She did have the brains to hang up.

Norma Lee's was not the number we were looking for. And neither was the next caller's.

Even to penguins, all penguins look alike. The mother penguin, I've read, knows her chick by his voice and can unerringly pick him out at one squawk from an atoll paved with penguin chicks. My children's voices too are unique. Even without what I thought, and eight weeks later still think, was a muffled giggle in the background, I knew at once and without hesitation that the child whose voice cried "Mother! Mother! They're keeping me—I can't get away! Help me! I'm at—" and then screamed as the line went dead, that child was not Lang.

This was my third Good Friday call. One doesn't have to be holy to be crucified.

Grove, whom I called at once and for whom I played the tape the second he got home, said flatly, "That is not Lang." And called Albert, who had South Central trace the call.

"It was not your son," Albert reported to us, together and separately. Who it was, I must trust his reasons for not telling us.

Grove wanted to destroy the tape as soon as we got Albert's report. I keep it hidden and secretly play it sometimes, searching for clues I may have missed. Grove thinks I should stop playing even the tape Mother sent back to us, the one Lang and I made for her last Christmas. When I hear Lang's voice I fracture like a diamond whose cutter has miscalculated, but what can I do.

I play the Christmas tape sometimes immediately before and after the Good Friday tape, for comparison, for reassurance that Good Friday's call was a prank, it wasn't Lang. The differences seem less striking now than they did in April, less conclusive, but I am certain, I am certain that plea was a hoax.

I had arisen Friday morning at once exhausted and unable to sit. I could scarcely engage in anything that took attention. Just barely, I could plan a meal. I couldn't write a grocery list.

Wednesday night we had eaten from cans. Thursday we'd eaten left-overs. Friday afternoon I was wondering how I could scourge myself to fix the kind of supper people under stress need, when Lorena Snyder arrived with an eight-pound warm-from-the-oven rib roast wrapped in aluminum foil. Lorena has eight children, and her husband, Eldridge, manages Hereward Farm; neither of them has spare time. "Grove is always tickled when he stops for a sandwich with Eldridge and this is the kind I'm fixing," Lorena said. Salad and potatoes were in plastic peanut butter buckets. Nothing needed returning, or even washing.

Her load set down on the kitchen counter, Lorena didn't seem to know what to do with her arms, and for a moment they hung like the arms of those wooden dolls she makes for her children. Then she put them around me. "Oh, honey," she said, and began to cry.

In the ten years I have known Lorena, that is the only time I have seen her shed a tear.

I remember comparing Lorena and her careless fecundity to the old woman who sat in the corner knitting, who never said anything, but every now and then threw out a sock. After the nightmare of Joanna's birth, as the long ensuing freeze gradually made itself undeniable, I lost my comfortable feeling of superiority. Lorena's assembly line babies seemed less certainly a burden or a joke.

As for now, a woman who has mislaid her only son doesn't laugh at a woman who has made and preserved four.

People tell you they know how you feel, but they don't. Lorena, who comes of stock who had accepted long before the Norman Conquest that it would endure more often than it would prevail, who made no claim, just stood there wetting my shoulder at our helplessness, our vulnerability, our burdens, probably came closest.

Something must have happened in those last days before we lost Lang that, if only I could recognize it, would provide the password out of this maze in hell. So I tell myself. And review them again. And again find nothing. If reliving recollections with the mind wore away their sharpness the way retracing an inscription with the fingers does, my memory's record of those last days would be as smooth and blank as an Etruscan tombstone.

The rest of that unholy holy week I try, unsuccessfully, never to call to mind. Three days of ringing—ringing telephone, ringing doorbell. Three days of "You must rest." "You must eat." "You must realize." You must hope.

Could no hope be much worse than hope? Grove was out with yet another search party, so the telephone's ring *must be his, calling to ask me if I'd like to speak to our son.* So I thought the first time, and the second.

"This is Lucille, Mrs. Brough," my fifth or sixth Good Friday telephone caller announced.

Expressions of shocked sympathy flowed into my ear while I tried to forgive Hereward Stud's new secretary for not being Lang. My hand hovered over my loud-belled timer. Lang's call would never get through if I were to accept lengthy telephoned condolences from everybody. I was about to set the timer to go off in thirty seconds, to give me a pretext for excusing myself, when Lucille said, "So I was wondering, Mrs. Brough, wouldn't you like me to keep Joanna tomorrow, so you can rest?"

My hand sank to my side. What would it take to let me rest? *No lullaby has occurred to me,* wrote Virginia Woolf, and walked into the water with rock-filled pockets. Helplessly I heard my silence.

"Honestly, Mrs. Brough, I don't have any plans for the weekend. She could stay with me till Sunday night, if you wanted her to."

With Joanna held fast in my lap, my gut hurt less. "That's really generous of you, Lucille, but I—but I think so much is upsetting Joanna right now, I—I should try to keep as many things as usual for her as I can." The fact was, I didn't want to see anyone, or more precisely, be seen by anyone. I wanted to close our doors on my disgrace, to grip Joanna securely by one hand, Grove by the other, and sit in a dark closet—with a telephone.

My mother had offered to come, but I was pretending not to need her. Secretly I yearned to put my head in her lap and howl, but to be responsible for one tragedy sufficed me. When Langdon was killed I was afraid she or my father or both would have a stroke, and Mother was only fifty-five then. Now they're both in their seventies.

Grove's mother had to be forestalled as well. When she'd realized I wasn't going to let her come and weep at me here, she wept at me on the telephone.

"Oh," Lucille was saying, "I do understand, Mrs. Brough. I know you're a marvelous mother. Dr. Brough is always talking about you. I admire you so much, Mrs. Brough. Listen, if there's *anything* I can do… Fran says we're closing the office at one today, and I'm not churchy"—Lucille gave a little self-deprecatory laugh in case I thought that was a fault. "I'll just be in my apartment. Let me give you my number, Mrs. Brough, in case—"

I marveled, as I told Lucille no and thank you one more time, that Fran was shutting the office down early. Both foaling barn and breeding shed were going full swing, and no way Good Friday was going to shut *them* down. The thought that it had anything to do with Lang didn't cross my mind, even though Lang was all I could think about.

Lang had disappeared from the world on Wednesday. Who could imagine that on Saturday I could be letting Joanna out of my sight?

Grove, as I discovered Friday evening.

"I think it's a good idea," he said when I reported Lucille's call. His words cut off my breath. "Lucille is reliable, and there's no telling what might be going on tomorrow. You might be called somewhere you wouldn't want to take Joanna. It might be like yesterday; I don't think it was particularly good for her to see all that boy scout business."

"She won't want to go," I began as soon as I could speak. My arguments were altogether reasonable, but in the face of Grove's

62

closed expression I didn't get far into them before I found myself weeping and incoherent.

"Now Ruth, it's obvious that you do need rest. Now, I want you to go lie down right now, and if you don't go to sleep, I'll give you a shot myself."

I was so furious I wanted to tear him with my teeth, but even in my dismayed rage it occurred to me that I would have an ally in Joanna, that when she heard her father's plan she would make a scene, so I for the present need make no more. "I'll call Miss Harper back," I told Grove icily.

"You don't have to do that. Go lie down. I'll take care of it."

~⚡12⚡~ {Albert

Late Good Friday afternoon, Albert spends an hour with Captain Ruben Davis, an administrator in the Lexington Police Department. Rube Davis is one of the LPD's 30 or 40 blacks (both he and Albert know the precise number, and Rube knows the name and nickname of every one). He and Albert were roommates their last three years at EKU's College of Law Enforcement.

Rube was a detective before he became an administrator, and Albert picks his brains about what steps he would take next if he were handling the Brough case. Rube is helpful, but what Albert carries away most clearly from their session is Rube's experienced opinion that the chances of finding a missing child alive drop about fifty per cent with each day that child is gone.

The conversation leaves Albert with no appetite. His younger sister and her husband, Jakba and Marcus Tiner, are expecting him for supper, however. Earlier in the day, Albert was on the point of cancelling, but thought better of it after he made his appointment with Rube. Leaving Rube, he reflected, he would be twenty miles closer to the Tiners' Lexington apartment than to his own in Paris. Now he realizes that he will be almost half an hour early, but he drives straight on. Marcus and Jakba are family, after all.

Jakba opens the door and exclaims "Oh!" even before she can have noticed Albert's tired clothes. She recovers and smiles warmly.

Albert is conscious of the skipped beat and apologizes for his inconsiderate timing.

"What are you talking about, early? You can't ever get here too early to suit us! Come on in here!" She hugs him.

For a second Albert thinks Jakba's uncharacteristic sweetness stems from sympathy for the strain he's under, but she doesn't know he's been assigned the Brough case....

Jakba is wearing a caftan, as always. Caftans complement her hair, which she has let go natural ever since the second year she failed to get elected to the all-white cheerleading squad at Paris High. She ushers Albert into the living room, where Marcus is shoveling documents off the coffee table into a briefcase. Marcus is a lawyer who specializes in civil rights cases; Jakba works for him as a paralegal. The pictures on their living room wall are framed photographs of Marcus Garvey and Malcolm X and—the gift of Jakba and Albert's older sister Maggie—a black angel done in acrylics by a member of Maggie's minister husband's congregation.

Marcus isn't discomfited that Albert finds him tidying up; he is older than Albert, and makes more money. Because he and Albert disagree on many things, however, they show one another careful courtesy. Marcus shakes Albert's hand, smiles, inquires after his health, and offers to make him "the usual."

Albert doesn't follow Marcus to the kitchen for his bourbon and ice water; he knows the kitchen isn't big enough for him and Jakba and Marcus simultaneously. Instead he ducks into the bathroom. That red and green caftan Jakba is wearing looks special, and Marcus hasn't changed from office suit to home clothes. Albert turns on the mirror light and straightens the tie he'd come expecting to stuff in his pocket as soon as he sat down. He leans closer to the mirror to consider his shave. His eyes, he sees, are bloodshot. "*White folks,*" he remembers Jakba declaring, "*don't look at us. White folks draw black people with big white eyeballs. Look in the mirror! Are your eyeballs white? Look more like turtle shell to me.*"

As Albert steps back into the living room, the doorbell rings and Jakba almost runs to let in another guest, a young woman. The two embrace, the young woman holding out of the way to one side what is plainly a bottle. It occurs to Albert that he might have spent his spare half hour buying his sister a box of candy.

Albert is surprised by the additional guest, but not astonished. Both his sisters are as anxious as his mother to see him married, and they do this to him as often as they can come up with somebody they consider appropriate. Their ideas of appropriate differ. Maggie favors young women who attend her husband's church. Mrs. Blount usually produces relatives of neighbors.

Jakba's candidate this evening is fifteen minutes early herself, Albert notes, assuming she was invited for the same time as he. Jakba's surprise, when she opened her door to find him, takes on a different meaning. Apparently he had been meant to arrive second. "Etta," Jakba says, "this is my biggest brother, Albert. Albert, this is my soul mate, Etta Hollamon."

Etta smiles and extends her free hand, saying in a pleasant voice, "Hey, Albert. How ya doing?"

Seeing a face move and speak that one knows as well as Abraham Lincoln's, and similarly only from a photograph, is unsettling for a moment. This face with its short-cropped, tinted hair, its Cherokee, not African, nose, has stared challengingly back at Albert from his *Herald-Leader* ever since that paper decided to add a regular column written from the viewpoint of Lexington's blacks. "Lexington *black*," Henrietta Hollamon hadn't even waited to be hired to correct her interviewer. "Nobody speaks for all of us." That had cinched the job, though she didn't, doesn't, know it. Ms. Hollamon, as her readers—who include Albert—have come to sense, prefers to think that whites find her assertiveness abrasive.

Etta is smartly dressed, in black slacks and a black-cuffed red jacket. The jacket is marred, in Albert's eyes, by large shoulder pads, which remind him of his brother. Cyrus Blount is a drummer with The Blues Supremes, who go in for shoulder pads.

Jakba protests Etta's gift. "Just to thank you for doing the cooking," says Etta, "which you know I hate."

"The crazy black woman who works for the *Herald* is here!" Marcus cries, stepping out of the kitchen. He too embraces Etta.

Albert and Etta and Jakba sit down in the living room and Marcus takes Etta's wine out to the refrigerator. "Appreciated some of the things you said in that piece you wrote on the Galloway case," Albert tells Etta. His words are carefully chosen, even though Marcus is out of the room. He knows that Marcus's take on that column will have differed from his own, that the things he and Marcus appreciated most in it will not have been the same. Sam Galloway, a black seventeen year-old pusher, was shot last spring on a Lexington street after pulling a gun on the white cop who'd stopped his car for running a red light. Word of a black teenager killed by a white cop had spread through Lexington like spilled mercury, and a two-day riot had left a lot of glass in the streets. Etta had been agitating in her column for more black police on Lexington's streets, and she repeated this demand the week of the shooting, but went on to condemn the riot. "I see racism in a community that refuses to hold one of its own responsible," she quoted the black attorney of the O. J. Simpson prosecuting team.

Marcus, Albert well knows, has no sympathy for the cop forced by the shooting into early retirement. Marcus wanted to sue him on behalf of the bereaved mother, but a white lawyer beat him to her.

Etta's wine is just what the buffalo wings Jakba has prepared for appetizers need, Jakba declares, and no one argues. Except for Albert's, spirits are high at the dinner table. Jakba has warned Etta that Albert is quiet. "Jakba tells me you live in Paris," she says to him. "That's Bourbon County, isn't it?"

"Yes," says Albert. "It's the county seat."

"They getting anywhere finding that little boy who disappeared Wednesday?"

"Nowhere."

"Suspects?"

"No strong suspects."

"Not enough blacks in Bourbon County for the sheriff to find one he can hang it on," suggests Marcus.

"Sheriff Maggard's not handling the case," Albert says. "I am."

The two young women lean forward as Marcus leans back. Albert's question beats the other three to the floor. "So what's your next target?" he asks Etta. He is not going to talk about Lang Brough.

Etta gets the message. "That Northside school with the 80%

66

black student body and the third world budget," she answers briskly. "Tell me that's coincidence!"

Albert doesn't have to tell her anything, because Marcus is off and running. Soon he has worked the subject around to his childhood in Frankfort, and the time he wanted to see Dumbo, and his grandmother had to explain to him that she couldn't take him because the theater showing it didn't admit blacks except to the balcony, and she couldn't climb stairs anymore. "I'm talking about our state capitol!" Marcus reminds everybody.

Albert and Jakba know the story by heart.

Albert is conscious of Jakba's displeasure when he begins to speak of going, barely thirty minutes after they leave the table. Etta has given up trying to draw him out; she is jotting down Marcus's suggestions for her school piece. Jakba sees Albert to the door. She is irritated. Albert is sorry. "I've got a date with a boat awfully early tomorrow," he apologizes to them all.

"Hope you hook something big," Etta says gamely.

Albert winces. "Don't know whether to hope that or not," he says. With a bleak smile, he goes out into the dark.

❧13❧   {Ruth

I know now how a woman might start drinking right after breakfast.

Saturday morning, Grove was scarcely back home from driving a beaming Joanna to Lucille's, before the fire department's cruelly blood-red engine arrived to search our pond. Grove's jaw set the moment the truck turned onto our lane. His determination and dropped g's Friday night, as he ruled for accepting Lucille's surprising offer to keep Joanna for me Saturday, fell into place.

"Nobody," my voice wasn't shrill as I began, but soon escaped me: "Nobody goes swimming in April!"

Grove bent to zip his boots, his face hidden. "Wait in the house. I don't want you down there."

"Lang went straight to the mailbox!" I hurried, but failed to get between Grove and his exit. "The dogs never lifted their heads!"

"Stay inside," Grove said, and closed the door.

I could have beaten it and screamed.

No Father React's Bedtime Stories about "Maybe they'll find his books, his jacket." They were after a body.

The enormous truck pulled up beside our house and a man got out. From newspaper photographs I recognized Chief Buddy Erbacher. He conferred soberly with Grove, whose back was toward my window. The engine door flashed like knives in the sun as the driver opened it and jumped down. The driver, a young man with carefully combed short hair, wore dark blue pants, a light blue shirt, boots, and an expression like Chief Erbacher's — grave as a mortician's. In a momentary mental picture, like the scene glimpsed as one's car rushes past a drive-in, I saw the two of them presiding over the hoses intruded into our silent pond. I felt as sick and weakened as if they were pumping the blood from my body.

I vividly remember the pumping of Charleston County's Adger Pond when I was a girl, after the police got a tip that the pusher they were looking for had been dealing to snapping turtles for a week. It took three trucks two days to empty Adger Pond at a thousand gallons a minute a pump. Langdon took me to watch, the second day. I never have told my parents.

The water lilies eventually bloomed thick as ever, but Adger Pond never had fish in it again.

Lang would never forgive us if we killed all his beloved bluegills.

When I jerked open the front door, every head turned my way. Then the young man became busy with something in the truck's equipment compartment. Erbacher clamped his mouth shut and looked at his boots. Only Grove watched me, with a contained, alert look that told me that he was going to let me speak once but, depending on what I said and how I said it, possibly twice and possibly not. He intended to protect me if he had to sack me to do it. "I don't want that pond bled to death," I told Erbacher. "Our boy is not in that pond." I was taking care not to look Grove's way. "There is no excuse for wasting—"

"No ma'am," Erbacher raised his eyes to mine briefly—as briefly as possible. "We won't pump your pond. No ma'am. We sure won't."

Now I did look at Grove.

"Albert Blount is meeting them with a boat," he answered my baffled eyes. "Will you go back inside, please?"

Does a happy marriage require that a wife remain a child? Furious, I left them. Then, like a bad child that finds a way to thwart its orders without directly challenging, I lugged my kitchen steps out onto the deck. From their height, with binoculars, I could watch.

The young man whose sleeves were the color of the innocent sky did the rowing. Chief Erbacher threw the grapnel, a small four-pronged hook such as his ancestors used to grapple grapes along the Rhine. The rope, fifty feet of skinny heron's neck, arced out. From the deck I could not hear the iron strike the water like a predatory beak, but I could see that each time it withdrew empty.

Under his carapace of a helmet, Chief Buddy Erbacher's cheeks are darkly weathered and deeply grooved; the corners of his mouth turn down. Thirty years of pulling children out of fires hasn't been like a career in viticulture. He reeled his empty grapnel in and cast again, impassive as a turtle on a log.

In the boat the younger man silently rowed, the elder silently threw and withdrew the iron hooks. On the bank the other three —Grove, Albert Blount, the man who had brought the boat— watched and waited. They, like the men in the boat, never seemed to speak to one another.

The night's frost was still bone-white in the shadows of our leafless maples, and I grew cold. I went inside and lay face down on the bed. How could I forgive any of them their willingness to find Lang dead? Apparently only I, when he telephoned—as he would if I lay still just one more minute—only I would be able to say that I had always known unfalteringly that he was not, could not be, forever lost. I watched myself run, triumphant, to the pond.

After awhile I washed my face in cold water and made the men coffee.

When I reached the pond with my thermos, they were beaching the boat. They had not found Lang with their ridiculous fruit-picker, and they were abandoning him. "You'll have to come back tomorrow and pump it," I said.

Chief Erbacher looked at Albert Blount.

"That won't be necessary, Mrs. Brough," Albert said.

The world tilted. Dread choked off my voice, but Albert saw my eyes fly to his beeper and was quick to forestall my question. "We haven't heard anything, Mrs. Brough. Because you have a pond, we wanted to check it off our list of possibilities, just get that line of thinking disposed of. There never was any reason to think we would find anything in your pond, but we've learned it's best to be systematic."

"I don't believe you will find our son by making gestures, Mr. Blount."

"The pond is too big to be pumped, Ruth," Grove said.

"The pond is too big to be properly dragged in the time you've been down here! They can't possibly have dragged every foot! And that *toy* wouldn't lift a pregnant possum!" I clenched my teeth because no matter how cogent your observations, nobody listens to you if you cry.

Chief Erbacher considered his insulted grapnel. "You'd be surprised what that can do," he said earnestly. "You lift that. It's heavy. It found that—fella—that drownded in the querry last year." I hoped Albert Blount hadn't noted the catch before "fella," for the quarry victim had been black; Albert would have known as well as I what Erbacher had started to say. "I found that one in just twenty-five minutes; maybe you read about it. He didn't have nothing on but a wristwatch. He was drunk, you know, and dove in like that. The hook caught him by the watchband, and I brought him to shore by his hand, holding onto his hand."

What had he felt with the cold hand of that unseen man in his? Less horror, apparently, than if he had pulled the body into the boat with him.

To this man, my beautiful child was a horror.

"The pond is not too large to be pumped," I said. "Zad Thacker could empty it with his irrigation pump in one day."

"What are you going to do with the water?" My persistence was costing Grove face, but he was patient.

I pointed to where the hoses obviously would have to be led to drain.

"And wash out Allen's entire field, and his barn, and his road."

The young fireman was helping the farmer load his boat. Blount and Erbacher stood still, not exchanging glances, watching me and, covertly, Grove. I was like a movie projectionist: I could control the action only insofar as I could freeze the actors in place. Permitted to move again, they would go on precisely as already directed by someone else. "Well, if Allen's soybeans are what's important to you," I said, and strode off toward the house.

The first pink-white blooms on the serviceberry the children see from their bunk had opened just that morning. My Virginia cousins call this graceful tree the shadblow because it matches its brief blossoming to their river's, to those few sudden days at winter's end when the water runs silver with excited fish. Kentucky's Appalachians called it the serviceberry because it flowered about the time the roads up to their little settlements became passable again after winter's isolation, and when the circuit rider came—to christen the babies born during the inaccessible months, to marry the couples who had publicly joined during that time, to preach the service for those who had died.

What did they preach for those whose bodies were not in lovingly marked graves, but who did not join in the singing? For those who vanished from berrying or hunting leaving not a limb, not a shred of shirt or skirt? What kind of service does the church provide for cases like that?

✤14✤   {Ruth

Albert's all-state bulletin describing Lang, where and when we saw him last, and what clothes Grove recalled he was wearing, had gone out by radio and computer to all Kentucky police agencies right after Grove called Sheriff Maggard, Albert tells us. Before he even got to our house, he says, analysts in Kentucky's Intelligence Section in Frankfort were sending all the information via computer to the National Missing Persons Center for national distribution. He means for us to feel encouraged. I feel mocked, it was all so futile.

Given Lang's photograph, Albert had gone to work again, and

as he left after dragging our pond, he gave us a stack of flyers he'd made. Gave Grove, I should have said. After my performance at the pond, I didn't come back outside until he and his firemen were gone. I can imagine the two of them, Albert explaining about the flyers, Grove accepting them, and the patient, sympathetic, resolute, *We-understand-women; we-feel-for-each-other; we-will-go-ahead-with-what-is-necessary* look on both faces. Grove had been a surprise and relief to Albert from the start, I suspect. A vet knows what it's like to have hysterical clients who expect omnipotence.

I had been good too, until Saturday, conscious of Joanna's eyes. So maybe Grove's hauling her off to Lucille for the day backfired, and serves *him* right. But not Albert.

"I've faxed one to every law office in Kentucky," Albert told Grove, "and to all the big newspapers. Take these and put one up anywhere you can think of. I'll give you as many more as you want."

Lang's picture on the wall with criminals, the petty, the vicious, I thought when Grove brought Albert's flyers in. At the same moment that I wanted to thrust one under the nose of every person in the world, I wanted to clutch the whole batch face toward myself and hide them and me. I laid them, face down, on the dining room table.

Grove brushed off questions about lunch and set out for every barn he's ever served, with a stack of replicas of his son's likeness over Albert's somber caption, face down, on the seat beside him. He made no comment on my behavior, but he neither kissed me goodbye, nor waved as the car passed the house.

I sat down and made two lists: where I could mount flyers at once; where I could mount some Monday.

Monday, the post office; the school cafeteria. *Today,* the library, open till three on Saturday. *Monday,* the banks. *Today,* the supermarkets; the trees along Clay Pike. (When I did get to the pike, I found that React had preceded me. They had been, I eventually learned, to more places in Bourbon County than I had ever gone in my ten years' residence.)

Today, the little shop around the corner from the school that sells chewing gum and pencils and candy bars and that I forbade

Lang to enter because it's such a firetrap. (Grove backed me up, telling me later that his concern wasn't so much with the unlikely chance of a fire as with the shop's clientele: "Anybody who makes a living in a hole like that is either making book or dealing.") Now I wish I had burnt it down. I wouldn't have to be asking myself if one of its hophead patrons took Lang.

"In 1945," Eva von Strehlenau's grandmother told me, "there was only one kiosk left standing in Karolinenplatz, and every inch of it was covered by notices from people trying to find their families. 'Whoever knows the whereabouts of my daughter Anna, 3, lost on the highway between Nuremberg and Munich during the air raid April 7, please notify…' Peter and Eva's Uncle Rolf was born just as the war ended; I would read these pleas for missing children and clutch him until he screamed. I didn't love the American army, but I was grateful they weren't the Russians, grateful the shooting was over. I would weep for those other parents, weep for my good luck. *Lucky, lucky,* Rolf came when he came, lucky not sooner!"

I had felt the same way about Lang. Lucky, lucky, American children don't die of measles anymore like five of Grove's great-grandparents' children; lucky, no war; lucky, no depression. We could give him every protection.

At quarter of one I had just finished my two lists when Fran Warren's Lumina pulled up in our parking area and Fran got out with a box of Kentucky Fried Chicken in hand. "Now how can I help?" she demanded. Her almost belligerent tone was unnecessary. I had been just about to ring Norma Lee and accept her offer to telephone-sit for me. Instead I left Fran ensconced at the front window with a magazine and a pair of binoculars, watching our pregnant mares, listening for the telephone, while I drove off with my first list and my flyers.

The magazine must have closed as I turned the truck out of our lane, because when I got back at quarter of four, Fran had vacuum cleaned the entire house. "You're sure you don't want me to stay?" she urged. "I don't have anything I've got to do today." A lie, I knew perfectly well. I used to work five-and-a-half day weeks myself. "Sure you'll be all right?"

73

"Yes, sure," I lied too.

I walked her out to her car, a sure sign I was lying. At the last minute she rolled down her window. "Stop blaming yourself," she ordered. "I know all about all that pressure on the victim to feel guilty. Takes the heat off everybody else! The victim's a damn fool to cooperate." Then she rolled up the window and drove away.

"The alcoholic's family," Fran said to me one day shortly after Max left her, "is expected to blame itself. We're part of 'the problem.' We have some conspiracy to keep our drunk a drunk; it's a game we play. I'm supposed to be bowed with guilt for something I could no more help than the Virgin Mary could help conceiving Jesus." But I am not religious enough to take a lapsed Catholic's comfort in blasphemy, and rationally, there is no way to escape self-reproach.

Fifteen minutes after Fran's Lumina drove out of sight, Grove telephoned to say that he couldn't be home for supper. Flyers in hand, he had walked in on an emergency. "One of the mares here has a twisted gut, it seems like. She's got to have surgery ASAP, and Roy's foaling a mare in Midway and Hank's halfway to a fracture in Versailles. I have got to go with her to the hospital, and I'll be with her till she's out from under. Will you be all right?"

Of *course* I wouldn't be all right. Did *he* want to be alone in our house? Why had he taken Joanna to Lucille? "Of course."

"Did you and Lucille talk about what time I would come for Joanna?"

"No, we just—"

"Tell her I'll be there before ten. If I can't, I'll call her."

I could have gone for Joanna in the truck, if he had called sixteen minutes sooner, while Fran was still there to man the telephone. Or Fran could have gone for her. Joanna loves Fran.

"Don't try to bring the yearlings in. Ervil can do it when he gets there."

I took two aspirins and looked up Lucille's number.

"It's not right," Lucille exclaimed, "expecting something like that of him at a time like this! But he's such a responsible man, Mrs. Brough."

I had given up reminding Lucille to call me Ruth. "Yes, he is. He's very dependable." I was ashamed. I had been thinking only of my own anguish, while Lucille had thought at once of Grove's.

"You can leave Joanna here all night if you want to, Mrs. Brough; we've having a lovely time. Really, why don't you just tell Grove to come in the morning?" I was Mrs. Brough; Grove was Grove.

A child who is apt to wake up screaming in the night should be in her own room with her own mother to turn on the light and lie to her. "That's really generous of you," I said, "but I'm afraid he's at the hospital by now. I'm afraid nobody can get in touch with him once that mare is cut open."

I was all too soon to learn that I was all too correct.

Might I speak to my daughter, I asked.

"Hi," said Joanna. "Lucille and me are decorating eggs. I have a surprise for you, but I *won't* tell you what it is. You have to wait and see."

Last Easter Lang, Joanna, and I dyed eggs five different colors, one color each. This year I said nothing about doing that again, and Joanna said nothing.

I was alone in the house with no suppers to fix, and two hours to go before time to bring in the mares. I knew better than to sit down and let myself think. I opened the laundry door, but the clothes on top of the stack to be ironed were Lang's. I had to get out of the house.

Thankless and her colt were supposed to get half an hour in their pasture, and Grove wouldn't be home in time to give it to them. I ran all the way to the barn.

The tack room phone was not ringing. I cocked both tack room doors open so I would hear it if it did, and I put the mare and colt out. The colt trotted so close to his mother that at any moment he could touch her with a turn of his head. Once in the paddock, she let him go nowhere until she had reconnoitered.

As soon as Thankless had assured herself that the fences between the paddock and the mares' field still stood, she paraded her colt up and down. Lagoon and Blithe Spirit stopped grazing and came running to see. I turned my back on the sight. Nowhere, I was learning, was any better than anywhere else.

I put Cat Chow in Troy and Katisha's nearly empty dish.

I won't think about what he is eating. I won't think about him at all. I will listen, but I will not think.

Half an hour was just enough time for me to clean and re-bed Thankless's stall, and that was better for my tense gut than sitting with my arms hugging my ribs, watching the telephone.

Half an hour was not, however, enough for Thankless. She drifted just beyond my grasp. When I persisted, she took the colt to the far side of the paddock.

If I went after her with the feed bucket, I just might catch her, but the telephone would be out of earshot. Meanwhile the air was growing chill, and she had led the colt twice as far as he should have walked. He could break down; he could get pneumonia.

I wondered if the first thing a psychiatrist would have said about me was that having lost my own son, I wanted Thankless to lose hers—that my strenuous efforts to care for the colt were merely an elaborate disguise to protect me from guilty knowledge of my own nastiness.

Disguise or genuine, as I watched the colt run shivering after his mother, tears ran down my cheeks. Any psychiatrist, lay or rich, is welcome to my considered conclusion that what I have suffered myself is the last thing I want anyone else to suffer, because I have so clear an idea of the depth of the pain.

Lagoon and Blithe Spirit had no objection to coming in to their suppers and once they were out of her sight, Thankless clamored for salvation. The shank I clipped to her halter as she pressed against the gate was probably superfluous: I could have led her in by an ear.

Back in the empty house, I switched on the TV. Even the news, with which I had lately stopped flagellating myself, would be a welcome distraction. I sat as close to the telephone as I could sit and still see the screen, and held onto my chair arms while I allowed the set to drown out the silence of the telephone.

Lang, I keep reminding myself, has known our telephone number since he was old enough to memorize *Mary had a little lamb.* So, in her turn, has Joanna. Name, address, telephone number, father's name: that, I told my mother, is their shorter catechism. I don't know if he would remember about area codes. A vision of Lang frantically dialing our number from a bus terminal or highway filling station and getting nothing but a *We-are-sorry-the-number-you-have-dialed...* recording is one of my stock torments now. Surely, I remind myself, each time, Lang would dial 0 or 911 and tell someone something.

The ticky-tacky of a teletype ushered in the long desk with the two young blow-dried commentators in their three-piece suits, and I leaned forward with a relieved sigh. "Good evening," said one smooth face sternly, and Lang's picture filled the screen.

I sank back in my chair. Through ears humming like an underwater swimmer's I heard, "Police are still searching for eight-year-old Langdon Brough, missing since Wednesday from—"

The picture, of course, was the one I had given Albert. In less time than the auctioneer gives a yearling, it was replaced by a beauty queen's radiant smile. I snapped off the set even before the telephone rang.

"Mrs. Brough?"

"*Yes.*"

"Go to the pay phone in front of the Paris Dairy Queen and wait for it to ring."

"What? *Who is this?*"

The man hung up.

For a second there was no sound anywhere, then I heard myself breathing. *Call Albert,* I told myself, like someone afraid to move telling herself to pick up her right foot. I dialed Albert.

"Drive slowly," Albert said. "If you're *too* slow, he'll get suspicious. He's scared. We don't want him to run, but try to give me time to get that pay phone monitored."

Grove's mobile unit number invited me to record. "Call your wife!" was all I could think to utter. I saw Grove bent over the laid-open mare, oblivious to everything but the gut under the surgeon's knife. I was on the point of calling the surgeon's wife and asking her to drive over and tell Grove that his wife was going out into the night to meet a criminal; then I imagined my caller dialing me back to make certain I wasn't doing just that, finding my line busy, and vanishing, Lang with him.

Despite Albert's instructions to stall, I was afraid not to start at once. Someone might be watching the house. I promised myself to give Albert his delay by holding the truck to thirty-five.

I had never fired Grove's one firearm, his groundhog shotgun, but I put my father's pistol into the glove compartment. Unfortunately, it was Langdon my father taught to shoot. The gun is the one with which my father won his fraternity the marksmanship trophy his junior year. Once when this farm's back field was empty, I set a can on one of its fence posts and did succeed in nicking the post twice, but Grove implored me not to practice anymore. "You and that museum piece will kill every horse on the farm!" Now I felt as if I had a time bomb in the glove compartment.

Clay Pike was built on an old buffalo trail. Propositions to widen and straighten it are annual, and I have opposed every one. Let the people who work in Lexington agitate for a commuter train, I said, not bulldoze two-hundred-year-old hand-laid stone fences. For ten years I had been telling Paris commuters to eat cake. Now, trapped by Saturday evening traffic in Clay Pike's almost continuous *no passing* zones, rarely able to drive anything approaching thirty-five, I felt mocked.

The scene at the Dairy Queen seemed unreal to me. The telephone booth in front was empty, but as usual on a Saturday night, the lot was full.

Nobody's routine had been disturbed by my child's disappearance. Anybody who usually went to Paris Saturday night was there as always. Just as always.

I drove around the corner to the deserted high school, parked, and ran all the way back to the booth. The telephone stopped ringing as I lifted the receiver.

How long might it have rung? I could see the kidnapper cuffing Lang at each unanswered shrill. If I called Albert and asked him what to do, if I tried to call Grove again (why hadn't I left the request that he call Albert?), the kidnapper might dial the booth again just at that moment. How would he interpret a busy line?

I tried to think what Albert would ask me; I wrote down the time: 6:36. Later I learned that a police car had driven up to the telephone company and let out South Central Bell's Carter Posey just as I replaced the receiver in the booth. "There hadn't been anyone on duty who could trace calls for us," Albert says.

The manager lives fifty miles away in Frankfort, but at least he was home. "The manager had a list. I began dialing," Albert says. "The first man had taken his wife to the movies, the baby sitter said; she didn't know which one. The second man's mother told me he had gone to spend Easter with his girlfriend's folks in Cincinnati. The third man was Carter Posey; his number did not answer at all. I radioed Sergeant Tackett and he went to VanHoose's bar and hauled out Carter Posey, and I talked to Posey on Tackett's radio as they drove to the phone building."

"An inspired guess."

"Oh, we know where they hang out."

Did *we* mean "we police," I wondered, or "we blacks"? ("We" meant "Albert," as it turns out. Albert and Carter Posey were classmates at Paris High.)

Paris's telephone booths are transparent nowadays, but the Dairy Queen's stank of urine anyhow. The sun had gone down and I was getting cold. Enough people were coming and going that I wasn't afraid I had been set up for rape, but what if one of these comers and goers wanted to use the telephone? I couldn't just stand there. I held the receiver to my ear and pretended to be talking, keeping the phone shut off with my other hand.

The man whose call I had just missed had hung up three seconds before Carter Posey started sprinting from his car to the telephone building. I, unaware of that, spun hopeful theories. Maybe the man had hung up because police had arrived to arrest him. Maybe in three more seconds Albert would arrive and tell me that Lang was secure and unharmed. Anybody who's ever waited for a traffic light knows how long one minute can seem. I waited for ten.

The telephone's ring socked my heart. The voice in my ear was the same man's. "If you want your little boy, bring fifty thousand dollars in hundred dollar bills to the water tower on Route 627 at eight o'clock."

"Put Lang on the phone this instant!" I demanded. "Let me speak to him!"

"Shut up and listen if you know what's good for him. Be at that

79

tower at eight o'clock. Come alone and drive your pickup. Park it behind the tower. Blink your headlights twice, and turn on your overhead light. Have that money in a freezer bag."

The booth seemed to be spinning. "But I don't have that kind of money," I protested frantically. "Not anywhere! And I don't have any money in the *house* at all! Let me speak to my child!"

Across the lot someone called to someone, and they both laughed.

"You can git it, Miz Brough. A big vet's wife like you. Nice house, big car, all them *thurr*-breds."

"The banks are closed! The banks are closed till Monday!"

"The bank will open for you, Miz Brough. Your kind of people got the banks all figured out; they're all working for your kind. *You* can git money. Just put your hand on your banker's dick the way you do when you want a new fur coat. Don't he always give it to you then, Miz Brough?"

A good vet in horse country is so necessary, so respected, so appreciated that as the wife of one, I had been wrapped in pink cotton for ten years, supposing—not supposing, because I had never thought about it: *feeling* that everyone was well-disposed toward me and my family, that I hadn't an enemy in the state.

"Now you listen good," said the voice. "That nigger's being watched. If he picks up a foot before I get my money, you'll never see your kid again!"

Albert sighed. "He's probably bluffing, but I'll sit here. Now what I want you to do is this."

Albert is a handy man for coming up with things—a tape recorder, a dog team, a boat—but five hundred hundred-dollar bills is something he doesn't keep in his desk. "What about the Smiths?"

Albert had interviewed the Smiths in the house Norma Lee's father built them. If I hadn't lent Norma Lee five or ten dollars a couple of dozen times, I, too, might have imagined that she and Fred had a wall safe.

"What about your banker: can you call him at home?"

The only unlisted Paris telephones I know of belong to a few beleaguered schoolteachers. Anyone can call our banker at home, but he takes his wife to her mother's in Memphis every Easter.

Several vets in this vicinity, who've been in the business long enough, keep a substantial sum in a wall safe in case some weekend, when the banks are closed, they suddenly want to claim a mare off the racetrack—which can only be done with cash. Not Grove's senior partner. Roy Bonnifred has never done anything suddenly, has never so much as blinked in haste, and never will. Standing in that upended plexiglass-and-aluminum coffin, I understood why holdup men destroy penniless victims. I hated Roy Bonnifred.

"Your husband will know how to get it," Albert said. "He'll have clients. He'll know which."

Dialing Grove's mobile unit number I had to start over twice. This time Grove answered. "Go home," he said. "I'll be there in half an hour with the money."

He had barely left the surgery. He couldn't get home in half an hour if he jumped into the car that instant and never touched four wheels to earth all the way and a genie flowed up and gave him the money through the window as he drove. I began to cry. "Ruth," Grove said: "Go home. The man may telephone again."

⚡15⚡   {Ruth

The man had instructed me to drive our pickup. I ticked off to myself what it has: no trunk, no backseat, and virtually no room in front of the passenger seat. No policeman could crouch on the floor. And—a short current shot through me—no telephone. Did he insist on the truck because of this absence of hiding places, or because he knew about our car's telephone? Who *was* he; *how much* did he know about us? While I waited for Grove, I played the tape of my first exchange with the man over and over, trying to recognize the voice, trying to hear something in the background— *a child*—or something to give a clue to where he called from. I succeeded only in making a totally strange voice sound familiar. At twenty minutes of eight I drove the truck around to the front of the house and remained sitting behind the wheel, a Ziploc bag on the seat beside me, my window rolled down.

Grove pulled the car up where it wouldn't block my exit. What looked like a college boy was sitting in the passenger seat; he leapt out before Grove's engine died and handed me the money. It could have been a box of brown sugar. The bills were in several packets, each secured with a rubber band. I began stuffing them into my little freezer bag. "You don't have to count it!" Grove snarled. "Get going if you're going!"

I'd started my engine just as soon as I'd seen Grove turn in at our mailbox; now I gunned it and left, sending gravel flying both sides of our driveway all my way to the Pike. I'd hoped Grove would lean in and kiss me before I left, but he was too furious at the danger he was obliged to be letting me meet.

Later I learned that Grove had driven directly to Malcolm Gurley, Lexington's best-known bookmaker, and signed a chit for the cash. *"What did you put up for security?"*

"The mare."

I didn't have to ask which mare.

The young man was one of Gurley's gofers. He had sat imperturbably all the way to our house, through all Grove's shouting, copying serial numbers off the bills. Grove had argued with Albert over the car phone all the way home. The police would protect me, Albert had said. He didn't say how.

Once the pickup had bumped over the desolate railroad tracks that cross Route 627 south of Paris's business district, the houses grew fewer, the sidewalks empty. Not soon enough and too soon, the water tower loomed ahead of me. It stood on eight legs like a UFO come to rest, its threat, like a UFO's, ungaugable. A stone fence was meant to keep vehicles like mine off this forbidding structure's landing pad, but the gate stood open. ("The padlock had been smashed," Albert told me later.) I paused. Twice the man had stipulated exactly what time I was to arrive. I had been too stunned to make certain that our watches read the same. When I thought of it, I had no way to call him back.

By my watch, I arrived five minutes early. Assuming that he was already at the tower, would he be more alarmed by my pulling in sooner than he was ready for me, or by the sight of me going by? Would he think I had arranged a rendezvous? *Would he kill Lang and flee.* I could see Lang's body lying in the cold wet grass under the tower more clearly than I could see the tower itself.

I pulled up as directed and turned off my headlights. I heard nothing, and saw nothing move. In the fields across the road the only life was grazing sheep; in the fields beyond the tower, not even that. Cherry trees were blooming along the empty pasture's roadside, ghostly in the darkness. When I turned my headlights on, they seemed to spring at me, like a Klan rally surprised. I turned the lights on twice and off twice, as instructed. No one came. The man had been so fierce about my punctuality, I had assumed he would be prompt. I grew cold, but the heater works only if the engine is running, and I wanted to hear every sound. The man had told me to turn on my overhead light. I felt like a staked goat.

My doors were locked, but I would have to open one to let Lang in. I kept telling myself that I mustn't stop to embrace him, but must instantly shove him down on the floor and gun the engine. The man didn't know we had recorded his voice, alerted the police. Lang and I would be the only ones who'd seen his face, and he might be planning to shoot us both the moment he had his cash.

Again, I was not really afraid of rape. There was no money in that, and he'd be in too big a hurry, I assured myself. I sat drying my hands on my thigh.

The face that appeared at my window came from nowhere. When I screamed, I thought the man would hit me right through the glass. "Shut your goddamned mouth, you bitch!"

He had no nose, no hair, no mouth.

He made a peremptory motion for me to roll down the window. I had slid to the far side of the cab; I leaned back and lowered the glass enough for us to hear each other better, but not enough for him to put in his arm and unlock the door.

"Where's the money?" The demand came through the stocking mask clearly.

"Where is my son?"

"He'll phone you as soon as I count my damn money."

"You said you'd have him here!"

"Am I gonna have trouble with you?"

Suddenly I decided to gamble that he was alone, to open the glove compartment as if for the money and pull out my father's gun. Not even Grove knew I had it.

The image of an accomplice nearby with a knife at Lang's throat, or even just a nervous foot on an accelerator, kept me sane. I rolled the glass down a couple more inches and delivered Malcolm Gurley's money.

"You sit here ten minutes," the man said. "If I hear that engine start before ten minutes, your brat has had it." He disappeared in the dark and the police closed in and arrested him.

He did not have Lang. He had never had Lang.

Blessed Albert was with the police and made time for me. "Are you all right, Mrs. Brough?"

"Will you please tell my husband."

I had tried to prepare myself for the worst: for Lang terrorized —hurt—for Lang dead. This was almost worse, and I had never thought of it at all.

"He knows, Mrs. Brough. We've been in touch with him ever since the man left his room. I'm sorry we didn't have any way to communicate with you. Are you all right? Mrs. Brough? Would you like someone to drive you home?

"Yes. No. Yes, I'm all right. Thank you. No one needs to drive for me." No, I was not all right; yes, I wanted someone to drive me home, to drive me home.

The man had seen Lang's photograph in the newspaper. He knew no more of Lang's whereabouts than we.

In the police floodlights, the shapes along the fence were cherry trees again. Only Tuesday my remaining springs had seemed too little room to see them hung with snow, but I could not endure even one more spring of Lang vanished, could not endure another Eastertide. After Langdon's death I had intended to face life prepared for ill and not for good, but I had let down my guard and taken a hit and lost too much blood.

When they took the stocking off the man's face I did and did not recognize him. He was the same sullen, bony, glaring Huck Finn, middle-aged and trapped, that I had paid in a dozen filling stations,

84

without ever having seen this particular one. He was a house painter who rented a single room in a boarding house on one of those residential streets that tolerate a laundromat and a mom-and-pop grocery, but no blacks. His landlady looked so guilty when she vowed he'd never given any trouble that I concluded he drank. At his trial she testified that he spent most of his evenings at the City Club, where she had supposed he was that evening.

I never pass the Club's door without an inward wince, a shrinking quite apart from the sick feeling that comes with any reminder of my dumb faith that I would be going home with Lang that water tower night. I picture the men in there, the men who throw their beer cans at our mailbox as they drive by, and I imagine them passing their sour comments about the vet's bitch screwing the banker, and I don't feel like that nice young Courtonne girl anymore. I don't feel anymore like the nice young wife of that nice young vet whom everyone respects and everyone is glad to have living here. I know they despise me only because they imagine they can't give their wives what they imagine I have, and I know I am not despicable merely for being despised. I know the whole scene is in my imagination. What I know is not what I feel.

Ervil was foal-watching for us. "Let me fix you a drink before I go for Joanna," Grove said.

"I thought I'd come with you."

I had wanted Grove to hold me so fiercely that I couldn't have moved if I'd wanted to, for an hour, maybe, or a day. I wanted to hear him sob between almost clenched teeth, like a modern, "vulnerable," movie hero, *Ruth-Ruth-I-can't-bear-to-lose-you-too!* But I had failed to bring him his son, and it was almost as if I had botched my mission. Of course I imagined this; "projecting," the word is.

I wanted at least to go with Grove to get Joanna from Lucille's. I had thought I would be holding Lang; I wanted to hold Joanna. It's a half hour drive, and I knew she would sleep in my lap all the way home.

"I think you should try to sleep," Grove said kindly. "You look like hell."

"I can sleep in the car. I always do."

He spoke more gently yet. "One of us should stay. I don't think Ervil's the one to handle the telephone."

And I did not question that, then, though if it had been true, Grove would not have needed to say it to me.

He left. I poured myself the drink he had offered to fix for me. There was no point waiting for him, I told myself. Grove never drinks in the evening, because he never knows which night some client is going to call him to an emergency and he's going to have to drive somewhere in the dark at top speed, and be wide awake when he gets there. I tasted my drink and made it stiffer.

I heard them drive into the garage and lunged for the door. Joanna was coming up the stairs on her own feet. "I made you a present," she said cheerfully. Maybe Grove was right; maybe getting her out of our grief-stricken house was what she needed more of. Maybe Lucille, maybe *anyone*, was better for her right now than I.

The egg she presented me was beautifully multicolored, one shade fading into the next as artfully as a rainbow's.

"Thank you," I said, relieved, as I accepted the gift, that my hands had stopped shaking. "Did you really paint this?"

"Uh-huhhh. Lucille helped me!"

I set down the egg and gave her a greedy hug. "Mmmm, don't you smell nice!"

"It's perfume!"

"Lovely."

"Lucille's boyfriend gave it to her. At least her used-to-be boyfriend. Lucille doesn't like him anymore because he's too young and silly. Lucille likes a man to be more responsivul. Lucille put perfume under my nose when I took my nap. Lucille says a little perfume when you go to bed gives you sweet dreams."

"And did you have sweet dreams?"

"Lucille says the best dreams come at night."

I met Lucille Harper almost her first morning at Hereward Stud, when I stopped by one Saturday to give Fran some horse tranquilizer for Grove. I knew Fran had been interviewing for a new assistant, ever since the old one telephoned from Christmas vacation that she'd married and wasn't coming back. The new girl spoke with a hint of Eastern Kentucky twang, but very buffered. Julia Roberts hair; turquoise eyelids; no lipstick and none needed. Skin still perfect fit—in fact, Miss Harper looked about eighteen, though I've learned that she's older. Short-sleeved pink cashmere calling attention to this or that, depending on viewer's age and sex. What caught *my* eye were smooth elbows.

I'd left a crockpot of chili simmering and it was nearly quitting time. Grove doesn't yearn for company in foaling season, but February to June was too long to wait to welcome a new Hereward Stud secretary. I invited Lucille and Fran both to come on home and eat lunch with us.

Fran had another engagement, Lucille had no car, and there was about an hour's work to do before either could leave, quitting time or no. The upshot was, I got hold of Grove on his mobile phone. He was indeed going to come home right past Hereward and could pick up Lucille, probably in an hour. I went on home to tidy up and light a fire in the fireplace.

As I drove in past the colts' paddock, I noticed that Uncle was limping. I am forbidden to lead Ten and Ten won't permit Uncle to precede him through a gate, so I had to wait for Grove to bring Uncle in. I pocketed a bottle of penicillin from our refrigerator and tramped back to the barn to flag down Grove and Lucille as they arrived.

At 16°, I had assumed that Lucille would sit in the car with the heater running while Grove and I coped with our beasts. Lang certainly hadn't protested being detailed to stay inside and watch Joanna and the fire. Lucille, however, crunched gamely through the crusty snow into the barn with us. "I want to see that summer sale yearling!" she declared. I gathered that Grove had bent her ear about Ten as they came.

I had no trouble holding Uncle for Grove to wash his wound, but that changed when Grove exchanged bucket and swabs for needle and syringe. At 118 pounds, I don't have much luck shoving yearlings against walls, but in the ten years I've lived on this farm, I've never developed the nerve to give a shot. It's absurd that I'd rather risk serious injury trying to hold a contrary 800-pound animal than jab a tiny needle into him for his own good, but Grove has given up telling me so. Trying hard not to look exasperated, he handed his needle and syringe to Lucille to hold while he fetched the twitch.

I stood back uselessly while Grove put the loop around Uncle's lip for me. As he gave the stick the final turn and I stepped forward to take hold of it, Lucille suggested that Grove just hang onto it while *she* gave Uncle his shot. "I've injected lots of horses," she said.

And clearly she had. A slight narrowing of the eye as the needle went in, a slight compression of the lips when it had to be rotated a bit, as it always does for anything as viscous as penicillin. "My Daddy was a vet," she explained. "Not a specialist like you, Dr. Brough. Daddy took care of everything in Rowan County that had four legs. That included a lot of Tennessee Walkers and Mountain Riding horses, and I used to help him some." Grove couldn't have looked more astonished and impressed if she'd announced that she'd come by her name playing first harp in the Lexington Symphony Orchestra.

Grove let Lucille and me out in front of the house, and drove the car around to the garage. In the foyer Lucille watched me switch from mucky boots to my waiting slippers and apologized for the condition of her shoes. "*I* apologize to *you!*" I interrupted her. "If I'd done my job, they wouldn't have anything on them worse than snow. Just leave them here and go on in by the fire. I'll fetch you slippers."

When I got back Grove was pouring three glasses of the chianti we drink with chili when we're treating ourselves. Lucille was sitting in an overstuffed chair with one shapely leg draped over the other; the children were opposite her on the sofa staring in frank admiration, and Grove was asking if Lucille had ever wanted to be a vet herself.

Lucille's dangling foot seemed to be considering her answer, slowly pointing first this way, then that. Her perfect stockinged ankle gleamed. "I didn't like the uniform," she said with a half smile at her foot, a smile which widened as she lifted her gaze to meet my husband's. Grove grinned back appreciatively, no doubt picturing, as I was myself, his heavy boots and shapeless smelly coveralls obliterating all that nylon and cashmere. "Seriously," Lucille said, seeing me in the doorway, "I saw how hard it was for Daddy to make time for my mother, and I thought, *me for a nine to five.* I don't think it would be easy for me to find a husband as understanding as your wife, Dr. Brough. If I were a vet, I mean."

"Will you cut that "doctor" stuff? Call me Grove, for cat's sake!"

Lucille rose smiling to accept my slippers. She is taller than I, but she stepped into my slippers with ease.

~⊰16⊱~   {Ruth

"Lucille says the best dreams come at night," Joanna told me placidly. That night I dreamed that our pond was paved with the skeletons of children, gleaming white as Georgia O'Keefe skulls; that our inoffensive mild-mannered soy bean-growing neighbor had been using it as a depository for years. "You can't prove any of them is Lang," I screamed at Chief Erbacher. And awoke to Easter.

I don't tell Grove my nightmares, and I think he's having some he's not telling me. There was a night when I awoke with the urgent conviction that someone was cutting the screen in Joanna's sliding door and that if I hurried I could scare him away before she too vanished. As my feet hit the floor I realized that this was nonsense, but being awake, I padded down the hall just to look at her. I do that a lot now.

The door to the wet bar was open and a bottle of bourbon sat on the dining room table beside a used empty glass. I couldn't reproach Grove. Wasn't I deviling Jake for Valium? Next morning when I came out to fix breakfast, glass and bottle were back in their cupboards. He is maintaining a confident front before the people who look to him, his wife, his daughter. He eats, he goes his rounds, he holds me when I weep, and tries to suppress his own tears.

As for me, I alternate despair with perfect certainty that Lang will roll back his stone and return to us.

This Easter Americans were urged to pray for our hostages in Iraq. The mother of one of them appeared on television making a gallant statement, one I would have admired a year ago. I left the room. "She knows where her son is," I said. Love is blind; fear wears blinders. Surely fear for a loved one must be the most selfish emotion a human feels.

I couldn't call Contel to have a telephone installed in the truck until Monday. I concentrated on getting through the holiday. Christ descended into hell, and on the third day, he rose, he emerged into light. We did not.

We are not church-goers. We arranged for our children to be christened in Charleston, to keep the local rector off our case. My mother was immensely gratified to be queen of these occasions, but she saw through our motives. "Living way out like that," she reproached me, "those children need you to arrange for them to have the society of their peers."

She has never abandoned this theme. "Lang," I pointed out last fall, "spends five out of every seven days in school. He's not exactly Tarzan."

"Public School children are not Lang's peers." My mother found out about Sayre School on just one visit up here.

Grove's mother had hoped he would marry a girl who would bring him back to Jesus. Then she began to hope that our children would save us both. She sees that Lang's disappearance is a setback. "The Lord tries us," she chose Easter to say to me, "but he never sends us greater trials than we can bear. His mercy is greater than our wickedness. You do believe that, don't you?"

"I believe that after what he let happen to his own son, I need not expect mercy for mine."

There was no gasp, just stillness. Then Grove's mother spoke louder and faster, exhorting me not to let "this" make me lose my faith. No one can utter what has happened. It is called "this."

Over the last two months I have come to wonder whether Mrs. Brough's fear might even be genuine, whether that grown woman may actually believe in a God who would burn me in Hell forever if his unspeakable cruelty to my child caused me to love him less. On Easter, I set the kitchen timer to go off loudly six inches from my telephone, and when it did, I exclaimed "Something's burning," and hung up.

Joanna had begun the day by pushing away her breakfast. Since before she was born, our Easter breakfast has been hardboiled eggs with our names crayoned on their shells in big red letters. Marking those three eggs and no fourth almost broke my heart, but I kept, and keep, reminding myself that Joanna needs demonstrations that life will go on, that she too matters to us, that not every good thing is over now forever. Maybe convincing her, I can persuade myself.

"I had boiled egg for supper," she said. Her real complaint was a little bit slower coming. *Lucille* had *shelled* her egg. "So I wouldn't burn my sweet little pink fingers," she explained critically.

"I can't write your name on a naked egg," I pointed out. She giggled at the idea of an egg's being naked, and that would have been an end to that protest, I think, but Grove, who had not spoken since coming to table, reached over wordlessly and peeled the egg for her. The look she shot me was feminine beyond her years, triumphant. Or maybe I was looking for grievances.

Joanna had gone to bed babbling happily about the care and production of rainbow eggs. I had been exhausted, more than ready for bed myself, but back in the kitchen, Grove had produced a bag. "Lucille sent you this." I could tell from his expression that he expected me to be pleased.

The bag, from The Chocolate Forest, contained two dozen individually wrapped chocolate eggs. "How nice of Lucille," I managed to say. I poured about seven eggs onto the counter beside the refrigerator, and started stuffing the rest into a freezer bag. *She can have one a day,* I was trying to think, but in the movie in my mind, Lang had come home and the four of us were dumping the entire bagful onto the dining room table and eating every egg.

"What are you doing?" Grove demanded. Lucille expected us to hide these eggs for Joanna. Monday morning she would be expecting to hear about Joanna's Easter Egg Hunt.

"Well," I exclaimed. "Those are thoughtless expectations!"

Lucille had been *outstandingly* thoughtful, Grove admonished.

She had imagined how distracted I'd been, how heavy-hearted. She'd realized I couldn't possibly have been doing any shopping. "Joanna needs our help," he went on to advise me. "She feels—"

"Joanna feels just like us," I interrupted passionately. "Are you in the mood for games?" I was leaning on the kitchen counter even as I spoke because I did not have the energy to stand unsupported.

Grove's tone became coaxing. "Lucille is closer to Joanna's age than we are," he said. "Maybe she has a better idea what Joanna would like."

"Are you actually saying that you think that *word processor* knows more about making my daughter happy than I do?"

Grove shrugged, no longer smiling. "You saw how she went to bed tonight."

Compared, he meant, with Wednesday, Thursday and Friday. I thrust the bag at him and left the room.

Sunday morning while I fixed breakfast, Grove hid eggs all over the front yard. Always before we have done this together.

I could not remember the last time we'd quarreled. Lang had been missing four days. What celibate first gave out that limbo involves less torture than hell?

❧17❧ {Albert

May of his junior year at Paris High School, Albert Blount had two plans: to outrun, in the coming fall's track meet, the Fayette County boy who had defeated him twice, and to advance, upon graduation, from summer help to full-time employee at Lochlann Farm.

Three things happened that summer that, to use his father's phrase, "put the quietus" on both plans. First a spurt of growth left Albert still wiry, but taller than his father, too big to ride young horses. Then, a loose yearling he was trying to head off knocked him down before his mother's eyes. Finally, Jack Rabbit Johnson got shot in both shins by a passing driver who, mistaking him for a member of a certain gang, aimed for his belly.

Mary Blount had always wanted college for her daughters, and after she had seen her eldest child bloody-faced on his back in Keeneland's sawdust, she'd started, Albert complained to his friends, "pushing it on me, too." Her husband had taken her side —not, Albert felt, because Albert had hit the sawdust, but because Albert had hit 5'9. Albert had three close friends at Paris High: his next-door-neighbor Nat Wrenn and, from a couple of streets over, the Gillum brothers, Junior and V. P., who as soon as Albert had grown old enough to slip his mother had taught him how to swim in the local creek, who now relied on him for help with their math homework. Albert trolled these three for their reactions to his parents' change of script.

Both football stars, Junior and V. P. barely managed to tolerate the classroom for the sake of the playing field. Nat was a good student, but equally unhappy, as was Albert himself.

From childhood, Nat and Albert had been exhorted and admonished to be better than they were, to be exemplary. "If you walk around dirty," their mothers chided, "whites will say, *Blacks are dirty.*"

"If you act dumb," their black teachers reproved them privately, "whites will say, *Stands to reason: blacks are lazy and stupid.*"

"If you break rules," warned their minister, "you will bring discredit not just to your family and your neighborhood, but to your entire race."

Every minute of the school day, Nat and Albert felt surrounded, observed, by these whites who had to be taught that blacks had no faults and no weaknesses. Nat played the sweetest clarinet in the conference, according to Paris High's band instructor, whose position he occupies today. Albert shone equally brightly on the boy's track team. But school for both was what Albert's work is now: every exchange a call for diplomacy, examined, guarded. *What will what I am saying be thought to mean, and what might come of that?*

"Eastern," he groused to Nat and the Gillum brothers, "just be four more years of the same."

There were jobs in the horse industry besides riding, the two-hundred pound Gillum boys pointed out, but Nat Wrenn, the son of a prosperous undertaker, didn't share Albert's doubts about higher education. He was going to Kentucky State University, the Commonwealth's formerly all-black college, to study anything, he said, but undertaking. In September, boosted by a track scholarship, Albert registered in Eastern Kentucky University's College of Law Enforcement.

Today, both the Gillum brothers drive horse vans. Albert prepares their tax returns for them every spring. Nat is married to a young woman he met at KSU; their son is named for Albert. In dealing with Ruth Brough, Albert keeps thinking of Nat's wife. What if the missing boy were Albert Blount Wrenn?

Albert's time at the Broughs' mailbox the first morning after their son disappeared did turn up the regular commuter for whom Albert had hoped, who could attest to Lang Brough's presence there Wednesday morning, and at a time about which he was convincingly precise. It was no breakthrough, but it had given Albert an inch of progress to report when he'd had to talk to Ruth Brough Thursday afternoon. That was nearly four days ago, and there has been no second inch. He knows she will call him soon, and he wishes she would not, but she will not guess this from his voice.

Neither will his voice evince sympathy. "When you're talking to owners about young horses," Albert's father had pointed out to him, "sympathy and encouragement, either one, can seem like promises. Keep your voice neutral and you can't be accused of promising too much, or caring too little." The warning is even more important for police work, Albert has concluded.

With some early help from state troopers, Albert has compiled interviews with everyone who lives within two miles of the Broughs — with Ervil Knecht, and Grove's partner, and the partnership's apprentice, with the Broughs' mailman, with Lang's teacher, and with every one of Lang's classmates. He has compiled a list of names two and a half pages long, with very little information on many of them. He submits each name by teletype to the National Crime Information Center and learns that no man or woman on his list is wanted by the police in any state of the union. He will learn nothing more from NCIC.

He has submitted each name for which he has a social security number to Army Intelligence, and learned that the army has a criminal record on none of them. He can learn nothing about any of them, therefore, from Army Intelligence.

He telephones the Kentucky State Police Information Systems, states his name and secret identification number, and reads them his two and a half pages. Half an hour later he calls back to learn what they've found.

Among the names for which Albert has no social security number or date of birth are two Smiths and a Williams. Frankfort cannot help him with these too-common names. Among the balance, three men have criminal records in Kentucky.

Albert spends the first half of Easter week finding out that all three have alibis for April the twenty-first.

⇜18↝ {Ruth

Early Easter afternoon baskets of lilies and white roses arrived. Norma Lee, I learned, was in charge of decorating her church all April, and had insisted that Easter's flowers were not to be shared among the parish sick as is customary, but were all to come to Grove and me. Joanna was enchanted.

Instead of weeping for her brother as I had dreaded, Joanna had kept up a petulant whine all morning about living in the country. Lucille's apartment house, it seems, is dense with children. Turn up the sun, and children bounce out of that house like popcorn from a hot popper. The arrival of Norma Lee's flowers did what Lucille's eggs had failed to do. I was too numbed by my own misery to take any small-minded pleasure in this. The moment, in any case, was short.

I wiped lily pollen off Joanna's enraptured nose. *NOW aren't you glad you came home?* I wanted to say. "Would you like to put a basket on your bureau?" I asked.

"This one," she answered. "No, that one. I want this one in my room, and can we take that one to Lucille?"

On the flowers' arrival, Grove had gone to our room. (Seeing Joanna's delight, he waited until the lilies faded and were thrown out to confess that they had looked too much like a Goddamned funeral for him to stand.) Now from our bathroom, he called to me: "Put nail file on the shopping list."

Grove is always losing nail files. He absently puts them in his pocket, then when he's kneeling in somebody's stall, they fall out in the straw. I followed his voice as far as the bedroom door and promised, "I'll pick you up a couple tomorrow afternoon, when Joanna takes Lucille her flowers."

"I don't want Joanna pestering—"

"We aren't going to bother Lucille at home. We'll take one basket of lilies to the office and thank her for keeping Joanna yesterday. I thought I'd do it about bus time." He frowned but cleaned his fingernails with his pocketknife and said no more. I didn't have to tell him that Joanna needed distraction at bus time.

And I? Monday, we'd agreed, Grove would resume his rounds. "The firm can't afford to be a man short in foaling season, and I'm just going crazy here." And I?

Monday morning wasn't so bad for me because it was taken up with calling Contel, and with the woman they sent immediately to equip the truck. For two months now, a succession of saints— friends, clients, some people I didn't even know beyond their familiar faces—have arrived at the door and said, "How can I help?" When I need to be out of the house, they sit with their magazines or their knitting, and wait for the telephone. After the fourth unanswered ring, our house phone records, and Lang is familiar with this. An additional telephone whose number Lang doesn't know may not sound like a big improvement, but now Albert and Grove can get in touch with me immediately. And, now that I know that the sitter also can get in touch with me at once, I won't risk my life and Joanna's speeding to get home because during any minute since we left, the call may have come, must have come.

Easter Monday afternoon, my volunteer telephone sitter had a last minute emergency of her own and called apologetically to beg off. Joanna and I went to Hereward at school bus time anyway. I had promised, Joanna reminded me strenuously. I had more than one child at risk, I once more resolutely reminded myself.

Fran was alone in the secretary's office. As Joanna and I entered, she stared and stood up. I felt like Lazarus. Anywhere I went, that first month, people were stunned to see me appear, simultaneously glad and appalled. Now, after two months, they are just embarrassed.

"Lucille's gone to the yearling barn," Fran said. Joanna's disappointment was a reproach to me. Of course I should have called ahead—but I was doing well to get the truck started, to stay on the road, to open its door and Joanna's, and walk up Hereward's brick walk. "She had to take the boys some registration papers," Fran explained. Summer Sale inspectors were on the way.

A week earlier that news would have started my heart to battering my ribs, because our farm comes shortly after Hereward on the inspectors' list.

What did shatter my heart was that when we got home, we found no calls recorded while we were out. I hadn't realized the real reason I'd taken Joanna and her flowers to Hereward. Only driving home, foot to floor, had I admitted the bargain I'd been making: I would leave no one beside the telephone for one hour, close to one hour, and Lang would call.

Lang wouldn't be put off by our answering machine. He simply hadn't called. No one had called.

Waiting for us in the mail was a card mailed Saturday from St. Paul's in Lexington. Mass would be said Monday morning for the safe return of Langdon Courtonne Brough. Tough, sardonic Fran Warren had gone where she had not set knee since her husband broke her jaw and left town with their joint savings, and her priest made clear to her what a poor girl's chances were for an annulment —*Fran* had gone on Good Friday and made "the arrangements." My heart welled with love for my good, my old, my faithful friend Fran Warren.

The mood was broken by the arrival of a man offering to sell me laminated copies of Lang on the Sunday *Herald-Leader's* front page. When I declined to purchase, this man inquired, "What's the matter—didn't you love your child?" and kicked the doormat into the bushes as I closed the door in his face.

Seven A.M. is early for callers, even in farming country. Anyway the man who rang our bell Tuesday morning was dressed for city, not farm work. "I'm Andrew Southgate," he said.

Standing in the open doorway, I heard the furnace come on. I wasn't dressed to step out into the chill morning fog. (How was Lang keeping warm?) I didn't want to ask a stranger in, even with Grove home. I didn't want to shut the door in his face while I went to get a jacket. I just stood.

He was a medium-sized, middle-aged man, his expression the sad, slightly harried look, something between reproachful and resigned, of someone who assumes responsibilities and takes them to heart. His eyes seemed to apologize for being there, but at the same time there was something not at all tentative about the way he stood on our stoop. Neither had he left his engine running. He had come to say something and he would do his duty however hysterical I might become. I began to feel sick.

His stress, in saying "I'm Andrew Southgate," had been on the "I'm." I was expected to have heard of Andrew Southgate. "Detective Blount talked to me." His speech was low-voiced but very deliberate. Numb as I was, I never had to ask him to repeat a thing that morning. "I pass your mailbox on my way to Lexmark every morning at five minutes past seven."

"Five minutes past seven" was stated perfectly seriously, and, looking at this neat squarish man without a loose thread on his Brooks Brothers overcoat or a flake of rust on the Mercedes that stood waiting behind him, I felt ready to believe that he knew exactly when he passed our mailbox every morning.

"Your little boy always waves to me. I told Detective Blount he was waving there Wednesday."

"Oh," I said. "You're Mr. Southgate. Come in."

"We've found a man who saw Lang beside your mailbox Wednesday," Albert had told me Thursday.

"What kind of man?" I'd asked, still just sufficiently self-aware to feel a bit rueful at how reflexively suspicious I'd become.

"Grandfather; Rotarian; Lexmark vice-president; sixteen years with IBM before that; not who we're looking for, I think," Albert had answered evenly, as if my question had been the most natural in the world. Albert has no idea what a comfort he is sometimes.

Of course I'd forgotten the man's name within the quarter hour. No one who couldn't be of any further help finding Lang was of any interest.

"None of those things would rule him out, of course," Grove had said after I relayed Albert's report.

"Well, Albert says he's clear," I had answered, annoyed.

Mr. Southgate followed me doggedly into the living room, but did not sit down. He was about to speak when Grove appeared.

"This is Mr. Southgate, Grove. He's the man who told Albert that Lang did get to the mailbox."

Mr. Southgate cleared his throat. "I was in the post office yesterday afternoon and I saw your son's photograph posted." His determined manner reminded me of those brave clients of my father's who required themselves to call on us after the telegram about Langdon came. "I wouldn't have known him. I've never seen him without his cap." Any vet knows how to look impassive and Grove is good at it. I was proud of him for showing no impatience with this intruder, who, I was convinced, meant well. Mr. Southgate squared his shoulders. "I was just driving by and I thought I ought to stop and tell you." His feet remained firmly planted but he turned his face from Grove's to mine. "I thought I should tell you that I wouldn't have recognized him without that cap." I looked at him, both of us straining. "That I saw him every day, but—"

I felt a surging compulsion to grip both his hands, but Grove sucks lemon when I am effusive, even with women; I clasped my own hands hard and leaned toward that good man. "Mr. Southgate, we'll see to it." Every second I had kept him patiently, doggedly standing, he was a second later to his desk. I wonder if he ever had been late to work before in his life. "Thank you. We'll see to that right away. We'll take care of it right away."

Every child on Weaver Radford's bus yearns to be the object of one of Weaver's running gags. Lang achieved this distinction after Grove took him to a game at Riverfront Stadium, and bought him a baseball cap. Next morning (and every school day since), Lang wore that cap, so Weaver congratulated him on becoming the Reds' shortstop, advised him daily about strategy, and demanded explanations when the Reds didn't take his advice. "We'll have to find a picture of Lang in his Reds' cap," I told Grove, "and I'll—"

Grove vetoed my rushing a capped picture to Sheriff Maggard and begging for a second set of flyers. I wondered if he would feel this same compulsion to be fair and reasonable if I were drowning, or if he would knock any man off his motorboat who wouldn't lend it to him, and speed to rescue me. I didn't care what other responsibilities the sheriff neglected for Lang's sake, or what fund he robbed.

I didn't debate the point with Grove. I kissed him goodbye as he left for his rounds, and sat down with a bottle of red ink and half my remaining flyers. On each, before it was time to waken Joanna, I had painted a slightly oversized Cincinnati baseball cap. No more widow's peak. No more eyebrows. Would anyone recognize a child from such a picture?

I would recognize *that* child with his back to me.

I never had felt entirely happy with how obliging Lang always was when lens covers were unscrewed, how eagerly he posed. This had been his way since he was big enough to stand on his own feet where the camera was pointing. I had kept telling myself it was the Only Grandchild (my side) Syndrome. I don't tell Grove all that occurs to me about this now.

I have told Albert. It was after React's visit, after my barn conversation with Roszell Randall, Burgerburg's cook.

Albert already knew about Lang and Breck's visits to Red McMain's Burgerburg, already had sounded Breck about anyone who might have befriended them there.

"Do you think he told you the truth?" I asked. "Do you think he might be too embarrassed to tell you something? Should I ask Mrs. Smith just to bring the subject up?"

"You can do that if you want to, Mrs. Brough." Albert's careful voice showed no defensive resentment, no impatience. "We never know what someone will tell one person and not another. If the boy is close to his mother.... But I've talked to Mr. McMain pretty carefully, and I didn't come up with anything. The boys don't seem to have *hung around* there. They went for food, which they took out. And they were always together, so Lang wouldn't have been the most vulnerable target for the kind of approach you're thinking about."

I had never set foot in Red's Burgerburg. I decided I would start there with my revised flyers.

I got Joanna into wrapper, slippers, and the bathroom, and started to lay out her clothes. I noticed her crayon box under her socks, which is not where she usually keeps it. I thought nothing of that, but I did remember the red crayon I had borrowed from her for Easter morning, still in my apron pocket. "Your orange juice is at your place," I told her. "Climb up in your chair and I'll come serve your oatmeal." Then I opened the crayon box. "Joanna," I called, very casually. "Would you come here a moment?"

When she saw the open crayon box, she froze in the doorway. I expected, "Those are mine!" but though her mouth was open, not a word came out.

"I wasn't snooping in your things," I apologized. "I was just putting away that crayon I borrowed from you Saturday, to write our names on our Easter eggs, remember?

"Now you tell me why your father's nail file is in your crayon box."

In her tears I recognized chagrin as well as the tension that racked us all. "I was saving it for when the dogs find Lang! I was saving it for when the policeman puts Lang in jail for running away! I was going to take it to him so he could ex-cape." At Lucille's, she had seen a TV comedy routine in which Bob Hope, bank robber, is moping in his cell when he receives a birthday cake from his gang. Out steps a beaming bimbo bearing a nail file on a satin pillow.

I promised that Detective Blount would on no account allow the police to put Lang in jail when they found him, but would bring him straight home. "Lang didn't intend to run away. He meant to go somewhere pleasant for a short while, and then he couldn't find his way back home yet." For a bad second, I thought I was going to break down myself, but Joanna stopped crying.

"Where did he go?"

"I don't know. That's why we're all looking for him, so he can tell us all about it."

Joanna ate her oatmeal without speaking or setting her spoon down once. She put her napkin in its ring without prompting. "I'm tired of reading," she announced.

"All right."

"Can we go look for Lang?"

"Yes. I'm going to put his picture everywhere I think anybody might go who might ever see him, so if they do see him, they can tell us where he is."

"Yes, and so they can tell him, *Go home before you get a spanking!*"

"Something like that."

Red's opens for breakfast at seven. I reminded Ervil to look at Chinese Lagoon every ten minutes and to forget any work that took him out of earshot of the tack room telephone. I showed him the truck's number, posted on the tack room wall, right under the fire department's. I drove with Joanna to Red's...where Lang had been, and we had not known it.

The jukebox was wailing, its colored lights pulsing and flowing. Joanna's hand tugged to be free of mine. "You can look at it from here," I told her. "I'm going to need you to hand me thumbtacks." I asked the two suety quasi-blondes behind the counter for Roszell Randall.

"Roz ain't here t'day," the darker of the pair told me apathetically. I explained what I wanted: to tack up two flyers, one hatless, one with hat added. "You can put 'em there if you want to," she said. "I guess." She exchanged looks with her colleague and they giggled. Neither looked back at me. The one who had spoken began studiously, if slowly, wiping the counter. The other drifted toward the kitchen.

"Is Red here?" I asked.

In a moment, Red came out of the kitchen, wiping his hands on his apron. "Mrs. Brough!" In every booth, heads turned. "You just put them up wherever you think. Yes, two, as many as you want. You girls!" He rounded on the sullen waitresses: "Every customer comes in, I want you to tell them, 'Look at those pictures.' Before they're served!"

The diners' stares embarrassed me; I reminded myself that attention was what I *wanted*. Much more zeal from Red, however, and I would have had Albert ripping up the Burgerburg's floorboards.

"Would you like a doughnut, sugar?" Red asked Joanna.

Naturally Joanna, who had risen from breakfast ten minutes before, was avid for a doughnut. "May I?" she asked me in the beguiling manner she usually reserves for her father. We did teach them not to accept treats from strangers. We taught them that in their baby shoes. We taught them that.

Foodtown, which stays open twenty-four hours a day, was our next stop. Here the irresistible attraction was a cart full of marked-down, plaster-of-Paris rabbits. "We will go look at them together when I've finished here," I told her. The store was jammed with people who had run low because of the holiday, people I didn't know. I can't tape flyers on a window with one hand, so had to let go of Joanna's. "Hold on to my coat," I told her.

"If I let go of your coat, will I get lost like Lang?"

I hugged her quickly to give myself time to think. "You certainly *won't* get lost if you *don't* let go of my coat."

Later I would add capped pictures beside the uncapped ones Albert had mounted at the post office, the library, the sheriff's office itself, but for now it was too early to go anywhere but home.

At the barn, Ervil couldn't look at me. Only one call: Dr. Brough wanted me to check in with him at Hereward Stud. Ervil mumbled thanks for the doughnuts we had brought him from Red's, and fled on the tractor.

Where can *I* fly?

⤙20⤚ {Ruth

I waited to act on Ervil's message till I got to the house, and the phone began ringing as Joanne and I stepped into the hall. "Honey?" Grove sounded harried. "I was supposed to bring Eldridge some blood results; he's got to have 'em to ship some horses this morning. They'll be either on my bedside chair, or on the bathroom floor. Could you bring them out here for me? I've got to be clear to Midway in half an hour." His voice changed. "You doing OK?"

"I'm fine," I said, by which we both knew I meant I was good for another six hours, anyway. "You?" He was doing fine, too.

Joanna sulked all the way to Hereward: Grove had said to leave the blood tests at Manager Eldridge Snyder's house, not at the farm office with Fran and Lucille. Of Eldridge and Lorena's eight children, it seemed that only Farrah was competition for Lucille Harper and Farrah is in kindergarten. I, on the other hand, was relieved. I didn't know what to say to Fran about that mass.

Lorena met me at the door in pompon-adorned house slippers and a red maternity pants suit, her youngest boy on one shoulder. Except that the large, no longer white daisy whipstitched above her heart had been well chewed, the pants suit looked new. Behind her, the stereo lamented tunefully: "I'm living on Valium, whiskey, and prayer." Lorena turned it off.

Joanna was dispatched to join the rest of the pre-schoolers. "They're watching TV in the little girls' room, honey. Tell Keziah to get you a soft drink." I, too, was given an Ale-8, and seated with my back to the fireplace and its flickering ceramic log, facing the wall Lorena has covered with her plate collection. Lorena sat opposite me, patting and jiggling her baby. The baby had begun to cry the moment I spoke, as if he knew the voice of a woman with whom a child would not be safe. "All he needs is his nap," Lorena apologized. "Just let me lay him down." The baby's screams followed her back from the nursery. "He'll stop presently," she told me. She sat feet apart, one hand resting on each thigh. Lorena's thighs are opulent but muscular; she played first-string basketball in high school. ("Now all my running is after these kids, and sometimes if I had a basket, I wouldn't mind shooting two or three of 'em right through it," she says, patting the nearest child fondly as she speaks.)

"Feels good to set down," she observed now. "This one's reaching the notice-me stage." She rubbed her belly. "It's the last. I told Eldridge, you get yourself cut, or you'll wake up one of these

104

nights tied to the bed and me standing over you with my doll knife!" She eyed my untasted drink anxiously. "You'd likely rather have a Coke or something, but there's not a soft drink in the house right now but Ale-8. The kids are saving the caps for a school contest. They fight over 'em. It's all they think about. If I didn't watch, they'd be pouring Ale-8 down the drain, just for the caps." Lorena swallowed and looked at me apologetically; she doesn't usually rattle. Her eyes shifted to a bleak examination of the pompon on her left slipper, and her voice dropped. "Honey, I just don't know what to say."

I shrugged, nearly sloshing my drink in my lap as my hands automatically started to make the palms up "empty" gesture.

I like Lorena, and I respect her. She is only months my senior, but her many children, and things she has told me (only half of them contemptuous) about growing up in the mountains seven children to the cabin, give me the feeling that she's older.

The details I've been willing to confide about my own childhood, she has heard with amused pity.

The baby, as Lorena had predicted, had fallen silent. "He'll sleep till dinnertime," she said. "When that back door slams behind Farrah, he wakes up." She smiled a little, brushing her long blonde hair back from her face. "If she ever didn't come home once, he might never wake up." As my heart constricted, I saw the realization of what she had said wipe her face. Once again it was up to me to comfort. What was I to say? Lorena's fists clenched. "I swear to God if I could get my hands on the creep that took your little boy, I'd jerk off his whatsis and wrap it around his neck."

The telephone in the next room began to ring. I was on my feet before I remembered that I ought at least to pretend that a call to Lorena's house might be on Lorena's business, not Lang's. Lorena answered. "Oh, *shit!*" I heard her exclaim.

I turned as cold as the glass in my hand. *Lang was dead.* My eyes closed to help me hear.

"If your Mama's sick, let Jessie take care of her! Old as she is, what's the matter with Jes— Well, what's Nelcie doing? Let her get her shiftless ass over there. Has it crossed anybody's cotton picking mind that I have got eight children and Nelcie has got N.O.

None? Let me speak to Nelcie. Put Nelcie on. What do you mean, can't: can't or won't? Do you mean to tell me your Aunt Nelcie is too drunk to come to the telephone already at this hour of the morning? Well, you just tell her I said sober up, Sister, because I am not coming. *What?*" Suddenly Lorena was speaking in a hoarse whisper. "*Swango,* you said *sick.*" I caught myself leaning forward, and rose guiltily to go make a bustle in the kitchen. I poured out the sweet, straw-colored drink (saving the ice in case Lorena should glance at my glass). When I could tell she'd hung up, I returned with the lying glass to my chair.

Lorena had not come back, but was dialing. "Annie? I need you real bad, this minute. Can you— No, the kids are fine; it's my folks. I've got to get to my folks just as quick as you can get here, and I don't know exactly when I'll be back. Might be a week! Can you— Well, praise the Lord!" She came back looking scared. "Ruth, honey, I hate the very *worst* way to ask you this with all you're under right now, but my half-wit sister's got herself snake-bit and I've got to get down there and help her kids *kick* her into the hospital. Annie's coming, but I could be halfway home by the time she gets here. Could—could you just set here till—"

With eight children and a well-paid husband, Lorena has her baby-sitter practically on a retainer. Annie is treated like family, and half the Snyder children think she's their grandmother. She herself often forgets that she isn't, I suspect, but even she can't get to Lorena's in much under half an hour. "Stop standing around," I said. "Pack."

"My sister's boy," Lorena told me as she threw things into a suitcase, "run to his aunt's house that's got a telephone, thank the lord." She was about to close the suitcase.

My hand was in my purse. "We've been putting these up, places," I said, pulling out one of Albert's Lang flyers, and one of mine. "Maybe—"

Lorena stuck out a hand. "Honey, give me a bunch. I've got this cousin, he's half the police force of Cotes, Kentucky. He'll paste up anything I take him!"

I beat it to the car for more flyers, and Lorena hurried down the hall to tell her children to mind Annie and their Daddy till she got back, and tell Farrah and them, that went for them too. She met me in the garage with her suitcase and one of Eldridge's hunting guns. "Hospital insurance," she said grimly. I had no trouble picturing Lorena getting her sister past Admissions with a shotgun if necessary. I thrust my flyers at her and she was off, breaking the farm's speed limit from the moment she backed out of the garage.

Lorena hadn't said which sister had been bitten, but I knew. It would be the eldest, Glenna. Glenna is the one to whom Lorena refers as "my sister." The other five are always spoken of by name. "Hawk Mountain hasn't changed all that much since we were children," Lorena will say. "My sister was a fool to stay. Quit school and married the first thing she seen. Married a *born-again*, just to get out of Mama and Daddy's cabin. Now she's hauling water and heating it on a woodstove just the way we did when we were kids. And Nelcie not a bit of help" (Nelcie being the other sister who "married a local"). "Squeaky little husband tight as wallpaper." But at least, it seemed, his wife had a telephone.

I had my own call to make. Serious as Lorena's conversation had sounded, I had been impatient for her to get off the telephone — *her* telephone. Ervil might have been trying to call me to say —

But he had not been. I explained to him that I would be late, told him not to leave till I came, reminded him to stay close to the phone, and went to check on the children. The five of them sat in a semicircle in front of the TV, a bottle of Ale-8 by even the three-year-old's knee. Not an eye turned toward me.

Since April twenty-first, a desperate feeling has afflicted me any time I am idle one minute, the feeling that if I were doing something, anything, it might result in finding Lang. I leaned against the doorframe, took one elbow in each hand and pushed my linked arms against my gut. "Concentrate on what is at hand," Jake Averoyne had advised me, after I'd asked for tranquilizers.

"I can't concentrate! Concentrate is exactly what I can't do!" "Try staring," he'd replied. Jake doesn't always give me the advice (or the prescription) I want. "Hold onto something and stare, and make a list, in your mind, of everything there is to say about what you're staring at."

What I replied to that does me no credit, but now I stood in the doorway, determinedly studying my mesmerized offspring, and Lorena's.

Joanna, except that she's blonde, looks nothing like the Snyder children. All the little Snyders have skin translucent like half percent milk, and sharp bones, and shiny straight blonde hair like their mother. Joanna's face is half eyes, half cheeks (her forehead being generally obscured by her curls). If I were to model her face, I would start by shoving together two balls of clay, and placing on top of them another, somewhat smaller pair. I'd mash the top pair once each with my thumb for her eyes, and the bottom pair once each with my forefinger for the dimples she and my brother got from my mother's father. If Delft made clear glass their famous blue, that is what I would use for her eyes. "Well, she may get cataracts," says my mother, who is not the grandmother from whom Joanna gets her lovely eyes, "but she'll never lose Father's dimples."

My mother is jealous that Joanna is named for Mrs. Brough. "Women named Ruth are supposed to cherish their mothers-in-law," I tell her.

"Do not speak unto the man," Naomi told Ruth, "until he shall have done eating." Of course Ruth cherished a mother-in-law who handed out advice that brilliant. My mother-in-law's advice is considerably less useful, but I don't say so to Mother.

The sound of Annie's car pulling up out front released me. I showed Annie Eldridge's blood tests and the note Lorena had left him, and filled in as well as I could with the explanations Lorena had been too hurried to make on the phone. At the words "snake-bite," Annie grew very still.

I prized Joanna loose from *Mr. Rogers' Neighborhood*, and hurried to leave before Annie should feel compelled to try to tell me how sorry she was about Lang.

Keziah waved us out of sight. Joanna returned only the first wave. Now, she was insisting, we should stop at the office and see Lucille. I said "no" twice and tuned her out. In my mind's eye I was seeing the seven Bailey sisters as Lorena has described them to me, going to the spring for water. "I was the smallest," Lorena says, "so they used to give me a little two-pound molasses bucket for each hand. The spring was a long way, and I was scared to death of snakes. All the way to the spring, I'd carry both buckets in one hand and a stick in the other so I could beat the brush my little legs had to pass through, but once them buckets was full, I couldn't do it. The water would already be a-sloshing without that. My little buckets was never more'n half full by the time I got home, and me always drenched on both sides. I wouldn't no more bring up my kids that way...."

None of you disappeared, I answered her now mentally. "Mama," Joanna protested. "Why is the truck driving so fast?"

I took my foot off the accelerator. "Tell me about Mr. Rogers," I said. She did so the rest of the way home.

The mail had come already: three bills, two supermarket circulars, six envelopes which from their sizes and shapes could only contain condolence cards, and a *Have you seen me?* postcard. I crumpled the last and stuffed the lot into my purse as fast as I could.

No calls. I managed not to seem to blame Ervil, and Joanna and I put the truck away. I hung up our coats and looked around. The telephone was silent, the driveway empty. Even Ervil was gone now. Joanna had stopped talking as we entered the garage. Now she stood where I had helped her out of her coat.

We could sit on the floor holding each other, calling his name and weeping. Or we could what? In Joanna's eyes, I thought I saw the same question. I marched to the kitchen, scalped half the carrots in the vegetable drawer with one whack of my butcher knife, and waved the tops at her. "Want to feed these to Thankless? Get your coat back on, then."

We have pretty well known since Joanna was born that there would be no more, but I congratulated myself that we were blessed with one of each sex; we would miss nothing. And they? My mother wrung her hands about "peers." *No cousins next door! No cousins across the street!* Given our animals, I firmly told her, our children could never be lonely.

Kat met us at the barn door, and as I held Joanna up to feed Thankless her treat, Troy wrapped herself purring around my leg so devotedly that as soon as I set Joanna down, I checked the cat food dish. Sure enough, almost empty. "That's a dumb name for a cat," I overheard Breck say once to Lang. "Troy is a dog."

"*Tray* is a dog," Lang corrected. "Troy was a city with nine lives." That a voice I can hear as clearly as if it were coming from the next stall might be silenced, never to be duplicated, is one of life's mind-blowing mysteries. I have come up against it before. That first time, when I was only nineteen, I could not have believed that my mother's agony was any greater than mine.

I dragged a bale of straw to where Joanna could stand on it and look in on Thankless's colt. "Stall is off limits till he's bigger," I reminded her, more sympathetic to her yearning to throw her arms around the foal than she knew. "That mare weighs fifty times as much as you, and her brain's no bigger than a potato. We don't want her to get excited and accidentally mash one of you."

I left her adoring through the bars as I fetched the Cat Chow. In that dark barn, with her head bent over her clasped hands, she looked like one of those angels whose glow lightens the manger in some Old Master's nativity. I set my box on the aisle floor and hugged her off her feet. *Ora pro nobis,* I thought. As I picked up the Chow again, the telephone rang.

"Mrs. Brough? This is the police. We've found your boy."

All the breath was squeezed out of my lungs by a heart suddenly doubling its size. "Lang!" I choked out. "Where is he? Let me speak to him! Lang?"

The telephone had gone silent. My reaction was primitive as an ape's. I lowered the receiver and looked at it, turned it over in my hand, baffled. Again at my ear, it remained still. "Hello?" I jiggled the recall button and got a dial tone.

I called the police. Their number rang twice and a woman said, "Police Department, Ship speaking."

"I was cut off! This is Mrs. Brough!"

"You were cut off?"

"I was just this minute cut off! One of your men called me. About my *child.* We were talking, and then he just went off!"

"Who were you talking to, ma'am?"

"He didn't say his name. He just said, 'Mrs. Brough, we've found your boy,' and then the line went dead."

"Did he say he was the Paris police?"

I was freezing; my hands were wet; my lungs were barely managing. I tried not to scream at her. "No, he did not say *what* police, but I—he—"

"Well, ma'am, I am the dispatcher, and no one had been talking out of our department when you called in. If you'll calm down and give me a minute, I'll ask if anybody knows who might have been calling you, but...."

"Thank you." I leaned against the cold cinderblocks.

Her voice returned, subdued. Someone must have pointed out the flyers on her own wall. *That* Mrs. Brough. Does anyone anywhere ever look at those flyers? "Mrs. Brough, I'm sorry. No one here has called you this morning. No one knows anything about it. Could it have been the state police?"

Of course, and I had wasted how long? As I hung up, I realized I hadn't even answered her.

The state police headquarters nearest Paris is halfway to Cincinnati. As I punched their number, the pictures in my mind succeeded one another like slides dropping in a viewer: a desk, a telephone, a dozen men in blue shirt sleeves, and Lang—hunched in front of the intimidating desk, tear-stained and pale; sitting on the desk chewing a carameled apple and acting smart; lying on a stretcher....

Nobody at state police headquarters had called me.

The sheriff's department wouldn't have called themselves "police." I backed up the tape and replayed the call.

Now I heard how young the voice was. I am old enough to realize that the clowns aren't going to get any funnier, and I know that there are gun-wielding police who weren't in kindergarten yet when I left Ashley Hall, but this was a voice so young it was new to its owner, new as the hairs on his lip. Now between the recording of my own first frenzied, joyous cry and my second, verging on hysterical, I heard or— after two replays — thought I heard a click.

I called Albert. The rings went on and on, a skein of birds flying south, their cries unintelligible except as a reminder of the long winter silence to come. I hung up and slid my spine down along the wall to the floor, leaned back and wailed like a Mafia mother, a Trojan woman. Howled.

I had forgotten Joanna. She crept around the doorway as cautious as the cats, who stared at me around her legs. "Mama?" I couldn't speak, so I just held out my arms to her, but though she came at once, she seemed afraid to touch me. "Did you fall down?" The cats sat twitching their tails in the doorway. Joanna began tugging at Grove's desk chair, trying to roll it to me. Bless the child, she spends half her own life on the floor; I needed a moment to comprehend her anxiety to get me off it.

Who would protect her if I stopped?

Believing I sensed the terror that was snuffling at her ankles, I tried to stand up before it could sink in teeth. "Don't!" Joanna screamed. "The amble-ance is coming!"

At lunch Joanna told Grove, "I thought Mama's leg was broken. I was going to call the amble-ance, but I couldn't reach the telephone, so I was going to stand on your chair, and then Mama got up!"

I had carried her all the way to the house. She is getting to be almost more than I can lift, but I wanted the impression made that I am still big and strong; I will still take care of her.

Better than I took care of Lang.

"Hang up your coat," I had told her, "and go to the bathroom. And wash your hands." I had gone in the bedroom, shut the door, and telephoned the Bell serviceman whose name Albert had given me, as I should have done in the first place. Then I had sat on the bed waiting for Albert to call and tell me what this man learned.

What would the Bell man do if, when he'd traced my caller, he couldn't locate Albert? The question put another knot in my gut. I couldn't rid myself of the dread that the caller had not been idle-minded, the dread that Lang had been in the room—unable to speak to me, but there. That the youth who had called himself Lang's discoverer had been his abductor. That if I had not scream-ed, I would have learned something. That my child was in the hands of someone nervous and unstable whom I had alarmed into flight when he was about to give me information.

How could I have forgotten to call the Bell man immediately?

Would a psychiatrist tell me, "You don't really want your son back"? Would a psychiatrist tell me, "You neglected him, didn't watch over him, because you wanted to lose him. He wasn't a baby anymore. He was getting bony, answering back. You just wanted to sit and rock your little girl, your fat baby seal, your pink and white bunny, not to be bothered with your son and his increasingly male demands"?

No, a psychiatrist would tell me none of these things, for they tell you nothing, Norma Lee says. "It's all questions. They ask, you answer. And they never tell you if you got it right—there's no grades."

So it would be, "How does it feel when you look at the bunk ladder he said he'd outgrown and made you take to the basement?" and "How did you feel, when he wanted you to stop kissing him good night in front of his cousin?" and "How did that make you feel, when he looked at his cousin and pretended not to hear you?" Only to the wife at supper, the colleagues over drinks, "I've got a patient, another of these women who only want a warm weight in their laps, detaches her kids once they learn to tie their shoelaces. Now she's been caught out, she's weepin' and wailin', but it's guilt, not grief."

Why did my imaginary psychiatrist drop his g's like Grove?

Why *did* I forget the Bell man?

If fire woke me in the middle of the night, would I forget where our doors are? Would I forget Joanna?

I sat waiting on the bed, my eyes closed. I could see a room, its bed unmade, its shade drawn, the cheap kind of shade that even a streetlight penetrates, its tears yellowed under the pieces of mending tape. In the near corner a small wastebasket spilling over with Tab cans beside a table with one drawer, its handle dangling half attached. On top of the table a plastic transistor radio the size of a deck of cards, and a worn magazine open to a picture of two young men wearing silver lipstick, nothing else. And in the other, far corner, a Lang gone feral.

Not seen was the youth whom my intensity had frightened into hanging up.

It might not be a bedroom, not a home at all. Every hamburger stop has a pay phone. How many miles—north, or south, or east, or west—could an unstable teenager have covered in—I looked at my watch, figuring the minutes that had passed. Waiting for the telephone to ring.

⤳21↩   {Wednesday, April 21

Lang hasn't seen Clint Penn since Zad Thacker fired him. Before then, Clint was always riding him, asking him when he was going to learn to shoot, when he was going to learn to smoke, when he was going to stop taking orders from his mother.

"You don't have to be ashamed of talking to the mailbox," Clint tells him. "Some people talk to theirselves; some people talk to mailboxes. If a poor sucker don't have a friend to talk to in all this world, I sure ain't gonna laugh at him if he talks to his mailbox."

"I've got a friend. Breck Smith is my friend."

Clint swipes his bangs aside and looks slowly in every direction. "You say so, Lang, I believe you."

"He lives a little way on."

"A little way. He's your best friend, huh, but you wouldn't walk a little way to talk to him—long as you got the *mailbox* right *here.*"

"I'm not allowed to walk on the road by myself." The radio sings dolefully of hungry children and drought-stricken crops. The Chevy's exhaust fumes assail Lang and he would like to back away from it, but he remembers how easily Clint is offended by anything he thinks anybody might be thinking about his car.

"Can't walk on the road withouten your mama," Clint says sympathetically. Lang's veins shrink at the insult. "How 'bout *ride:* your mama let you *ride* in a automobile withouten her? I'll carry you where your friend lives."

Lang may not get in a stranger's car.

Lang thinks that his mother has met—he *knows* that his *father* has met Clint. Clint reaches across and opens the passenger door for him. The three right claws of the dragon on Clint's forearm grip a skull: Lang has admired this before. "No need to make that ol' school bus stop twicet," Clint says.

As Lang gets in, the radio commences a louder tune. Lang would like to ask Clint to lower the volume, but is afraid this would be heard as criticism. When they get to Breck's driveway, Clint does not slow down. "Here," Lang says: "This is the—that was the place."

"I thought you said you wanted to go to school."

"Turn around here. You can turn around here."

Clint decelerates. "What's the matter—you forget something you want to tell the mailbox? You told me you wanted to go to school, didn't you? That's where I'm a-taking you."

Twenty miles south of Paris, Lang sees a Texaco sign. He has been watching the gauge for twenty miles; it is close to empty. He edges nearer to his door and becomes very still. Between him and Clint the radio sings of faithless love and death in the morning. "Hey, Lang," Clint says softly. "Did you see where Zad Thacker had him a far?" Lang watches the Texaco sign grow larger and the stillness that has numbed his knees and elbows seems to expand like freezing water. "How do you reckon that hay shed come to catch afar like that?"

Clint is waiting for an answer. Lang flushes, mumbles, too proud to answer, too frightened to keep silent.

"I set that far, Lang." Clint spits out his window. "Zad Thacker, he thinks he can run me off, thinks him and his girl is too good for me. Pig shit. She ain't nothing but country just like me. Hair on her legs that long." Clint is no longer looking at Lang; he glowers at the road ahead. "Ol' Zad he come in there a-hollering about his 'baby.' His 'baby' didn't do nothing with me she wasn't dripping for. Big enough, old enough."

Clint glances Lang's way again. "I like fars, don't you?" At the bullying sarcasm in Clint's voice, Lang feels his face heat again. The Texaco station slides past. "Zad's wasn't too good of a far; wasn't nothing in that shed but a litter of cats, and a cat don't hardly stay around a far long enough to get warm. You take a mare, now, you set a light to her straw, she'll stay right in her stall. It's home to her. She might scream when her tail whooshes up, when those burning pieces drop on her back. She might thrash around, fall on her foal, maybe, when that smoke starts to choke her, but she'll stay right there where she thinks you're gonna keep her safe. She trusts you. She knows you won't let nothing hurt her, long as she's in her stall. She'll scream an' her foal will scream, but they'll be right there when the coals blank out. What's left of 'em."

Lang is refusing to look at Clint. He stares at a small asymmetrical hole in the Chevy floor, at his school shoes, at two empty beer cans and a piece of crumpled paper.

"I might just go back to Bourbon County, Lang. If you want me to, I might. There wasn't enough noise to suit me when Zad's shed it burned." Clint pauses. "I know a barn up the road with three mares in it."

Lang will not look at Clint, but his nose is stinging; he must raise his chin or snivel. He scowls blindly out the window.

"When somebody thinks they're too good for me, that's when I get to thinking far." Clint looks from the reflection of the Texaco pumps in the car's mirror to Lang's averted face and back with a smile to the road. "When somebody thinks they're too good for me, cuts out and leaves me, that's when I get to thinking what good company a good far is." Now his voice changes and the hair at the base of Lang's neck rises light and stiff as hoar frost. "If you leave me, Lang, you better stand outside your daddy's barn ever night till the rooster crows, from now on till you hear I'm dead. I'll burn your daddy's barn, Lang. I'll burn that barn with ever mare in it."

"A man with a horse barn," Lang's father has said often, "cannot afford an enemy." Lang's ears have begun to hum; his neck is rigid.

A self-service station has appeared and Clint pulls over. He is the only customer. From his booth the attendant looks at Lang without interest. Lang pretends to be asleep.

Sixty miles southeast of Bourbon County, the land begins to hill, and the deer outnumber the horses. If a man has a hook and some string, and is willing to tend a little vegetable patch, or has a boy to tend it, he can live all summer. Provided a trap or two, he can survive months without traveling the ten or fifteen miles that may separate his hilltop cabin from the nearest cluster of neighbors, the nearest store. The number of lawmen who have made their way to these hilltops is greater only than the number who have made their way back down.

Somewhere after the land has begun to rise, fall, and rise again, Clint makes Lang lie face down on the car seat. When Lang—who cannot say for sure that his foot moves at his direction—kicks Clint, Clint stops the car, drags Lang out of it, takes off his belt and beats Lang, no worse than Clint's father routinely beat Clint until Clint got his growth; lifts Lang bodily and dumps him, face down, in the back seat, and drives on.

The next time he stops, he tells Lang to get out.

The car has been climbing for what Lang judges to be an hour. (It has been fifteen minutes.) They are in a flattish clearing just big enough for a car to turn around in, maybe halfway up a hill that, so far as Lang can tell, is entirely covered by trees. The road seems to have ended.

Clint picks up a carton of what appears to be clothing off the back seat and jerks his head toward the beginning of what Lang can see must have been a footpath uphill, though scrub cedars and young saplings are reclaiming it for the forest. The spring growth is beginning in the underbrush. Lang trips occasionally as he precedes Clint up this trace of a trace, but he continues to walk as fast as he can because he doesn't like the feeling of Clint close behind him.

At the top of the hill, there is a cabin. "In there," Clint says, and Lang steps inside, Clint following so close Lang can smell him. At once Clint drops his carton on the floor and strides to the bed that stands in the darkest corner. It is in Lang's mind to run. "Git over here," Clint says.

Clint's eyes are gray as fish belly. They hold Lang against the wall like nails as Clint drags the bed a short way out of its corner and kneels where it has stood. From beneath a loose board he withdraws a twenty-two rifle and a pouch. The rifle he places on two pegs above the cabin's one window. He hangs the pouch by its strap over one of these pegs. Ashes lie on the blackened stone hearth. Clint begins to arrange kindling. "Git some wood," he says, and jerks his head toward the cabin's back door.

Lang knows he has slept three nights in Clint's cabin, but he does not know for sure what day of the week it is because he is confused about what day it was that he got in Clint's Chevy. He is also confused about what he should do. "Don't confront them," Lang heard his father caution his mother once when she reported noticing suspicious-looking men with suspicious-looking sacks beyond the pond where the mower can't get and the wild hemp grows taller than Lang. "And don't call the sheriff. Make your presence known. They'll leave, if they see you're around. Put a salt block in the truck and drive it down to the back field, or something—but don't ever antagonize that kind of man."

"I can take care of myself," Lang's mother had protested.

"No, you can't, and even if you could, you can't take care of the barn. People like that will fire your barn quick as look at you. A man with a horse barn has no protection."

Lang is running away from Clint anyhow. This is the first time Clint has left him alone by daylight, and he is heading down the footpath, or what used to be the footpath when Clint's family lived here. The going is more difficult than he expected. He has already skinned one knee and torn his school pants. He stoops to lift a branch so he can duck under it and a stunning pain stabs his free arm. The shock runs clear to his armpit. He lurches backward, looking around horrified for the snake. After a moment he realizes that he's brushed against some kind of nettle.

The pain lasts and lasts, and spit is no help. Lang keeps walking while he rubs. Once he finds the clearing, there will be a road, and though he doesn't know where it leads, it will, he reasons, lead somewhere that other cars are.

The barn will have to be guarded. Burying mines around it to blow Clint up, the way North Koreans do, has to be ruled out. Even if no horse ever got loose, how would the two cats be kept off them? Once Lang has explained to his parents, they will be sure someone sits in the tack room every night until Clint is caught, just the way they do when a mare is due to foal, except now with the light out, of course. Picturing Clint's capture, his astonishment and humiliation, Lang fails to hear Clint coming up the path.

Clint declares himself with a heavy slap to the side of Lang's head even before he asks where the hell Lang thinks he is going. The belt he was wearing the time Lang kicked him is coming off; Lang turns to run and gets nowhere.

⁓⋊23⋉⁓   {Clint

The first morning back in the cabin, Clint got up from his parents' iron bed before sun-up and visited his car for help organizing his ideas. The Chevy's trunk is stocked with the cases of bourbon Clint bought in Lexington, which unlike Wolfe County, permits the sale of whiskey by the bottle. That first day and a couple more, client appointments kept Clint tied to his yard, which was all right; good, in fact. Let the boy's parents worry.

Saturday, Clint composed his letter, and after sundown drove all the way to Lexington to mail it in one of the drop boxes in front of the main Lexington post office. He wasn't stupid enough, he congratulates himself, to mail it anywhere in Wolfe County, and he certainly wasn't stupid enough to show his face or car anywhere near the Broughs' mailbox. Horse people are as likely to be prowling around at midnight as at noon, foaling season.

Clint has seen enough TV to know that letters like his are not written, lest the writing later be hung on the writer. He began by cutting the words he needed out of a newspaper bought for the purpose, and taping them onto a piece of lined paper from the pad in Lang's book bag. He is a slow reader, and got fed up before he found the fourth word. Composing these words letter by letter was just too painfully tedious. He is proud that when he ended by printing, with a pencil also taken from Lang's book bag, he printed left-handed. The lettering can never be pinned on him.

IF YOU WANT BOY, he printed, PUT $100,000 IN $100 BILLS IN KROGER SACK IN BACK OF PICKUP TRUCK. PARK TRUCK BEHIND MORGAN MALL KROGERS NOON THURSDAY GO TO MORGAN RD PHONE BOOTH FOR CALL FROM BOY. ANY TRICKS AND BOY WILL BE KILLED.

Of course there will be no call.

Contemplating this note, Clint had reflected that he should have specified an *open* pickup truck. It would be just like those bastards to walk away from a covered pickup with seven cops waiting inside. By the time he scrawled a second version, his hand was cramping and he was enraged with Lang, the cause of it.

Brough Farm, Clay Pike, Paris, he managed to print. He knows the right zip code, from having worked for Zad Thacker for over a year. *40361,* he finished, relieved to be done. The Broughs should get his letter Tuesday, he figured, except that he doesn't know whether the bastards at the post office work on Easter Monday. He had allowed an extra day in case they don't, and another for the Broughs to get their money together.

Easter Monday Clint sits in the front seat of his Chevy, thoughtfully drinking out of the bottle and considering what he will do with the money. Lang is locked in, and Clint has set all the chairs outside. Finding the little bastard on the path Saturday morning was a surprise: Clint had been gone only long enough to drive to the nearest general store for scissors, Scotch Tape, newspaper, envelope and stamp; he hadn't expected Lang to have the gumption to pull a chair up to the window. Maybe he should have. At Lang's age, Eddie, Clint's sister Mae's boy, had feared nothing—nothing but his father and his nightmares. Clint tilts the bottle, welcomes the lava flow down his throat. He had been right to count on Lang's inability to find his way to a tree in a rainstorm. In the time it had taken Clint to drive to the store and back, the kid hadn't traveled half a mile.

That precaution with the chairs is unnecessary, now that the owls are stirring. Clint didn't bother with it when he stole out again to mail his letter after Lang was asleep Saturday. Lang won't walk six feet from the cabin in the dark.

He should have had the Broughs' money for Eddie. Things would be different for everybody. Eddie never had anything. The soles of Lang's feet are so pink they make Clint want to hurt him. The little bastard is just the age Eddie was, the spring Mae's husband finally beat her one time too often. Mae brought Eddie home to the cabin, where Clint and his mother were the only ones left. There was frost the day Mae and Eddie arrived, Clint remembers, and Eddie was barefoot. This rich vet's bastard has always had everything.

The cabin contained only two beds, but at first Eddie couldn't be persuaded to share Clint's. Mae, of course, had shared her mother's, and Eddie had slept on the floor beside her, where she could reach down and take his hand if his nightmares threatened to keep the lot of them awake. Clint had been amused that his sister could be regarded by anyone as a protection against anything. Mae was such a small woman, Clint could have grabbed her by the hand and swung her around his head.

Eventually Clint had changed where Eddie slept.

Clint doesn't want to think about Eddie. He will think instead of all the women he will have when he gets the Broughs' money. Clint hasn't had a woman since Zad Thacker caught him in the hay shed with Milly and fired him. The sun has been down long enough that the car is getting chilly, but Clint doesn't want to go back to the cabin, where Lang is.

There are services tonight at the Word Alive Church of the Resurrection. Everyone will come—all the women, certainly: there is a visiting preacher. James MacBee, pastor of the Pine Hollow Church of God With Signs Following, is here from Signal Mountain, Tennessee for all Easter week.

Clint's first score was from going to church. *To,* not *in*-to; it was a morning service, and he had stared through the window till he'd caught the eye of the girl he had in mind and she had slipped out as soon as the speaking in tongues got going good. They had done it in the woods. He had known for years that this was how it was done, because his brothers had told him, but you needed to be tall enough to look through the window. Ever since that summer, when Clint has felt horny, he has thought of church.

Clint has not been to the church in years, but little has changed. The same plain glass windows, three on each side and two flanking the coffin-friendly front door, their curtains drawn tonight against the April cold. The same hard pews, two sets in rows with an aisle between. In front of the foremost pews, a row of folding chairs is set up awaiting this evening's expected overflow, and the rows of pews to the left of the aisle have been lengthened into the aisle by the addition of one chair per row. Clint takes the chair nearest the door. He isn't bothered that this puts him in Sinners' Row. In fact he suspects that will make him more attractive to the girls.

The choir that soberly contemplates the congregation from behind the pulpit wears its dresses below the knee, its hair long and caught back with a ribbon, a bit of string, a shoelace. Clint could be looking at his mother and his grandmother. The carpet he remembers is gone; he puts his foot over the knothole that was sending cold air up his ankle. In front of the pulpit, a man and a youth are singing "Church in the Wild Wood," accompanying themselves on guitars. They are earnest and spirited. They face each other like dancers. When they get to the line *"Come, come, come, come, come, come, come,"* Clint smirks at the pretty girl across the aisle, but she turns her face away.

Two men sit a little in front of the choir, to one side of the pulpit. Clint judges the younger—a dark, spare, stern man in khakis and a flannel shirt, long-sleeved but tie-less—to be the regular preacher, Ned Selden, and the elder to be the Reverend MacBee. The latter rises at the end of the hymn and beams at the performers and their audience. Like his host, he is clean-shaven, with an almost military haircut. He has sandy hair, a reddish face, and a big, solid-looking nose. He is about Clint's height and almost as muscular, though fifteen or twenty years older. He is wearing blue jeans, a blue zipper jacket, and brogans. "Praise God," he says, "for that singing. Wasn't that fine? Didn't that make you feel good? Wonderful. Praise God. The Lord *wants* you to feel good. The Lord *wants* us to have a good time, enjoy all the things He's given us. The Lord didn't put us on this wonderful earth of His to suffer. We do suffer. You suffer; I suffer—but that's not the point of it. Come on, let's just hear those Combs boys again, praise God."

"Amen," somebody says, and the Combs boys, who have made no move to sit down and who don't seem surprised, take off with "Stand Up, Stand Up for Jesus." This time the choir joins in, and after the first verse, MacBee gestures with widespread upraised arms for the congregation to rise and sing too. The girl Clint has been staring at hands him a hymnal across the aisle. He holds it open at the place she has marked. MacBee holds no hymnal. His strong steady voice can be heard by everyone to the last chord.

Right of the pulpit is a small table on which lies a wooden box about the size, Clint judges, of an insurance salesman's briefcase. His eyes narrow as he makes this appraisal; he has a special grudge against insurance salesmen. The Reverend MacBee's hand sometimes rests on this box as he sings, sometimes strokes, sometimes taps it. His eyes never waver from the Combs boys. When the latter seat themselves in two of the front row chairs, he steps behind the pulpit, where a spotlight illuminates him, and faces the congregation. "Praise God!" he says, cocking his head, "you-all got you a good choir here! These sisters can sing! They sing so you don't have to wonder if they mean it. They sing so they let the *Lord* know they're singing." The choir begins to hum "Shall We Gather at the River."

Near a window, scuffling breaks out between two of the many children in the room. The Reverend MacBee seems unconscious of them. His head is thrown back; he is gripping the pulpit, possessed by the music, or praying. The spotlight shines on his closed eyes. Now the choir is humming "Rock of Ages." When they fade into silence, the Reverend MacBee recollects himself. His hands continue to grip the pulpit, but his chin comes down. He stares compellingly at the congregation for several seconds. Then his right arm rises, stiff and straight. "And these signs shall follow them that believe," he declares. His forefinger points at the ceiling somewhere to the right of Clint's head. Reflexively, Clint glances up. "In my name shall they cast out devils!" The pointing hand jerks to the Reverend MacBee's throat; he unzips his jacket with a gesture like ripping. "In my name shall they cast out *devils!*" He throws his jacket on the table beside the pulpit.

Several women have brought babies. Set off by the shouting, two or three of these infants begin to cry. In the row in front of Clint, a mother puts her red-knuckled hand over her protesting infant's mouth; Clint watches the baby's face darken, its neck veins bulge as the Reverend MacBee's are bulging. Clint wonders detachedly if the mother will suffocate her child before she will release its roar. She has three other children—two boys, and a blonde daughter bigger than she is herself, old enough for Clint's inspection, especially since no man is sitting with them. The girl is miserable, the boys impassive.

"*Devils!*" Macbee shouts. His tie lands on top of his jacket. "They shall *cast out devils!*" Then his voice softens and his face is full of wonder and promise. "They shall speak with new tongues." His voice drops to a whisper: "They shall take up serpents."

In front of Clint, the baby is sniffling spasmodically on its mother's shoulder. The red-knuckled hand pats the exhausted back.

The Reverend MacBee moves over to stand again beside the little table where his jacket lies. The congregation leans slightly forward. "They *shall* take up serpents!" the Reverend MacBee repeats. "They *shall.* Not, you can if you want to. Not, you can do it if somebody, your brother or your friend or somebody you're trying to impress, dares you to. They shall. Hear that, brothers? You hear it, don't you, sisters? That's the *Lord* speaking. Those were his words. You can't get away from it. That's not your brother or your friend or somebody you're trying to impress daring you, that's the *Lord* daring you. He's daring you to show him your faith in him, show the *devil* your faith in him.

"And you can do it." Gently, MacBee's hand strokes the wooden box. There is no more scuffling among the children. The congregation seems to be holding its breath. "You can show that ol' devil that his power is nothing to the power of the Lord. It's nothing to the power of a man or woman who believes on that Lord." MacBee smiles on the congregation as gently as a father tucking his child under a quilt. "They shall take up serpents." On the baby's back, the red-knuckled hand lies still.

One side of the box on the table is a Plexiglas door secured with a small padlock. The Reverend MacBee removes the padlock and lifts out a five-foot rattlesnake. There is a collective sigh as the congregation sits back.

Clint doesn't shrink or wince. He never has seen a snake in church before, but he has seen boa constrictors twice that long in Panama.

Circling the pulpit, MacBee holds the rattler loosely in both hands like an offering to the congregation, the choir, the congregation again. A woman in the front row moans. Other women join in; they begin to sway like the mourners at Clint's mother's wake, but the moaning is in a different, eerie, key. Their men don't make a sound, don't move. The Reverend MacBee circles the pulpit again. The moaning grows insistent. Clint realizes that in spite of himself, all his muscles have grown rigid.

"Praise God!" a man shouts. He has risen and is pushing, stumbling, over the feet of his neighbors, toward the aisle. "Praise God!" The Reverend MacBee stands still. The snake's head turns from side to side; its eyes stare unblinking hatred at the congregation.

The man, he wears overalls and stiff leather work shoes that come up high over his ankles, is advancing on MacBee. His face is pale, exalted. He takes the snake from MacBee and raises it triumphantly over his head. The spotlight glitters on the snake's scales.

The man is holding the snake too close to its head, Clint judges. Clint's daddy taught him to hold a snake by the tip of its tail, so it can't turn around and bite your hand. Choked like that, it's only to be expected that the snake will try to free itself, will sink its curved fangs into the offending wrist. There is so much moaning, Clint cannot hear if the snake is rattling, and now MacBee begins to speak again.

"They shall take up serpents," MacBee says, "and if they drink any deadly thing, it shall not hurt them; they shall lay hands on the sick, and they shall recover."

"They shall recover—but only if the holy spirit is in them. You can't do it just because somebody—your brother or your friend or your neighbor or somebody—dares you to. You can't do it because somebody you envy just a little bit does it, and you don't want him to be any better than what you are. The Lord won't protect you if that's your attitude.

"He'll know. You can't fool *him.* You can fool me. You can fool your neighbor. You can fool that pretty girl you think might be impressed. You can even fool yourself, sometimes. But you can't fool the Lord. If you take up that serpent and have not faith on the

Lord, have not faith that the Lord is your savior, and will stand by you, then he won't do it." MacBee smiles a little, shakes his head. "You have to have that faith, and brother, sister, you better believe me, that faith has to be strong." The moaning from the congregation has never ceased. Softly, the choir begins to sing: "Not as I Will, But as Thou Wilt."

Suddenly the woman in front of Clint thrusts her baby into her daughter's arms and rises. She almost darts past her two boys, out of her pew. She reminds Clint of his sister Mae, small, quick, and determined. She is headed for the man with the ecstatic face and the rattler. Her steps are amazingly fast. Her mouth is slightly open and she stares at the snake as she takes it into her hands, but then she lifts her face and there is no telling what if anything she sees. The choir begins to sing, "Wait a Little Longer, Jesus."

The woman holds the snake loosely. Its head, its tongue, flick from side to side. She allows it to glide where it will—up and over one shoulder, around her neck, down the other shoulder. She walks —slowly, now—from one side of the church to the other. The worshippers in the front row do not move. Deliberately, majestically, she returns to stand before the pulpit. Her eyes glitter like the snake's. She starts down the aisle.

When she reaches the rear of the church, the woman turns again toward the pulpit and stands still. She is very close to Clint. Clint sees the snake's piggy nose, the fork in its flicking tongue, its cold stare. The woman does not restrict it. It coils around her waist and Clint can hear the buzzing of its vibrating tail as its flat head glides upward toward her breasts. He does not feel himself lean forward. A snake, his daddy told him, will milk a cow. The snake's head seems to caress first one breast, then the other. Clint feels himself begin to sweat and the saliva collects unswallowed in the bottom of his mouth. Not even aware that he causes it, he feels his chair hitch ever so slightly forward. Suddenly its right foot goes through the knothole and he is pitched against the woman in the aisle.

The woman screams. She screams again, and the second scream is different from the first.

Clint is putting his chair back on its feet and the younger Combs Boy is holding the wooden box for the Reverend MacBee to put the rattlesnake back in it, and the woman is staring up speechless into the home preacher's face. The preacher's Adam's apple is jerking. The choir's singing has broken off.

The woman's daughter and younger son are crying; the baby is crying. "They shall lay hands on the sick, and they shall recover, praise God," the Reverend MacBee says calmly. "The Lord's will be done." He and Selden, the home preacher, lay their hands on the woman's head, her arm. Her own hands clasp her breast. Through her spread fingers, Clint sees a quarter-sized bloodstain.

The law will not be called—not now, and probably not later, but Clint is taking no chances. He eases through the people clustering around the woman. As he steps out of the church into darkness, he hears the choir begin to sing again: "I'm Getting Ready to Leave This World." He is hornier than ever.

~⊰24⊱~   {Lorena

Lorena crosses double solid lines and passes a logging truck going uphill. Tuesday traffic, she reflects, isn't the worst.

Her nephew Swango—she had pulled the information out of him over the phone—hadn't gone to the school bus stop with Kyle and Jessie. Swango is only thirteen to Jessie's fourteen, but he has longer legs. By agreement, the moment the three children were out of sight of the cabin, he had run to their Aunt Nelcie's. Her husband had gone to his barbershop already, so Swango had called Aunt Lorie. Why, Lorena had demanded, hadn't he called last night? "After what I done, Pap wouldn't let nobody outen the house." Swango had already got one beating.

"*Who told on you?*"

"He seen the marks."

Ned Selden, Swango's father, had gone to the privy almost as soon as the men had laid his wife in her bed and, at his insistence, left. Kyle, who is seven, had stood guard at the back door, and Swango had cut their mother above the puncture marks and sucked out the viper's poison and spat it into the dishpan Jessie held so there would be nothing on the floor for their father to see.

Swango hadn't needed her to hold their mother down. Glenna was already feeling weak. Swango had cut and sucked, cut and sucked, until Kyle's hiss. In her fruit box in front of the fire, the baby had never stopped crying. This morning in spite of Swango's work, Glenna's chest is badly swollen.

Lorena finds Swango and Jessie waiting for her as planned at the school bus stop. Jessie and Kyle had gone ahead and waited there while Swango ran to their Aunt Nelcie's. Although Swango had run to join the other two just as soon as Aunt Lorie had promised to come at once, the bus had arrived before him. Jessie had lifted and shoved Kyle onto it, and warned the driver not to let him off until she got him to school. Jessie has been waiting in the cold for more than an hour. When Swango first joined her, he was hot from running, but now he's as grateful for the station wagon's warmth as she.

"Who-all's with your mama?" Lorena demands.

"Just Daddy," Jessie says. She is a big girl, bigger than her mother, but fair like all the Baileys. Fear as well as cold has drained her face almost blue and she is half sniffling. "Preacher MacBee, he offered to take turns setting up with Mama overnight, but Daddy, he would not hear to no man setting in Mama's bedroom." Preachers, in Ned Selden's opinion, are no less inclined to sin than other men. *He should know*, Lorena thinks balefully, *being one*.

There are two cars in front of the Seldens' cabin, but one is on blocks, and the other Lorena recognizes as Ned's aging Chevy. If any neighbors have come to help, Ned has run them off. Lorena turns the station wagon facing out before she puts it in park, and leaves the engine running. Sections of a cardboard packing case have been laid out to make a sidewalk to the cabin steps. So much mud has been tramped onto them, the improvement is small, but Lorena is interested only in whether the improvised walk will lie still underfoot.

Ned meets Lorena at his door. He is tall and dark, gaunt from his sleepless night. His hair is cut short as a Parris Island drill sergeant's and he is clean-shaven. Lorena has Eldridge's shotgun in her arms. "I'm taking her to the hospital," she says. She can hear Jessie's nervous breathing behind her, but Swango doesn't make a sound.

Ned's eyes blaze like a challenged hawk's, but his Adam's apple rises and falls only once before he steps back. Lorena keeps the gun on him while Swango and Jessie carry their mother to the station wagon, Swango at her shoulders, Jessie at her feet. "Harlot," Ned calls Lorena grimly. "Ye have taken the ways of the world." He stands motionless in his doorway as Lorena backs across the muddy yard toward the station wagon.

When Jessie slams the door after her mother, Ned starts toward her. The children glance fearfully at their father over their shoulders, run to the other side of the station wagon, and jump in. Ned crosses the porch. Something Lorena's hand is touching clicks, and he stands still again on the top step. Glenna is scolding weakly as Lorena slams the driver's door and shifts gears.

"Let me suffer it out," Glenna pleads. "My faith is stronger than e'er a viper." She is still complaining as she is carried into the Marcum and Wallace Memorial Hospital emergency room. She has to rest between arguments.

❧25❧ {Albert

Albert sits on his single bed to tie his shoes. His feet are on the rug his sister Maggie passed on to him when her husband's church carpeted their parsonage, and he is sitting on the green chenille spread she rushed to Sears and bought him after she came to deliver her rug, and discovered nothing over his sheets but an army blanket. Except for Maggie's rug and spread and three pictures, one on the bureau, two on the walls, all gifts, Albert's room might be described as Twentieth Century Monastic. At the head of the bed stands a table of a size to accommodate his telephone, lamp, alarm clock, weather radio and not much else; his books crowd a small set of shelves against one wall. These books include *Martin Luther King, Jr.: a Documentary; Montgomery to Memphis,* a gift from his other sister, Jakba; Milton Cross's *Complete Stories of the Great Operas,* Albert's own purchase; no detective stories. Albert doesn't necessarily prefer austerity, but he is in this room an average of only six or seven hours out of twenty-four.

In the warmth and casual clutter of Nat and Suzanne Wrenn's house, where he is a frequent supper guest, he relaxes and expands. He is going there now, but the promise of Suzy's good and plentiful cooking, his namesake's adoration, his old friend's genuine interest in his life, fail to soften his somber mood. Lang Brough has been missing for seven days. The fire department has drained every pond as much as three feet deep within a mile of the one Ruth Brough first urged them to drain, starting with that one. Like the bush by bush county-wide search that preceded it, this effort has produced nothing whatsoever that could be connected with Lang Brough.

Albert's teletype inquiries have yielded nothing, and there has been no useful response to the flyers he or the Broughs or React have mailed or posted, nor to the publicity Lang's disappearance has generated on TV or radio or in the papers. For a change, Albert rather dreads Nat's intelligent questions about his work. At the same time, he doesn't feel he has the energy to forestall them by thinking up distracting questions of his own.

The Paris Band Boosters, he remembers, have a rummage sale every April. Nat and Suzy's basement fills with donations months ahead of it every year. He can ask how collections are going.

Albert is too tired to jog to the Wrenns' as he usually does. Nat and Suzy live one street over from where Nat and Albert grew up, the street where both men's mothers still live. Albert's bed-and-bath apartment is in another neighborhood, close enough that he can be a help to his mother, too far for her to notice his hours and worry.

Albert had been in the state police five years and was posted at Dry Ridge, near Kentucky's Ohio border, when his father suffered his first heart attack. Maggie at that time was already living in Lexington with two children under four, plus all the duties of a minister's wife. Their brother Cyrus, a drummer with a band that plays the R&B circuit, was in Detroit. Their younger sister Alice was a senior at UK. Since her announcement that from now on she would be answering only to "Jakba," and *just* Jakba, no slave surname, she and her father had been spending all their time together baiting one another. Albert's mother could use him back in Paris, Albert concluded, and except that his father's death last year leaves

130

his mother more time to concern herself with his bachelorhood, he has never until now felt the move to have been disadvantageous. Now he reflects that if he hadn't been in the courthouse when Dr. Brough's call came, this racking case need not have fallen to him.

In the Wrenns' foyer, Albert hands Nat his coat and turns smiling to Suzy. "So how's the junk business this year?"

Suzy gestures, laughing, to the living room. It is full to the gills, as Junior Gillum would have said, with contributions for the benefit of the band: a pair of faded chairs stacked seat to seat; a decade's worth of *National Geographics* tied with baler twine in parcels of twelve; boxes full of newspaper-wrapped items which Albert knows from previous years' sales will be of the sort dubbed "Collectibles" because they are neither Valuable nor Antique. "I tell Nat to please just leave Ali and me a path to the door so we can leave him when I can't stand one more donation," Suzy says. Albert Blount Wrenn is known variously as Ali, Ali Cat, and Big Al, the last because Albert, when Nat and Suzy asked permission to name their baby for him, stipulated that the child was never to be called Little Albert.

Nat takes Albert's coat to hang and returns with his son by the hand. Big Al has on his white rabbit pajamas; he has been permitted to remain up to hug Uncle Albert good night. "What's happening, man?" Albert cries. "Gimme five!"

The child strides forward and slaps Albert's palm soundly with his own. Albert picks him up for his hug. At Suzy's request, he walks to the staircase before putting Big Al down, on the third step. This brings the boy's face level with his own. "Hey, man," Albert demands, "how'd you get so tall so fast?" The child giggles happily.

With a combination of firmness and sweet talk, Suzy gets her son started up the stairs before Nat and Albert take seats in the living room. Otherwise she knows she would have to remove him from a lap.

"So how's it going," Nat asks Albert soberly as soon as the child is gone. "You're looking for that vet's kid, aren't you.... We read about it."

Albert knows Nat's inflections as well as his own family's. He can hear that Nat is trying to make his question sound casual. Nat wants Albert to tell him that Nat's son is not in danger, that Lang Brough's disappearance is a tragic freak, not a signal that Bourbon County families are besieged. It comes to Albert that this may even be why he was invited tonight. "I'm looking," he says.

"Any good leads?"

"Not a clue, man. Nothing."

"All those posters and not one call?"

"Oh, calls. Lots of calls. You can't put a person on TV without twenty people seeing him at the supermarket. The last guy I was looking for was arrested holding up a filling station in Los Angeles and I'd had three positive sightings of him within fifteen miles of here that day, one in Lexington, one in Cynthiana, and one in Carlisle."

Suzy comes back downstairs and enters the living room smiling. "Sorry to put demands on a tired man but I've got a child upstairs who can't sleep until Unco Abber reads him a story."

Albert is pleased with this interruption, even though he knows his relief is temporary; Nat and Suzy will pin him to the subject of Lang Brough at table. Halfway upstairs he smiles, ruefully, at the thought of how he will feel when the realization comes to Ali that Abber is not Albert's name, and he never again calls him Unco Abber.

Ali has propped himself up expectantly on his pillow. "She Come Bringing Me That Little Baby Girl" lies on the chair by the head of the bed. Albert glances quickly through it and concludes that the answer to the question that had occurred to him when Suzy greeted him at the door in a new and waistless outfit is *Yes*. Two weeks ago he would have grinned.

Unfortunately, the book choice turns out to be Suzy's. "Don't read that book," Ali commands. "Read the pebbo book."

"Man, I've read you that pebble book one thousand times. This book here is a good book. Let's read *this* book."

"Mama already read me that. I want the pebbo book."

Up to this hour, when Albert has read Ali William Steig's parable of the donkey child who finds a magic pebble and turns into a stone, he has thought of it as a study of autism and love, but tonight it has become what it is, a story of parents whose son has disappeared. "Tell you what. I'll read you this book first, and then I'll read you the pebble book." Ali, Albert hopes, won't stay awake long enough to collect on this promise.

Ali does, however. There is a break in Albert's voice when Ali silently slips his hand into Albert's. The pause is not shortened when Albert realizes that Ali has taken his hand to give comfort, not to seek it.

Suzy has fixed red rice, which she knows Albert loves. She waits till he's eaten half a plateful before commenting quietly, "Nat says you haven't had any breaks looking for that little boy."

Albert lays down his fork. "No breaks."

Nat is studiously buttering his cornbread.

"What will you do?" Suzy asks.

"I'll start checking on who's been paroled around here lately, and where he was the first three days last week." From the Department of Corrections, Planning and Evaluations in Frankfort, Albert has obtained a list of all the parolees who have been released in Bourbon and the six neighboring counties in the last six months.

"Will there be many?"

"Sixty-one," Albert says. "And I'll go to each one's parole officer and get the dates and times the individual checked in the first three days this month. If the individual has a job, I'll go to his employer and find out if he came to work those first three days, and what time. If he's a renter, I may check with his landlady: Was he home those nights? I may talk to his family; I may talk to the individual himself. Or herself."

Now Suzy too has laid down her fork. "All that for sixty-one names?"

"Depends on what I learn, how far I go with each one."

"How long do you guys work on a case like this," Nat asks, "before you give it up?" He is careful to sound matter-of-fact, but Suzy cannot conceal the fear in her eyes.

"We never give up on a missing child. A missing child's case is either solved or it's open. But open is one thing. Active? There will come a day when I have to leave it be while I do something else."

Albert pauses somberly and looks at his plate, away from Suzy's eyes. "The day will come when I have to tell that lady I can't find her son, not even his body."

Albert thinks he can rely on the boy's father to help him when that day comes, but it will not be enough, even if he could count on it. He hasn't got the feeling from either of the Broughs that they think a white detective would have found their son by now. On the other hand, you never know what a white actually thinks of you. Albert's roommate at Eastern was a white boy from Harlan County. The boy hadn't blinked when Albert arrived, and by Thanksgiving, Albert had begun to relax into what he thought might become a friendship of a kind he had never thought possible back in the days of Paris High. The thought even had crossed his mind that it had been no fairer of his parents, his teachers and his minister to say "whites will" than it is of whites to say "blacks are." Then the boy's parents had driven up to bring him home for the holiday, and he had begged Albert to make himself scarce till they were gone because he never had told them he was rooming with a black.

Suzy is pressing Albert to take more rice, more cornbread. "No more, thank you, Suzy," Albert says.

❦26❧ {Ruth

"You can have your first wish in life, but not your second," Eva suggested to me once, after a letter from me griped that Grove seems to feel no urge to visit Europe, indeed hasn't left this farm overnight since our honeymoon. (Grove's idea of a vacation is a long afternoon fishing at Cave Run.) Once I read him half a page of the Shaw biography he'd given me for Christmas and teased that he ought to trade our mares in on giraffes. *Get rid of the dogs and buy a giraffe*, Shaw urged Mrs. Patrick Campbell, who wouldn't return to England and star in his play because her dogs would have been quarantined. England doesn't quarantine giraffes.

"Unlike Mrs. Campbell's dogs," Grove responded, "our mares are worth money. Shaw would side with me."

My thought at the time was that Shaw might be right about Mrs. Campbell but wrong about us. Now I think he was wrong about Mrs. Campbell, too. Lang gone, I hold Joanna more than ever, and I can feel this physical contact easing my gut. I have changed my mind about widows; they are wise, not fatuous, to get lap dogs. If Joanna, too, were to be torn from my arms, it would be healthier for me to wrap them around a sofa cushion than to let them dangle. Mrs. Patrick Campbell was sager than Shaw, I think, as I pull out a book to read to Joanna just as an excuse to hold her in my lap.

Nevertheless, and although my love for my daughter is boundless, my patience with her is not.

"This oatmeal is cold!" she informed me rudely.

I had not been thinking about her. She always knows.

I had been gazing out the window at the purple martins. Easter Monday, they had returned. Every one of them vanished from Clay Pike last July, but they were back now, all of them back. I could feel the edges of my eyelids tightening, then Joanna recalled me. "You should eat it more quickly," I said.

"I can't eat it now. It feels like snot."

Reminding myself of the stress the child is under, I said quietly, "I'll reheat it for you."

"Don't stir it! I like the milk on top. I don't like it all mixed in. I don't want oatmeal *soup.*"

Again suppressing the first reply that came to mind, I promised, "I won't stir it any more than I have to, to keep it from scorching, and then you can put more milk on top if you like."

That is not what my mother would have said to *me*, but then my brother didn't disappear from my life till I was nineteen. *Temper the wind,* I admonish myself, every time my shorn lamb starts acting like a piglet. But I am bleeding from the same shears. I thumped her bowl back in front of her, saying, "Now if *this* gets cold, you will eat it cold, and if you find you can't eat it cold now, you will get it cold for lunch."

Which wouldn't have been much worse than what we did get: my uneaten Easter-breakfast egg sliced onto lettuce, and some dissolved bouillon cubes served in brown bowls, so we wouldn't notice that it looked like steeped bark. I was determinedly serving meals on schedule, requiring myself, or trying, to eat portions of the size I would have offered another adult. The fatigue of those first weeks is hard to remember now except in details like this: I felt that I could not stand up long enough to peel and chop three potatoes into our soup. Grove meant to be kind, coming home for lunch when he could—or maybe he himself needed comfort, needed to see that Joanna and I were still there! Either way, I owed him a better meal.

Grove emptied his bowl without comment, then asked, "Can I do anything for you before I go?"

Every Wednesday afternoon, any bagged trash left beside Clay Pike's mailboxes is collected by a compactor truck. There are weeks when more than half of our contribution consists of what I have picked up along our road front. "Let me hitch a ride to the front gate," I answered Grove now. "I forgot to pick up cans yesterday." Of course I hadn't forgotten.

"I'll do that; you go lie down."

"I need the distraction," I lied again.

The night before, telling Grove about the secreted nail file, I had deprecated Lucille's choice of TV shows.

"Seems to me for her own mother to get hysterics and come apart right in front of her face is a hell of a lot worse for her than anything Lucille's going to let her see on a box!" he had instantly rejoined. "I've been wondering if she'd be better off spending more time with Lucille, till you can get hold of yourself!"

The telephone company had traced the bored dropout in minutes, and that is all he was. I had let this account for Grove's outrageous outburst at the time, and now supposed that he was trying to atone for it, coming home for lunch, not complaining at my bouillon cube soup, offering to make himself late back to work for the sake of my footling neglected chores. I was willing to take the deed for the word.

Joanna, who'd asked to be excused, was back before I finished clearing the table. She'd put on her jacket. "Where are you off to, princess?" her father asked.

"I'm going to help Mama pick up cans."

Lang's job.

Every Tuesday after school, dragging a discarded feedbag, Lang helped me clear the front line of beer cans, vodka bottles, styrofoam hamburger chrysalises—the motorized ape's banana peels. At eight, he seemed old enough not to go dashing onto Clay Pike because he saw a bunny rabbit in the far ditch, but I always walked between him and the road. I told him this was because he, being shorter, was the one who would be slithering under the fence to get the occasional projectile that had made it into the pastures.

Joanna was presenting her front to her father to be buttoned up. I looked across the mares in the front field to the Pike, where a car was passing. One is all it takes.

Grove saw my glance. "Do you mean to tell me I've got to palpate David Trimble's mares all by myself?" he demanded. "Here I was countin' on you to go along!"

Joanna has yet to make the connection between her father's dropped g's and subterfuge. I wondered how old she would be before that silent g would sound louder to her than any word he spoke. Now she looked anxiously from his face to mine, trying to gauge which of us would miss her worse. She is very protective of us now.

I let them give me a lift to the foot of the driveway. They drove away, and I was alone in the last place Lang was seen. The last place Lang was seen by anyone willing to tell us. There I was, and I could choose. I could run out in front of the next fast car, or I could clean the front line.

I cleaned the front line, deposited my bags at the gate for Gordon Barry the trashman, and went back to the house with the mail: two advertisements, three more of those stiff square envelopes, and a letter from Mother, heaven bless her.

I have continued to clean the front line every Tuesday for the last seven weeks. Since Grove's nephew Tad arrived for the summer, he has helped, but we two have not been companionable this year. At the gate he heads west with his bag and I head east with mine. We fill our bags, deposit them at the gate for Mr. Barry, and walk, only more or less together, back to the house, each privy to his own thoughts. Mine are of things to tell Lang that I found or saw on this job, while he was away. Tad's may be anything from incinerating terrorist bombers to lunch.

In April, alone, I took twice as long at the job as I ought to have taken, because I paused to stare at every vehicle that passed, sick with the feeling that one of them contained someone who knew that Lang should have been at my side, someone who had taken him from me. *The poor little dauphin was just about Lang's age when he was wrested from his mother and taught to call her a **damned whore**, taught to deny his name. He never saw his parents again.* Almost as bad were the other cars, the cars whose drivers had no thought of Lang, no knowledge of him. Then I stared at them thinking, *They don't know about us. They don't know that this is a place where Lang was, and is not.*

But on that first Wednesday after Easter, I cleaned the front line, and I kept an eye on Chinese Lagoon, due in seven days and not grazing, but standing with her rump shoved into the fence. "Wait till your doctor gets home, will you?" I begged her silently. All I needed was to have the most valuable mare on the farm decide to foal with nobody there but me.

"Four more like Lagoon and I can retire," Grove began saying after Ten's older brother won a big stakes race last September. His goal, he confided one day last winter, was to have the band up to seven by the time Lang finishes high school. "No telling what Lang will want to do with himself," he said, so offhandedly that I stopped scolding the colt I was trying to hold still and listened closely. I couldn't see Grove's face because he was wrapping the colt's leg. "If Lang should decide he wants to be a vet, it would make no sense to expect him to help with college expenses."

I know, from the people who've begged for Grove's help, that getting into vet school is harder than getting into med school. The first B stands for *Blew it.* The top of Grove's head, where he will soon be bald, looked so vulnerable that I wanted to let go of the shank and hold him. He has never repeated or referred to that day's diffident disclosure. If Lang should announce that he wants to be a lepidopterist, Grove will say fine. Love means caring enough to lie.

My feminist friends would fault me for not having pointed out that Joanna might be the one who sends us bills for pre-vet courses.

Perhaps I was influenced by something Peter von Strehlenau told me and Eva years ago about Napoleon. Napoleon, Peter claimed, declined to open his mail until it was a week old. That way, he said, most of its questions had answered themselves. At the time, I laughed.

~~27~~ {Ruth

Grove and Joanna didn't make it past Trimble's mares. Chinese Lagoon went into labor as I deposited my sack of detritus beside the mailbox, and I was on the barn phone to Grove before I even fetched her in.

Delivered a week sooner, the new colt would have had us dancing in the barn aisle. Joanna, at least, was diverted, babbling all the way back to the house. As I unbuttoned her jacket, I heard the guttural groan of the weekly garbage truck. For some reason, it had turned into our driveway.

I knew as Gordon Barry stepped out of his cab that this was a condolence, not a business call, because his mouth was empty. I left Grove to see to the door while I eased Joanna into the sewing room and settled her down with a stack of picture books and orders to stay put.

The jaws of Mr. Barry at work always grip a cigar. Observing this, my first year on the farm, I gave him a box of Dutch Masters for Christmas. "You're spending too much," he protested. The cigar wasn't part of his uniform because he liked to smoke, but because its smell protected him from the garbage stench. "Just get King Edwards, if you want to give me something." Every subsequent Christmas, I have presented him with two boxes of King Edwards. After Norma Lee told me about his alcoholic wife, I felt satisfaction in giving him something so patently all for himself, nothing she could share. These days I'm having second thoughts.

Mr. Barry was carrying something in a tightly gripped paper bag, which he shifted to his left hand as Grove opened our door to him. I hoped Grove's bloody coveralls would put him at ease about his own clothes, but he wouldn't sit down. "I have to go right back on the route. If I fall behind, my wife starts getting calls and it worries her. She's always afraid I've had a heart attack somewhere."

I suppose he never knows when she's going to answer drunk and insult a customer.

"Never sitting down is exactly how you and I both are going to get heart attacks," Grove told him. "The customers can wait long enough for us to have a cup of coffee."

Later I tried to remember Mr. Barry's answer, for I did remember that the look the two men then exchanged communicated something which I did not, and was not meant to, comprehend. Mr. Barry took a sparkling jar out of his bag. "My wife makes the best green pepper jelly," he said with obviously false heartiness. "If you're having a little drink in the evening, try some on a cracker."

It gave me a pang, that "little drink," so bravely casual—like me now, asking about my friends' children.

"My wife wanted to come with me, to say how sorry we are for your trials, how much we hope you find your little boy quickly."

Everyone, myself included, has taken to calling Lang "little." Tall for his age, bony, knock-kneed Lang, "little," when even Joanna bridles at being called so.

"I wouldn't let her come out in this cold. There's not a blacksmith has worse arthritis than my wife. I told her you'd understand."

I understood.

Grove walked Mr. Barry to his truck and I went to invite Joanna to come have a cup of cocoa with me. Grove came back inside and kissed me as I followed his daughter down the hall—unlike Mrs. Barry, I was not a dipsomaniac. I helped Joanna into her chair and began measuring milk and cocoa mix.

I could hear Grove opening and closing drawers in Joanna's room. He doesn't know how the children's clothes-space is divided. He was liable to open a drawer to Lang's, and he'd had no breakfast. I was half running to forestall this when he left Joanna's room and began deranging things in the hall closet. Shortly he came to the dining room bearing a faded wring-out hat which apparently had spent the whole winter dirty on the closet shelf. "Chuck it in the laundry," I said, but he had already placed it on Joanna's head.

"You look like Paddington," he told her. "Go look in the mirror." That is something Joanna is always ready to do; off she padded. "Is this Lang's?" he asked, bringing his other hand out from behind him.

I snatched the red baseball cap he held out, and my stomach heaved. But it was not our son's. "No, it's not!" I said. He says I yelled. "I lettered Lang's name in the front binding of his. Where did this come from?"

"Barry noticed it on his Tuesday route in the trash of a guy who he knows doesn't have small children."

So the jelly had been a blind. Poor Grove! Even knowing that Lang never went to school without his cap, he had been looking for it, desperate for *proof* that this torn, stained object could not be Lang's.

"Whose trash?"'

"That's none of our business," Grove said, so I knew he knew. Joanna was coming back, preening herself in the grimy wring-out. We put our conversation on hold.

Why hadn't Mr. Barry gone to the police; why had he done this to us? What if it *had* been Lang's cap? What if it had been Lang's body, a hand breaking through the side of an extra-strength Hefty bag, a lock of fair hair escaping through the twine at the opening—would Mr. Barry have come flapping his vulture wings straight to us?

I waited until Grove and I were alone in our bedroom to demand, "Why did Mr. Barry bring that to us? Albert knows Lang's name was inked in his cap. That's part of what I wrote out for him. There was no need for us—"

Grove interrupted me so loudly, I jumped to close our door. "Everybody's not as impressed with that blackface Charlie Chan as you are, Ruth! I mean, what's he doing? What in *hell* is he doing? Lang's been gone more than a week and I don't see this country turned upside down!" By now he was crying, but when I hurried to hold him, he hurried to stop, to wipe his eyes and turn away—a cruelty, for I had gripped him as much to take comfort as to give. "Now you tell *me*. A boy doesn't just vanish. A boy doesn't just vanish off the face of the earth!"

But he does.

Blithe Spirit broke water April twenty-ninth. I called Fran on the tack room telephone to say that Grove would be late to Hereward, then hurried back to the foaling stall, where Grove was feeling to see if the foal's presentation was normal. "One foot; two feet; nose," he counted out reassuringly. The telephone rang before I had time to congratulate him. Ervil: I relayed his message that his pickup wouldn't start and he didn't know how late he would be. "Mmm," said Grove, not taking his eyes off Blithe.

Blithe was placidly eating hay, showing no signs of labor. I removed her water bucket and went back in the warm tack room to watch her and Grove through the window. Minutes passed while Blithe simply went on munching. Grove scowled at his watch. When he led Blithe away from the hay to stall center, she just stood. "Come hold her for me," Grove called. "She's not having contractions. I'm going to have to pull it, and she won't lie down."

Grove tugged gently, first one forefoot, then the other. I was shifting from foot to foot myself; even through straw, the stall floor was cold. With no help from Blithe, Grove advanced the foal to the point that its head was free. I wanted to ask if it was alive, but kept my mouth shut. "It's huge," Grove said. "I'm going to have to use chains."

A foal-pulling chain has a handle on one end that's easier to grip than a slippery forefoot. The other end loops over the pastern, between hoof and ankle. Grove has two pairs of these chrome-plated chains; one in the trunk of his car, the other hanging in our feed room with the shanks, pitchforks, Ervil's coveralls, and such. Taking long strides, Grove fetched the latter.

By the time Grove had pulled the foal's shoulders free, his face was flushed and shiny, and Blithe's chest and shoulders were soaking, but she still neither helped nor lay down. The foal's head and forefeet dangled. "Now it's the hips," Grove said grimly.

I heard a car pull up in front of the barn. Grove, his feet planted like an archer's, his arms pulling so hard the tendons stood out, ignored it. When the car door slammed, however, Blithe determined to walk, and for a minute the best I could do was steer her so that the foal flopping out under her bandaged tail didn't strike a wall. A barn door rolled open and Lucille Harper, snug and immaculate in a cherry red coat, appeared at the stall window. One look at us and she scuttled away. I got Blithe under control and Grove went back to work, his jaw clenched so tightly I could see the movement of the little bone in his temple. The next thing I knew, Lucille had helped herself to Ervil's coveralls and stationed herself at Grove's right hand. "I'll catch it when it comes," she told him quietly.

"Get back, it'll be awhile," he said, panting. "Get back; you'll get hurt."

Blithe didn't take kindly to a stranger in the stall and dragged me a few steps away from Lucille despite my tugging and jerking. "That's good, that's fine!" Grove cried. "Keep her there!" I tightened my grip and took a deep breath. Blithe was now standing where Grove's heel could brace against the wall behind him; he grunted as he pulled. Despite me, Blithe lurched forward. With a sudden swish the foal's hips were free and Grove was staggering backward empty-handed and Lucille, who had stepped forward just in time to get both arms under the foal, was down on the straw with the foal on top of her.

Grove helped her up. I thought he was going to hug her. He stood beaming at her, his chest heaving. When he could speak he said, to Lucille, "That drop would have broken its back, most likely." She smiled at him. I could have been in Zanzibar.

"Can I let Blithe go now?" I asked.

"Yes, let her go, let her go. I need the iodine."

I reached just outside the stall for the bottle I'd set there as soon as Blithe broke water. Grove took it and bent over the foal. "It's a filly," he said. I couldn't tell if he was informing me or Lucille.

"It's *big*," she murmured.

The filly's protest as Grove sloshed her umbilicus with the cold iodine was startlingly loud; Grove and Lucille exchanged delighted smiles. I'd wedged a bath towel between the stall bars as I'd come to deliver Ervil's message. Lucille cleaned her hands on it, then handed it to Grove, who began drying and chafing the filly's rump while Blithe licked its head. His eyes were shining. I felt a rush of gratitude to Blithe for the ordeal that I could believe had totally engrossed Grove, at least briefly freeing his mind of our own. "I owe you one," he said to Lucille.

"We both do," I seconded.

She glanced at me quickly, maybe for the first time, and her smile was perfect.

"How did you come to be here?" Grove asked her.

"Eldridge needs your signature on those three-year-olds' papers so he can ship to Churchill this morning. Fran didn't know how soon you'd be free here, so she sent me over in her car." Eldridge, I noted, was "Eldridge." I wondered if Lorena was Lorena, or Mrs. like me.

"C'mon, I'll sign them now," he said, and the two of them walked out of the barn.

The moon had been shining when I'd left the house for the barn. By the time Grove and I walked back together, it had faded to a vaccination scar on blue skin.

Usually the year's last foaling makes us jubilant. Grove changed clothes almost in silence, pecked me on the cheek and left on his rounds.

I was all right till Joanna's naptime. When Lang was our only child, waking or sleeping, he filled the house, but now I felt alone in mid-ocean, desperately glad to see Lorena drive up.

She wanted to apologize again, thank me again, for bridging the gap between her and Annie. "That fool sister of mine is going to be fine, no thanks to that crazy ignoramus she married. Had to drive her clean to Estill County to get her looked after."

I was so grateful to see Lorena, I wanted to grip her hand, keep her sitting in my living room till Grove got home. She didn't seem to want to talk about Glenna. "I hear Eldridge shipped a couple of fillies to Louisville this morning," I ventured.

"Ugh, that pair. Bred like champions. Haven't won the first thing. Eldridge says three years old, time they were mamas! But Mr. Dag wants to give them a chance at Churchill."

"Well, lucky for Grove and me," I said. "Fran sent Lucille over with their papers this morning. Grove was just pulling a foal out of a standing mare and he thinks it would have broken its spine if Lucille hadn't stepped in and caught it. The cord broke, of course; the foal was a bloody mess, but Lucille didn't bat an eye."

"She's something else!" Lorena said. "You'd expect with her looks, all she'd be thinking about would be a husband, but my cousin in Morehead knows her family real well. She says there was this boy crazy to marry Lucille, dated her all through high school —didn't roll into town on a watermelon, either; father owns his own drugstore. But Lucille is like me at that age; she wants to see a little of this earth before she gets covered with it." Lorena grinned. "She told my cousin's daughter she didn't care how many drugstores his daddy aimed to give him, she didn't intend to marry any boy fixing to spend his whole life in a town where the best thing in the museum is dog hair place mats." Lorena paused, put her hand where I guessed her baby was kicking her, and sighed. "I burned like that to leave Hawk Mountain, but I miss those hoot owls. I cover my wall with pretty views because when I look out the window, I see flat land and empty sky.

"Well, I don't think anybody as sweet as Lucille is with children is set on some big career. She sat for me a few times when Annie had jury duty. I think my Ezra is in love with her."

"I know Joanna is," I said.

Leaving, Lorena looked uncertain. "I shouldn't just drop in, but I didn't like to call you, honey. I know what's going on in your mind every time that telephone rings."

Grove was due home so soon after Lorena drove off, I didn't go for the mail. He always checks.

～29～   {Clint

Clint pulls into Morgan Mall shortly after sunrise Thursday morning. The mall is old, shabby, not particularly clean, qualities more conspicuous at this bleak hour, empty of the bustle of customers. Clint is pleased to see the front parking lot empty. He drives around back. A few unlucky early-shift employees have parked their Toyotas in the smaller, rear parking area; no one is in these cars. That's what Clint is here to be sure of. He doesn't trust that bastard Brough not to set him up, have a dozen cops in six parked cars just waiting for Clint to pick up his money before they close in on him. Clint intends to monitor the situation all morning. It sweats him to leave Lang alone so long by daylight, but this time he's tied the brat, and told him what will happen when Clint gets back if Lang messes his britches.

Clint parks where he can observe who drives in, who drives out, who doesn't get out of his vehicle once it's parked. Anybody left sitting in a car will be suspect. Clint, he congratulates himself, isn't stupid!

A tractor-trailer as big as Clint's cabin is backed up to Kroger's for unloading; the driver probably thinks he's a big shot. Clint wouldn't have his job. When he gets his money, he won't have to have any job. He leans back, stretches his right leg over into the passenger's side. He considers shifting seats, but he'd have to move the food he's laid in for the morning: a couple of cans of Pepsi, already room temperature; a couple of packs of peanut buttered crackers; a couple of sacks of potato chips; a fast-food box containing slaw, hamburger, french fries, little bladders filled with mustard and catsup; a package of doughnuts. He keeps his seat.

Not even a stray cat moves on Morgan Street. Litter is spilling from the overfilled trash bin back of Kroger's; a plastic tray blows and skitters around its base like a crippled bird. It gets on Clint's nerves. Clint left the cabin too excited to eat breakfast, and broke the speed limit all the way up to Lexington, but now the prospect of sitting in the cold Chevrolet for almost seven hours is drearier than any sentry duty Clint has ever pulled. His next car will have a heater. The thought of the new car he soon will buy cheers him and he opens the package of crackers.

He means to eat lunch at quarter of eleven: for that last hour, nothing must distract him. The Chevy clock doesn't work anymore, but he checked his watch on the drive up by the radio. For an instant he thinks time has moved along, but then he sees that he was mistaking the second hand for the minute hand. He shifts his legs again. He opens the doughnuts.

A couple of the mall pigeons are going into their act; they sound as if they were upchucking. Clint would like to shoot the damn things. He thinks wistfully of the gun hanging over the cabin fireplace. The damn birds will drive him crazy.

The tractor-trailer grinds out of the lot; its driver looks tired and angry. The bread truck arrives from the bakery on the north side of town. Clint has eaten his last doughnut.

The tension that relieved itself in speeding on the way up needs an outlet. Clint would like to open a bottle, but he needs to be cold sober for this job. He is both, sober and cold. He clenches and unclenches his toes.

Just as he will not go into his trunk, he will not light the joint he cannot get out of his mind. It would relax him, and he would like to be a little more relaxed. It would help fill the time. He checks his watch. If he turns on the ignition to play the radio, he has to do it at the cost of either the battery or the gas tank. This is no day to risk having the car conk out on him.

The sky is overcast; his windows aren't going to warm the car any. He needs to piss, and he figures he'd better get to it, before the lot starts to fill. He waits for the Rainbo truck to leave. The walk to the wall next to the garbage bin warms him some.

At five minutes past nine, a pickup truck pulls into the lot. It parks eight or ten spaces from Clint, and the driver, a man Clint's age, goes into the mall's hardware store. The passenger, an older man, remains in the truck. He looks too old and too country to impress Clint as much threat, but now Clint is reproaching himself because he never till now thought that people may conceal themselves inside one of the stores, awaiting the moment to rush out at him, jump in their vehicle and take out after him. He pictures these things, again stops his hand on his way to the pocket with the makings, opens a bag of potato chips. He can't taste them. He eats them all without once taking his eyes off the pickup. He wipes his fingers on his pants leg. At nine-twenty-five, the young guy comes out of the Hardware Center and drives his truck away, the old guy still in it.

By ten o'clock, Clint has eaten his lunch.

Customers begin to arrive for the department stores just before ten-thirty. They all sit in their cars, waiting for the doors to open. Clint has heard of cops who dress themselves like women to tempt bag-snatchers and poor bastards looking for sex. He watches the department store customers as narrowly as the pickups. Now his stomach is churning.

Around eleven, light rain begins to fall. Clint never thought of this possibility. What if it picks up; what if his money gets soaked? He should have told those bastards to put it in a garbage bag.

At quarter of twelve, the rain ends.

Clint smells his sweat becoming acrid. He hasn't stunk like this since Panama. He keeps his mind fixed on the parking lot entrance, barely remembering to breathe.

By twelve-ten no one has come with Clint's money. The rain, Clint thinks, might be what's made them late.

At twelve-eleven there is still no pickup truck in the Morgan Mall rear parking area. By one, three have come and gone. Clint is incredulous, baffled, furious, and finally, appalled. What do they expect him to do now?

A police car drives into the lot, then a second. The second pulls up beside the first and the two cops have a quiet conversation. Clint watches them, his hand on the ignition key, his heart pounding. Then both cops drive away. Clint knows he should get the hell out of there but he continues to sit. They will come. They have to come; he has their boy. What the hell is Clint to do with him?

Like its text, the address on Clint's letter—Brough Farm, Clay Pike, Paris 40361—has been scrawled by pencil, left-handed. The bar code reader at Lexington's Nandino Boulevard main post office having taken Clint's 4 for a 9, Clint's letter is on its way to the West Coast.

It took the Radfords nine days to get up the nerve to call on me. I wished it had taken forever. Weaver was ashen, his age suddenly showing. He walked stiffly, slightly bent, his hat in his hands, and glanced often at his wife. She stuck close to his side. I seated them on the sofa and offered them coffee; they accepted politely. I sat opposite them, thankful that Joanna was making rounds with Grove. Their untouched coffee grew cold.

Weaver's yellow bus full of laughing children had continued to pass our farm every school morning as always, rattling east toward Bourbon Central. Every afternoon it rattled back. Every time I saw it, I wanted to move to some steep Kentucky hill where there never are any school buses. I did my best to comfort the Radfords, but I was desperately relieved when Albert arrived.

Albert accepted a chair but declined coffee. The Radfords were grateful, I saw, to take the arrival of another person as an excuse to leave.

Albert clasped his hands in his lap and gave me bad news, which he tried to make sound like progress. Checking the April whereabouts of the latest five dozen of this area's parolees had so far turned up nothing suspicious.

We are not in a position to be pleased. Which is worse, Lang in the hands of a recidivist, or Lang no one has any idea where? My faith, probably as a direct function of my need, didn't waver. By Albert's next visit, I told myself; by his *next* call. I didn't cry, as I sensed he dreaded I would. I asked if his wife forgives the terrible hours he's putting in on Lang's case. He didn't smile as he denied a wife. This could mean displeasure at my asking a personal question, or it could mean that he regrets being single, but he smiles so rarely anyway, it may mean nothing.

I am sure that if Albert were white, he would be married. He is handsome, intelligent, dependable, kind, and has an instinctive rapport with children. I suppose sophisticated black girls think a detective's pay is unexciting, and unsophisticated black girls think a black detective is an Uncle Tom—or they're afraid their friends will. Maybe Albert smiles so rarely because he regrets going into police work. As a high schooler, he's told me, he wanted to become a ring-handler like his father. Albert's accent is what my Ashley Hall classmates used to call "dry-cleaned." It's better than Station WMCD's token black's; better than Zad Thacker's. He permitted himself a rare grin and slid with gentle self-mockery into dialect, though, as he described his boyish yearnings to put on them flared black trousers, them black leather gloves, take a-holt of some of them million dollar studs. "Did you ever get to help your father at the auctions?" I asked.

"Oh, yes, in the ring, not on stage, I was allowed to do my stuff —with a shovel and dustpan. I was *working up*."

"You got discouraged?"

"My mother got discouraged; she got real discouraged. She was there the day somebody let go of a yearling and I wound up on my back with a hoofprint in the middle of my forehead."

"So that scar isn't from police work."

"That scar is what sent me into police work, indirectly. Or directly, if you're one of those folks who think you have to be kicked in the head to go into police work.

"Actually, the colt only nicked me, but my mother was so upset she got with my teachers and she found me a scholarship and she fired me up for college."

I hope Mrs. Blount doesn't think Danger has the laugh on her, now that her son is with the police.

When Albert brings Lang home I am going to give him the most beautiful black leather gloves on the market.

❧31❧ {Albert

Albert takes the Brough driveway slowly, so as not to scatter its gravel. "In this uniform," he tells black rookies, "when confronted by racism, you must learn to be neither surprised nor enraged." The school bus driver and his wife had left the minute he sat down, abandoning full coffee cups. Once this would have set Albert to brooding. Today he advises his black sergeants, "Set yourself the challenge of ignoring racism. It's a fact of life, but if you become obsessed with it, your work will suffer. Acknowledge racism, then forget it and walk on, work on." Fastening his seat belt, Albert realizes that tension has given him a stiff neck.

Ruth Brough's manifest regard for him, Albert dismisses as impersonal: obviously faith in him is vital to her. She is a lady, however, and he wishes he had wonderful news for her. He turns on the car radio.

Its music banishes from his mind his neck and even, for a minute or two, Lang Brough. WEKU is broadcasting the first act of *Don Giovanni;* he has picked it up in the middle of Zerlina's duet with the don.

The young woman Albert hopes to marry is in Germany, trying to establish herself in opera. Albert fell in love with her at a University of Kentucky production of *Don Giovanni,* in which she sang the part of Zerlina. This was the first UK opera Albert had ever attended; his ticket had been given him by his sister Alice/Jakba, on the grounds, of which he is now suspicious, that she had a test the next day. The young soprano's name is Juanita Wrenn, and she is Nat's younger sister; that's why Albert suspects Jakba's story.

The skinny child who was living next door when Albert left Paris for Eastern is unconnected in his mind with the beautiful creature who stepped onto UK's stage and blew him away. He had not seen her in ten years. "It was your wig," he teases her. She tells him she'd had a crush on him for years. She tells him that alone among her brother's friends, he had always been polite to her. He hopes this is true. He doesn't remember.

Albert and Juanita "have an understanding," but haven't made it public. No date has been set for a wedding, and Juanita has told Albert not to give her a ring "just yet."

When Juanita agreed to marry Albert as soon as she graduated, in less than two years, Albert felt no unease. He would make lieutenant within two years, he correctly estimated, and would be in that much better position to support a family. Juanita, he supposed, would teach music, which she could do almost anywhere, just as he could get police work almost anywhere. They would not have any trouble choosing a location that suited them both. Several months before she graduated, Juanita broke it to Albert that she was determined to launch a singing career, even if it meant going abroad "for a little while." She has been in Germany three years.

Nameless tenors, faceless baritones, people Albert's dreams. He has allowed his family, and Nat, to assume that the Juanita affair ended three years ago, to spare himself humiliation if she ditches him. Currently, she is singing Micaela at the Munich State Opera; on his bureau is a picture of her in that role in an earlier, provincial production. The last time any of Albert's womenfolk got into his room was when Maggie brought him the bedspread, *ante Micaela,* and on the rare occasions when his brother Cyrus is in town, the picture goes in the top drawer.

Albert reaches Clay Pike and turns west. His next interviewee works for a nursery in Georgetown.

⌇32⌇ {Ruth

Saturday's mail had brought word from a Lexington bookstore of the arrival of some books I'd ordered back in March for Joanna's birthday. I wasn't afraid of seeing anyone I knew at a bookstore— they'd all be at the Dags' Derby Party, where we'd gone ourselves for the last nine years. I was in no mood to watch the Derby even at home. I went to Lexington as soon as I'd fed Grove and Joanna lunch.

Among the Owl and the Pussycat's own stock, I spied the latest *Encyclopedia Brown. Encyclopedia Browns* come out like flapjacks, and that's how Lang and Breck devour them. Encyclopedia is scarcely older than they, and he solves crimes unfailingly, with an ease that leaves grown-ups gaping. For a second I wanted to stick *The Case of Two Spies* at the clerk and ask her where was the quick solution to my son's agony, now that such stories had taught him to expect one. Instead I got her to gift-wrap it. Books are something Lang gets to share with Breck instead of the other way around, and a child who's been unaccountably missing for more than a week needs his re-entry eased, needs his self-confidence boosted, needs to know that his mother loves him—no matter what has been done to him. No matter what has been made of him.

I stopped at the Supervalu on the way out of town. I kept count of what I took off the shelves so that I could get in the *12 Items Only* line. I counted the items in my basket again as I waited my turn, and recounted them. Counting things, as Jake Averoyne promised, helps me not think. I didn't notice Lang's picture till I was next-but-one to check out.

I turned cold, stupefied.

If I made a movie, I could make its audience feel my shock at unexpectedly coming face to face with Lang's flyer. I would show them Lang's posted face as if they were seeing Lang himself, his face only gradually becoming a mounted photograph. In that line at the Supervalu, I had to grip my cart for support.

The poster was taped onto the front window. Men and women came and went in front of it without once looking up. The people behind me in line were bending to count their own items, or straining furtively to count those of any cheaters ahead of them. I felt my throat closing. Did we need someone with a bullhorn to stand in front of every flyer? The old man behind me nudged his cart up till it pushed my calves; the checkout girl said "Ma'am?" and I realized there was no one ahead of me. "I forgot something," I said, and wheeled my cart out of line.

I bought crayons.

At first I didn't connect the questions with me, and went on crayoning, but the voice grew sharper and louder and I glanced around at a woman who was glaring at me, through lenses so thick they made her face a frog's. "What do you think you're doing?" she demanded.

"I'm putting a hat on my child."

If she had discovered mouse dung in her butter, her face could not have registered more repugnance. Before I could appease her I saw, or thought I saw, the idea begin to infuse her indignant stare that I might be dangerous. She retreated and I resumed work.

"Could I ask you what you're doing, ma'am?" The manager, the bespectacled woman at his elbow, shone with the white-of-eye anger of the frightened. His meager shoulders and pale skin spoke of growing children, second mortgages, early openings and late closings. Customers must not be antagonized, scenes not made. Anger stretched his skin glaze-thin across his face and pinkened the tips of his ears and nose, and only some of it was at the woman who'd summoned him to the hot spot. His revulsion for me was so plain, I felt my own ears pull back.

"What if it was *your* child?" the woman demanded around his elbow, like a pup that plants himself between your feet and then barks bravely at the other dog. Behind them the checkout girl bagged groceries resolutely, never glancing at me, her face rigid.

My eyes scalded at the realization that they were all on my side. "I *am* the child's mother," I said. I fumbled, trembling, for my driver's license. "He never takes his cap off outside the house. His father gave it to him. His father took him to Cincinnati and got it for him."

People were beginning to stare. The manager looked at my license aghast, checking my address against the one on the flyer, but the woman didn't wait for that. Her arm was around me. "You poor thing!"

"I've got five kids myself," the manager stammered.

As the door swung open for me, I knew better than to look back, but I have the neck of Lot's wife. There must have been a dozen people staring after me. I almost stumbled to get out.

It's comforting to think that the Yahoo who goes to draw a moustache on Lang's face will be confronted by angry women with umbrellas. I was shaking inside long after I drove away, but I was comforted, too, in another, less rational, way. I have no idea who put Lang's unretouched flyer on that window. Somebody cares that he is missing. Somebody knows that it is awful.

Monday morning I mailed that Supervalu manager an unretouched flyer to go beside the one I had crayoned a cap on. Already before Grove had left for his rounds I had put under both truck and car seats a stack of both kinds. Now wherever I go I have both. Maybe people take them down the minute I drive away (and there was the day I was pulling every notice off Kroger's big front window and in their stead, putting up all my flyers, one after another, and Grove had to come and take me home). Maybe somebody

154

takes down my flyers, but I have never anywhere been refused permission to post the pair.

In May this seemed urgently worth doing—but how much longer will a picture of Lang taken last summer be worth posting? I look at every child. My eye corrects for altered hair and clothes without blinking, but time's disguise? At nine—for we must believe that this month is Lang's ninth June, that he has had his birthday—at nine he could not be expected to keep his baby fat much longer, even in a cage behind a gingerbread house. At eight, he was still more baby than boy, but even this spring his face was already less the dicotyledon than Joanna's. Between her fat cheeks, Joanna's baby nose makes me think of the sprout that emerges from between the big halves of a lima bean, and grows as they shrink. So Joanna's nose will grow as her cheeks diminish. But though the shape of the vine to come from the bean's tiny sprout is somewhat more predictable than the shape to which Joanna's anonymous nose will grow, Joanna is unlikely to metamorphose into a stranger as little boys do. The one feature of Lang's face that nothing can change is his changeable eyes.

Lang at eight was still pretty as a Renaissance angel. Studying both children at the supper table this April, I found it strange to think how well I knew those faces—better than my own—yet how little I could imagine how Lang's would look in fifteen years, or five. I sometimes had the giddy feeling that I was harboring a masked stranger. Already predetermined for Lang is a certain man's face, destined for him already before his father and I knew even whether his name was Langdon or Joanna. Already those curls that shone in his cradle like marsh marigolds, that I could never resist twisting around my finger, had subsided into a faintly wavy pale topaz, and I kept my hands off except when he had to let me give him a haircut. (His friend Breck, he mentioned twice this spring, goes to the barber.) Already the cherubic legs were hardening, perfection giving way to knobby awkwardness. Next his jaw will angulate. How soon will he be unrecognizable?

At just short of two years, Chinese Lagoon left our barn for a trainer's. At three she returned to her mother's paddock. If they knew one another, they gave no sign.

Lang is moving one of the chairs. Clint is snoring on the floor; the bottle beside him is empty. He did this yesterday, too, and slept through suppertime. Lang fried himself some ham, and as he took the pan off the heat he burnt his hand and dropped the skillet and even that didn't waken Clint. Lang stuck his hand in their drinking water until it quit hurting, and ate his ham. Now Clint seems to have passed out again, and this time Lang isn't going to waste time eating.

The mares have all foaled without him, colts or fillies, he does not even know. Probably his sister's been allowed to name them. How's he going to explain that to Breck? He's bragged to Breck that he names the colts; they've agreed that he's to name the next one Slugger.

Probably his sister's looked at all his things. Probably his mother believes he's run away because he doesn't love her. When Lang imagines his mother crying, he cries; if Clint guesses, Clint jeers at him.

He has watched, without seeming to, where Clint stows his car keys: in the cartridge pouch. With one eye on Clint, he climbs up on the chair he's brought and lifts the pouch down from its peg. If he knew how to load the rifle, he'd take that too. He pockets Clint's keys. Now Clint won't be able to come after him in the car. He intends, moreover, to reach in and release the emergency brake, let Clint's old Chevy roll where it will. He puts the chair back. No use advertising where he's headed. He gets the butcher knife. His heart is pounding, but he makes it across the cabin clearing and into the underbrush where the path begins, without a sign from the cabin.

He hasn't been on the path since that one time Clint left the place in the morning, and it's changed. Only a few steps and he's bewildered. Wilderness has flowed over the trace, submerging it under vine and briar, nettle and poison ivy. The shrubs have leafed; you can't see around them. Trees close off the sky. Lang soon has to admit that he doesn't know for sure whether he's on the path.

The knife he brought for the occasional obstruction—an inconvenient rope of honeysuckle; a nettle to take vengeance on—he is using almost continually.

From time to time he stops hacking and listens. Clint won't take him by surprise this time. He hears no human sound. He has heard no human sound but his or Clint's since Clint brought him here—not a car start, not a dog bark. How far does this forest flow, over how many miles of hills, how many valleys?

By late afternoon Lang is exhausted, and he knows that he's lost. He and Clint didn't take anywhere near this long to walk from car to cabin. He's had nothing to eat or drink for hours. Woodpeckers jeer at him from the trees. He has no idea where he is. A few times he's come upon a wilting vine that he's recognized as one he cut himself—another minute further and no one alive might ever have stood where he is standing. His breath comes hard and fast; he has to keep blinking the sweat out of his eyes. The sweat on his back begins to chill him; the woods are getting darker. The realization spreads through him that he's going to spend the night in these woods. His heart begins to pound again. He wants to sit with his back against something, now. He stands still, looking for the place, holding his breath against panic, and Clint steps from around a tree.

"I am going to beat the shit out of you," Clint says, and takes the knife away from him. It's hard to swing a belt there, and Lang never has to give Clint the satisfaction of seeing him cry. Back in the clearing, Clint gets a look at Lang's scratches and welts: the little bastard is as ragged as Eddie, now. Clint smiles grimly, and doesn't bother to beat Lang any more. "You're lucky I didn't shoot you," he tells Lang later. "I was about to. I thought you was a bear, thrashing around in there. I shot a bear under that very tree one time—when I was about your age," he adds cruelly. He knows that Lang's father has never taken him hunting.

Clint is baffled at the Broughs' behavior, furious. What is he going to do? He dismisses the notion of a second set of orders and threats as often as he thinks of it. The bastards are playing some game, and until he figures it out, he's afraid to move. Every time he wakens, the tightness in his gut and throat are already there waiting for him to remember that there's a boy in the other bed, a boy whose parents know Clint. He wants to think that last morning in the Bluegrass all through again differently. He does so, several times. He must give that up once and for all; he must make plans. He must do something immediately.

Clint raids the Chevy's trunk whenever he thinks about Kelly Moss, the last murderer Kentucky fried at LaGrange; about his own poor chances of hiding Lang's body successfully, and poorer still of hiding himself, if he were simply to abandon Lang and run. Changing your name is easy, he has reason to know, but he was counting on having money. He must do something, immediately.

He will take Lang hunting. If he tells Lang to go in front and flush something, the sucker will never know what hit him. The cops can't dig up the whole mountain.

~34~ {Ruth

Saturday morning Jake Averoyne's nurse telephoned to remind me that Joanna was overdue for a booster shot. I had never let that happen before. Every day for ten years I had consulted my desk calendar before I washed the breakfast dishes. I stammered something as I began flipping expired calendar pages. "You don't need an appointment, Mrs. Brough," Nurse Pritchard said, as if she could see my shaky fingers. "Dr. Averoyne says just bring her in when you can."

If I took Joanna to a Lexington pediatrician the way Mother thinks I should, I would never hear a sentence like that, but Jake Averoyne is my best friend in Paris, and Joanna's oldest; he delivered her. Like all doctor's wives, Caroline has had to accept that many women hold her husband in particular, even fervent, regard. Even my mother likes him—the blood I lost birthing an abruptly early Joanna was almost enough to kill me, and it was Jake who was on duty in the Bourbon County hospital's emergency room that night, who saved me.

Joanna and I found Jake's waiting room full, as always, but we didn't have to sit two minutes before Nurse Pritchard led us off to one of those examining cells, gave Joanna her shot and told her she was a brave little girl. I could see in Joanna's face that she was considering taking a stand about that "little," when Jake stuck his head in the door and asked me to step into his office for a minute. "Take Miss Brough's blood pressure," he instructed Nurse Pritchard.

Straight-faced, Nurse Pritchard began wrapping Joanna's arm in the brown fabric boa constrictor, and I loved her, because I knew she would keep it there, solemnly puffing air in and out, until I got back.

Joanna's file lay open on Jake's desk, beside the photograph of Caroline and Angie. Jake smiled, waved his thin, tanned hand at the obvious chair, and waited for me to sit before taking his own. Jake looked tired around the eyes, as usual. This is a trick of his wrinkles; he has the energy of a cricket. "She's lost weight, Ruth," he said. "You don't look so good yourself, but Joanna maybe we can do something about. My father would have taken one look and put her on cod-liver oil, but we both know you're feeding her properly, and winter's over. You need to do something for her morale."

"Sure."

"Have you thought of sending her to visit one of her grandmothers?" I was gathering words, but Jake registered my expression. "Just an unconsidered thought. Does she have anyone to play with? Could you take her to the movies? Put your mind to it. You'll think of something."

Back home the telephone began to ring as I was about to hang up my shoulder bag. I dropped the bag and ran.

But it was Norma Lee. Her voice sounded subdued. "How's it going?"

"Oh," I said. She understood that it was an answer.

"Have you learned any more about that creep that called you?"

"Just a bored drop-out who reads headlines." When I began to tell her Albert's report on the creep's polygraph tracings, I got the feeling Norma Lee wasn't listening.

"Hot for May, isn't it," she said.

"I actually had the air conditioning on awhile," I agreed, not adding how guilty I'd felt, because I can only guess what Lang's air is like.

"There's something I hate to tell you," Norma Lee said.

I closed my eyes.

"Daddy thinks it's not good for Breck— Daddy thinks Breck is too— well we're going to move. As soon as school's out. Daddy's bought another franchise over in Scott County, so really, we won't be so far. I hope you'll come see my new house. Daddy just thinks Breck's gotten morbid about Lang, you know? Summer without Lang is going to be very hard on Breck, and Daddy thinks a change of scene is necessary."

I wish she'd hated telling me enough not to tell me.

Jake's advice—his warning, really—couldn't be shelved, however my frantic, exhausted mind shied away from it. Uneasy over what Grove's response would be, however, I didn't report it to him right away.

Pointedly in time for Easter, my mother had sent Joanna an organdy dress. I had helped Joanna try it on the day it arrived, but since then it had hung in her closet. I had seen her stroking it one morning when she hadn't heard me come down the hall, and I'd felt a rush of remorse at that yearning caress: of course I had forgotten the dress. The ecstatic unwrapping had taken place just one week before Lang disappeared and I began taking no smallest action without calculating in what way it would, might, could lead us to him. Now I brooded over Jake's admonition. Joanna was born on May the twenty-second: I took a deep breath, talked it over with Grove, and suggested to Joanna that she invite six friends to share her fifth candled cake. (Seven is how many croquet mallets we have in our basement.)

Grove's mother, I warned myself, would be scandalized, stunned that I could be so unfeeling. (What she is hoping is that our tragedy will bring Grove and me to Christ. Honey, as any Bible student knows, can be reaped from the skull of disaster.) My mother would side with Jake.

When Joanna was several months old I took her to Charleston to show off (she was hard enough won). Mother arranged a christening party to rival my debut. Ever since, she's been agitating for me to give "the poor child" another party. "Anybody brought up away from her family needs friends."

Everybody knows the vet's children. Secretaries take them home to decorate eggs.

Mother has always thought I wasn't fitting my children to take their place in society. *Their place* requires a social ease which they have not been getting, Mother feels, stuck on a farm, acquiring no polish and no connections. One of the intermittent pictures in my mind now is of my mother sitting in Charleston thinking that if I had married the right diplomat, my son wouldn't have been standing on a country road.

"Maybe," Joanna suggested, "we'd better see if I can still wear Grandmam's dress. Maybe I've grown."

I was jolted by the self-absorbed way Joanna preened before the mirror, but the whole idea was to get her as involved in her party as possible. I should have rejoiced. I did rejoice.

Secretly, I bargained that if I devoted myself to preparing a party to distract and console Joanna, Lang would be found, restored in time for the candles.

I make these bargains every day. If I get up at once, not snuggling into Grove's warmth for thirty more seconds; if I wait to answer the telephone on the third ring....

Joanna's adoring hands smoothed the pink skirt over her hips as if it were velvet, her fingers held stiff, not profaning it. If ladies be but young and fair, they have the gift to know it; into her mirror smiled my undeniably gifted child, my Baroque cherub with the dimples I didn't inherit from my grandfather. Those generations our Huguenot ancestors found refuge in the Netherlands (before our grandsire Gerrit Courtonne killed a man for spitting in his pipe, and removed to South Carolina) have given Joanna hair the yellow of wild persimmon blossoms. She is a Christmas card child, *my* mother's God keep her.

Joanna and I hadn't heard Grove's car, but we heard the back door slam. "Hey, Jo," Grove said: "You look ready for the ballet."

Joanna smirked, turning to show her transformation from other angles, watching their effect on him over her shoulder like some schooled coquette.

"Do you know what time it is?" Grove asked her.

Joanna gazed intently at the clock on the bureau. "T-w-e-l-v-e o'clock."

"It is not twelve o'clock. Didn't I tell you yesterday, if you're going to expect us to believe you're five years old, you'll have to learn to tell time?"

As I started to murmur something protective, Joanna lifted her bare wrist, studying it. "I need something closer to tell time," she said, and brushed back her curls as if casually with the other wrist. Grove swallowed his laughter and I wanted to hug her; no one had laughed in this house for weeks.

"I'll tell you the time," Grove said. "It is three o'clock. What time did I tell you I'd take you to Hereward with me, if you were ready?"

Joanna gasped. The appointment was news to me, but I had her back in slacks in five minutes. I waved her and Grove off with the kind of smile one makes by drawing one's lips back from set teeth. Grove hadn't seen me hysterical once (the Kroger flyers came later), but a careful succession of plans held my head above water. I hadn't planned for an afternoon alone.

I had never heard Grove call Joanna by any name but his mother's. What did it say for his faith in Lang's return if he was going to make a *Joe* out of his daughter? I could not have hope where Grove had none, and I could not live without hope.

I hung up the organdy dress, realizing that the sooner I got out of Lang's room, the better for the pain under my ribs. I awoke with this pain, it lived with me, but suddenly it was pushing harder than ever, filling me with a cold black unspecific terror. Suddenly what I craved was to sit in Grove's lap and be completely enveloped, held fast against the undertow. Failing this, I had an unarticulated feeling something like that if I could make someone think about me I wouldn't drown, that a voice directed to me on a telephone would be like a hand held out through the water. I telephoned Mother. While the number rang I hunched on the bed scraping my underlip with my teeth to try to get some moisture in my mouth. I forgot to remind myself that if I talk, Lang can't call. I forgot everything but getting somebody on my line. When Mother didn't answer I dialed Lorena Snyder. I reached Eldridge's answering service.

The bathrooms are the only windowless rooms in our house. I closed our bathroom door on myself and lay sweating on the bathmat with my knees drawn up and Grove's towel over my head—it seemed important that it be Grove's towel—until I heard him and Joanna come home.

Joanna ran to hang up her coat. I threw my arms around Grove. When he answered with his own around me I wanted to cling like a limpet at ebb tide, but he relaxed his grip after perhaps one second and when I didn't let go, he gave a spurious grunt—to lend his embrace an emphasis his arms weren't giving. He looked at me pointedly, his expression asking, *is that enough?*

I let him go.

"I have to catch Hereward before the girls close the office," he said. "I remembered some things driving home I was supposed to tell them." He went to the bedroom phone and talked business with Lucille Harper until the truck arrived with his oats order and he had to hang up.

~❧35❧~   {Ruth

Sometimes I see myself as a wireless telegrapher who sits in her tent, who doesn't know that the "land" she is camped on is an ice floe that has silently detached itself and drifted beyond transmitting distance of the signal for which she waits. It is night and she is alone in the glittering cold listening to a disconnected set.

Other times I break the speed limit driving home with the groceries because I hear so clearly Lang's voice, which I am going to find recorded beside our telephone. Grove is going to be waiting in the yard, and he is going to drag me out of the car to hear what Lang has said to him. I don't *wonder if*, I don't *hope that*, I *know*, the way for two or three years after Joanna was born I used to know every month that I was pregnant. Even after I felt something, and went with held breath to a private place to look, I knew the spots would be colorless, not blood. You'd think someone to whom that has happened month in, month out for one or two or three years would learn that it is always blood.

Send me a picture of my godson, Eva von Strehlenau closed her Christmas letter, the letter I had started to answer in April, just before everything I might have said became obsolete.

In May, I confronted this letter again. Everything I wanted to say was so self-pitying, I hope I couldn't have written it even if I'd had the energy. In the end I folded up a flyer and sent it to Eva airmail with only three or four sentences.

Eva's reply was swift.

Everybody says she knows how I feel, but she doesn't. Eva did not say it. Eva wrote three pages without making one of those blunders that everybody makes to people who, in Grove's doggedly fair phrase, are not in a position to be pleased.

The last half of Eva's letter was a story she had never told me before.

Many times when Peter and I were children, our cook told us how she came home from work to find her apartment building gone, and no one who knew where her baby was. She put a notice on a board near the railroad station, but she had no picture; her pictures had all been lost when the bomb destroyed her apartment. There were many such notices by the station, and no one answered hers. She went every day to be sure it was still there.

Before the war, she had worked for a Swiss family, and in her last Christmas card to them she had put a picture of her little boy wearing the sweater they had sent him. Now she wrote to them. When they sent that picture back to her, it was the only one she had of her child.

She glued it to the board with her plea.

That Sunday, strangers brought her baby home. He was wearing the sweater the Swiss woman had knitted. The old woman who took care of him while his mother worked had put it on him just before she carried him to the bomb shelter. When the shelter was dug out after the raid, none of the survivors knew whose the baby was. Someone took —

Fortunate mother — her baby hadn't outgrown his sweater before someone who knew his rescuers saw his picture. Is Lang still wearing his red cap? How much will his face change if he is ill-fed? Has his hair been dyed, shaved off? Was his jacket slashed to ribbons the first night and flushed a shred at a time down a toilet?

"When you lose something," Eva's brother Peter used to say, "always replace it with something nicer." What could he say to me now?

The next letter was Grove's, from his sister-in-law.

I knew at once what it was about. Long ago we promised to keep Tad again this summer while Velma goes to summer school again. Naturally she would think I wasn't up to it.

She was tactful to write Grove privately, I thought, instead of putting me on the spot. I began to compose brave answers for when Grove told me. Velma is working on her master's degree. Once she gets it, her school board is legally bound to raise her salary, and having fed Tad last summer, I don't need to be persuaded that she needs to earn all her union can extort for her. Her own mother is in a retirement home, and heaven knows I wouldn't wish Grove's mother on any boy.

I wondered if Grove would even give me the chance to keep my promise, or if he would put Velma's letter in his pocket and say nothing until he'd answered it.

That first month I tried to spare Grove every finite additional distress or anxiety. I would have warmed his wristwatch for him before he got up every morning, except that he sleeps in it. I ought, I thought, to volunteer at once how glad I was to help his brother's widow.

"Honey." Grove looked up.

I hoped Velma's alternate plans were so firm I couldn't overrule them.

"Honey, can we keep Tad a couple of weeks extra, so Velma could take a vacation? She's got a chance to drive to Mexico with some friends after summer school. It's a real deal for her, but there's no room for Tad."

For a few seconds I couldn't make a sound. "Why doesn't she wait till it's official?" I asked.

Grove looked at me.

"I realize that mothers of sons have a right to demand services from the less useful, but why doesn't Velma wait till they find Lang's body to start demanding mine?"

"Hey, Ruth."

"Does Velma suggest Tad might be a comfort to me?"

He frowned down at the letter.

Smug, self-serving bitch! Tad is no disgrace as a cousin for Lang, but as a substitute, he is infinitely less than worthless and any suggestion to the contrary is either disingenuous or unsurpassably opaque.

"I thought it might be good for Jo," Grove said gently.

"Jo*anna* does not need a thirteen-year-old boy for a role model!"

"Did I say one damned thing about role model? I just think—"

Velma was Grove's sister-in-law before I was Grove's wife. His feeling of responsibility for his brother's son and widow was one of the things that attracted me to him. If I had a nephew, I would want Langdon's brother-in-law to be like Grove.

I'm glad there's another boy who carries some of the same genes as Grove.

"Of course we can keep Tad," I said.

Velma, I reflected, is a person who makes it easy for people to be generous to her. Life has dealt her such a blow that everyone yearns to help her, and she isn't stingy about letting people know how they can. Touchingly, she counts on our goodness. With shining face she confides what a marvelous thing is to be had, what joy it would give her. Who could deny her such enormous pleasure, purchasable at such small cost to himself—small relative to the enormity of the pleasure to Velma? When I see Velma looking radiant, I check my pockets.

"Listen, Ruth, nobody wants you to feel pushed."

Velma's eyes are naturally wide, and as she sees you start to calculate costs, they quickly get wider, like her smile. Dazed by your goodness, she is dazzling.

I had never thought like this before. Maybe it's harder for Velma to bring off her act by mail. "Nobody wants me to feel pushed. Everybody wants to push me and have me swear I don't feel it."

Grove looked at me steadily. I was meant to infer reproach, to recognize its justice, to retreat, to apologize. I have to hand it to

166

Velma. She can make more of an impression on my husband with a letter than I can when I'm close enough to hit him. I lifted my chin, smiled, and blinked my eyelashes rapidly in a parody, which I don't think he recognized, of Velma saying thank you.

He abandoned his look of patient injury. "You know Velma's not like that, honey." He didn't address the question of whether he is like that. "It's just that I doubt if she's had a vacation since Ted was killed. She's excited as a kid." An indulgent grin was beginning to sabotage his reproachful pose. "And Mexico, you know, that's *Abroad*. 'Abroad' is a big word to Velma."

"I hope 'these friends' Velma wants to vacation with is going to make Tad a good father," I answered. "I'm getting really tired of you in that role." *Lang*, I wanted to weep—you're *Lang's* father. We *have* a son, *we* have a son, we *do*. Unfortunately, the telephone rang. Twenty miles away a foaling mare was impacted, and the question of Tad was laid aside with Velma's letter. Grove hied him to Falada Farm, and I sat down with paper, pencil and Joanna to decide on six guests.

All parents vow to avoid their parents' mistakes. I had been hostess at several parties by the time I was Joanna's age, but I'd had no voice in their planning. My mother knew every family from Broad Street to the Battery, and half of them were related to her, she knew precisely how. I could never have had a party for only six children. Just neighbors and cousins my age filled our parlor—and effectively shut out anyone extraneous. Anyone, that is, I might have made friends with on my own.

"Whom do you want to invite?" I asked Joanna.

"Lucille!"

My pencil hand sank of itself. "This is a party for girls your age."

"Wellll." Joanna is convinced that silence will lose her the floor; she keeps the gavel from falling with a series of "Welllls," interspersed with little breath-snatching grunts, for as long as it takes her to think of what she might say. "Wellll, uh, uh, wellll, girls my age will like Lucille."

"I don't think Lucille would enjoy the kind of games little girls play."

"Yes she would; Lucille likes games. She's younger than you,

167

and you play games with me 'n—" She shrank the way she does when she's waiting for something she has jostled to crash. Of course she had been going to say "me 'n Lang."

If I hugged her, we would both burst into tears. "And besides," I said quickly, "Lucille doesn't get off work till 4:30, and your guests are going home at four, remember? Think of somebody you'd like to ask who doesn't have a job. We can invite Lucille another time."

Bonnie Earlywine, Amy Herndon, and Zad Thacker's youngest, Kimberly, were Joanna's first choices.

Amy's inclusion especially pleased me. Amy's father is the young vet interning with Grove and Roy. He and Amelia Sr. will appreciate any help we can give Amy with making friends, and not just because their move here is so recent. Five years are too few to civilize what is born of woman, and Amy, being cross-eyed, is a natural butt. Her lenses are as thick as bookends and—perhaps from her constant effort to see what she looks at—she hunches. She should have a life belt of friends before she's thrown overboard into the public schools. I know Grove is hoping he and Roy can offer Hank Herndon a permanent job. Anything I can do to make Amelia want to stay here will help. In May, I still wanted to help Grove.

"Georgia Winnall," Joanna said.

Georgia is the daughter of Jim Winnall, who introduced me and Grove to each other. Last fall, after Chinese Lagoon's first colt won the Vanderbilt Stakes, *The Blood-Horse* sent Jim to photograph her. Jim's praise of our lovely mare won Grove over, and he has forgiven Jim for knowing me first. Georgia is welcome.

"Two more," I encouraged Joanna.

"Well. Uh, uh, wellll...."

Maybe Mother is right. A five-year-old should be able to think of more than four friends. As Joanna's "welllls" continued, I reflected that Claudette Callet hasn't been living in the Bluegrass much longer than Amy Herndon, and probably needs friends just as woefully.

Twelve years ago, when I went to my classmate Margot Dag's wedding to Chuck Callet, I didn't expect ever to pass between

Hereward Stud's stone gates again. That I would marry Hereward's vet and that Margot would bring her two children home to live, were equally unforeseeable.

I used to take heart at the gap between Margot's son Charles Junior and his sister Claudette —seven years is longer than I've been trying—but it turns out that Margot had decided one was enough. Claudette was an accident gone through with. "Biggest mistake I ever made," says Margot. "No. Marrying Chucklehead was the biggest."

Charles Junior is twelve now, and refusing to be confirmed. ("Chuck blames me. Can I help it if I have intelligent children?")

Charles Junior is refusing to do so many things that Margot has sent him off to military school. That leaves Claudette even more on her own than Joanna. "I would worry," Norma Lee prods me, "if Fred had as much business at Hereward as Grove does, and Margot out there re-bounding all day," but what Margot is doing all day is drinking. Hereward Stud, so full of horses, hounds and Snyder children, must be very lonely for Claudette.

"How about asking Claudette Callet?"

"No. She thinks her shit don't stink."

"Shit" is a noun I do not believe that I had ever uttered, and Grove is touchingly careful what he says in front of his daughter. (I remember when he was careful what he said in front of me.) "Joanna, she what?"

"Farrah says she's stuck on herself."

Ah. Farrah is Hereward Stud Farm Manager Eldridge Snyder's daughter, and unlike the owner's granddaughter, has lived on Hereward all her life. "Farrah should be more charitable to her juniors. Maybe if you got to know Claudette, you might like her better than Farrah does."

"I don't want to ask Claudette. I want to ask Farrah."

I reminded myself of my vow not to make my daughter my social instrument. I hadn't foreseen that I would find myself not inviting my classmate's child, while inviting that child's nearest neighbor. What's more, my classmate's parents are my husband's number one employer. If anyone had suggested to me, when the Dags lent us their Saratoga cottage for our honeymoon, that I would one day find myself denying hospitality to their grandchild, I would have answered in words of one syllable.

I thought of Santayana's definition of a liberal: someone who wants his child to wash behind her ears because she wants to. I dropped the subject of Inge Dag's granddaughter Claudette. How much that contributed to what Margot did to me this month I might learn one day, if Margot sometime sobers up.

"Farrah goes to kindergarten, dear. How about Keziah instead?" Keziah is Farrah's next younger sister, exactly Joanna's age.

"No, Farrah. She only goes to kindergarten in the mornings." Joanna must have mistaken my surprise at her accurate memory, for doubt. "See, she told me Ezra 'n them have to eat that shitty school lunch, but *she* doesn't stay all—"

"Joanna, do you know what shitty means?"

Coloring, my four-year-old began carefully rolling her napkin ring and began to roll it carefully on the table, without letting go of it or lifting her eyes. "Farrah said it."

"'Shit' is what Ervil spreads on the fields every morning."

I saw her eyes round with delicious shock, but her face quickly went blank before she looked at me. "You mean straw and things?"

"I mean things. Now then. Farrah makes five and that leaves one place. How about Keziah?"

"I don't want to ask Keziah."

"Oh, why not?" As if I didn't know that contemporaries are competitors; that of the eight Snyder children, Keziah is probably the hardest for Joanna to like.

Joanna resumed the close consideration of her napkin ring. "Her name is too funny."

"Farrah Fawcett Snyder" doesn't seem at all funny to Joanna.

I shrink from the picture of Farrah, scrubbed and curled— maybe even in a dress—the bearer of shinily wrapped treasure, setting out with merciless self-importance to Dr. Brough's house, and Keziah, all sicklied o'er with the pale cast of murderous envy, sniffling in the shadows. "I want Angie Averoyne," Joanna said.

I wrote down Angie Averoyne. "It will be a lovely party," I promised.

"Will Lang come?" she asked.

Lang never finds the car keys in the cartridge pouch any more. He doesn't know where Clint keeps them now — not under that loose floorboard; not in the ground coffee. He has quit searching. The nearest town, Clint has told him, is a hundred miles away; he and Clint aren't even in Kentucky any more. Where are they then? Clint won't say. The biggest tracks Lang saw by the creek where Clint took him hunting were raccoon, but now when he is alone outside he is always listening for bear. He knows from TV that any bear can outrun any human. Clint has promised to take him home as soon as Clint finishes 'the little bidness he come up there to do.' Lang has thought a lot about what might have happened if he had got completely lost those times he tried to run away, so lost Clint never even found his body. If he had died of starvation or a bear had torn him apart, his parents never would have known they had to guard the barn, and Clint would have burnt up Lagoon and Thankless and Blithe and both yearlings and all three foals. Now that Lang has decided to wait for Clint to finish his business, not to try to run away any more, he has stopped dreaming about the mares' eyeballs exploding from the heat the way Clint has told him they do.

The little bastard has got shaggy. From behind, he looks just like Eddie, faded torn clothes and all. Clint raised his rifle and could not shoot. Next time, he thinks, he will have a drink before he and the little bastard leave the cabin. Tomorrow.

Who deserves shooting are the poor kid's parents, who are crazier about their money, Clint figures, than about their kid. How could they just ignore his message? How could they do that?

Six days after Clint dropped his note in a mailbox, the note arrived in Inglewood, California. The envelope is addressed to *Brough Farm, Clay Pike, Paris 40361*, no state, no return address, and Clint's scrawled 4 looked as much like a 9 to Inglewood's human postal employees as it had to Lexington's automatic bar code reader. Inglewood has no Brough Farm, no Clay Pike, and the zip code numbers don't reach any higher than 90312. Clint's note has accordingly gone to Philadelphia's Mail Recovery Center.

⸙37⸙ {Ruth

As I had promised Jake, I took Joanna to Lexington's largest department store to get her autographed *Lion King* poster. In the children's department, Pumbaa stood signing one poster after another from a stack almost as high as himself. Joanna and I stood in line half an hour waiting her turn for one. What, I wondered, was under the make-up artist's job?

John Wayne Gacy dressed like Pogo the Clown to attract small boys. The first twenty-seven bodies were found under his house.

Many of the children in the room were without their mothers, who had gauged the line's speed, put their youngsters in it, and dashed off to make one quick purchase in some other department. I was standing with Joanna by the hand feeling grimly wiser than they when I glanced at the elevator across the floor just as its doors began to close, and saw a fair-haired boy.

I felt a shocking surge and drop of blood. My inner ears closed and opened like gills. I know I called out his name. I know I told Joanna to wait; I know I told her I would be right back. Anyway, I know I ran.

The elevator doors closed before I had run two steps, and pressing on the button did nothing, and there was no one there to help. I ran for the escalator. On the escalator I crowded past people— "I'm sorry, I'm sorry"—never knocking over anyone. Those steps that were empty, I ran down. When I got to the first floor elevator doors, the elevator had emptied and started back up and Lang was nowhere to be seen. I called his name three times, each time louder. People turned to look, and when I ran for the outside, people got out of my way. Across the nearest lot, a stout woman was slamming a car door after a small blond boy, not Lang.

I walked around the building so that I could re-enter through a different department, and so that I would have stopped crying first. When I got back to the second floor, Joanna was screaming like a child on fire. "You lost me," she sobbed. "You lost me!"

Somebody at the store mailed her a poster next day. I was moved to tears by this thoughtful kindness, but I find I can't look at the poster.

John Wayne Gacy shared his thirty-three victims between the earth beneath his house and the nearest river. None of those boys, Grove reminds me, was as young as Lang. The Lindbergh baby, I do not remind him, was younger. Three hundred and eight children are listed at Frankfort's Missing Child Center, Albert admitted to me when I insisted on knowing—more than a hundred of them for over a year. "Children are trusting, greedy, and optimistic," says Albert. I waken with no saliva and my gut clenched, and though I wake to the fact of my son's void every day, it is less horrible than my nightmares.

I do not believe in an anthropomorphic god, yet I feel that Lang was taken from us for my faults and sins, and further, I feel that he will be returned to us safely because I have not been that wicked. Sometimes I think, *it's nonsense that he was taken for my sins: his father is suffering equally, and his father is a good man.* All the time I know it's all nonsense, because I don't believe for a second, am unable to believe, that there is a God. But I know God will forgive this and return my son, because He understands why I see through the scrim to the empty stage.

Meanwhile I stage things myself, like a party for my daughter.

"What do you want to serve?"

"Birthday cake!"

"What else?"

"Ice cream!"

"What else?"

"Popcorn!"

Our popcorn maker was our wedding gift from Peter von Strehlenau, which was not his style at all, except for the card that came with it. I certainly wouldn't have expected a wedding gift from Peter, but Eva had told me he was sending something. "My lips are sealed," she wrote. Venetian glass, I thought ruefully. Beautiful, expensive, easily shattered—like the moonlight bliss of a holiday love affair.

Peter's taste is exquisite, informed, and impatient with ersatz. For my birthday the year we met, he sent me an illuminated page out of a book of hours, the page for my birthday month. I would have predicted that any gift chosen by Peter would be something old, or something made by an ancient craft. His wedding gift, however, arrived by UPS from Sears, Roebuck. "To Ruth," the card said, "when she marries her farmer: 2, 14. *Dein* Peter."

The winter after the summer I toured Europe with Eva and Peter, Peter flew to the U.S. *To see me,* I thought (and so, I am sure, thought Mother). Officially, he was part of a trade mission. He took his one free weekend to fly down to Charleston. My father found him reasonably congenial. My mother was captivated. *I* quickly realized that what I had thought was his pretext for coming to this country—this mission he claimed was too dry and boring even to tell me about—was indeed his reason. In Peter's *Michelin,* I rated only two stars—*worth a detour,* not *a journey.*

By the time of his dig about the farmer, I was so well recovered that I could smile. To paraphrase Peter himself, having lost someone, I had replaced him with someone much nicer. The "2, 14" puzzled me—February 14 was neither a recent nor a significant date. Then I remembered earlier references Peter had made to my Biblical namesake, and I read Chapter 2, Verse 14. "And she sat beside the reapers, and he reached her parched corn, and she did eat, and was sufficed...."

I suppose if you happened to be giving someone a corn popper, that would be a pleasant inscription, but if I know Peter he ordered me the popper so he could use the verse. If I know Peter, he read the book of Ruth looking for some way to needle me.

Once Joanna's menu occurred to her, the popper had to be brought up from the basement immediately. This was how I wished her to feel, I reminded myself. I kept my back to the horseshoe box (*by the water heater*), the fly rod (*on the wall beside Grove's*). Joanna's eye fell on the croquet set. "Let's set it up now!" she urged.

"Might be better to wait till the day of the party," I said, "when we'll know whether we're going to have rain." And when it wouldn't entail several days of looking at a game which no brother was going to come home from school and play with us.

"OK, but let's clean it up now."

I joined her on my knees, wiping a winter's spiderwebs off the scuffed, scarred balls. I did my best to shake the picture of Lang with a similar rag stuffed in his mouth in some other ill-lit basement.

"Farrah can play with the green mallet because she has green eyes," Joanna dictated. "Which color do you think goes best with my dress?"

"Well, blue goes with pink."

"I think white. I get to play with the white, and Angie can have yellow because...."

Last year on her birthday, Lang lost his temper because she got through the middle wicket ahead of him. "You give her too much handicap!" he accused. "It should be smaller now than yesterday; she's a year older!" He had his revenge once their cousin Tad arrived. Joanna is too small to pitch a horseshoe, and horseshoes was what Tad and Lang and Breck played for eight weeks.

"What color do you want your cake?"

"Pink!"

"You shall have peppermint icing," I promised. "Now, let's take this popper upstairs."

Later, hearing effortful breathing, I dropped my mending and hurried to Joanna's bedroom. She was practicing blowing out imaginary candles.

There's this much to be said for inviting only a closed circle of friends: if you're going to be blowing on their desserts, better just invite children whose faces you've been breathing into all week anyway.

But Joanna had a sickness too dread even for that.

The Earlywines were going to be out of town, but the other five accepted. Then the day before the party, Lorena Snyder telephoned. "Honey, *all* my children have the flu. Little Ezra is the only one helping me carry trays. Farrah is so mad at me for calling you, she's screaming every word she's ever heard her daddy say. I had to tell her, 'If you get out of that bed, I'll whip your butt!' I can't let her out of this house with a temperature."

"Keep her in bed," I said. Keep them in bed, that's what I tell all my friends. Keep them in bed and don't leave the room; don't turn your head; don't blink.

⚘38⚘   {Ruth

Beside Joanna's breakfast plate: from me, two books and a box of crayons; from her father, a Mickey Mouse watch; from her Courtonne grandparents, which is to say my mother, white gloves embroidered with rosebuds, just the kind to wear if Joanna is ever flower girl in a White House wedding, otherwise, I feared, destined to waste their sweetness in the bureau drawer. I was wrong: Joanna put them on that very afternoon, two hours before her first guest was expected. Finally, from Grove's parents, one of the two envelopes that had come, separately, from them.

"I know you will not be celebrating Joanna's birthday," Grove's mother had written. "I know you would not want her untying ribbons at the very moment when her brother may be crying for mercy.

"Joanna is old enough to understand that she will never be asked to give up more than Our Lord Jesus Christ, who sacrificed his precious blood for her.

"The Lord has his reasons for every one of our trials, and it may even be that He has sent us this suffering to help Joanna realize the vanity of worldly hopes.

"I do not want to be critical like other mothers-in-law; I know you are not entirely to blame that Joanna seems to take no thought at all for the hereafter. I know how little my son's heart inclines toward the ways we took such pains to bring him up in. He has never accepted his brother's death in a Christian spirit. I pray every night that our Lord will be patient with his bitterness. I don't want to believe that any sin of the father is being visited on little Lang."

From Grove's father I received a twenty dollar bill. Cash, not a check. The envelope had been stamped by office meter. "Tell Joanna her grandmom and granddad love her," his note said.

I didn't tell Grove about his mother's letter, and Joanna gloated almost indecently over the money. *Children are trusting, optimistic, and greedy.* I leapt up and went to the kitchen for jelly, which nobody needed, till my face was fit for a happy scene.

Joanna could not have admired her watch-adorned wrist more if Grove had given her a diamond bracelet, and when I suggested that she wait to take white gloves out of their box till her breakfast things were cleared away, I might have been trying to put them in a time capsule. "I have to see if I can still see my watch when I'm wearing them!"

Traditionally, our birthday breakfasts have been followed immediately by measuring. Last year, Joanna could hardly eat, she was in such a swivet to have her hopes confirmed that she was "as tall as Lang now," meaning, as tall as Lang at four. The marks are drawn and dated on the closet wall, Joanna's lower than Lang's on every comparable anniversary. Joanna has burned over this for as long as she can remember. This birthday, that found us in purgatory (for I am determined that we are in purgatory, not hell; how could I go on if I thought our sentence was final?) — this May, nobody mentioned the yardstick.

"So," Grove asked Joanna, "what time is it?"

How long will Lang have to be gone before I paint over those eight marks on the closet doorframe that stab me every time my eye slides over and past them? And if the day ever comes that I paint over them, will the day ever come when the fresh paint will cease to stab me in exactly the same way? I was grateful for Grove's read-your-watch lesson. Too soon he pushed back from the table.

Joanna isn't one to lose her audience without a struggle. "Now read me my books," she suggested firmly.

"I have to go to work," Grove pointed out. "Talk to your mother. She gave you the books." She had already asked me twice how much longer was left before time for her company. I congratulated myself for the distraction of new books.

Nell Winnall's call interrupted *Simple Pictures Are Best* between the one-eyed cat and the turnips. "Ruth, I don't know how I *could* have forgotten. Georgia has an appointment with her dentist this afternoon, and it's exactly the wrong time for Joanna's little party. The dentist's secretary just telephoned to remind me; it had entirely slipped my mind."

"Oh, too bad! Maybe he'd do you the favor of arranging a trade for—"

"I'm not a *favors* person, Ruth. I like Georgia's dentist to know he can always count on her. I think that's so important, don't you? Georgia will be so sorry to miss meeting Joanna's *fascinating* rural friends, so different. I know they'll all have a lovely time."

Someday, I told myself, Nell Winnall will realize that there was never anything to Jim's squiring me around all those years ago except that we were both out-of-towners working for the same magazine.

"Mrs. Winnall has choked eyes," was Joanna's only response when I formally told her what I knew she'd overheard, sitting right beside me. For we never sit down far from a telephone.

What does Joanna know about how the eye reacts to strangulation? How would a five-year-old come to such a grisly comparison for Nell's exopthalmos if somebody (Lucille Harper!) hadn't been lax about the kind of TV she watched?

After I had read both books twice, I pled the necessity to stir up a birthday cake. I let Joanna lick the beaters, then sent her to wash the batter off her nose. She returned, lugging her little cane chair, just as the pans were coming out of the oven. She had changed into the pink dress, the first time she had ever put on a dress by herself, and she was wearing her gloves. She set her chair in front of one of the dining room windows and sat down to watch for her company, who were coming at two o'clock.

Amelia Herndon telephoned as I was stirring nuts into nougat filling (Joanna's choice). "Ruth, I'm just getting Amy's coat. Hank's mother had an 'incident' last night and Hank can't possibly go, so it's up to me."

Hank's mother is in a Louisville nursing home. "We'd be delighted if you'd like to drop Amy off here for the day," I offered. "If you think Mrs. Herndon—"

"Oh, I have to take Amy with me. Something to hug is the best therapy, and Amy can be something to hug for her grandmother. I want my child to learn to be a caring human being, Ruth; we—"

Caroline Averoyne didn't call till after lunch. Didn't dare till Jake was out of the house again, I guess. "I'm just as sorry as I can be, but Angie can't come to Joanna's party."

"Oh, I'm so—"

"Jake's had just an awful weekend, just hectic; we've never known the flu to hang on like this. He's been working eighteen-hour days, and of course I can't sleep when he's out of this house; I just lie awake thinking about if anyone would come while he's gone, what would Angie and I do? I haven't had a bit of sleep. You don't know what it's like to have every good-for-nothing in the county think your house is a drugstore. They killed one of Jake's classmates in Buffalo last week, broke in at night, and he was on a call and came home while they were still—you can imagine what my head feels like. I'm just going to have to go back to bed. I can't keep going another minute."

"Look, Caroline, I hate for Angie to miss the party, and Joanna especially asked to invite her. Let Joanna and me come get Angie. Joanna would love to have her spend the afternoon."

Caroline's words came a trifle faster, a trifle higher pitched. "Alice Earlywine is taking Bonnie to the puppet show at Turfland Mall this afternoon, and she said she'd take Angie too, so I could sleep, and I've packed Angie off already."

Joanna was subdued, but I am a believer with the Japanese that an aesthete doesn't need a Williamsburg-style centerpiece: one chrysanthemum alone has more beauty than ever can be adequately appreciated. Kimberly Thacker was coming, I reminded Joanna. Two little girls and a mother who is willing to play the assigned mallet can have a fine party.

The day after Joanna's birthday, Lexington's Sears had a children's shoe sale, and Joanna and I stopped at the nearest supermarket afterwards, one where I've rarely shopped. I was as surprised to see Idella Thacker as she was to see me. "Ruth! I've been going to call you. Kimberly was so disappoin'ned to miss your little girl's party,

I don't think she'll ever forgive me. I just couldn't get that ol' car to start, and Zad he was out on the tractor; won't nobody to hep me. I'm sure it was a grand party; did your little girl have a nice time?"

Joanna and Kimberly had their own conversation, and driving home, Joanna told me Kimberly's version. "My mother doesn't like to come to your house; it gives her the creeps, because of Lang. She's afraid I'll have nightmares."

Flu (which Lorena's children really did have) is nothing to the disease of having a missing brother.

~❧39❧~   {Ruth

Joanna began to wet her bed.

The year I turned five, my father went to Denmark for seven months, the guest of Copenhagen's Royal Academy of Arts, and I became a bed-wetter. Behind Mother's back, our maid reproached me in Langdon's presence that my lapses were due to my being too lazy and selfish to get up, and told the cook about "this baby's" accidents even as I begged her not to. Forbidden by Mother ever to speak of it in front of Langdon again, she always contrived to be removing the sheets from my room when he would see. She ostentatiously aired my room on such days, and I was sure that all our neighbors knew exactly why my window was open when all the others were closed. The son of the neighbor on my side of the house was a Citadel cadet who took Sunday dinners at home. I walked up and down our garden every Sunday hoping he would notice me, except on open-shuttered Sundays, when I didn't show my face.

Waking in slowly heavier dread to a furtive damp tickling between my legs, then, is one of my earliest memories. Then was worse than now, because now I am troubled only once in four weeks, reliable as a digital watch, but then fear was part of every wakening. I always lay very still, especially my legs, and tried to decide (because until air from outside the covers hits you, you can't always decide) whether my warm bottom was wet or dry.

When I was Joanna's age I would stealthily ease a forefinger between my fat thighs, then look to see if it shone wetly. Now I reach with equal stealth for a Kleenex from my bedside bureau and see whether it stains.

My menses are not painful, but for the first day or two I am fogbound and morose. I feel singled out for disproportionate burdens —disproportionate to my strength, to my deserts, to the burdens of others. This feeling is, of course, exacerbated now that it's accurate.

The morning after Joanna's birthday I wakened to the suspicion that once again, regular as the moon herself, as always.... I lay rigid on my back and considered whether what I felt was sweat. Moving my arm only, I felt for the Kleenex box. Grove, when I got up to see to myself, gave no sign of awakening; he always shows me that courtesy.

Jake Averoyne warned us not to expect a third child. Yet every single month I am surprised.

Surprised, but this time, not so sure I was sorry. Could I do well by another child? How well am I doing by the two I have? For surely Joanna too is at risk! A beloved brother, as taken for granted as blinking, disappears. A pair of supposedly omnipotent parents are exposed as helpless. What is this doing to her? What can I do about it?

Grove's sister-in-law Velma would know how I feel.

Several years ago Grove and I got a letter from Velma praising Tad's school counselor for uncovering a terrible worry that Tad had concealed from everyone for years.

When Grove's brother went to Beirut, Velma and his infant son moved in with the Broughs. After his death, they stayed until Velma got her teaching certificate and the job she now holds in a small town up near Columbus, Ohio. On Tad's fifth birthday, his grandmother made him a beautiful cake. His grandfather, whose hobby is his basement darkroom, took copious pictures. Unfortunately, he went down to develop them the minute Tad went to bed. Grove's father is a wise and kindly man and his whole family could have used him that evening.

Tad, naturally, had eaten too much. When his stomach began to hurt, some time after he was supposedly asleep for the night, he padded out to find his mother. He found her in the living room, in his grandmother's arms, weeping. Velma had been overcome by thoughts of how her husband never had shared a birthday celebration with his son.

Tad had never seen his mother cry. "I'd been so careful!" Velma says. Now the sight of him—that his father never had shared—only made her sobs come harder. "He was terrified," Velma's letter went on. "He began to cry, and that stopped me, of course. While I got hold of myself, Mother Brough carried him back to his bed and did her best to comfort him. I went in to him as soon as I could." Not soon enough to know that his grandmother had explained to him that his mother was grieving for his father, whose death had come by hideous chance on Tad's first birthday, a detail which of course Velma had never inflicted on him. "He was confused," Velma lamented. *"He got the idea he was responsible.* He got the idea that seeing him made me unhappy because he had caused his father's death! How could we have guessed that? What should we have done?"* What should *I* be doing?

The Dags sent a colt east to run in the Dumbarton Handicap this year, a first for Hereward Stud. Once Grove and I would have been excited. A couple of days before the race, Joanna and I stopped by Hereward to give Fran some insurance certificates Grove had signed. Fran was wearing her usual brown slacks and sweater, but Lucille's blouse was the color of our euonymus hedge in autumn. Joanna plainly found her ravishing.

Lucille stared at me. I'm getting used to that. My friends stare because they think that if I loved Lang, I would have hysterics every ninety seconds and are waiting, baffled and a little disapproving. Semi-strangers like Lucille are examining me for clues to what kind of mother would recklessly expose her eight-year-old. I was in a hurry to finish with Fran and get out even before I heard Lucille moaning over Joanna and realized that she was getting the lowdown on my incredibly bungled birthday arrangements. Fran saw me glance their way and shoved her chair abruptly back from her desk. "How'd you like all those macho llamas last night, pal?" Fran and Joanna are nature film fans.

"I did!" Joanna beamed. "Did you see where all the llamas were *spitting?*" she asked Lucille, "and two of them *boxed?*"

"No, honey, I didn't see anything on TV last night because my set broke and Barney swears he absolutely can't have it back to me for at least a week. Honestly," she turned to Fran and me, "when I heard I wouldn't get it back in time for the Dumbarton, I just about died!"

I knelt to tie Joanna's shoelaces.

That night Grove suggested inviting Lucille and Fran to watch the Dumbarton Stakes with us. Joanna's "Oh, yes!" cut me off at the gap. I realized that Grove, like me, was looking for ways to alter occasions which otherwise set us up for anguish, occasions we four had been celebrating in just the same ways for the last five years, together. (I had deliberately scheduled Lexington errands so as to miss the Derby.) *I should be grateful to Grove,* I thought, but I hoped neither Fran nor Lucille could come. All I wanted to do was lie down with a mask over my eyes and a telephone under my hand.

I called Fran first. If she said *No can do,* Lucille would have to be fetched by one of us. Grove's response to this, I figured, would be, "Oh, let's have her another time, when Fran can come."

"Love to come, Sweetie," Fran said. "Let me bring my strawberry dessert."

So they came. Joanna hugged them both, Grove busied himself with the cocktail shaker, and I resisted the urge to hole up in the kitchen.

Every time I looked at Lucille unexpectedly, her blue eyelids seemed to have stuck wide open, like elevator doors being held for me. *She thinks if I loved Lang I'd be in bed taking sedatives,* I thought, angry that I couldn't be. Fortunately this anger was hard to maintain in the face of the friend who had closed Hereward Stud's office in breeding season for surely the first time in its history and gone to pray for Lang in a church where she hadn't lit a candle since Max ran off to San Francisco with its choir master, and in her car. Fortunately too, Grove seemed to be bearing in mind that the invitations were his idea and to accept, apparently, some responsibility for acting especially lively and cheerful and welcoming, which even in normal times has never been like him. I was grateful.

"It's so nice of you to have me in your home, Mrs. Brough," Lucille said. "I get so tired of my little apartment."

"I used to have a Lexington apartment myself," I told her. "I know how they can make you miss home!"

Fran laughed.

"There's really not a lot to miss in Morehead," Lucille demurred. "Well—I sort of miss baseball. My best friend's father coached at MSU, so she and I got to go to all the games. And I miss fishing at Cave Run with my father. I really enjoyed that."

Grove looked wistful. All his life he's gone fishing with his best hometown friend, Ken Staunton, who lives now in Cincinnati, only an hour away. After we married he expected me to make their excursions an enthusiastic threesome, but as with baseball at Riverfront, I was a good, rather than spontaneously enthusiastic, sport. We were both glad when Lang got old enough to supplant me on these trips. Last summer, of course, Lang and Tad both went along. It's been two years since Grove expected me to be part of his Cave Run excursions, but now he said vaguely that maybe we should all go together sometime. "I would just love to!" Lucille told him. I was too unprepared to say anything.

"We have a filly!" Joanna informed Fran. "My father dropped her and Mama's hands were full and Lucille caught her!"

"That's right, Fran," Grove chimed in. "You probably didn't know those business college folks taught your assistant how to catch foals in between filing invoices."

"Lucille knows a lot they don't teach in business school," Fran said.

Lucille looked at her for a second, then laughed. "I learned about foaling from my daddy. He looks after everything in Rowan County from French poodles to Vietnamese pigs, and after Tom left for Auburn, I got to go along on Sunday rounds. I guess that's the only other thing I miss. I just love animals."

Tom would be an older brother, I guessed. Grove seemed to know.

"*I* ride with *my* father, every Sunday," Joanna boasted. "You can come with us!"

"Wouldn't think of it, Sugar. That's quality time for you and your Daddy."

"Jo and I will take all the help we can get," Grove said heartily. "You should go with us sometime—get to know some of Hereward's clients."

This time Lucille turned brightly to me. I felt obliged to smile. "I'd really like that," Lucille told Grove.

I saw Fran looking at me thoughtfully. "Let me take those strawberries off your hands," I said, and escaped to the kitchen.

"When I retire," Fran confided to me some time ago, "I'm going to be a caterer. Or sooner, if Hereward goes belly up."

"Hereward Stud?" I protested. "Never."

Fran grinned wisely. "You can say 'never.' I've had the rug jerked out from under my feet once already. When Max drove west, he drove 'never' out of my vocabulary."

Fran is preparing for her next vocation, building up a repertoire of receipts for which my fortunate family is often the guinea pig. Her Strawberries Fayette (sliced sweetened strawberries, crushed pineapple, brandy, puréed peaches, and whipped cream) we have long regarded as heaven; Lang inhaled it like a vacuum cleaner. I put Fran's dish in the refrigerator spot I had waiting for it and vowed to make myself eat some, Fran being present.

After lunch Lucille sprang up from the table. Her "Let *me* carry these out for you, Mrs. Brough," was so solicitous, I had a vision of myself feebly lifting a tray full of our empty sherbet dishes and snapping my spine.

"Just leave them there," I told her—pleasantly enough, I thought. Grove says I was peremptory. Anyway, I managed to convince Lucille of what Fran already knows, that I prefer just to put the food in the refrigerator and leave the rest for after the guests have left. Fran joined Grove in the living room and Joanna dragged Lucille off to the sewing room to hear her read, an accomplishment Lucille could not get over. "Did you really make up these fantastic lessons yourself, Mrs. Brough? Oh, I just admire brilliant people so much!" She brushed her glistening hair back off her shoulder and smiled across the room at Grove. Grove smiled back, a fatuous, avuncular smile.

I came along about ten years too soon to have learned to feel at once smart and sexy. Lucille's chatter about my brain made me feel dried out. Fortunately, turning on the TV distracted all of us. The Dags' horse didn't hit the board in the Dumbarton, but they were interviewed in the walking ring, and Margot's hat was stunning (literally), so it will be a good memory for them. Unusually helpful Grove and always reliable Fran kept the afternoon if not sailing, at least afloat, and if I overlooked or misread a lot of signs, it should be recalled that the situation developing was one quite new to me, even had I not been numb.

Once Fran and Lucille left, Grove's own anguish presented its bill for all that geniality. The soup had been too peppery. Joanna had hogged the stage; I was spoiling her. I shouldn't have declined Lucille's offer to help; Lucille is a sweet girl and I hurt her feelings.

"She made me feel like a palsied great-aunt who can't be trusted with the crystal," I said, expecting him to laugh, and when he did not, "After all, it's my crystal."

"Yes, Miss Courtonne, we all know you grew up with crystal. You grew up with everything and you've been everywhere: we all know."

Lucille Harper didn't grow up poor either, but Lucille isn't the one who mislaid Grove's son.

When Lang disappeared, my body stopped permitting itself the amount of sleep it needs. "It thinks it should be up looking for him," I told Jake, who finally gave me a prescription and told me to try not to take it. "You buttered the wrong side!" screams Joanna over her toast, and it's all I can do not to scrub her face with the "right" side. I want to scream too; every time anybody crosses me, even Grove or Joanna—*especially* Grove or Joanna. I want to scream, *It's not my fault,* and *It* has nothing to do with the matter at hand, and none of us would have to have that spelled out. When Grove snarled at me about my great-aunt Ruth's Waterford, I thought I understood. I said nothing. I admonished myself not to brood about it. Mistake.

Tad arrived Friday night, Memorial Day weekend. Velma hadn't lost a minute. Tad, thirteen now, has changed over the winter from a small boy who took my services for granted the same way Lang and Joanna did, because they've never thought about it, to a youth almost my own height who has absorbed notions about what man is due from woman. "Put on shoes before you go in the barn," I reminded him his first morning.

"I don't like shoes," he answered.

As humorously as I could, I told him some of the colors various hoofs have turned various of my toes even through leather and thick socks, but found myself at last obliged to say, "I am not asking you, Tad. I am telling you."

"You may be telling me, but you're not making me."

He was both right and wrong. I can't make him do anything, but he obeys Grove, and there have been no more bare feet around the horses. He avenges himself by bucking the house rule that barn foot gear comes off at the front door. I pretend not to notice: manure is easier to wash out of a bedspread than out of smashed toes.

Last summer, the three boys naturally never included Joanna, but Tad was at least kinder to her than the younger two, having less to prove. Joanna was enthusiastic about his arrival this year. Tad had never seen Thankless, or any of our foals!

Tad was willing to accept Joanna as guide so long as, by shared looks, Grove and I acknowledged that he was only bearing it. Briefly I entertained the hope that his coming would be good for Joanna, as Grove had said, but poor Tad. Last year I was delighted to have him. This year, putting him in Lang's room bothered me. Last summer when Grove urged me to show Tad whatever, make this or that dish especially while Tad was with us, I was enthusiastic. This month, helplessly, I have resented them both.

I have always despised Abraham for letting Sarah make him turn his back on Ishmael, the boy who was kin to him but not to her. *I will not be Sarah,* I began admonishing myself in May. *I am Ruth.*

187

I will let parched corn suffice me. I tried. I know Tad is here because Grove feels guilty that he was safely listening for mare-gut motility while his brother was listening for terrorists.

But Grove, I brooded, isn't the one who launders the bedspread Tad lies on in his boots.

It wasn't Tad or Tad's laundry. It was what I felt Grove was making of Tad, and of me. It was Velma.

Grove, of course, craves to make amends for surviving his brother. Myself, I have made peace with my conscience for the near-infinite sperm I have somehow annihilated. Until April, even before Joanna was born, Lang was enough, my answer to all those stilled wrigglers, my answer to all my shortcomings since my birth. Even had Joanna never been born, Lang alone in my scales more than balanced anything that could be counterweighted. Now, nothing I can ever put in the scales can make up for the weight of Lang lost, not even Joanna. Certainly not Tad. The idea that I might be expected to compensate for not serving my son by serving Velma's was intolerable.

Tad's laundry didn't bother me last year. Tad's laundry wouldn't bother me now, if Velma had died with Ted—or instead of Ted. Grove's motherless nephew could be grappled to my heart, but, I told myself furiously, I am not going to be Grove and Velma's slave ant, their worker bee—the sexless one who exists to serve the queen.

⟿41⟿   {Ruth

Sleeping on the sewing room cot now that Tad is here doesn't bother Joanna; it's just like last summer. (Nothing is at all like last summer.) Lying on her back with her arms flung out, a favorite pose, she looks as if she'd been pushed off a roof.

This used to amuse me.

Once she wakens, she's bad-tempered till she eats. I restrain my impulse to embrace her when she inveighs that she hates me, hates me *for the rest of the day.* I feel obliged to remember that what's cute in a puppy can be deadly in a dog, and that I have a duty to those on whom I shall unleash her. The morning after her desolate birthday I fixed her toast and egg, which she regards as more grown-up than oatmeal. "You buttered the wrong side," she grumbled.

"Bread isn't like saltines. There isn't any wrong side."

"Yes there is! I can't eat it! You spoiled it! You did it on purpose: you buttered the wrong side *right on purpose!*"

Do I really want to shake a five-year-old until she acknowledges that yes, I am bigger, stronger? "I'll make you another; you can butter it yourself. I'll eat *this* one *my*-self. You will say *Excuse me, Mama, for being rude.*" Instead she put her head down on the table and sobbed, such a hopeless lament, my heart despaired. It wasn't the party, though she may have thought so, and there was nothing I could do for her. I see her coming up the barn road, sobbing, forever, and I am at the end of it and she thinks there is something I can do.

Tad has found me equally useless. Of course he misses Lang horribly. He has avoided me, afraid, I think, that I'm going to cry, like his mother, all those years ago. I'm afraid I'm going to cry too, but I haven't ever in front of Tad. I wish this could be a pleasanter summer for him. Even Breck is gone now, and when I invited Margot to bring Charles Junior, hoping the two boys would hit it off, Margot informed me that adolescent boys are shits, and that she has sent hers to stay with one of his military school friends as long as that boy's mother can stand him, whereupon he is to visit another.

As for us, I can't see that Tad's presence has been the help to Joanna that Grove hoped it would be, but it is some help to Grove. In June, the urgent, scarcely meetable demands on horse vets of April and May begin to ease, finitely, and that heretofore welcome relief is hard on Grove this summer. Doggedly living up to his responsibilities through those heaviest foaling months is what kept him from breaking under the desperate strain of there being nothing whatever he could do for Lang. Time to breathe is time to think. The evening meal was especially hard on all three of us the whole spring. Supper is the one time of day when Lang has always been present, when the four of us have always been together. Sitting at table with just Joanna and me, there was no way Grove could pretend not to be thinking of Lang, and so to keep up the confident front he feels it is his role to keep up, not just before Joanna, but me too. Now the terrible silences can be filled by man to man talk with Tad.

I have tried to make up to Tad for his being left so much with two females by not bugging him unless driven to it. About his room, for instance. The only thing that doesn't go on Tad's floor are his used towels (which go on his bathroom floor). In fact, there's so much on Tad's bedroom floor that he's almost stopped using his hall door, which opens inward, and is mostly using his patio door, which slides on its track.

Possibly Tad goes and comes via the patio because he is fed up with my asking him please to leave his boots on the stoop when he comes in. Possibly he imagines that if he comes in the back way, I will never know that he lies on his bed in said boots.

Last June Tad and Lang and Breck were always outside together. This month a good deal of Tad's day has been spent lying on his bed, with or without boots. He has helped Grove and Ervil in the barn, particularly with Uncle, his favorite. Once the men leave, however, he vanishes behind the closed doors of his bedroom. Joanna's reading lesson is punctuated by the electronic squeaks that indicate touchdowns or base hits. In personal worldly goods, Tad is certainly far less the pitiful orphan than the only grandson —Velma's side.

I do not permit myself to think of him as the Broughs' only grandson.

Meals are received like fill contributed to Zad Thacker's sink-hole: nothing has been found inappropriate, or sufficient. Tad eats more than Joanna and I combined, although I am trying hard to regain the weight I have been losing all spring and summer. Calling him to lunch is nevertheless a challenge, because his ears are blocked with earphones. These are such a constant that his automatic response to being addressed is "What?" even when his headset is on the floor. I bang on his door with my fist and he stumbles out smelling so strongly of the chocolate he doesn't dream we realize he has that I wonder Joanna doesn't cry. His luncheon conversation consists of answers to Will-you-have offers: "What? Yes;"

"What? No." Last summer he or Lang was always talking, usually both.

At supper, Tad will talk to Grove about the yearlings, very male to male. I have wondered whether his often-expressed scorn for the much bigger price Grove counts on getting for Ten isn't just a thirteen-year-old's need to oppose a father figure on safe (innocuous) ground. "Uncle is more beautiful," he says firmly, "and he has better sense."

Uncle *is* easier to handle than Ten, but even I can see that he's less well-made.

What Tad wants more than anything else is to be treated like a man, but he can't resist childish stunts. Before I realized that Margot had sent Charles Junior away for the summer, I invited the Dags and Callets to drinks on the patio Tad's first afternoon here. Margot didn't even bring Claudette. Tad perched unseen in the nearest maple for an hour, waiting, he explained afterward, for us to consume enough ice to allow the frog he had put at the bottom of our ice bucket to jump out at us. Nobody told him that chilled frogs hibernate. Nils and I were drinking bourbon on the rocks, Margot and Grove, Bloody Marys, and Inge, elegant in white linen, tomato juice. Inge's was the groping hand that encountered the slimy inert body.

The frog, I believe, was Tad's revenge on me for having ignored his stuck-out tongue when I put two mugs and a pitcher of cider beside the five grown-ups' glasses on the patio table. At bedtime I could tell from Grove's dropped g-preamble that he too thought I had been too doctrinaire about alcohol and thirteen-year-olds. "Dad used to give Ted and me a taste of whatever," he told me. "Kept us from thinkin' liquor was some big deal." I didn't want to argue at bedtime: getting to sleep is a major problem for us. I pretended to hear Joanna call.

I checked Joanna's covers leisurely enough to give Grove time to forget about my reluctance to serve Rebel Yell, however dilute, to visiting children. The telephone rang as I was returning. I ducked into the kitchen and snatched up the receiver in time to hear Albert Blount ask Grove for Lang's dental records.

191

The telephone was deathly silent until dinner the next evening. Grove and I both spilled something when it finally rang, but no, Albert said: the body was not Lang's.

My relief was the qualified kind one might feel as a six-shooter's first bullet flew past one's head. This body wasn't Lang's, but that left all the floorboards in the world yet to be ripped up.

Friends tried to help. Neither they nor we had any idea what would help. We should have ducked the Bonnifreds' invitation. I wanted to. I knew it was kindly meant. Roy being Grove's senior partner, his was the first table that had welcomed us as a married couple, and now I could almost hear Agnes thinking *Ruth cannot be allowed to sit beside her telephone forever. Ruth must be* drawn out.

We had gone to the Dags' annual *So Long, May* dinner dance. Nils throws big, deductible parties, which Grove, who hates big parties, regards as obligatory. I was surprised to be invited to this one. Probably Nils and Inge hadn't known what to do. We have rules for the duration of mourning a dead child, but what are the rules for a child who has vanished? We'd planned to skip the Dags' bash this year; those drinks on our patio were meant, partly, to make amends for this plan (though I can't swear I'd have been so conscientious if I'd known Charles Junior was in Nashville for the summer). After Tad wrecked that afternoon, Grove and I talked the situation over, guardedly. The meal at Hereward would be buffet. We could make an appearance, and stay just long enough to be polite.

We left the "So Long" party as planned almost at once, but not soon enough to prevent my having to go straight to bed with a headache like a concussion. There could be no similar retreat from a sit-down dinner such as Bonnifreds'. On the other hand, I told myself, there would be no crowd. We were being asked to spend a quiet evening with two people who had always been kind to us, who wished us only good with all their hearts.

Agnes and Roy's house is older than Bourbon County. In the past, just stepping into Agnes's garden has been as good as a martini to me, it reminds me so of Charleston. We went, and it did its best. Butterflies fluttered over the alyssum that lines its brick walks. A praying mantis with eyes like Tad's earphones ogled us severely from the daylilies, where dozens of bees were loading their legs with golden pollen. *He is very allergic to bee venom. I took him to Jake monthly for shots. Now it's been nine weeks since his last shot.* We sat in the shade of antebellum maples where Agnes's Ruby Muirhead had glasses and an ice bucket and cold shrimp laid out for us. I had supposed that Grove and I were to be the only guests, but the partners' apprentice and his wife, Hank and Amelia Herndon, were already there. Amelia's face had a prepared expression, as if Agnes had warned them that Grove and I were coming, or maybe I've become paranoid. Amelia is always uneasy when she has to leave Amy with a sitter. (She's afraid someone will tell Amy ghost stories or feed her refined sugar, or even administer unconstructive corrections. Or maybe, like me, she's afraid her child won't be there when she gets back.)

I knew when Stoy Littleton joined us that there would be another woman coming. Stoy is a widower. He fixed himself a drink and took the chair between Amelia and me.

Stoy Littleton runs the most successful horse insuring agency in Bourbon County. "Got a call on a mare of yours this morning," Grove told him. We both had learned to start conversations with other people. Otherwise, they sat in frozen misery, not knowing what to say, what tone to take, or even, it often seemed, where to look.

"You mean the one boarding at Linville's, got herself lightning struck?"—Stoy, nervous, relieved.

Grove nodded. "Actually, lightning got two mares. Same bolt hit both, I imagine—one of Linville's own, and the one you insured."

Stoy shook his head, a preacher watching a heathen drummed to the scaffold—trying to look sorry, calculating the advertising. "I tried to sell Linville protection on his horses. But he told me, 'A man can't stay in the horse business unless he's lucky—and if he's lucky, lightning won't strike his horses.' What can you do?"

Hank Herndon laughed. Stoy didn't.

Stoy never speaks of *insurance.* "Give your mares the *protection* they deserve," his ads urge, as if the right policy would inoculate your herd against every danger.

"Maybe Linville's got something," Hank joked. "He had fifteen mares in that field, but only one of his own got killed, and she was barren." Hank must learn never to make jokes with undertakers or insurancemen. I, pondering the expendability of the barren female, probably looked no more affable than Stoy.

"May we expect," Roy inquired, "that for insurance purposes, our frugal friend now would be deemed, as it were, lightning proof?" When Roy talks, one lip caresses the other as if they were lovers loath to stop. "Lightning, as is well known, never descending twice upon the same target?"

"Well," Grove said, "I read recently that if the first bolt doesn't *remove* the object, the object is virtually certain to be struck again."

I read that article too. It also related a myth of the cloud goddess Tien Mu. Tien Mu carries a mirror in each hand and whenever their two reflections cross, lightning flashes. One day lightning knocked an old woman into her rice paddy, breaking her arm. As she lay dazed in the mud a voice from the clouds cried out, "I have made a mistake!" With that, a little unguent pot appeared at the woman's elbow. Her friends rubbed the unguent on her fracture, and she scrambled to her feet, miraculously healed. When they tried to secure the pot, however, no amount of effort would lift it. At last they gave up, whereupon the pot floated up to the clouds.

Where is the goddess who will cry, *I have made a mistake,* and lay our son beside us in our field?

No one heard Margot Dag Callet's Mustang arrive; she came walking around the house toward our voices. While Stoy poured her a drink, Margot took the chair he'd been sitting in between Amelia and me. Stoy seated himself on Amelia's other side, and Amelia resumed telling him about her "para-professional work" at Amy's school.

Grove and I honeymooned in the Dags' Saratoga cottage, a generous wedding present that may have owed as much to my friendship with Margot as to Grove's professional connection. I knew Maggie Dag before she pledged Kappa and became Margot and a redhead. By daylight, Margot looks a little older now than we are, but eye-catching still. Smoking and alcohol have wrinkled Margot's face, but Margot's body isn't bad, in a *Voguish* way. Her dress that evening was a large-patterned green silk that left one shoulder and most of her back bare; the kind that makes a flatchested woman look sexier than if she were bosomy enough to need a brassiere. Stoy looked as if he would rather have been talking to Margot, as very shortly I wished he had been myself.

"We're trying to teach the children to stay in touch with their feelings," Amelia explained to him. "In my opinion, it's totally related to a lot of different things."

"Shit," said Margot.

Amelia looked startled, but Margot was only commenting on having sloshed a little cold bourbon in her lap. I fished her a handkerchief out of my bag.

"We do," Amelia persisted doggedly, "want our children to be *fully human*, don't we?"

Margot handed me back my wet crumpled handkerchief. "I hope your headache wasn't anything serious the other night," she murmured. "You were smart to leave. That crowd got louder and louder and not a damn bit funnier."

We had arrived at Hereward calculatedly late. The party, as we stepped out of our car, had been a Brueghel-with-sound and had had sent me home feeling like one of Tien Mu's mistakes. I'd turned in at once. Grove had closed the bedroom door on me and slept on the sofa, and I had been grateful.

"I would have telephoned in the morning except I knew Grove wouldn't have come back if there was any cause for worry." Margot's eyes were on my face. "He was so dear to come back, even if he couldn't spare me one dance. Daddy appreciates anybody who helps him keep up the help's morale, and seeing other people letting go encourages everybody to have a good time." A current shot through my chest. Margot took out her cigarettes.

I put my arms casually on the cold iron arms of my chair and waited, sure that Margot was going to tell me who the help was, the requirements of whose morale left Grove with not one dance to spare his host's daughter.

I had a feeling I wasn't going to be surprised.

They looked so cute doing the twist together, Grove and Daddy's little secretary. "He may have thought I was too drunk to stay off his damn feet. Honey," Margot gripped my arm (did she think I would flee?)— "by the time they popped the last balloon I was, I mean *I was,* nigger kissing drunk!"

My heart lay at the bottom of an elevator shaft; my head was humming. Margot patted my hand and stood up.

Grove had never told me he *hadn't* returned to the party.

Grove was talking earnestly to Hank and Roy about contagious equine metritis. Stoy, trapped beside Amelia, had put his expression on automatic pilot. Agnes had gone to the kitchen to tell Ruby that all the guests had arrived. "I need some more ice," Margot announced, "but nobody's going to give me any until I check out that bucket." No one laughed harder than Margot as she told about Tad's frog. "Of course, if Mamma'd had anything in that tomato juice, she wouldn't have got so hot and bothered, but Mamma thinks alcohol is the devil's own piss."

How long ago was it, that time I said something about not feeling much enthusiasm for supper fixing, and before I knew it, kind Grove had me lying down resting, with the promise that he and Joanna would drive somewhere for their meal—and Joanna told me happily later what Lucille fed them? And I didn't ask how that happened, but Grove told me; Grove carefully told me.

"Well, you have to laugh at Mamma whatever happens," Margot said cheerfully, "because she's just too dumb to roll downhill, but if your little nephew sends any dress of mine to the morgue, Grove Brough, I'll kick his arse so far up his tail he won't know whether to hiccup or fart. I don't know how poor Ruth puts up with him. Boys that age aren't human."

So now I was poor-Ruth. The earth had swallowed Lang and I did not become poor-Ruth, but now I was poor-Ruth.

"My nephew is here, because his mother—" Grove began, and suddenly I was interrupting him.

"Tad is here because the most ominously powerful union in the United States next to the teamsters finds it beneficial to keep the schools of education making money in the summertime. And also because his mother can write more emotion than I can scream." Later I remembered that Roy and Agnes's daughter teaches elementary ed.

Margot stirred her Wild Turkey and grinned. Roy threw an anxious look over his shoulder toward the door through which his wife was just reappearing. Stoy and the Herndons, with palpable effort, looked blank. Grove began explaining about Velma and Tad.

"In the Old Testament," I interrupted again, "a man was *required* to marry his brother's widow. Grove's just a hero born out of his time."

"Dinner is served," said Agnes, who never had struck me as telepathic before.

Grove was wrong when he accused me of saying every nasty thing I could think of that night. I do remember comparing the busts and portraits in Lexington to something Peter von Strehlenau had said to Eva and me in Copenhagen. "Never cross the street to look at a statue in Denmark," Peter had advised. "Either it's somebody you never heard of before and won't again, or it's Hans Christian Anderson and you have already seen fifty."

In Lexington, substitute Henry Clay for Hans Christian, I suggested at Bonnifreds' table. So it's to Agnes's credit that we got all the way to dessert before she reminded me that Grove and I still have Joanna. (In case we hadn't noticed.) "You have a lot to be thankful for, young lady."

To which the proper junior partner's wife responds with sweet humility, *Yes indeed.* "Nobody ever told Marie Antoinette's head to be grateful that it still had quite a lot of teeth," I said. Everyone but Margot looked stunned. How, Grove afterward asked me reasonably (though not in a reasonable tone of voice), were they supposed to go on eating after that? (Margot, I thought, seemed in excellent appetite.)

For ten years my thinking had been that Grove works hard any hour, any day, any weather—strenuous, often dangerous, work, and—because thousands of dollars depend on his judgment, work done under considerable strain. Anything friendly I could do for his clients' or his colleagues or their wives was little enough, my duty. That's what I'd thought. *Had I been a chump for ten years?*

I was asking myself, but also, *Was having been a chump for ten years an excuse for turning into a virago now?* Agnes Bonnifred hadn't hired Lucille Harper. And poor Amelia! It's for what I said to Amelia after dinner that I'm the sorriest.

Agnes commented on my continuing weight loss. I admitted I wasn't sleeping. Amelia assumed her caring, involved expression. Had I considered *seeking help?*

From someone else, seeking help could mean anything from looking for a cleaning woman to calling in the FBI. From Amelia, "seeking help" means just one thing. "Psychiatry won't find Lang," I answered, "any more than it'll cure crossed eyes." I wish I could say I was sorry the moment I said it, but I was too angry. I'm sorry now.

I have been advised to "seek help" before. I was advised to "seek help" years ago, by people who knew that we had not intended Joanna to be our last child.

"Which of you by taking thought can add one cubit unto to her womb?" was Jake's considered response, one of the reasons I love and trust Jake.

Grove didn't wait till we got all the way home from Bonnifreds'. By the time he worked his way to Copenhagen, I was looking out the window and he was driving dangerously. "You're always talking about your trip to Europe—why don't you take another?"

"While Tad takes care of Joanna, and Joanna answers the telephone?" *And you go dancing.*

"While Tad makes rounds with me and we hire somebody grown up to take care of Jo and answer the telephone."

"You've given up on Lang!" In that enclosed space my suddenly raised voice seemed like a yell even to me.

"Will you talk sense?"

"Who's this 'Joe' you keep talking about? You'll ruin Joanna's life if you try to make a son out of her!"

"Make a— Oh, for Christ's sake, Ruth. *You're* the one who's ruining her, trying to turn a sturdy little girl into a mamma's baby! *'Hold onto my skirt.' 'Take hold of my hand.' 'No, you can't go there*—the poor kid can't go around the corner to piss without you! She'll be as nutty as a fruitcake—she'll be as neurotic as *you* are if you just keep it up!"

"Margot says you drove Lucille home after the dance."

"So?"

"The night I was sick."

"So?"

"You didn't tell me you went back to the dance."

"So?"

Striking the driver is mortally perilous, but fortunately Grove continued speaking this time. "I don't tell you a lot of things, but I'll tell you one right now. I'm worried about you. It won't be as much as ten years before Jo starts going out, and that's always a difficult time for a mother, and I don't know if you're going to be able to handle it. You're already showing signs that you're going to have trouble. Lucille is half your age; she could be my daughter. If you're jealous of *her*, what are you going to be like when Jo turns gorgeous just as you hit forty-five?"

43 {Ruth

Parched corn is one thing: *shit is something else.*

Our days were correct, conversationless. We did not touch each other. My mind was like a stall-walking horse, a beast that no sooner fetches up against one wall than it wheels and stalks back to the opposite wall. Grove's little after-Bonnifreds' speech was fit only to flush down a commode—*but:* what about my behavior at dinner? I wasn't proud of embarrassing Grove about Tad—*but:* How many times when I thought he was looking for Lang was he with Lucille?

I had turned off the light before Grove got back from taking the baby-sitter home. Our exchanges next morning and after were confined to basic civilities. Grove looked grim and self-righteous. "Max hated me," Fran Warren told me once, "because he couldn't make himself believe the lies he told me." Remembering these words made me shiver. What lies had Grove told me? Everything

I'd ever observed about him, I reflected, I'd interpreted in the light of certain apparently mistaken assumptions. All must be re-examined. Was Lagoon's September stud fee Grove's only spur to getting Ten into the summer sale, or had he obligations I hadn't dreamt of? Should I be suspicious of bookie Malcolm Gurley's swift help? Did the rock-steady Grove I had thought I married exist?

Half Fayette County knows who Malcolm Gurley is, even the ones who never get near a bookie, and everybody in the industry, certainly all the bookies, knows all the vets, and probably everybody in Lexington saw Lang's picture on the *Herald-Leader's* front page. Grove's going straight to Gurley didn't convict him of anything.

Nothing had happened that couldn't be explained. Margot is a bitter drunk; why pay attention to her? Why, after ten years of trusting Grove, was I jumping off the window ledge over one alarming ticker tape? Would anybody else who'd known Margot Dag Callet for seventeen years leap at her bait?

Margot's marriage displeased Nils and Inge—Margot was too young, Chuck too Catholic. However, the pig Margot and a sorority sister had shoved through the front door of the Sigma Chi house three hours after dorm closing had turned out to belong to the basketball coach. Both girls had been suspended. "If I hadn't married Chucklehead, I'd have had to spend that semester at home," Margot says.

Last Christmas, when Margot came back to Hereward without Chuck, Norma Lee warned me against her.

"If Grove didn't like women, he wouldn't like me," I answered Norma Lee flippantly. I knew I was prettier than Margot, younger looking. (That was two months ago.) I didn't worry about Grove's giving Margot a thought. I was too stupid to see that his not giving her a thought could be a problem too.

I would have soaked my head in mineral oil before I asked Margot one question about what she'd told me at Bonnifreds', but I decided to sound out Lorena. She and Eldridge would have been at the Dags' party till the music went home. I waited till afternoon, to be *certain* Grove had finished at Hereward and moved on. "Let's stop and see Lucille!" Joanna suggested as we passed the farm office. Something about the way I said *no* stopped her from asking again — or maybe it was just that school was out and Farrah would be home.

Lorena and I didn't have to ask our offspring to let us talk; our supervision is the very last thing Farrah and her brothers want. Eventually the biggest boy made a furtive trip to the kitchen. Otherwise the children were just a variety of sounds down the hall. Tad, I had left at home with the telephone — after stashing his earphones in the truck's glove compartment.

What have you heard? I wanted to ask. *You're right here where she works, where he comes every day. Your husband spends more hours with him a week than any other man in the industry. What do you know?* I talked about my brush with extortion. Would Lorena have guessed, I asked innocently, that a presumably hard-bitten professional illegal gambler would thrust a boxful of folding money into Grove's hands on the strength of an oral promise?

"Malcolm's a good ol' boy," Lorena said comfortably.

"You know him?" I tried not to sound the least disapproving.

"Eldridge knows him pretty well." Lorena grinned. "I don't worry. I'd rather have a husband to gamble a little than to chase skirts." As if one insured against the other.

Lorena's remark was a *non sequitur,* unless, I thought, she was hinting at something, waiting to find out if I knew anything before she spoke plainly. I told her what Margot had told me about the Dags' affair.

She did not deny it. I tried not to reveal my dismay, but I must have looked smacked.

Lorena hadn't expected me to pick up on her chasing skirts remark, but she carried the situation off with no apologies. "If it was Eldridge, I'd skin him alive!" she declared. "But don't be too hard on Grove. He's all tore up over your little boy, and he's needed — he's needed a lot of extra — and you've been — well, honey, we all understood why you might be —"

Why I might be a witch on a broomstick, I mentally finished for her. My mind flew back to that day Velma's letter had come asking that I look after Tad while she went to Mexico. As at Bonnifreds', my anger had welled up despite all I could do, compelling as vomit.

None of my victims deserved my fury—none of them had snatched Lang—none was glad of our torment—and Lorena was of course right: Grove of all people, now of all times, was entitled to soothing sympathetic kindness twenty-four hours a day. I wished I could give it to him. I wished he could give it to me.

Lorena admitted nothing in so many words about Grove, and shifted swiftly from my case to her own. All men, she seemed to be saying kindly, are the same.

Eldridge Snyder had given up horse training and moved into Hereward Stud's farm manager's quarters, Lorena told me, because Lorena wouldn't marry a traveling man. Now, eleven years later, he and she have eight children, plus one on the way. Eight rather than nine because, Lorena informed me, laughing merrily, "That was the year I wasn't speaking to him, honey." The unsociable "year" referred to commenced that August when Nils Dag sent Eldridge to Saratoga to buy yearlings, while Lorena, too pregnant to travel, stayed home.

Saratoga yearling auctions are held at night. Afternoons are for the races, and Eldridge, who had the use of the Dags' box, attended them all, a redhead on his arm. That redhead, I now learned between explosions of Lorena's laughter, is why there is a Snyder a year older than Lang and one a year younger, but none Lang's age. Word of the redhead beat Eldridge home. "I met him at that door and I read him his pedigree! I told him, 'Get the hell outta my footpath, you bedswerver! Don't you bring me your leftover seed!'

"Honey, he just turned around and walked out. Didn't say one word, just give me one mean look and banged the door behind him. I thought he'd left me."

Lorena had no rights to Hereward's manager's house except through Eldridge, but she was prepared to stare that fact down. "Crawling back to my parents' was no part of my plan, I can tell you! Live in that little shack with all my sisters and their kids coming back and filling up the floor whenever they take a mind? Good night! I wouldn't go back to all that noise and fighting for *nothing!* Let *him* go somewhere—he was the one straying."

Eldridge had gone to Sears Roebuck. Through the kitchen window, Lorena watched him return with a brass bedframe—a single bed, she emerged to confirm as soon as he drove away again. This bed now stood in the nursery. The awaited baby's clothes were stacked neatly beside its crib, in the hall.

"Well, honey—it really wasn't such a big deal to either one of us to be in bed together right then, I was so close to my time. Eldridge he could climb up there, but then he'd paddle them arms and legs like a turtle stuck on a rock. His thing wouldn't hardly reach mine, and I was like to suffocate—and little Ezra hitting back as hard as he could swing." Another peal of laughter as a muffled thud from the kitchen drew our eyes to little Ezra himself, listing across the kitchen from the weight of the eight-pack of Ale-8s he had just extracted from the refrigerator. Lorena's voice rose good humoredly to include her first-born. "He meant to strike his daddy, but who he was getting was me." Little Ezra's face was a mask as he ducked out the door.

Every morning when Lorena rose she would find Eldridge's breakfast things left for her to wash, and every evening when he came home he would find his supper waiting. They lived that way for months before they both happened to get drunk the same night. "Well," Lorena confessed, "maybe I wasn't as drunk as I let on."

I was forced to speculate on the implication of Lorena's confidences about herself and Eldridge, for about Grove she confided nothing. Lorena, I concluded, wouldn't lie to me, but would volunteer nothing. Faced with information already in my possession, she would resort to diversionary prattle, going to some lengths to try to make it comforting. "You aren't the only one," she seemed to be saying. "Look how Eldridge did." Unfortunately, that was a tacit admission of Grove's guilt.

Though of just what, I wasn't forced or permitted to know. I never had taken seriously the Biblical injunction that lust in the heart is as bad as lust accommodated. Now, burning to know which I was confronting, I could feel my attitude waver.

In my car was the dish in which Fran Warren had brought us her strawberry spectacular on Dumbarton Day. I sought Lorena's permission to leave Joanna "to see the rest of the cartoon special" she and the Snyder children were watching, while I returned Fran's dish. If Lorena very well knew why, she didn't let on.

"How're you holding up?" Fran greeted me, rising from her desk chair. I had intended to make a coffee date with her, but since Lucille was running errands I already had Fran to myself. "I looked for you at the boss's shindig. Got there late. Somebody told me you'd come and gone already."

I waited but she clearly meant to stop there. Dear Fran. "Yes," I said, pulling a chair for myself over beside hers and sitting. "And I'm told that was unwise of me. Fill me in, for auld lang syne."

Fran sat back down. "Don't take it personally, chum. You can't fight pheromones. And that one's got 'em. She's already been to *Dr. Wade Roe's* clinic once, which you didn't hear from me."

I felt myself go rigid.

"She brought the problem to the Bluegrass with her," Fran supplemented casually. "You know the kid sister."

Fran has a sister whose screaming face turns up in Lexington and Louisville newspaper pictures of sign-wielding picketers. It seems that she stopped by Hereward one morning this spring to get Fran's signature on a school-aid petition and recognized in Lucille someone on whom she had forced photographs a year or so before—someone who had rendered herself memorable by coolly crumpling the gruesome pictures into a ball and stuffing them down their donor's blouse front. "I was invited outside and informed that I had hired a *murderess*," Fran said cheerfully. "I think I was expected to fire the girl before lunch. I told Sis it was none of my business, and none of hers. But I'll tell you, I'll be glad when Miss Hot Pants gets herself a man and gits. Her own man, that is, and not somebody else's. She doesn't seem to recognize the difference."

I folded my arms so that they could push unobtrusively against my stomach. "I'm not just losing on the pheromones front," I said. "Grove seems to have decided that where I'm incompetent, it's because I feel too good for animal husbandry. Your 'Miss Hot Pants' is a veterinarian's daughter."

"It's not you, and it's not her," Fran said. "Grove is furious because he thinks he's failed you. If I learned nothing else from being married to Max, I learned this: when a man can't do as well by his wife as he thinks he should, he'll hate her. Grove can't find Lang. And he can't comfort you—you probably get more help these days from your doctor and that good-looking cop. A man would rather punch his woman in the nose than have her feeling he's failed her. That or get another woman."

This was supposed to comfort me? I collected Joanna and went home.

"Mrs. Callet wants you to call her at this number," Tad informed me. I waited till he'd gone back to his room to throw Margot's number in the wastebasket.

Who I did telephone was Amelia. I wanted, I pretended, her advice about kindergarten. Amelia was overjoyed. I let her tell me what she and her gurus recommended in more detail than ever. Working around from there to babysitters was easy. "Does Lucille Harper ever sit for you?" I eventually asked.

The answer was a moment slow coming. "She did a few times, back when she first came to Hereward."

"She certainly seems to love children. I bet she volunteered — right?"

"One day Hank offered her our symphony tickets, one time when I couldn't get Amy's sitter. He never should have told her that was why! When she told him she wouldn't take the tickets, she would sit for us, he *accepted*. I didn't know what to do! I hadn't even met her." Amelia uses only one sitter for Amy, a part-time Montessori teacher who engages Amy in meaningful play. "Hank thought it was terribly sweet of her. He said he just assumed I would think so too.

"Well, I didn't want to offend her. Fran told me she'd never missed a day's work, and the people at Fugazzi told me she stood very high in her classes."

Fugazzi College is one of Lexington's business schools. I felt reproached. Even in the face of Hank's endorsement, Amelia had made inquiries before entrusting Lucille with her child. *Amy* will never be picked off some roadside. "Well, I'm sure Amy loves her," I said. "Joanna does." I paused before adding — as if the question were just coming to me — "But did I understand you to mean she doesn't sit for you any more? You didn't have a problem, did you?"

I could see Amelia's lips press together, her chin lift. "You can't always put a name to what isn't positive about a situation, Ruth. To be judgmental isn't *me*, but I just couldn't see it working out."

Maybe those inquiries to Fran and Fugazzi came after the fact, after Amelia had begun to wonder whether this oh so helpful baby-sitting was a Trojan horse. Maybe they were made in the hope of learning something that could be used as an excuse to Hank for not having Lucille back. Even if so, Amelia was still more watchful than I—watchful of her husband.

Supper that night was virtually silent. Immediately after, Grove and Tad left for a lecture on the pros and cons of Caslick's surgery, which was obligatory for Grove, and to Tad apparently preferable to an evening at home with only females.

I had not returned Margot's call, but when she showed up just after I put Joanna to bed, I let her in.

One doesn't offer Margot coffee. I fetched sherry; I opened a can of brown bread. We sat facing each other across the coffee table in the living room.

When Margot thinks anybody's pitying her, for her failed marriage, for her obvious disappointment in life, she is venomous—but *Margot* pitched *her husband*, as she puts it, not the other way around. I could see that she felt this put her one up on me. Now that she has seen to it that I must see this also, she can be kind. There are women who would have drawn lines around their personal business, would have stopped Margot the moment she stepped over one. Good for them. I despised myself for not being one of them, but I wasn't one of them. I sliced and buttered brown bread, so as not to have to look at Margot, and listened with my whole strength.

"Look, Ruth, that *harper* is no angel. She went after him, and he's not the first. Talk to that cute apprentice, the one with the psychobabbler wife and the ugly kid.

"My old Morehead drinking buddy told me an earful. Her oldest daughter and Lucille were classmates since kindergarten. Calculating to their toenails, that pair. Lucille led one poor bastard on all the way through high school, milked him for all he was worth and dropped him cold the day she left for Lexington. He thought till the day she left town they were going to marry as soon as he graduated from MSU." Margot laughed. "His daddy owns a pharmacy where they still sell ice cream, and he's the lucky one going to inherit; can you imagine a girl turning her back on all that?" Margot stopped to light another cigarette and I pretended a need to pick up some crumbs I'd deliberately spilled on the floor. I didn't like the picture of myself motionless, unwilling, in my need, to interrupt Margot with so much as a syllable. "My friend's daughter said Lucille just tolerated the sap for his car and his prom orchids and his Christmas cashmeres, said she never had any intention but to get out of Morehead and never come back except to thumb her nose. Well, can't blame her for wanting to get out of Morehead. Wanted to get out of Morehead myself, from the day Chuck and I drove past it trying to find it."

All Margot's life she has wanted to get out—out of UK, out of her parents' house, out of marriage.... Once I felt loftily immune to Margot's virus. Now I didn't feel so smug, so safe. I didn't walk Margot to her car.

Grove and I had not conversed (different from not speaking) since we'd slammed the car doors after arriving home from Bonnifreds'. I hadn't spent every hour since reviewing his shortcomings; I'd taken a conscientious interest in my own, but by my reckoning, I came off better than he. The cold selfishness of his embarking on an affair when I was fastened to the rack of Lang's disappearance, the hypocrisy—the *pomposity*—of his defense, made him quite another person from the one I had blissfully constructed in his image. Clearly I had married and lived for ten years under serious misapprehensions.

Those who remember the past are condemned to revise it. I began to revise.

Of course Lucille is more than half my age. Thank God I'd had just enough self-possession to resist being drawn on that issue. Whatever nasty squelches Grove had in mind for when I protested, he didn't get to use.

I hadn't had to listen to them, but I could imagine some, making myself as angry as if he *had* treated me to them. Fair enough, since he'd benefited from all the noble, worthy things I *used* to imagine about him.

Some things I know about Grove can be documented. He went straight from public school in Chillicothe, Ohio, his birthplace, to Ohio State University. Thirteen semesters later he graduated from Ohio State's vet school, and became Roy Bonnifred's apprentice. Unlike Roy's earlier succession of apprentices, who were all sent forth to seek their fortunes elsewhere after two years at most, he became Roy's partner. His wedding trip, to Charleston and Saratoga, is the longest he has ever taken—a fact with which he seems aggressively content. He doesn't like to fly, he says.

I love to fly.

But I was staying put. Over and over, I put myself through the arguments, always fetching up against these: Did Grove deserve to lose both his children? I couldn't kid myself that he loved Joanna any less than I. Grove might not love me, but he loved his son and daughter. And they love him. Was I willing to drag our already scarified little daughter through anything more? Over and over I made my daughter a solemn promise: whatever I learned, I was not going to leave her father.

Yet in my fantasies of finding Lang I had begun to leave Grove out; it was beginning almost to seem as if Lang were someone whom I had loved in a dream in which Grove played no part.

⚡44⚡ {Albert

Albert doesn't have time to pay much attention to art, but he once went with Juanita to an exhibit at UK's museum by an artist whom his sister Jakba called Dead-white-European-male-number-2000, but who had called himself Mauritz Escher. "Some of these pictures," Albert commented as, elbows touching, he and Juanita studied every one, "remind me of police work. You think you know what something is, but imperceptibly, it's turning into something else." Later Juanita gave him the Escher print that hangs now where he can see it when he lies in bed.

Jakba had already given him a painting, a leopard on a jungle limb. The signature almost hidden in vines is Jomo Shivutse. "That cat," Albert's brother Cyrus volunteered on one of his rare passes through Paris, "never been out of the Cincinnati zoo." The leopard hangs above Albert's bed, looking every night as if it were about to jump on his head, and that reminds Albert of police work too.

This morning Albert sits beside his bed, unconscious of either picture. Last night he brought some of the Brough boy's file home with him. The child has been gone more than six weeks. Albert has done everything that cried out to be done and has heard nothing in return more substantial than an echo. He re-reads his interview notes.

"Start with the neighborhood," Ruben Davis, Albert's Lexington Police Force friend, has told him, and, "If the day comes when looks like you're getting lost, get back to the neighborhood."

Clint Penn isn't the only untraced man who was discharged on Clay Pike this spring, nor even the only one discharged for stealing, but he is the only one discharged for stealing from a farm which has subsequently suffered an unexplained fire. Albert resolves to pay another call on the Thackers.

Zad and his eldest son, D.B., are working at their forge and can't be expected, Albert reminds himself, to be glad to see anyone of any color. Albert's life is a succession of these self-reminders. At first Zad goes on hammering and lets D.B. do the answering. He straightens up when Albert asks if Clint Penn drank. "Not on my farm, he didn't!" Zad is wearing faded overalls and he eyes Albert's neatly pressed seersucker resentfully.

"Do you know if he went to any bars, any bar in particular?" A man will talk more when he's drinking, Albert knew before he was taught.

The Thackers are teetotalers; they can't connect Clint with any bars.

Albert has determined that Clint has left no forwarding address at the Paris Post Office. No mail, the Thackers say, has ever come to the farm for him.

"How did he get to work?" Albert asks. "Did he come with a group? Did somebody drop him off?"

"Had his own car," Zad says shortly.

"Do you remember the license number?"

Of course they do not, but D.B. remembers that the car was a blue '80 Chevy with Scott County plates.

Albert once parlayed a witness who remembered an out-of-state license on a car leaving a crime scene into help from the FBI, but that was when Albert had a friend in the bureau. D.B. is firm in his recollection of Clint's Kentucky license plates. Albert records his words impassively.

"Did he ever speak of having any friends around here? Did anyone ever come here to see him? Did you ever see him with anybody?"

Father and son shake their heads, and Zad makes sure Albert sees him looking at his cooling metal. "Didn't nobody ever come to the farm for him," D.B. says. "He was kind of a loner, you know?"

D.B.'s last words send a tiny jolt to Albert's heart, followed by a sick heaviness in his gut. LONER he prints, and goes on with the interview. "What exactly did he say about being in the army, as well as you remember?"

Without a social security number, Army Intelligence had been unable to tell Albert whether they had a criminal record on Clint Penn, or even whether Clint ever actually bore arms. "Have you got a birth date?" Albert had been asked. "No birth date either. Without that social security number or at least a DOB...." Albert had known that before he called.

Zad and D.B. can add nothing to what Zad told Albert in April. The unfriendliness on Zad's face deepens at the suggestion that Albert should interview the rest of his family. "Me and my boy done told you all we know," Zad says. "The women and children don't know nothing about the boys I har."

"Sometimes a person knows more than he thinks he knows. Sometimes a person doesn't realize what he knows, till you ask him the right question. A man will say things to a woman, a girl—" Albert sees Zad's face and corrects himself—"in front of a woman or a girl, that he wouldn't say in front of a man. I'm trying to find the little Brough boy," he reminds Zad.

Milly Thacker wears cuffless shiny orange shorts and a yellow T-shirt stamped with a black bat logo. The wings stretch over her breasts. Albert's notes say that she's fourteen. Without them, Albert would take her for anywhere from fifteen to eighteen. She doesn't once look at him, but sits sullenly pushing one sandaled foot back and forth on the kitchen floor, an inch forward, an inch back. The Thackers have ushered Albert in through the kitchen door and have ranged themselves on stools or chairs or against counters around the room. A stool has been left empty for Albert; he doesn't take it. He needs these people's help. The smaller children stare at him. Milly, except for covert glances at her glowering mother, stares at her red-nailed toes. She answers only those questions put directly to her.

"Do you know where I could get a picture of him?"

"Couldn't nobody make a picture of that ugly thang," Milly says, eyes on the floor. "He'd break ever camera."

"Did he ever say anything about where he used to work?"

"Said sumn 'bout settin' tobacco," Milly says barely audibly, and shrugs. Her mother seems to swell.

"Did he say where?"

"He never did say where."

Under the fiercely glinting eye of her mother, this is the most Albert will get out of Milly. He moves to the counter and sets about producing a composite likeness of Clint from the Thackers' descriptions. D.B. and the younger children come closer to look over his shoulder and help.

~≈45≈~   {Lang

In July, when it's too late, a worker at Philadelphia's Mail Recovery Center will deal with Clint's note to the Broughs. Like everyone before her, she will mistake Clint's 4 for a 9, and since her computer will show no location in the entire United States with the zip code 90361, and since her computer will turn up eight towns in the United States named Paris, she will open Clint's envelope. She will see at once that the note must be turned over to the Postal Inspection Service. In July, this will be of no help to anyone.

Clint has told Lang that he will take Lang home when school starts up again in August. Lang feels sure it's already June, because he and Clint planted their corn long ago. Lang is worried that his teacher may make him repeat. If it is indeed June, he has missed some of April and every bit of May.

Lang is also afraid that one of the mares has had a colt. If all three have had fillies, Lang is OK. He only told Breck that he gets to name the colts. This was a fib; names are chosen by vote, and he gets one vote just like Joanna and his parents. But if there are no colts, Breck won't find out.

Clint is absent again tonight; night is when he meets his customers. The stills are nearly all gone from this county, Clint has told Lang, careful not to use a name. His daddy had one when Clint was Lang's age, "but got so it won't hardly worth the trouble." A few men still prefer their own brew the way a few women still make apple butter, but it's so easy for Clint to fill the Chevy's trunk in some wet county and sell the load locally for three times what he paid, why should he go to all the work his daddy went to, only to be stabbed to death by a black in LaGrange Reformatory? Clint's daddy never had minded LaGrange, where he periodically paid his dues, "until the one time." Clint, he has told Lang, hates niggers, and fragged the only black bastard who tried to give him orders in the army.

Clint has known all his customers since he was born or they were; he doesn't even take the rifle. Lang's first thought, the day Clint began to teach him to hunt, was of shooting Clint, but the idea hushed quicker than a sneeze. How would he ever get back to Kentucky if Clint died?

Lang has also discarded the idea of holding the gun on Clint and forcing him to march directly to the car and drive directly back to Bourbon County. Clint could march just anywhere he chose until Lang dropped; Lang wouldn't know where he was being led. Or, say they got to the car, Clint could drive anywhere he liked until there was no more gas, and all the rifle in the world wouldn't make the car go. What then?

If Lang is careful not to concentrate, he can recall his father's face, but often he cannot call up his mother's, and this terrifies him.

Lang knows that it's got to be June, from all the flies. "I'll be nine June ninth," he has told Clint.

"Well you've got another week to go, squirt," was Clint's response.

Behind Clint's back Lang put a little stone in his pocket. Now he is doing this every day. When he has seven creek pebbles in his pocket, he will know it's his birthday.

The awful quiet of the dark hills overwhelms Lang. Sitting on the steps with the twenty-two on his knees, waiting for whatever may assault the garden, he tells himself that so long as his backbone touches the top step, no ghost can snatch him. He prays that no animal will rustle the garden and force him to move. He doesn't want to find out whether he is more afraid of ghosts or of the beating Clint will give him if something spoils the garden.

One night, when a waxing moon held the floating dead at bay, Lang shot a raccoon.

Clint agreed that the skin should be his. Lang imagined wearing to school the hat his mother should make of this skin, imagined telling Breck how he himself shot the coon. That hat would have been enough to shut Breck up. Clint didn't tell Lang he should tan the hide, and the skin was stinking before they even finished eating the meat. Clint laughed and told Lang to bury it. Then he sat down with one of those pint bottles and Lang picked the skin up with a stick and threw it in the creek.

The creek is too shallow to bathe in now, and buzzing with every kind of stinging insect come to suck mud. Lang is happy to be spared his monthly allergy shot, but remembering his pumpkin-sized head the last time he was stung, his difficulty breathing, he gives the wasps and bumblebees plenty of room. Similarly, he is pleased not to have to wash his face and hands every time he eats, but he is always itching now. He thinks a cool shower would help the poison ivy on his forearms, and of course that time he fell in the nettles he wanted nothing so much as a tub to sit in up to his neck. He can thank the United States Congress, Clint says, that there's no plumbing. "They're the clowns that voted to bring all them people over here that's been killing American boys and give 'em a house, where they won't give a veteran shit."

When the sun is playing in the beech leaves, Lang minds the cabin's isolation less. The crows that investigate the garden are North Koreans, and Lang imagines telling Breck how many he has killed. Left out of these imagined boasts are the weeds from which he also must guard Clint's garden; the spotted red larvae that soundlessly defoliate wherever they hatch, stretching their skins tighter and shinier like ticks as they fatten; the inch-long earworms Lang pulls off with thumb and forefinger and smashes between stones. Sometimes he imagines that he is smashing Clint Penn.

46

{Ruth

Margot Callet's motive in coming to see me the evening after "Bonnifreds' Night" wasn't clear to me. Did she come to enjoy the condition to which she'd reduced me, or was she contrite? As the level in the sherry bottle sank, her mood darkened. *I should leave the bastard: the place for Joanna and me was Charleston.* "Don't tell me you have to patch things up 'for the children's sake,' Ruth. Wake up and smell the sour mash. Children don't stick around *themselves;* children leave you. Children grow up, Ruth." Her voice grew harsher. "It's not just Lang you're going to lose. Thirteen years from now, your Joanna and my Claudette will both shake our dust from their feet, and you'll be be faced with another fifty years with that bastard, another fifty years on this farm. Doing what?"

I look down the road, Mother's cook used to sing, *and the road looks narrow, long and lonesome.*

I have been thinking, since that night, about the things I love on this farm, the things that fifty springs will leave little room for — things like the soft muzzles of the foals searching earnestly under my chin for milk; the dandelions that turn into goldfinches and fly up laughing as I step into the pasture; the cherry trees in our orchard "hung with snow." I'm glad I didn't think of a one of them that night. Such a list would have sounded defensive, the lady protesting too much. Instead I said the first thing that came to my tongue, words I hadn't even realized were in my mind. "I'm going to be a reading teacher."

For an instant, Margot was brought up short. She set down her glass. "Just like that."

"Just like that," I agreed, trying to sound self-possessed while I listened to my mind racing to tell me things I didn't know it knew.

I have gone on listening.

To friends who in the past have questioned my not having 'chosen a profession, with all my education,' I have replied, "I chose my profession before I could read, and I chose well, too, because sure enough, I like it." Now I know I was deceiving myself when I said to my sleeping family, "You are my *without which nothing*." That is a statement no one can afford; to make it is to risk the head in the oven. *Without you, what?* every woman must ask herself.

Margot's needling startled me into my own answer, not that I thought it all out sitting across the coffee table from her.

I concede Margot's point: as a career, child rearing is similar to professional baseball—between the last pitch and Social Security is a long stretch. And I don't need Fran to tell me about rugs jerked out from under feet. But I have skills, and there's time for credentials.

I wrote my own texts for Lang and Joanna. I can write a text for whomever it is I'm helping, of whatever age and background. Hard workers who don't necessarily have to charge are popular. I'll pile myself into my car with my texts and tape-recorder and portable blackboard—and the carry-out lunch I'll buy from *Fran's Catering*—and go where my work is needed. I am good at it. I like it. It's important.

Grove and I continued to show each other the most punctilious courtesy, not touching except by accident. Joanna burst into helpless tears over trifles. Tad kept more than ever to his room. At night I lay beside my silent husband and tried not to think of the heat-stricken chickens the headlines told us were dying by the hundreds in Arkansas, lest I dream of Lang blistered and thirsty. And I realized every morning once again that it was not Lang's ring that had wakened me, but only the birds helplessly greeting the rising scourge.

Every year the Snyders have a potluck on the first Saturday in June, and we of course are always invited. This year I didn't even reply to the invitation, and Lorena, bless her, didn't bring it up when I called on her the morning after "Bonnifreds' Night."

At breakfast Saturday Tad asked, "Are we going to Snyders' this year?"

Food and fireworks: of course he remembered.

Grove and I hadn't even discussed the possibility of going; I had just assumed that it was the last thing either of us could bear. Now to my momentary surprise, Grove answered Tad, "We always go."

Yes, and Hereward's secretaries are always there. Suddenly I was determined to go with him.

Suffering, William Wordsworth tells us, "is permanent, dark and obscure"—to which I would add that joy is fleeting, dazzling, and unconcealable. As I listened to the laughter from our bathroom, where Grove was painting faces on Joanna's stomach with shaving lather, I realized that these happy sounds were the first I had heard in our house since Lang had been snatched away.

Eldridge and his boys had set up tables in the shade, where the temperature was only 90°. Lorena bustled around waving flies off the plastic dish-shrouds. I scouted for an empty spot for my spoonbread. There was already more food laid out than we could have eaten had we all stayed till the Fourth of July.

God knows what Lang has eaten since April.

Fran Warren was wearing blue jeans, a wide-brimmed straw hat and a loud Hawaiian shirt, not tucked in. "Is that spoonbread?" she greeted me. "How long do I have to wait?" She gave my shoulder a hug.

I had decided that Joanna could be safe out of my sight here. She'd gone off with Amy Herndon and Farrah to watch all their fathers play volleyball, but when Fran and I found lawn chairs and sat down to talk, she came running. In that heat, the players had stopped after one game. The chow line was forming. "I'm hungry!" Joanna urged; "I *need* some food! I NEED a hamburger!"

"I'll join you shortly," Fran said; "I NEED a beer first."

"You may have anything but shrimp," I told Joanna. The platter I had nudged to make room for my spoonbread contained huge Texas prawns. Under them, crushed ice had melted like the vows of passion, with one fly already struggling in the tepid water. "No shrimp."

When I realized who was headed for the line just ahead of us, I put my feet in low gear. "Come on," Joanna urged, "there's *Lucille!*"

Doubtless I only imagined that Lucille's matching cries of joy were pitched to reach Grove, a couple of people up the line. She looked perfect, the first person I'd seen who wasn't sweating. This will have owed something to the fact that she wasn't wearing enough clothes, as Langdon would have said, to swab a shotgun. In white hot pants, and a halter the color of pomegranates that made her breasts twin fertility symbols, Lucille was Dressed for Success. "Did you bring these *huge* shrimp?" I asked her brightly.

"Oh, never on my salary, Mrs. Brough. I brought the aspic; it's my own recipe. That's mayonnaise, in the little green bowl; I made that too. Which dish is yours, Mrs. Brough? I know it'll be good; with all your experience, everything you cook would have to be good."

I pointed to the culmination of my awesome decades of experience, and helped myself to a civil serving of Lucille's aspic. The mayonnaise, I risked foregoing, not because I don't need to regain some of the pounds I've lost, but because in marked contrast to my daughter, I am not one who greases everything she eats. I do not butter my peas or put whipped cream on my gingerbread, and I did not put Lucille's mayonnaise on Lucille's aspic.

Ahead of us, Grove had swiveled. "You made that?" he asked Lucille, reaching back in front of two people for a square of trembling red mold, which he then plastered with the spoon in the little green bowl. I knew this was for my benefit. Grove doesn't like any gelatin salad. Mayonnaise, he has entreated me to leave off the table until there is a little more belt threading through his buckle. Later I saw his discarded plate, a puddle of untouched aspic filling one compartment, the mayonnaise spreading over it like skywriting at sunset.

"Let me give you some aspic, honey," Lucille cooed at Joanna.

"Which do you like better, bunnies, or kitty-cats? You have your own kitty-cats at home, don't you, doll?" Lovingly Lucille drew a large mayonnaise cat-face on Joanna's aspic.

"You know what? I climbed that tree."

"Did you?" Lucille marveled in that special upper register some women require for children and the retarded. "That high tree?

"It's so wonderful to see her having a good time, poor little thing," Lucille confided to me over Joanna's head, children being notoriously unable to hear anything spoken in a normal tone of voice.

I carried Joanna's and my plates over beside Fran and her Stroh's, but Joanna soon deserted us, having licked the *itty-bitty kitty* off her aspic and gone to have Lucille succeed him with a *runny bunny.*

"So he said, 'Vengeance is mine, saith the Lord,'" Fran related cheerfully. She was telling me about her priest's visit to her in the hospital, after Max slugged her. Looking at Joanna's and my plates had reminded her of the five weeks she'd spent with her jaws wired, since when apparently she can't look at melting gelatin without laughing. "I had a notepad for writing anything I absolutely had to tell anybody," she said. "*God will smite him,* I wrote, *but I can't wait.*"

I was glad when I saw Amelia and Amy Herndon heading our way. Amy's presence, I thought, would lure Joanna back.

Joanna did return, bringing Lucille with her.

Joanna joined Amy on the grass and Lucille sat in the last empty chair beside Fran and Amelia and me, but not so long as she would have liked. "Now make a horse," Joanna commanded, thrusting her plate of still untasted but again clean-licked aspic perilously close to Lucille's lap.

Lucille glanced at me.

I smiled. "Oliver Twist wants more."

The sandals on Lucille's shell-pink feet had three-inch heels and she had been teetering on them for an hour. "Oh," she stalled — "have you seen *Oliver!* Mrs. Brough? Wasn't it fantastic?"

"Well," I trotted out, "'I haven't see the video, but I read the book.'"

"Please will you," Joanna jiggled her plate of aspic up and down over Lucille's white hot pants, "draw me a horse, please?"

"Honestly," Lucille turned to Amelia, "Mrs. Brough is so intellectual, she's read everything."

But Joanna was as merciless as Lucille herself.

I hoped it wouldn't occur to Lucille just to bring the mayonnaise bowl back with her.

What did we think, Amelia wanted to know, of the senator's patting his wife's pregnant forefront for the TV cameras last night?

Fran belched.

"I think it shows a healthy attitude," I answered reflexively. Actually I think it's the usual political couple on the make, but I don't want to be accused of sour grapes. "I'd love to be as young and pretty and pregnant as our senator's lady." And that was reflexive too, because as things stood, I was jolly glad I wasn't pregnant.

"I didn't know you had a problem," said Amelia. "You seem like the last one who ought to. I mean, I admire the way you've decided to realize yourself just through motherhood, and you and Grove have such a beautiful relationship." Lucille and Joanna were closing in. Lucille was the last person to whom I wanted my personal deficiencies exposed—assuming Grove hadn't told her already. "Have you ever considered adoption?" Amelia asked.

Lucille, arriving in good time to hear the question, resettled her voluptuous bottom in the chair beside mine, assumed an expression of heavy sympathy, and focused her long-lashed eyes unwaveringly on me.

Fran belched again. "Time I got some food," she said, and stood up. "That plate looks like it could use a refill," she observed of mine, and taking me firmly by the arm, marched me away. You see why I love Fran.

By the time Joanna was three, I more or less conceded to myself (never to Jake) that if Grove was to have any more babies, they would not be mine. I wanted more children almost as much as I believed he did. I tentatively decided that once Joanna was in school, we should approach an agency. Now I didn't know what he thought anymore, but being robbed of Lang had changed my own attitude entirely. The putative adoptee became not a simple addition, but a recompense, and there could be no recompense; a substitute where there could be none. *Unique human being* is one of Amelia's phrases. "If everybody's unique, what's special about it?" I have always forborne to tease her, and just as well. *If you lose something, replace it with something better*—but if what you've lost is perfection, infinity?

We are not in a position to be pleased, Grove had cautioned me the very first day—frightened, outraged, but still judicious. (Infatuated is apparently something else.) Before I began turning away from my friends, or turning on them, I reflected, I should arrive at what it is I want to hear them say. I should formulate what I would say to someone in like circumstances.

All I wanted to hear was: *Upon investigation we find that you have been a good mother. Your child was not taken through any fault of yours. He is in excellent health and we are sending him back in the morning.* What I could say to any other victim I could not imagine. No, it is not tolerable. No, it does not get better.

⤳47⤳ {Ruth

Night settled over the farm like a steaming compress on an infected wound. So as not to have to go to bed when Grove did, I watched the news.

Alarmed citizens of Osprey Point, Massachusetts, are finding that they could more easily rid their town of seagulls than of a guru and his dupes. Seconds before the camera narrowed from the phalanx of smug robots to a spokesman for their involuntary hosts, I saw Lang. Closing my eyes and mentally re-running the scene showed me, yes, the guileless face of an eight-year-old, but on the body of a youth of seventeen. I loosened my clammy grip on my chair arms and opened my eyes.

In Oklahoma, cattle sucked mud. In Dallas a woman walked up to an ice truck and without a word to the driver, lay down on the cargo. I lay down beside my unmoving husband and pondered, as painfully as if my decision would determine Lang's fate, whether I would rather our son had been put out of some furtive car to stumble for help on some scorched southwestern road, or had been brain-sucked passive by slave-seeking cultists.

As soon after Lang was born as I could walk, I hobbled to the hospital nursery to see whether I could pick him out. For seven months I had worried that having our baby in a hospital was going to lay us open to catastrophic error. Could we be sure the baby we took home was ours?

I hadn't seen Lang since the two of us left the delivery room, separately, both groggy. To my exultant relief, I didn't have to ask any nurse anything; I recognized him instantly. He looked nothing like any of the others.

At nine he still will look like none of the others, but will he look like himself? *Would* I pick him out of a crowd on TV? Sometimes last winter I would sit absorbed in imagining different family features superimposed on his face until, looking up from his trough to grunt for more, he would misinterpret my gaze and wipe his chin.

As a child I wanted meals to end, so that I might escape my parents' critical attention. As a parent, I used to find supper the best part of the day. The family was all together, under at least some control, safe.

Since this April, of course, there is no best part of the day, no *safe*.

I remember that back when Lang was crowding my bladder, I observed wearily to my mother how glad I would be when this child was born and I could sleep through the night in peace again. I misread her answer, "Honey, you have had your last full night's peaceful sleep." I thought she meant four o'clock feedings, but she knew how soon I would learn that no mother is ever more than half asleep. I can't prove that Joanna has never moaned in her dreams without waking me, but the morning after the Snyders' potluck, I was up before Tad reached my door. "Joanna's whaled up Jonah all over the floor," he said. Then he lurched back to bed and was snoring long before I had her in a clean nightgown.

Grove never wakened.

I knew that Joanna had eaten too much. She came home too grumpy for simple fatigue; we all did. Grove was somber, presumably thinking about Lang, possibly not. I was brooding about

Lucille's expression when Amelia blathered about my "problem." And Tad, naturally, hadn't wanted to leave before the fireworks.

Expecting Grove to skip grooming the yearlings because of the potluck, Tad had gone to the barn right after lunch and curried Uncle till you could have mistaken that rawboned creature for the summer sale colt. (Ten, Tad affects to scorn. Uncle is his favorite of all the animals on the place, including humans.) When Grove got home from his rounds, however, he declined to omit a single swipe from Ten's toilette or a single circling of the barn from his exercise, and much worse, for Tad, he declined to pretend that June's afternoon sun is temperate, so that we could put Ten and Uncle out for the afternoon just this once. They remained in their stalls as usual while we were at Snyders', and that meant we had to come home long before anyone else, because shank-leading after dark is hazardous.

Truth is, neither Grove nor I wants to leave the phone, let alone go smile at people—joyfully shrieking children least of all. Now poor Joanna was feeling anything but joyful, but she did assure me that she felt much better, which I could well imagine, and we both went back to bed.

I was dreaming that Lucille had fatally poisoned Joanna so that Grove would feel free to divorce me ("*I* could give you a son," she was telling him), when slowly, like blood seeping through a bandage, the realization seeped into my nightmare that the gagging I heard was actual.

This time the carpet escaped; Joanna was hunching miserably on the toilet, the victim of simultaneous urges. She was ashamed and embarrassed and her insides hurt and giving her a hot water bottle did not, she whined, make them feel any better. Looking at her watery eyes and flushed cheeks, I believed her and took her temperature. "What you need is a little cold cider," I told her. With Joanna, I didn't call Jake for anything under 102°.

The clouds beyond the barn were a bloody flux; the mist was rising in discrete layers, the kind of striated fog in which a motorist rushing to his work strikes a child walking along the roadside and drives on, supposing he has killed a dog. The alarm clock would ring within the hour. If I went back to bed I would only wake

Grove, not get back to sleep myself. I sat down on the floor beside Joanna's cot, to reassure her that I wasn't disgusted with her as she touchingly feared, and to hand her cold cider on call.

I can't sit that way fifteen minutes without going numb in one leg or the other, but no problem: we were up again in ten.

Who, if Lang were sick, would hold cold cider for him?

Joanna was really sick. A little cold draft blew inside my rib cage. I began to calculate, to read my wristwatch every several minutes, to feel as if I were listening to her breathe with more than my ears —my elbows, the hairs on my arms. Shortly after six I heard Grove running water for his coffee. Another outburst from Joanna brought him down the hall. I had spread a beach towel on the hard bathroom floor, its colors a sky of fireworks around the moon-white toilet. Silently Grove stood watching us, kneeling together on our towel. With nothing left to bring up, Joanna went on retching. "This is more than too much fudge cake," I said. "Jake leaves home for hospital rounds at seven: I'm going to call him at twenty of."

"If you think you should call him, call him now."

"That's all right, Ruth," Caroline Averoyne said aggrievedly. "You're not the first. The Crocker boy drank antifreeze an hour ago. It eternally mystifies me, the things some parents leave around. Is Joanna sick?"

Grove's face had the pinched look it gets when a foal won't nurse. "You go on and feed," I told him. "Jake will call as soon as he gets out of emergency. Wait till Tad comes out of there, will you, and tell him he can use either the barn toilet or ours today, but this one's to be kept for Joanna."

I wanted to sit by the telephone, but Joanna began to have chills. Her head hurt, she wept. In her eyes I could read her bafflement that I didn't correct these things. Lang had been gone more than six weeks yet she still expected me to be omnipotent.

When she could lie still, I sat again beside her cot and held her damp hand and considered how she and I compared. Despite all my doctor could do, I had been helplessly empty five years, and still I was desperate for that same doctor's call because I counted on him to walk into my house and make my child well.

When Joanna and Lang were babies, Grove and I congratulated

our priceless luck in having our children now, when there's a shot for everything. No longer does typhoid or scarlet or a dozen other fevers sweep out a town's children like the vengeance of Moses as happened in our great-grandparents' day. No longer are proper Charleston children forbidden to swim at Sullivan's Island all summer for fear of polio. Automobiles were going to be the major threat, I thought, and for Lang, the army.

This was before Albert Blount admitted to us that the latest federal study's figure for non-family-abducted missing children in the United States is 3900. ("Whatever he tells you," Grove tried to console me, "you can be sure it's worse than the truth. That's the kind of number cops and social workers and politicians all love to inflate, so the taxpayers will kick in." Even if I believed Grove, it wouldn't help. Even if only one child were missing, so long as that child is Lang, the number is infinity.)

A cold or two were the worst upsets Joanna's health had ever suffered. I had never seen the color sink from her lips before, nor felt her hand in mine lie limp. Fear was a little cold blind worm in my gut. I held my watch to my ear. Its ticking belied its reading, scarcely advanced from what it had registered when the hospital had promised that Jake would call.

Another watershed, I thought, will drown me. I can not lose this child, I told myself calmly. I leaned back with my head against her bed as my nose began to run. *I cannot lose this child.* My breath began to quicken, my body to rock back and forth. I hadn't made a sound, but I suddenly realized that I was close to screaming and I wasn't at all sure that I could stop. The next thing I knew I was stuffing Joanna's bathrobe into my mouth and lying face down on her floor beating her carpet with both fists and my forehead.

When I heard the front door opening, I ran to the bathroom and locked the door, turned on both faucets and the shower full strength and crouched in the furthest corner, sobbing and gagging.

As soon as I could, I rinsed my face.

Luckily Tad had stayed behind to feed the outfielders, and I did not think Grove's mind was registering anything he heard or saw except Joanna. As I appeared, he rounded on me. *"Where the hell is Jake?"*

The telephone rang.

Grove was the nearer to it. "I can't get there before tomorrow," I heard him say, so it wasn't Jake. "I'll send you Dr. Herndon."

I wanted to tell him not to call Hank Herndon on that phone, not to tie up our line, to go use his car phone.

"One of David Trimble's summer sale fillies ran into her gate last night," he told Hank, "and she's got a big swelling on her chest. It'll have to be drained.... Some bastard threw a string of fire-crackers at her.... Nah, she'll be flat as you by September."

I hustled Joanna into the bathroom just in time.

When we came out, Grove counted her pulse. "Come on, we'll take her there," he said. I reached for her coat and the telephone rang again.

After Jake hung up I realized I hadn't thought of Lang at either ring. "Botulism," Jake said, "wouldn't have shown up for a couple of days." Then he asked if I'd called Lorena. Which I ought to have done immediately.

"I'll be there in ten minutes," Jake said.

Lorena and Margot and I called every family on Lorena's guest list, but Joanna was the only one with a temperature of 102.6° and cheeks that had lost their convexity with their color, eyes that no longer looked as if they expected anything from any of us.

Two years ago, Paula Vaughn's six-week-old died of her whooping cough booster-shot. Last summer, Breck Smith's cousin was taken to a hospital in Maryland in a coma, and we learned about Reye's Syndrome. Both those children were much younger than Joanna, with much less reserve strength. I repeated this to myself like prayer as we waited for Jake.

"Let's do some blood work," Jake said. "It looks to me like salmonella. I'd have expected more than one case, but two people can eat the same contaminated food, and one will be violently sick and the other not at all." He looked at Grove's gray face. "It's not as serious in children as in foals. If it's salmonella, she'll be jumping rope next week."

"Meanwhile," he turned to me: "what I gave her should help the

225

vomiting, but I don't really want to attack the diarrhea full force; I *want* her to get the toxin out of herself. So keep on fighting the dehydration. Cider's fine. You're doing the right thing." Jake is reassuring me, I thought, distrusting him. "But don't wait for her to ask for it. She should drink a little every ten minutes. I'll call you as soon as I get a lab report."

Grove walked Jake to his car, and I stood at the window watching them talk and imagining the things Jake couldn't bring himself to tell me. Grove returned and denied them all.

Tad came back from filling the creep feeder, collected his radio, and retreated to the barn.

The sun climbed. The thermostat clicked and the air conditioner gasped, at first frequently, then ceaselessly. Now when Joanna needed to go to the bathroom, one of us had to carry her. It was as if our robust child had been nothing but a thin layer of paint on a balloon and that balloon had been infinitesimally pricked, and there had never been anything but air, an illusory child, now leaking away before our eyes. Grove laid her back on her bed and we sat down on the floor beside it and waited. In my mind I saw Joanna in an oxygen tent; then the tent was taken away. In my mind Jake came to us with what we knew, as he got out of his car, were the lab results. "From them that have not," he said, giving Grove the paper and turning his face aside. *Shall be taken even that which they have.*

Beside me on Joanna's floor, Grove rested his head in his hands, his elbows on his knees. When I leaned toward him enough for our shoulders to touch, he reached over and gripped my hand, and we sat there wordlessly.

Around 10:30 I remembered that Tad had had no breakfast, and Grove took him two peanut butter sandwiches and a carton of milk.

Around eleven Joanna went to sleep and didn't waken even when the telephone rang. "Salmonellosis," Jake said. "I was virtually certain it was. For somebody else, I would have held off on the blood, but you two don't need any extra questions on your minds. Get out that jump rope."

I hung up the bedroom phone in tears; if Grove hadn't been

listening on the kitchen extension, he would have thought Jake's news was fatal.

I had never dressed, and he hadn't shaved. As he came through the door I turned to embrace him and we tumbled onto our bed. We clung and thrashed as if we were drowning, and then I was floating like a water lily on a Chinese lagoon. "I do love you, Ruth," he said.

Little else has been said. After ten years of marriage, intimacy can sometimes take the place of explanation. I don't consider it superior to explanation, but it beats confession all hollow. Which is one way of saying that carnal intercourse is often a substitute for unarticulated questions and unformulated (or unforgivable) answers. In the two weeks that have passed since that morning, we have never discussed Lucille.

"There is no honest country," I remember Peter von Strehlenau insisting. I wonder if that could equally well be said of marriage. Who would have suspected Grove's and mine? But I am certain that Grove wanted to cleave him unto Lucille for awhile and that she was more than willing. I'm not certain that he did.

I tell myself that Grove's feelings were my fault, as Lorena gently tried to suggest, because that would give me some hope of control over my life. Grove needed comforting and his wife was withdrawn, edgy, bad-tempered, frantic. If this is the explanation for Lucille, then my future is in my own hands — if I am loving, Grove will be true.

Then I remember that laugh on the telephone the night the sirens howled past on the way to Thackers'. I remember the elaborate explanation, next day, of why Grove couldn't come home to lunch, though I never said I expected him. Lang was safe, that night, that morning; I was myself. So. Will Grove ever put us in this kind of stew again? I have to realize that he might.

Albert radios his dispatcher at the Dry Ridge State Police Post, who tells him that there is no record of a Kentucky driver's license to anyone with any name enough like "Clint Penn" for the state computer to have thought of it.

Albert resists asking the dispatcher to look again. He checks both Scott and Bourbon counties for a possible record of a traffic violation by any variation of the name Clint Penn that their computers can come up with. There is none, not so much as a parking ticket.

At the Bourbon County Clerk's office, a deputy clerk punches every variation of Clint Penn that Albert can suggest into her computer. No vehicle, the clerk tells Albert, has been registered in the state of Kentucky to any of the submitted names in at least the last twenty years.

Albert realizes that he has a growing pain at the base of his skull. Clint Penn could come from anywhere. He wouldn't necessarily have a Kentucky driver's license, if he's lived in Kentucky less than a year, or if he's driving with an expired license. He could be driving a father's or a brother's or a cousin's or anybody's car. There are pages of Kentucky vehicles registered to Penns in the state of Kentucky.

Some niggling human error as little as a dropped period after an initial could have wiped Clint's record out of the computer.

Or, Clint Penn is not this man's name at all.

Albert's neck muscles have gone rigid: he rubs them once or twice. Beside his composite likeness of Clint he types:

Possible suspect in kidnaping case
Clint Penn: May be an alias
     Description
Age: Approx. 24, date of birth unknown
Height: Approx. 5 feet 7 inches
Weight: Approx. 135 lbs
Eyes: Gray

Hair: Sandy brown; curly
Race: Caucasian
Identifying marks: Tattoo on right forearm: dragon gripping skull
Occupation: Farm laborer; believed to be a veteran
Subject has been known to operate this type of vehicle: Blue 1980 Chevrolet 4-door possible Kentucky Scott County registration number, numerals unknown. Last known location: Bourbon County. Direction of travel unknown.
If located, please notify the undersigned COLLECT by telephone or fax.

After Albert has made as many photocopies of this page as he thinks he'll need, including a stack for the Broughs, he turns to the fax machine.

Even on the telephone, once Albert has spoken a sentence or two, he detects, or thinks he detects — is always braced to detect — a wary stiffness in the people he has called. There is something about the very meticulousness of his speech, his scrupulous r's, the way each gerund tings like a dime in a parking meter. "You some citify nigger!" his brother Cyrus, the drummer, tells him. Albert returns his brother's grin because both are conscious that it's the brother's speech that is studied. Mary Blount, who has been teaching English at Paris High School ever since integration and had been teaching it at Western for three years before that, did not tolerate what she called "Befo' de wo'" talk from her children. Her younger son, a pragmatist, chooses how he will speak depending on his mood and audience. Albert is equally adept at slipping into the cadences of a brother, but that is not the patois he has needed most often on this case. He *can't* make himself sound like a good ol' boy. The fax machine is the most relaxing tool he uses.

Without uttering a consonant, Albert faxes Clint's description above his own request to the radio room of the Dry Ridge State Police post, whence it will be forwarded via computer nationwide to every agency connected to the National Crime Information Center.

From Bangor to Los Angeles, police post the Thackers' description of Clint Penn.

A few flyers, Albert faxes individually — to several Kentucky racetrack security offices, and to the sheriff's department of any county within a day's drive of the Bluegrass that he knows or suspects is not connected to NCIC. He personally posts a flyer at the police and sheriff's departments in Bourbon and Scott counties, and at the Paris and Georgetown post offices. By this time it is too late to get to Frankfort before the Department of Vehicle Regulation closes for the day. Given his headache, he is almost glad that that will have to wait for morning.

The Wolfe County sheriff's department studies Albert's flyer carefully, and posts it on the wall.

⤳49⤶ {Clint

When Flynt Ward quit Johnson Controls and left Scott County, he left an unpaid room bill and a girl who was beginning to act like she might be pregnant, or fixing to claim she was. Driving toward Paris, Flynt heard the same tobacco warehouse commercial three times. Penn Brothers, it said, was the largest warehouse in the world. Penn seemed like as good a name as any to Flynt. *Clint Penn.*

When he left Zad Thacker and applied at Williams Machine Shop, the dumb bastards wanted references. He did not need that Bourbon County asshole bad-mouthing him, and he had a clean record at Johnson Controls; nobody fired him, he quit. He told the dumb bastards that his name was Flynt Ward and that he had last worked for Johnson Controls, Inc. He gave the social security number he'd had ever since he went in the army. Zad had never asked for it. Zad always paid in cash, and that suited Clint Penn.

What had Flynt been doing since he left Johnson Controls, the dumb bastards wanted to know. Flynt told them he had gone home for a spell.

The wild cherries are ripening, their flesh as soft as darkness around their subtly poisonous hearts. Lang has told Clint that he wants to go home now, in time for his birthday. When Clint does not wish to hear something, he pretends to be drunk or he orders Lang to weed the garden and goes hunting without Lang or he threatens to hit Lang if Lang doesn't stop his mouth, sometimes all three. Lang can hear his father saying, "If you wanted presents on your birthday, you should have come home on your birthday. Now you'll just have to wait till Christmas."

Lang wonders what Clint is going to give him. Clint has plenty of money from selling whiskey, and before that runs out, he'll be digging ginseng. For a little ginseng root you wouldn't bother scraping if it was a carrot, Clint can get twenty dollars, Clint says, and he has a whole patch nobody outside his family, except Lang, has ever seen. Clint's daddy planted the first seeds for this patch when Clint was Lang's age. He scattered them on the shady side of a deep gully under some beech trees. He waited two years to see if any meant to come up. He waited four more before he dug the first root. Nobody has ever dug a plant from this patch before it had six years' growth to it and its berries were blazing ripe, Clint says. "That's the way to make a patch pay." His daddy's special narrow-bladed hoe hangs on a peg across from Clint's rifle just waiting for this summer's berries to flush. August is when ginseng ripens.

Anybody who would dig sang before it gets its growth and before it ripens is a fool or a son-of-a-bitch, Clint says, but the hills are full of such. Many's the man has gone out of a morning and found every plant in a patch he'd been watching gone, not just this year's but next year's and the next's. The only lies Clint ever heard his mother tell, Clint says, were when somebody asked her where his daddy dug sang.

If anybody was to come poking around his sang, Clint says, Clint would shoot him.

The night I heard the sirens on Clay Pike, I had hurried dishwashing lest Grove, tired as he was, think he ought to look in again on Lagoon before I went over. When I went for my coat, he was asleep in the bedroom's reclining chair.

The moon reduced the children's night light to a glow worm. Lang, on the top bunk, had one arm thrown over his eyes to shield them from the flooding moonlight that Joanna, in the bottom, had turned to face. I stood in their doorway, victim of a happiness so fierce it scalded my eyes. I had everything I wanted. I knew that all too well. I'd lived for years in perpetual astonishment and underlying dread, dread lest God call me April Fool in a whisper of thunder and snatch one of these three from me.

Any impartial outsider would counsel me as Lorena did, to make allowances for Grove because he is especially vulnerable right now, blah blah. "When a man thinks he falls short," Fran claims, "he imagines his wife thinks he does too, and that makes him hate her. Max thought I despised him for his problem, and I didn't even know he had it. Grove's problem is Lang. He feels helpless. He may not know he believes you despise him, but that's what he dreads."

At the time Fran said this, I went right on thinking about Lucille.

Peter's work, Peter von Strehlenau said to Eva and me, trains him to forget justice, and just do the best he can for his country. We were talking about the deliberate bombing of population centers in World War II, about certain virulently anti-Semitic Polish priests who were martyred at Dachau, about baby-smashing Cherokees setting out on the infamous Trail of Tears. "The world has been wicked so long, there is no untangling all the wickedness, no getting back to the fair status, no finding an innocent nation. Both sides of every war have been vicious, and this will be always so. When a war is over, the loser claims moral superiority. 'Unfair' is the complaint of the weak."

If Peter were right, what did that make me? I was outraged, furious with Lucille for going after my husband because I turned my back to look for my lost child. Had not, in other words, played fair.

Was I merely weak? Hadn't I a right to expect better of Grove?

I am a grown woman; I know that no perfect reading of another human being exists, that we construct everyone we know from insufficient material, like scholars constructing the mastodon from the toe, the Hercules from the foot, the pot from three little shards. Can a woman ever know much more of her husband than about a foot's worth? The Grove I lived with for ten years was a Hercules of my own construction. I shouldn't blame him, should I, if I got some parts wrong?

Our wedding anniversary week before last was not joyous. It falls, as I've mentioned, on Lang's birthday. Nine Junes ago, we took that coincidence for a good omen. Not every spectacular eastern star is an earnest of good, as Mary, not to mention Bethlehem's innocents, learned.

My heart stabbed me when I saw the very small box beside my breakfast plate. How could I ever wear anything Grove gave me this particular summer?

Sitting in the velvet-lined box were two tussling hand-carved ivory cubs, and a card that said, "Bear and Forbear—Love, Grove."

⊰52⊱ {Albert

The heat is already oppressive by eight in the morning, and sleep has not completely banished Albert's headache. Before he sets out for Frankfort, he telephones the Thackers. D.B. agrees to come to Paris and look at mug shots, but Albert must come and get him since his car is at the shop.

None of the pictures Albert and D.B. are shown looks like Clint to D.B.

Taking D.B. home, Albert tries probing him for any useful detail he might remember about Clint, but D.B. only repeats what Albert learned from his first Thacker interviews. Stolen tack is what stands out.

Leaving the Thacker farm, Albert bypasses the turn to Frankfort

233

and drives on into Lexington. Considering Zad's belief that Clint was fencing Zad's halters in Lexington, Albert has decided to give his Clint flyer to the Lexington Metropolitan Police Department pawnshop detail. These four detectives daily inspect the purchasing records of every pawnshop in the city and will be able to tell him within two days whether any Lexington pawnshop admits to ever having done business of any kind with Clint Penn, or with anyone who looks like Albert's attempted portrait of Clint Penn.

It's about a thirty-mile drive from Lexington to Frankfort. Albert presents himself at Kentucky's Department of Vehicle Regulation and requests from the current Scott County registrations a list of blue four-door 1980 Chevrolets. The computer turns up twelve names and addresses. None of these names is anything like Clint Penn.

Flyer in hand, Albert begins to visit the twelve addresses.

It's slow going. About half are empty during the work day and must be revisited in the evening. "Do you know Clint Penn?" Albert asks at each address. "Do you know anyone who looks like this?" Some look at his flyer reluctantly and answer grudgingly; some are eager. None knows Clint Penn, or anyone who looks like Albert's composite likeness of him. Albert says thank you in his even voice and goes doggedly on to the next address.

~❧53☙~

{Clint

Clint doesn't admit to himself that he's come to count on the boy's company. He wishes he'd never laid eyes on him.

Clint's last Friday in Lexington he loaded his trunk. Saturday was a half workday for him, and he was planning a weekend trip to Wolfe County. Friday night, a friend from his days at Johnson Controls came by. The friend's name was Odis Reavely, and he was wearing a new suit.

Clint is still wearing army pants. He has pointed out to Lang that if he had went to prison, they would have give him a suit when he got out, but since all he done was serve his country, they given him nothing.

The first couple of years after Clint got back from the army, he made enough to get by setting tobacco May and June on a big horse farm down near Georgetown. After his sister Mae showed up with her eight-year-old, he felt even less like taking a steady job.

As a boy, Clint got more than enough of being youngest in his family. Even Mae gave him orders in those days. He enjoyed teaching Eddie to mind him, as he had been obliged to mind his brothers; to run his errands, as he had run theirs; to cuss like a man. Sometime in midsummer, after Clint had begun teaching Eddie to catch and clean fish, Eddie had moved up off the floor beside his mother's bed into the iron bed beside Clint. It was after this that Clint learned that Ronnie Minton had done more than batter his little boy. Clint had wanted to go looking for Ronnie with a gun, but had put it off till he could get one of his brothers to go with him. He had been on a rare trip to the store the day Ronnie showed up and marched Mae and Eddie at gunpoint down the hill to Ronnie's car. Clint and Mae's mother had been afraid to fire Clint's rifle after Ronnie for fear of hitting Mae or Eddie.

Ronnie had driven his wife and child clear to Swango Fork before he shot them. Clint regrets that Ronnie then shot himself. Clint would have liked to do it.

That August his mother had a fever the coldest spring water would not assuage and pain in her belly that made her cry out like a woman in childbed. Before Clint could get her out of the house, the faith healer came.

Hours later Clint's mother wept as Clint drove the faith healer out of the cabin, out of the clearing. Clint carried his mother down the hill toward his parked car. Halfway down her pain suddenly ended and she declared that prayer had cured her, but Clint took her to the doctor and the doctor sent her to the hospital to be cut open and there she died before morning.

The hospital doctor was an English nigger from Bombay. "It was her appendix," this nigger told Clint. "Why didn't you bring her in sooner?"

Then Clint didn't want to stay in the cabin alone, and took a job making Toyota parts at the Johnson Controls plant near Georgetown. That's where he, Flynt Ward, met Odis. Now Odis pretends that working at Johnson Controls is all right, but Clint is sure he minds the noise and confinement and bossing almost as much as Clint hated it. When rumors of layoffs rustled through the plant, Clint quit. Nobody was going to run him off like a dog, he told Odis. Clint became Zad's hand for $4.35 an hour.

Clint seriously considered killing Zad the day Zad fired him in front of Milly, but when Williams Machine Shop told him what they paid, he saw that Zad had done him a favor. He felt sorry for Odis, who was probably living somewhere on unemployment. Then Odis came to see him, in his new suit.

Clint took Odis out and showed him what was in the Chevy trunk, and with a lordly gesture, extracted a bottle just for the two of them.

Next morning, Saturday, Clint was half an hour late punching in. By eleven he'd broken three tools and a machine, told his boss what he could do with the parts, and been fired. Odis, who'd passed out on Clint's floor, went home when Clint's landlady came to remind Clint that there were to be no drinking parties, which she had clearly.... If she had to speak to him again, he would have to. All this she told Clint when he got home.

Clint hadn't planned to tell Odis he'd been fired. He'd been fed up with making bolts anyway, but at least, unlike horse farm work, the job had left him enough time on weekends to run his other business. Clint has known his customers all his life, but he doesn't kid himself about their loyalty. Neglect them and somebody else would move in on him. Another seven-day-a-week pitchfork job, therefore, was out.

He did not look forward to asking some bastard for work.

He could live well enough in his cabin just on what his business and the mountain could provide, except for the loneliness. He'd had a taste of that after his mother's death. Town is better, even at the price of a job. But he was in no shape that Saturday morning to start looking for one. Monday, he would start.

Wednesday morning Clint counted the empty bottles in his room. He counted them again, then went out to the Chevy for another pint. Sunday night, he remembered, he'd gone for a drive. Tuesday he'd slept. Monday he didn't remember. He drank slowly. Perhaps not Sunday either; perhaps some of his seeming Sunday memories were only part of Tuesday's dreams. The pint still sloshed a little when he decided what he would do; he stuffed it in his pocket. Leaving the empty bottles for his landlady, he put everything he owned into his car and drove to the nearest Hardee's.

Coffee and the cold wind through the car window sluicing his face made him feel some better except that, undreamlike, his Sunday nightmare kept getting clearer, and by the time he came to the last curve before Thacker's, he'd sweated through his shirt. The car in the Thackers' driveway jolted his lungs.

He'd meant to go by just slowly enough to glance at Zad's shed, but now he eased his foot off the accelerator. He wasn't close enough to read the little round Farm Bureau Insurance sticker on the intruder's dash, but he knew whose salt-pork face he would see if the spindly figure in its dry-cleaned suit should turn away from Milly and glance his way. Zad's straw-storage shed was ashes, all right.

Milly was pinning skivvies on the line and laughing up at that four-eyed shit-head, her breasts lifting and subsiding with her arms as she reached for the line, the basket, the line—a little trick she did on purpose. Clint imagined backhanding her. Where was her mother, who never let *him* hang around Milly two minutes? Looking out the kitchen window drooling down her warty chin, he bet; anybody that worked in a tie seemed like Jesus come back, to that pitiful family. Clint accelerated so hard he had to brake mid-curve to avoid a sycamore. When the empty beer cans rolled over and bumped his shoe, he kicked them back so hard he dented them.

By this time he was in sight of the horse vet's prissy little show-off farm.

Clint had been in the army just seven months when his battalion found themselves called on to capture the headquarters of the Panama Defense Forces. Clint had sweat blood and dodged bullets, but a man didn't get rich serving his country. *Grove Brough had set in them air-conditioned classrooms, learned how to make hisself a millionaire sticking his arm up horses' asses, got hisself a wife too good to give a working man a ride. In Wolfe County people died because wouldn't no doctor live up in the hills, where down in the Bluegrass they fought one another for the chance to treat a bunch of goddamned shitting animals that all they done was to chase their goddamned tails in a goddamned circle.* Clint decelerated so as to empty his pint and throw the bottle out the window. Then he saw the boy.

His first thought was that if ever he had known a sissy that never would be worth a damn if somebody didn't take him away from his mother, it was that stuck-up bitch's stuck-up boy. Eddie was worth ten of him, but the little shit-head had always had everything, where Eddie never had nothing. Clint can't remember which thought came to him first, that one Bluegrass-ass anyway ought to get a little taste of how mountain people had to live, or that he would be doing the boy a favor, jerking him loose from his bitch-mama's skirts — his daddy's skirts, if it came to that. And then: *what wouldn't they pay to get him back....*

That would take care of the damn job hunting! Vivid as lightning the picture had flashed through his mind of himself driving up to Thackers' in his shining black Lincoln Continental. One blast on his horn would bring Milly running out, all smiles. He, laughing in her face, backing the car out of the driveway and gone. Milly in the yard, her fat mouth hanging open.

Then he'd revised the scene. He would pull up beside Milly and she would leap into the Lincoln; Zad would be the one left standing there looking stupid, Zad and that pukey paper peddler in his dry-cleaned suit.

That his ransom note could be ignored never crossed his mind. Nor had it immediately occurred to him that because Lang and Lang's parents know his face, he could never show it in Kentucky again once Lang went free. What to do now he has no idea.

Stuck with the boy, Clint considers that he has done well by him. He has taught Lang to shoot, to take an animal out of a trap without blubbering, to get through a day without working his yap like a woman. He has treated Lang like a little brother, shared everything, even — Lang's one shirt and pants having become filthy rags — Eddie's clothes.

He has taught Lang things he had been planning to teach Eddie.

Clint despises himself for having served under a black in the army.

Claiming that he fragged the son-of-a-bitch soothes him a little, and if he repeats it often enough, he may come to believe it and feel better. Burning a barn with animals locked inside is something he believes only a lunatic would do. Like the non-venomous "puff adder," which when challenged, hisses and spreads its neck to look as if it did have poison sacs, Clint learned young that an aggressive bluff usually clears the path, and his had certainly worked on Lang. Clint's father was at LaGrange when he should have been pointing out to Clint that the puff adder's second commonest reward for bluffing is a swift death.

Clint knows that he is in trouble well enough. In fact, he feels more imperiled than he felt his worst day in Panama. Increasingly, he stays in an alcoholic stupor, but this morning he has drunk nothing. The gash on the boy's foot is infected. What kind of country boy nine years old would use his foot to steady something he was chopping on? Play farmers, that's all in the world horse people are. "Pour a *little* kerosene on it," he'd told the boy plainly. So the dumb little bastard takes and douses the whole foot, and the skin blisters.

Clint personally mixed lard with soot and spread it on the wound thick as mortar, and the bleeding stopped right quick; it wasn't a bad cut. Clint has sure seen worse. What he sees now is that he ought to have some of that yellow salve. If he could trust the boy, he would take him along to the drugstore, get the gunk on him twice as fast. Clint had a cousin who died of blood poisoning. If he could trust Lang never to tell on him, he would take him down to Mountain Parkway before dark.

What Clint wants is not to walk down the brush-choked gnat-thick hillside to his car, but to take a bottle and sit with his back against the walls of the darkest corner in the cabin.

Once Lang goes home—if Lang goes home—Clint will be a hunted man. He will have to leave these hills, change his name again, go he does not know where. He has been trying to remember what he can of a conversation that came up one day at Johnson Controls about South Africa. That was a place, somebody claimed, for a white man who could shoot. He could fill his tank, put Lang out in front of a hospital or YMCA, and take off. Or, give himself

more time, just leave Lang here, be out of the country before anybody started looking for Clint Penn. The kid wouldn't starve. Clint
has taught him how to catch all the catfish a boy could eat. This
drought won't last forever.

Other times Clint knows that whatever he does with Lang, he
can never let him go. He has become Lang's prisoner. They are
manacled together until one of them dies.

～⚡54⚡～

{Ruth

I knew better than to ask Jake for something to make me sleep, but
I thought he might give me something for a headache that sleep
wasn't relieving, nor bourbon neither. In a way, he did give me
something. He listened to me.

I cannot talk to my mother or Grove's about Lang. I feel too
guilty. I have lost their grandchild, and I of all people am not entitled to whimper to them. To friends, I mustn't even speak of him;
he is as taboo as if he were himself obscene. I realize that this is
only because their powerlessness to help me is so painful to them
that they consider it indecent of me to bring it to their attention.
With Jake I could talk and talk about Lang, and Jake assumed the
burden of realizing and understanding and making allowances that
had been my burden for almost two months.

I even found myself explaining how much more than Lang I have
lost, how from the day Lang was born—disclosing his sex, acquiring a projectable personality—I began to dandle his children on
my knee. And to placate his wife. If I wanted lovely grandchildren,
Lang must be a good father, i.e. good husband, i.e. a man who puts
his wife ahead of his mother. I went into training that day. None of
this have I been able to say to anyone else in all these weeks.

"You're spending too much time in the house," Jake said. "You
need to get off the farm some. What would Grove say to your
working for the *Blood-Horse* again?" Seeing my face, "Part-time."

I said nothing. No need to tell Jake I'm listening for the telephone;
he knows that. That, presumably, is what he wants me to stop.

Albert works doggedly through his Scott County list. At three addresses, he finds people who have lived there only a few months, and only one of these has a forwarding address for the departed tenant. Albert is determined to find those two remaining Chevrolet owners. One of them, he can't resist feeling, is going to make everything else he has done worthwhile. He takes a break to call his friend on the Lexington police force, Rube Davis. His news release seeking Clint has drawn a blank, but he has an idea he wishes he had thought of weeks ago.

Every Monday Lexington's daily paper runs a plea in its magazine section for help locating the division of police's "Wanted Person of the Week." A photograph of the quarry is published, if possible, otherwise the best sketch the police can come up with. Cash is promised in return "for information leading to the arrest of this individual." With help from Captain Ruben Davis, Albert arranges to have his likeness of Clint Penn given this *Crime Stoppers* spot on June the 21st, two months to the day, his gut tightens as he reflects, after Lang Brough's disappearance. June 16th he hands in his *Crime Stoppers* submission and dials a Lexington number.

"Hello. Etta? This is Albert Blount. I don't know if you remember me. We met at my sister Jakba Tiner's apartment."

Etta Hollamon's "Sure I remember you, Lieutenant" is cautiously warm. Seven weeks have passed since their meeting, and this is Albert's first call.

"Say, I liked what you had to say about those Northside swimming pool closings."

"Thanks. My mail's been running about two to one against. Not everybody appreciates my take on the local scene."

Albert chuckles. "No, I imagine not, but they read you. They read you."

"I guess." Etta, meaning to sound unconvinced, sounds pleased.

"Etta, I have a favor to ask."

"Most people who call me do."

"I can imagine," Albert says sympathetically, and at once regrets the possible implication that he wouldn't expect Etta to attract personal calls. (Had this been true, he would have thought in time to avoid the implication.) He frowns and keeps talking. "You know I'm working on the Brough case; that little boy who disappeared in April."

Etta, who had been hoping that the "favor" was going to be dining out with Albert, answers with a brisk, "Well, I understood you were doing a little of that, in between fishing trips."

Albert realizes what she's been thinking ("I've got a date with a boat," he'd said), but he has disciplined his voice all his life. "I did drag some ponds," he says evenly.

"Oh, Albert, I'm sorry!"

"I didn't come up with anything, but now I'm trying something else." Maybe it's good that she spoke tartly, Albert thinks; maybe remorse will make her more obliging. "I've been getting some assistance from the Lexington division; Captain Davis has helped me arrange to have Monday's *Crime Stoppers* run a description of a suspect I'm looking for." Albert has dropped Rube Davis's name deliberately, confident that Etta knows the name of every black on the Lexington force. "So what I want to ask you: you have a lot of readers, and you have a lot of readers who never look at *Crime Stoppers*. A column from you on the Brough boy that came out the same day, if it called attention to that 'Wanted Person', would help that item reach a lot more people. Could you do that for us, Etta?"

"I've already written my Monday column. I work on my stuff; I don't toss it off in a couple of days."

"Five days."

"What do you mean, five? You think I sit here tapping my fingers and the words just pop up in your paper by magic one second later? Ever hear of editors? Ever hear of deadlines?"

"I've heard you've got a lot of clout at the *Herald-Leader*."

"And I keep it by never crowding a deadline, and sticking to my turf. This Brough kid isn't black."

"I am," says Albert.

In Albert's experience, newspaper accounts of police activities are exasperatingly inaccurate, whether the writer is friendly or hostile.

Willingness to lay himself open to mention in a newspaper column is a measure of how urgently he needs help. Lang Brough has been missing two months and Albert is getting nowhere. "Every day a child is missing," Rube Davis's words are a burden to remember, "your chance of finding him alive goes down about 50%."

"Have you got any idea how many times a week my telephone rings and it's somebody wants me to do something for him, 'because he's a Brother'?"

"Etta, will you do it?"

Monday morning, the *Herald-Leader's* "Wanted Person of the Week" is "Clint Penn, possible suspect in kidnapping case." Albert's drawing of Clint is flanked by the Thackers' estimates of Clint's weight, height, and date of birth. That same morning, Etta Holloman's column is an eloquent evocation of the grief of the mother whose nestling has disappeared, whether feathered or sweatered. "Shenelle Washington felt it three years before little Langdon Brough started school," Etta has written, taking the name of a black Louisville mother from 1991 headlines, "and Ruth Brough feels it now. This is one of those times when color isn't in it. When mothers' hearts bleed," Etta reminds her readers, "the blood is all the same red."

Etta's column tells Lang's story, what Albert Blount knows of it. Anybody with information about the man pictured by *Crime Stoppers,* magazine section page 2, is urged in Etta's final paragraph to call their number or Lt. Albert Blount's or hers. Etta provides all three. "A mother and a Brother need your help," she concludes.

❧56❧ {Lang

Lang has learned to watch Clint's moods carefully. Today, Clint has been wordless, with a tight look around his mouth that Lang hasn't seen before. Noon has come and gone with nothing said or done about eating. Finally Clint tells Lang that he and Lang are going hunting—how long has it been?

The cartridge pouch is empty. Lang wasted most of the cartridges on bad shots yesterday, and forgot to return the rest to the pouch. They're still in his back pocket, which suddenly feels heavy, bulging. Lang keeps his back turned away from Clint.

Lang doesn't like wearing the cartridge pouch; the strap chafes his neck. Yesterday, it had been so long since Clint hunted, Lang decided he would try. He is sick to death of salty ham. Clint, Lang knew, would have jeered at the idea if he'd been there, but after all, Lang had killed that raccoon. He never had succeeded in hitting a rabbit, but he might. He didn't think to put the cartridges he had not wasted back in the pouch when he finally gave up. Now the look on Clint's face is so cold and hard, different from his usual loud rages, that Lang is afraid to tell him this.

Clint, first hefting, then opening the empty pouch, curses Lang without looking at him, curses him quietly, viciously, not the usual shouting Lang is used to. Lang is startled silent, and the longer he says nothing, the harder it is to confess. Were Clint to start taking off his belt, Lang would produce the cartridges, but instead Clint abruptly strides out of the cabin and down the path, not even glancing back. Well, it's not all Lang's fault, Lang tells himself. Clint has been strange all day; he was acting different even before he found that the pouch was empty. For one thing, he hasn't had a drink, and drinking is all he's been doing lately. Lang stands at the window and watches Clint go, hating him.

Clint is a liar. Lang knows that for sure. The receipt in the bag from where Clint bought coal-oil and flour last week said Catesby, Kentucky. Lang read it again and again. His cut foot is hot, swollen shiny like a potato bug. He hasn't had his shoes on in weeks, so he's surprised to discover that he can't even get his left foot into one, let alone the foot that's swollen purple. As usual, he doesn't know how much time he has. Clint never does say where he's going, when he'll be back. Clint counts on Lang's fear that if Lang starts down the path, Clint will meet him.

If the creek were halfway full, Lang could put his throbbing foot in the cool water.

Lang knows a doctor should look at his foot. He thought Clint might be fixing to take him to one. Clint didn't even ask if the foot was better this morning. Clint isn't going to take him anywhere; Clint has been lying about taking him home.

Clint didn't take notice of his birthday in any way, either. Scowling, trying not to cry, Lang stuffs a couple of the runty June Apples Clint has set on the windowsill into his side pocket. Lang has tried to eat a June Apple only once. He threw that one away, it was so sour, but he has no way to carry water. Two apples is what his pocket will hold. He fills the pouch with sliced ham, which is all there is, and hangs it around his neck. Right now, he is too keyed up to eat, but he has no idea how far he will have to walk.

Ain't nobody here can go down this lonesome road with me, his mother used to sing. Lang had never told her that it always made him feel like crying. Even *then.*

In the flush of spring, no one could have found his way through this woods who didn't, like Clint, know it as the hand knows the way to the mouth. Drought has changed that. Lang will be able to steer by the sun the way he's seen Clint do, coming home from hunting. He bets Catesby isn't any hundred miles away, either. He bets he can find it.

He takes down and loads Clint's twenty-two.

Wasps are building over the cabin door again. Lang is no more afraid of them, he tells himself as he limps warily under them, than he is of Clint.

The path is as hard as the cabin floor and setting his sore foot down on it hurts, but off the path is uneven, and after trying it for several steps Lang decides that's worse. The ups and downs trick him into putting weight on the foot, and every unexpected time he gasps.

Lang would much rather be setting off after sundown—cooler, easier to hide. He feels a different heat remembering Clint's jeers back when Clint saw that after twilight Lang was afraid to go a decent distance from the cabin to piss. Now he goes cat-fishing with Clint any night Clint wants to go, or did, before the creek dried up.

Lang is beginning to be sorry he took Clint's rifle. It just keeps getting heavier. It isn't even good for a crutch. He wishes he'd dumped those cartridges, put a couple more apples in his back pocket. Already one's gone, and his mouth is as powdery as his nose and throat. There's a grapevine on the path-side tree he rests against; its hard little green grapes are a mockery. Lang closes his eyes. Maybe hunger's what makes him feel light-headed. Perhaps it's lunchtime. His head feels something like the way it felt the night Clint taught him to smoke pot.

The ham nauseates him. He walks away — like his mother's barn cats, the thought takes him by surprise, who cover their feces but not their puke.

Sweat runs salty into his mouth. Gnats surround his head like a school of fish. He unloads the leaden rifle and leaves it behind in the path.

Coming upon the rifle there will tell Clint much sooner than he has to find out that Lang has left. Lang stands still as this thought comes to him. All but crying at the extra painful steps, he limps back and hurls the rifle as far off the path as he can.

Not far enough. He hobbles after it, and now he is crying.

He will hide the rifle in that wild raspberry tangle.

The raspberries are dried to little knots of hard seeds, but their thorns are as protective as ever, guarding what not even a bird would want now. Lang has to sit down and stop crying to find the thorn that gets into the heel of his good foot. The hurt one is so swollen, his toes are white sausages; he can't wiggle them. He runs a dry tongue over his lips as he looks for his path again and does not see it.

Of course he sees it when he stands up; he knew he would. Even if he hadn't, he wouldn't have been scared, he tells himself. He knows how to steer by sky language now, night or day. He's thirsty, though. He wonders if he has a fever; his forehead feels as hot to his hand as his hurt foot.

The path seems to peter out. Lang doesn't remember walking around any rocks the day Clint brought him. He can tell he's going downhill, though, and that's the main thing.

He knows he's lost when he comes upon a patch of ginseng as wide as a mare's shadow, with plants so many-pronged he's sure no one has ever discovered it but himself. These plants aren't ready to dig, of course, but if Clint or anybody were to come upon them when the berries were red, he wouldn't waste time wishing for his hoe. He'd break off a tree-branch and poke the roots out of the ground; he'd go down on his knees and dig them out with his hands. No one ever has passed this way.

Not scared. If he just goes in one direction always, he has to get somewhere, and he has seen no trace of bear. There aren't any bears on this hill; that was just another of Clint's lies. Lang is not a bit scared. He's not sick either. If he just had some water he'd be fine. He is telling himself these things half out loud, keeping his face turned up to see that the sun keeps to where he has decided he wants it, when he trips over a broken branch and falls flat on his stomach. He will stand up when he feels less dizzy, he tells himself, and closes his eyes.

⤙57⤚ {Lorena

The week she graduated from high school, Lorena left Cotes, one of the stagnant little towns like Catesby and Trimble that encircle Wolfe Country's Hawk Mountain, for a job at Lexington's Turf Catering. That's where she met Annie, who was an old hand there, showed her the ropes. "You have to get to Cotes on purpose," Lorena used to joke to Annie back then. Sixteen years later, you still do. "And more and more, anymore, Lorena observes to Annie, calling to tell her bad news, "the purpose is getting to be some-body's got to be buried.

"You shouldn't be driving all that way in your condition, honey," Annie chides, "in this heat. Everybody knows you loved her. They'll understand. Don't tell me Eldridge is going to let you go."

"Eldridge left for Belmont before dinner," Lorena replies, "and Nelcie just called me about the funeral twenty minutes ago. It's months till my time, and I want to see Glenna."

This trip Lorena is driving a four-wheel drive Jeep Cherokee from Bill's Save-a-Lot Rental. Her station wagon would be handy taking relatives to the funeral, but, she confided to Annie, negoti-ating those narrow winding roads in her station wagon, as she did in April, scared the shit out of her.

Lorena drove the station wagon last time only because she had not known what shape Glenna would be in, how she'd have to be loaded. She'd known what shape the roads would be in: the same as when she was a little girl, she reported to Annie, "except there's a sight more litter."

Today drought has lowered the creek in which she once nearly drowned to where she could wade it; the lowest bushes along its banks look decorated for Halloween from throwaway diapers and styrofoam. There aren't more people in Wolfe County now than when Lorena lived there to account for all this trash. Fewer, her daddy claims, but admits he doesn't know it for a fact. There were 8000 when Lorena was in fourth grade. She can tell you that for a fact, has told Eldridge a dozen times about the arithmetic question she missed, kept her from getting 100 on the test. She can see the question on the blackboard to this day. *Wolfe County is 230 sq. mi. large and has 8000 inhabitants. How many people per sq. mi. live in Wolfe County?* Lorena divided and got thirty-five, which she knew to be nonsense. From her home to the school bus stop was a mile, and not another house did she and her sisters pass the whole length of it. She left that question unanswered. When the test papers came back, her teacher tried to explain to her about "on the average."

"The average square mile in Wolfe County ain't got nothing living in it but skunks and skinks," she told that teacher flatly. Next report card's Deportment grade would have got her a whipping, but she hid in the chicken house till her daddy fell asleep in his chair and forgot about it. Glenna sneaked her some biscuits.

The funeral isn't Glenna's, as Lorena is certain it would have been except for herself. Who has died is one of their aunts who never was healthy: sugar on the blood. Lorena has sent flowers-by-wire, and she intends to go by the funeral home ahead of the Visitation this evening and make sure the florists haven't cheated her. *First,* she is going to the Seldens' cabin. She's had no word about them since the doctors swore to her that Glenna was out of danger, and she settled the hospital's bills and came home. The Seldens have no phone, and none of the Bailey girls is much for writing.

Lorena hasn't seen Ned since she removed his wife from his house with the aid of a shotgun. Looking after that baby while his wife was gone surely will have cooled his readiness for widowerhood, Lorena and Annie have assured one another. In any case, he will be at the sawmill this time of day. Lorena wants no trouble.

The spring afternoon Glenna quit high school and ran off with a dark growthy sawmill hand, Lorena thought Glenna was a fool. She can sympathize a little better now that she has a houseful of young'uns. Glenna, as the oldest, had borne the greatest burden of helping their mother. Ned's cabin, in Lorena's opinion, hasn't been much of an improvement—though undeniably quieter than a house full of sisters. Ned's quiet ways probably made him romantic to Glenna. She could imagine that he was *thinking* anything at all that she was wishing he would say. Glenna bragged to Lorena early on how Ned looked like Clint Eastwood. After Ned married her, she changed to that church of his, and Lorena didn't see much of her.

The sawmill where the Seldens' preacher worked got into some kind of trouble with OSHA, and the preacher moved to Detroit. Ned took over his place in the church, just like that. *And Glenna*, Lorena remembers bitterly, *fool enough to be proud of him for it.* Sitting in Marcum and Wallace Memorial Hospital's waiting room, Swango and Jessie had told Lorena about the visitor their church had had since Easter week, a Tennesseean with a box full of copperheads and rattlers. She had driven straight from letting Swango and Jessie off at their school to hunt Tricks Bailey down and give him, along with little Lang Brough's flyers, a piece of her mind.

"It's been going on for 2000 years, and it'll be going on in 2000 years," Tricks had told her.

"Not in Wolfe County it hasn't!" she had retorted. "If you had the guts of a lizard, you'd run that snake-toting Tennesseean right off this mountain. You ought to care about your family, even if the law don't mean anything to you."

She had lived, Tricks had accused her mildly, too long in the Bluegrass to realize how some Hawk Mountain folks felt about that particular law. "I can't do a thing without a warrant, which nobody who has to get elected around here is going to give me.

There's one thing I know, Lorie, and you used to know it too: if Hawk Mountain folks want to worship with snakes, the President himself isn't going to stop them."

"I'd like to stuff that carney-barker in his own box and nail down the lid and Tricks Bailey with him!" Lorena reported home to Eldridge. Glenna is her favorite sister, the one who took up for her when she was little.

Lorena isn't worried about Ned. She will have come and gone before he gets off work. She doesn't anticipate any excitement on this trip except what she intends to stir up herself if her Cousin Tricks has failed to put a stop to this snake nonsense. She had asked Nelcie, when Nelcie called to say that their aunt would be buried Tuesday, "What's going on over to Glenna's church these days?" Nelcie had professed to have no idea. Lorena believes her. Nelcie is getting to where she doesn't know much. (That's another thing Lorena means to tackle while she's down here.)

Linda Ronstadt is singing *Blue Bayou* on the Jeep's radio. Homesickness has never been much threat to Lorena, but the song gets to her so bad she has to turn the radio off. It brings a vision of little Lang Brough, Lord knows where, longing with all his baffled and desperate heart for his mama. Lorena's Dwaine is just six months younger than Lang. If Dwaine were missing, Lorena knows she would go out of her mind. Ruth never was one to tell anybody much about her feelings, but she is thinner every time Lorena sees her. She has given Lorena some more flyers from that detective, on a suspect this time, for Lorena to give to Tricks. Lorena doesn't tell Ruth what she thinks of Albert. "The wrong detective has that job," Annie believes, and Lorena is afraid she agrees, though for different reasons. Annie is afraid a black detective won't do his best to find a white child. Lorena has been interviewed by Albert and thinks he is decent, but thinks that no man is going to find Lang Brough.

"A man can't find a jar of pickles in the refrigerator if it's behind the milk," she has pointed out to Annie. "Why does anybody think men are going to find children? What we need is woman detectives. Then we'd start to find some of all these children."

Lorena means to run Tricks down as soon as she's checked the arrangements at the funeral home, but right now she's going to Glenna's, and from there to Nelcie's husband's barbershop. All the moved-away sisters are coming for the funeral: Shirley and Lorena are to stay at Nelcie's, the other two at their parents'. (Seldens, Nelcie didn't need to point out to Lorena, have only three beds and a cradle for the six of them.) Lorena wants a private word with Nelcie's husband, and a private word is impossible in a house containing Nelcie and Shirley.

Pines shade the cabin. Drought has stilled the customary June buzz and whir of insects, the rustlings and calls of the birds that fed on them. But for the rusting Ford on its cinder blocks, the clearing is empty. April's cardboard sidewalk has been removed from the now hard-swept yard, and the flowers in Glenna's hanging basket are sticks. They make the cabin look uninhabited, and though Lorena announces her arrival with a toot on the Jeep's horn, no one comes to the door. She is relieved, when she gets almost to the porch, to hear the baby crying inside.

Ned opens the door.

For a moment, Lorena doesn't hear the baby, though its crying is louder than ever, through the open door. Ned's face is dark with anger. He stands wordlessly blocking the way. Lorena hears Glenna or Jessie shh-shhing the baby. Ned's jaws, where he's shaved that morning, are the color of gun metal; the skin is stretched tight. Lorena can't see around him.

After the air-conditioned Jeep, the heat is an assault. Lorena sets her tricolored but sensibly heeled sandals about a hand's breadth apart and leans back slightly to balance the load she is carrying in front. "Glenna!" she calls, in her carrying mountain voice.

There isn't a sound from within the cabin. Even the baby stops crying. Ned folds his arms.

Lorena calls "Glenna" again, and puts one foot on the bottom porch step. Ned's arm rises. His work-hardened hand is flat; its creases look as if they would imprint themselves on Lorena's face the way the potter's hand imprints clay. "Cross me in my own house," Ned growls. "You think you're too good to beat."

If anything, Lorena leans toward him. *"Please do,"* she says. *"Please* do lay your hand on me *one* time. *Eld*ridge will *kill* you."

Neither moves until Lorena feels satisfied that she has made her point, then she turns and walks with head high back across the yard to the Jeep. Ned watches silently from the porch. There is not a sound from the cabin.

Through her bedroom window, Glenna watches the retreating Jeep.

Glenna will not forgive Lorena for cheating her of the glory that would have been hers had she been allowed to conquer the viper's sting on her own. She would not have died; her faith is strong. Jezebel, that's what Ned has called Lorie.

Lorie has taken the ways of the world. Glenna turns from the window. For a while she stands as if studying the can of purple ironweed. Glenna soaked the wrapper off the can, which came with mackerel in it, and gave it to Kyle, who loves the beautiful shining fish. The purple flowers are the only weed the drought has not shriveled, and Glenna has not had Swango this summer to pump water for her garden. Ned has forgiven Glenna for her weakness, and Jessie got off with a belting, but *the son who uncovered his mother's nakedness—the son who put his lips to his mother's breast! Him Ned will never allow to set foot in his cabin again.* Swango has lived with his grandparents since April.

Glenna holds her sleeping baby in her arms but is not comforted. Lorie, she thinks, always did think she was better than any of them, with her high school diploma and her Lexington job, and now it's all them colored shoes, all them plates on the wall. Lorie has shown Glenna camera pictures of every room in her house. But for the hope of seeing Swango at the funeral, Glenna would not go, Lorie having come.

Lorena takes care to park on First Street, around the corner from her brother-in-law's "Sanitary Barbershop for Ladies and Gentlemen." Elburn is obsessed with the spaces in front of his shop, thinks they ought to be for his customers only, by law. Lorena has been steeling herself all the way from Lexington to tackle Elburn about sending Nelcie to Charter Ridge Hospital, and making him furious wouldn't be a Jim Dandy way to start.

"Nelcie," Elburn tells Lorena, "is very well."

Nelcie tells all her sisters that Elburn is tighter than wallpaper, but Lorena thinks maybe that's because any money he does give her seems to go to a bootlegger. In any case, Lorena is prepared to pay all the costs, if Elburn will just cooperate with her. Nobody ever crossed a river, her daddy always said, standing on the bank. She holds her nose and dives in.

The dive is a belly-flop. Bleached patches appear on Elburn's nostrils. He is not aware that Nelcie has any needs that are not being met at home. Nelcie is not sick. She gets tired. She needs a lot of rest.

Lorena sighs.

Elburn intends to say no more; he clasps his hands. His fingers are as pink as a rabbit's nose, Lorena notes scornfully. "Hon, no one would have to know your wife went some place to get dried out," she coaxes. "You could tell your friends she was visiting me."

A slow flush seeps up Elburn's neck, over his face and back to where he still has some hair to hide it. "Your sister has everything she needs at home, Lorena," he says. His thin lips set and he stares at her as if he dares her to speak another word.

He is afraid of Nelcie, Lorena realizes. He is ashamed to admit that he has no control over her at all. "What," she proposes, "if I just ask Nelcie to visit me? Don't even say anything about this business till I can show her the place?"

Elburn turns to pick up an immaculate face towel from the perfectly square-edged stack on the shining counter beside his big white plastic basin, signaling that he has given Lorena all the time he can spare. "You must do as you please, Lorena," he says. "Nobody seems to be able to talk to you."

Lorena doesn't know which Cotes brother-in-law she'd rather choke.

Elburn watches Lorena cross the street to the funeral home. The "home" is the newest, finest building in town; if its customers did not so frequently spill over into his customers' parking places, Elburn would be pleased that his shop is on the same block. He is humiliated, furious, and what he sees on his own side of the street does nothing to brighten his mood. His pole, which isn't one of these modern poles that's had a blue stripe added to it, but a genuine barber's pole, his pole has bird droppings on it.

Walleye Lykins is seated as always, barring hail, on the bench in front of Elburn's shop. "Don't know what you need that pole for, long as you got Walleye," Nelcie taunts Elburn. "You could sell it to one of them antique stores in Lexington, get you a good price. Walleye shows up just as far down the street as that ol' candy cane, and you ask anybody in Cotes where the barber's is at, he'll tell you it's where Walleye sits and spits."

Elburn has gone before the town council and asked to have the bench and the parking place in front of his shop reserved for his customers, but the council is too small-minded. All Elburn can do is check the tires of any non-customer who parks in what ought to be his space, and call the town's patrolman, who is Nelcie's cousin, if any tire is over its line. Walleye, with nothing better to do than collect his black-lung checks and pass comments on Elburn's customers (before and after), continues to pre-empt the bench, and people going to Finkerman's Sporting Goods next door continue to take what ought to be Elburn's parking space. Funerals like Nelcie's aunt's tomorrow will continue to hog all parking the length of Main Street for hours, but at least there's an up side to funerals. Already several of Elburn's patrons have come in this afternoon who might have put off their trims a week or two longer if they hadn't had a burying to be seen at, and Elburn has stayed open later than usual in the expectation of more.

There's no up side to Walleye. Elburn puts soap in a bucket and lets the water run into it so hard, the suds foam up to the brim. He sets his shoulders and goes out to clean his pole.

Walleye doesn't even take time to spit before asking, "How's Nelcie today, Elburn? She all right?"

Elburn answers with dignified brevity, and wipes the side of the pole that causes his back to be turned to Walleye's bench.

"Sue told me to be sure to ask. Sue didn't see Nelcie at Circle meeting last night." Walleye pauses. "She was just wondering. If Nelcie might be sick again." Walleye speaks the word "sick" with such insinuating solicitude that Elburn would like to empty the bucket over his head.

The pole is clean and the bucket emptied discreetly into the street before an approaching car distracts Walleye. A rusting artifact with its radio going full blast, the car takes the place smack in front of the barber shop. Elburn's suspicion that it contains no customer of his is confirmed when the driver gets out. The kinky hair that radiates from that head has never been the customer of any barber. Elburn sets his empty bucket down and folds his arms, the better to project disapproval. The driver, who is filthy, passes Elburn as if *Elburn* were dirt. He walks the way he parks, halfway between a slouch and a swagger. His sleeveless shirt flaunts his tattooed arms. Finkerman's is welcome to him.

"Hooo-ee!" says Walleye, when it's safe. "Have to hold that one down to count his ears! How much you charge him for them curls, Elburn?"

Elburn is already on his way to telephone Nelcie's cousin, the law.

~58~ {Albert

Monday afternoon Albert Blount receives a collect call from a furious Lexington woman. "That man you're looking for," she announces without preamble: "his name's not Penn; it's Ward."

There is a hum in Albert's ears as if he were swimming under water. He grabs for his pen and presses his wrist against the desk to keep his hand from trembling as he writes. "What is your name and address, Ma'am?" he asks. He has had informants change their minds and hang up before telling him all they knew, leaving him with no way to trace them.

The woman is annoyed by this interruption, but sufficiently anxious to have her say to answer. "My name is Hazel Maynard, and I live at 63 West Grierson Street. Flynt Ward is a piece of trash. Let a room from me and cut out owing me two weeks rent! Left my room filthy as a nigger's!"

Albert takes a deep breath and asks his next question without inflection. "And what was that date; can you tell me exactly, Ma'am?" Anger has taken the tremor out of his hand.

"Yes, sir, I can tell you exactly. It was exactly the day Etta Hollamon says that lady lost her little boy!"

Little points of light dance in front of Albert's eyes. He blinks hard before writing, *April 21, suspect moved, no forwarding address.* "Do you happen to know where Mr. Ward worked, Mrs. Maynard?"

"*Mister* Ward worked for Williams Machine Shop, and they ain't seen him since April themselves!" Mrs. Maynard has followed Etta Holloman's instructions and turned to *Crime Stoppers.* She knows about the reward. She wants it. "Two weeks' rent," she reiterates, "and I had to hire that room scrubbed!"

"Yes, ma'am. I understand your feelings."

"Well, I called them so-called *Crime Stoppers* five times, and all I got was this record said call back 'Monday through Friday, nine to five.' This is the first I ever heard Monday ain't Monday!"

"I understand your feelings," Albert repeats. Now he is aching for the woman to hang up. "I'll get back to you, Ma'am; you've been a great help. You're not planning to go out of town in the next week?... Good, that's good.... Yes, yes, there is a reward.... Yes, I definitely think you would be. Of course, no one is accusing Mr. Ward of anything. He may have no connection to the Lang Brough case. But I'll be in touch. Thank you.... Yes—thank you, Mrs. Maynard."

Flynt Ward ceased to be employed by Williams Machine Shop on April 21, 1995. Their address for him was 83 Grierson Street, Lexington.

A Kentucky driver's license bearing his social security number was issued to Flynt Ward in Wolfe County on April 25th, 1991. Flynt Ward's address at that time was Route 1, Catesby, Kentucky. The license expired four days after Langdon Brough disappeared, and has not been renewed.

A 1980 four-door Chevrolet was registered to Flynt Ward in Fayette County in May, 1994, and this registration has not been renewed, nor has he registered any other vehicle.

Flynt Ward is wanted nowhere by the police, and has no civilian or military criminal record. He has an honorable discharge from the army.

Catesby's police chief is named Garvis Winslow; Albert has had no dealings with him. The drive will take roughly an hour and a half, Albert estimates, but he will go rather than telephone. Albert is familiar with inbred small towns and their sociable police offices. He won't risk having somebody tip Ward off that a police detective is inquiring about him. He leaves at once.

~≥59≈~　　　　　　　　{Ruth

Walk toward a shy yearling and it will walk away from you. Keep that up long enough and when you turn and walk away, it will follow you, Eldridge Snyder says. This morning, before I opened my eyes, I calculated for the uncountedth time since Joanna's birth how many days have passed since last I tore open a Tampax. Tomorrow will make thirty. It has been years since I gave up taking conscious, deliberate steps to achieve such a count. Perhaps I am at last about to learn that turning the back does work sometimes. Only it's the Monkey's Paw again. Do I want another baby now?

A sensible person nibbles at a question if it's too bitter to take by the mouthful. I have tried to reach an answer by taking short rational steps. Would I want a third child if Lang came home tomorrow? Maybe. If yes, then why not if he does not? Because I can't bear the ceaseless terror? Because trying to keep hold of Joanna, to keep her in sight, to keep her breathing, already takes more than my strength?

Every night of my two stays in the maternity ward, the last thing I did before closing my eyes was rehearse in my mind the route I would take if fire obliged me to snatch up my baby and run. Never did I take the sleeping pill the nurse brought me nightly. Although I felt guilty at the selfishness of my plans—no stopping to give a general alarm, no grabbing two babies, one under each arm—these plans remained confined to my own child, first Lang, then in her turn, Joanna. (I needed that other arm to open doors, to protect their heads, to hold onto the rails of steep fire escapes.) Anyone who marries a horse breeder develops an extra dread of fire, but I believe that the obsessiveness of mine dates from Lang and Joanna's nights in the hospital nursery. Since April, I am worse than ever. Now I never waken in the dark without sniffing for smoke. Now I get up and walk to Joanna's bedside, putting my hand on walls as I go.

So do I want another baby?

"Sufficient unto each day," Mother would say. Why rack myself with these questions before I'm positive they matter? If the drugstore's test says *yes* after twenty-eight days, believe it, Jake has told me. "If the over-the-counter test says *no* and you definitely think otherwise, come to me and we'll do a serum test." I will go to the drugstore tomorrow.

Today's lesson took up the diphthong *ou*. "Joanna likes to bounce and bound around and about the mountain ground," she read, while I gazed out the window at the white cabbage moths fluttering around and about the jade-green asparagus fronds—at the low cloud of pink cosmos billowing beside them and the cumulus of butter-yellow fennel above, and in a perfect sky a white and blue moon, round as the eyespot on a butterfly wing.

Once under a full moon in the valley of the Loire I sat with Eva and listened to Peter declaiming,

> *"Füllest wieder Busch und Tal*
> *Still mit Nebelglanz,*
> *Lösest endlich auch einmal*
> *Meine Seele ganz…"*

which he then refused to help me translate. "Translations are like women," he said. "If they are beautiful, they are not faithful; if they are faithful, they are not beautiful."

"It's Goethe," Eva told me later: "The first lines of *To the Moon.*" For Christmas I received from Peter a collection which contained the whole poem. Like a love affair, the beginning is best.

Goethe's was a night moon; Joanna's and mine was a water lily floating on a French Impressionist's sun-drenched pond.

By late afternoon, our Monet had become an El Greco. Great

ash-gray clouds passed over the garden and house one after another, fleeing an inexorable seeping blackness beyond the barn. Like praying Arabs, the asparagus fronds bent eastward to the very ground. The treetops' tempo quickened from the billowing up here and subsiding there of stewing tomatoes to the full rolling boil of jam, and I heard the deck chairs collapsing on the patio. Thunder preceded the rain and I wished Tad had an extra set of earphones so I could clap them on Joanna, who is sensibly terrified of lightning.

Tad, after a boa constrictor's lunch, habitually staggers off to his room. I don't doubt that when he holed up there today, it was his intention not to emerge until Ervil came to feed and put the colts out for Grove, who won't be home in time this evening. Ervil is walking the yearlings an hour apiece every morning, to put muscle on them, and while he has each out of its stall Tad removes the piles they've dropped since Grove's bringing them in for the day and refills their water buckets and hay racks. These labors, plus what he engorges at table, obviously necessitate that he lie down. In this state, and in his headset, he isn't likely to be disturbed by thunder. I wish Breck hadn't moved away. There must be things he and Tad could do together that would be better for Tad than lying on a bunk with a computer game propped between his gut and his thighs (and with the door shut so I won't see that he has on his boots).

He will go home when Velma completes her course, and Joanna will move back into her room. I haven't decided which will upset her more, for me to remove Lang's remaining things, or leave them. I packed his woolens like everybody else's.

I haven't inflicted on Joanna the news that she will be losing Lucille as well. Cross that bridge when we come to it, Mother would say. Lucille, Fran informs me, has given notice. Margot's doing? If so, Margot will tell me so, sooner or later. Officially, Lucille's leaving is Lucille's choice, she having an offer she can't refuse from an Ocala farm manager she met at Keeneland's spring meet. Plausible enough, considering all *Lucille* offers. Meow. Meow, hiss, spit; I can't deny I'd like to scar that lovely face. Grove never utters her name, and with this parched corn I am resolved to be sufficed. "Any time you quarrel with him over her, she is beating you," Mother says.

A scorched smell in this evening's air has me brooding again about Zad Thacker's fire. Lang's disappearance seems to have put Zad's shed out of everyone's mind but mine. Zad has never wanted to talk about it. "He's embarrassed," Grove says. "He's figured out Milly did it with a cigarette butt." Once a person's inborn feeling of invulnerability is lost — destroyed, in my case, by my brother's murder—every further mischance is sinister. I think Zad's reticence means that Zad thinks what I think: it was arson. Now in my mind is a picture of Lang returning to find this place ashes. Are we three part of those ashes? Then my parents will take him in, I tell myself, businesslike in my wildest fantasies. I've already made sure Albert knows how to get in touch with my parents. Tomorrow I will tell Jake, too. This afternoon's lightning hardly eased my fears of fire.

When Tad staggered off to his room after lunch, Joanna and I retired to the sewing room. We are making her a skirt and jacket like the ones worn by the young woman who reads the news on Channel 18. Waistless, Joanna must keep her skirt on with the help of shoulder straps. She is alive to the significance of this, but points out that when she wears the jacket, no one will see the straps.

The new outfit, though she doesn't know it, is my amends to her because I can't bring myself to send her to kindergarten next month. It is out of the question, whatever Grove says.

Keziah is going, and has a new dress, not a hand-me-down from Farrah. "Keziah lives in Fayette County," I explain disingenuously. "Some things there are different from Bourbon County."

Keziah's new jumper is green "corderoy." Joanna chose her own fabric, dark brown, like the sternest of the Channel 18 newswoman's. I have only the hem to finish. "Put this on," I said to her just before today's storm peaked, "so I can mark the length." This distracted her from the frightening window scene, and permitted me to concentrate on it.

Through glass turned pre-Colonial by rain, I watched flash after terrifying flash of great river systems of lightning irrigate the sky. Raindrops hit the ground so hard they bounced and ran across the drive like relays of bayonet charges. At each momentary illumination, I scanned what I could see of the south field. At last I found the mares, huddled too close together to count, where they'd taken the foals to low ground.

The yearlings, at least, were safe in their stalls.

Leaves splatted against the window like personal insults. I tried, for Joanna's benefit, not to recoil from the thunder. My eyes on the dramatic waving of the branches of the ancient hickory nearest the barn, I saw the bolt that hit. My scream was simultaneous with a thunderclap of unprecedented ferocity. For a moment, I didn't actually know all that had happened. I thought the window had shattered, expected glass in my eyes, rain on my machine. But the roof above the barn was what blazed.

Even while screaming, I heard Tad's boots hit the floor. Joanna's mouth was open to howl. "Don't leave this room!" I ordered, and lifted her out of my path. From our doorway, Tad took one look out our window and turned without a word. The front door slammed behind him before I reached the kitchen phone.

In my office, Joanna was wailing. "You *stay there*," I yelled as I hung up, and ran after Tad.

I got to the barn just as Ten broke away from him.

How straw and timbers can go on burning in torrential rain I do not know. Uncle was screaming and rearing in his stall, and Ten knocked Tad down getting back to *his*. The barn was full of smoke. I rolled open Uncle's door so that he could run anywhere at all, if only he would, and jerked off my skirt. After I threw it over Ten's head, he let me take hold of the shank Tad had put on him, let me lead him to his paddock. As I latched the gate I heard the first roof trusses give way and crash and my heart exploded. I turned around and saw Tad leading Uncle out of the end door.

He had wrapped a rub rag like a firing squad's bandage over Uncle's eyes.

The Bourbon County Fire Department is five miles from our farm. I had just time to put on my soaking skirt before their trucks howled up our drive.

Nobody in the Fire Department drinks anything but cold water or hot coffee on duty, but no guest ever departed from my home happier than those men. Immensely pleased with themselves, and with a look of pure love for me in their eyes because they had saved me, they shook Tad's hand (for which I, in turn, loved them) and waved to Joanna out of sight. I opened one of the bottles they had conscientiously turned down, and turned to Tad. "Split a beer with me?"

"Sure," he said, as if we'd been doing that all month.

Had there been no beer I would have offered him whiskey.

I don't remember when it struck me that he had moved first to rescue the summer sale yearling ahead of his favorite. I shall always remember the responsibility, the loyalty, of this choice. Especially, I hope, when Velma writes to dump him on me again next year.

He leaned a wet, blackened shirt against the white refrigerator and listened to what I told Grove over the phone.

"No, the colts are fine; just the roof is hyperventilating.... Not a singe. Tad got one out and I took the other." I could see Tad's quickly turned-away grin reflected in the window glass. "Yes, but we wrapped their heads. (Don't ask.)"

The storm passed before sundown. Joanna, who had remained safely glued to the sewing room window as ordered, was sandbagged by her reward—all the ice cream she wanted—and for once permitted herself and Snoopy to be put to bed early. Tad confessed he was ready to follow suit; a nice boy who hasn't known how to deal with a hostess half out of her mind with grief. Now in dry clothes, I am waiting between the two colts' paddocks, nursing my second beer and watching the western sky settle into a bed of coals. Grove will come to this spot first, I know—even before he inspects his sodden barn. "If I'm asleep when Uncle Grove comes, will you call me?" Tad requested as he went to take his first voluntary shower since his arrival.

I am waiting for Grove.

Last night an apricot moon turned, slow as a flower opening, to silver, and the mockingbird that has not visited our roof since spring, sang until dawn.

The lights of a car on Clay Pike gleam and are gone; not Grove, but his will be the next, and if not, the one after.

Ten years ago in Saratoga, the garden under our window was all moon-blanched roses—*so various, so beautiful, so new*—and we poor wise brave amputees both of us, perhaps not thinking of our brothers very much that night but because of them knowing how little certitude or help for pain we could expect from the rest of the world, swore to be true to one another.

I scratch Ten between the ears and move Grove's Stroh's so that his pet doesn't knock it off the fence post. I walk over and pat Uncle, too. The colts routinely spend June nights outside. So far as they are aware, they have now just what they had this time yesterday, and they will never be happier.

And I?

Tomorrow will make thirty days. Those rational steps I urged myself to take in search of my answer to this turn out to be like the sober analysis I lay down and closed my eyes to give all my mind to, after it occurred to me that if I continued to see Grove Brough, I might fall in love with him. I should stop seeing him, I cautioned myself, if marrying him was a poor idea. What would be the arguments against marrying this man, I asked myself solemnly. None, I answered just as solemnly.

Tomorrow will make thirty days and I will go to the drugstore. Maybe this resolve will bring things down tonight; maybe what I have is a tumor; but Jake himself has told me it makes sense to check after twenty-nine days.

I will not be there before 9:30; I will not give the impression that I have been just waiting for the shop to open. Should the results turn out negative, I will call Jake for that serum test he said was more accurate, but I will not make a fool of myself by pleading for special consideration should Jake's book be full for awhile. It might give me bad luck. Us, bad luck.

So I'm waiting for more than Grove.

But Grove first.

He will come first to the paddocks to see his colts. I will be standing here in the moonlight, with his drink. Sweet is the night-air. And if Lang calls, the tack room telephone is sooty but functional; the doors are open.

When Lang telephones, I will hear it.

Tricks Bailey is exultant. The blue Chevrolet Elburn Meece has called him to has a Scott County plate and not only is one tire well over the line, the sticker on the plate expired May 30. That costs out-of-town cars one hundred dollars.

The catch is, these people from away throw the summons out the window as they turn the corner, and simply never come back to Cotes. First the Chevy's driver will claim that he has his new sticker but just hasn't put it on. Then he'll go on home to Scott County, and Tricks will never see his hundred dollars. Tricks will never see even the two dollars that are owing for parking out in the middle of Main Street.

What Tricks does see through the Chevy's open window, however, restores his mood. The open ash tray is stuffed with rolling papers. In plain view.

An Army fatigue jacket, frayed and dirty, lies on the Chevy's torn front seat. "That's a mighty nice jacket," Tricks observes to Elburn and Walleye, "to be just laying around in an unlocked vehicle." Tricks can guess what would fall out of its pocket, he tells them, if the law allowed him to give the jacket to Elburn to hang on his rack "for its own protection" until its owner returned. "Not too many people roll their own cigarettes anymore."

At the suggestion of permitting such a garment on his rack, Elburn's lips press so hard they blanch.

Elburn is safe. The law will *not* allow Tricks to so much as touch Clint's jacket, whatever his suspicions.

Tricks considers, however, that these suspicions will stand up in court. *Poss. marijuana* is fifty dollars and costs, which with the hundred Cotes would collect for the expired sticker, would be an excellent day's haul. And it takes only one ounce....

When Clint returns with his box of cartridges, the uniformed law awaits him.

"This your car?"

"Might be."

"You got a license to operate this vehicle?"

"Might have."

Those rolling papers in the ashtray, Tricks informs Clint, give him a reasonable suspicion that he would find an illegal substance in Clint's car, if Clint were to waive his rights and let him look. If not, then Tricks will just have to hold Clint until he can go and get a search warrant.

Clint hasn't said that the Chevy is his. He folds his arms. He knows the fine for possession, and he doesn't have it on him.

He could strangle this hick cop without working up a sweat, only the bastard is toting a gun.

Clint's money is under his floorboards. There is no one in Cotes he could call to come bail him out so he can fetch it. There is no one in the world he dares to send to his cabin.

Tricks kicks the Chevy's near wheel with calculated contempt, but Clint continues silent. "Well, whose ever this car is," Tricks remarks, "if you want to call it a car, it might not be theirs much longer, because it is a potential traffic hazard, and I am going to have it hauled away and impounded. Won't take many days storage to eat up a piece of junk like that."

Across the street, Lorena is coming out of the funeral home well pleased. Her flowers are prominent, and the corpse looks nice. The woman setting up the guest registry for the Visitation as Lorena arrived turned out to be a high school basketball teammate, and after a decent exchange on the subject of the just departed, she and Lorena have talked at good humor-restoring length about victories Lorena thought no one remembered but herself. Now Lorena looks across the street and sees her cousin Tricks in front of her brother-in-law's shop. She has rehearsed what she intends to say to Tricks, and Ruth's flyers are in her pocketbook. Her sandals slap across the street.

The fourth man in front of Meece's Sanitary Barbershop is a stranger to Lorena, and after one glance, that is all right with her. She notes curiously, as she gets within hearing distance of the men, that none of them seems to be speaking. Had to stop telling dirty stories because of her showing up, she bets. She could teach them a few; she smiles. Then she sees the dragon on Clint's arm.

Lorena has read Albert's flyer closely. She remembers that the suspect had curly hair, and that his car was an old blue Chevrolet. She stares at Clint, who scowls back. "What's your name?" she asks in a tone of accusing wonder. "You're Clint Penn, aren't you?" In a moment, Clint has kicked Tricks in the groin and bolted.

Almost before Tricks can breathe again, a tree root that has broken through the pavement in front of Donnie's luncheonette trips Clint and drops him on his face. Before he can rise, Walleye is on him. Tricks isn't far behind.

Lorena feels a need to sit down, and does so on the pavement. Tricks, putting the cuffs on Clint, hears her shrill demand: *"Where does he live?"*

Of all things, Trick thinks. *Where does he live? —* as if that were the first question Tricks needs to consider. Hysteria, Tricks has observed before, affects people in ways you'd never figure.

⇜61⇝

{Lang

When Lang wakens he is sweaty, stiff-necked, and electrified. He has heard voices.

These are the first voices besides Clint's that Lang has heard since Clint turned his car radio off that day. He sits up to prove he isn't dreaming.

Two boys are coming up the hill. Lang's mouth opens and in his mind he hears Clint saying, *When somebody else is talking, you're the one learning.* Clint used to tell him that all the time, before Lang caught on. One of the approaching boys is much bigger than Lang, the other no smaller. Lang's mouth closes, and though his heart is pounding like a post driver, he waits for the boys to see him, waits for them to say the first word.

The taller boy—he's as tall as Clint, but very skinny—carries a hoe, and from its narrow blade, Lang knows what is in the sack that swings from the strap across that bony shoulder. The younger boy carries a pronged stick. They are jumping the ginseng season, Lang thinks scornfully. His scorn turns to malice as he imagines Clint's face should they find Clint's planting.

When the pair see Lang, they stop in their tracks. Lang stares back.

They are wearing overalls, the younger boy's a size too big, the legs rolled up. His shoes have burst their side stitches. Neither boy wears socks or shirt. Their faces are sharp and brown as deer. Lang sees the taller boy's eyes narrow, his Adam's-apple move, and he senses that he is about to be challenged. "I know where there's a whole big patch of that 'ere sang," he says.

~≈62≈~   {Albert

It's Albert's birthday; his mother is expecting him to supper. His sister Maggie and her husband and children will be there, each child with a gift for Albert that Maggie has bought and wrapped, besides her own. Marcus is in Washington this week, but Jakba will be driving over. Albert doesn't look forward to thanking Jakba, as he must certainly do, for the introduction to Etta Hollamon that ultimately netted him this morning's column on Clint Penn. He remembers Jakba's displeasure at his early departure from her apartment that night, and so will she.

The exchange with Jakba, when it comes, will be merely uncomfortable; telephoning his mother that he isn't coming is going to be painful. Albert doesn't stop to do it before heading out the door. He will call her from his car.

Traffic isn't heavy, for a Monday afternoon. Half an hour out of Paris, Albert is making good time east on the Mountain Parkway. Too good, he realizes, letting up on the accelerator, which he had not been conscious of urging. He can't help the feeling—instinctive? reflexive? superstitious?—that five minutes makes a mortal difference. He knows better. He knows that after two months, minutes are what his mother would call "neither here nor there." At night, Albert still dreams vivid dreams of taking Lang Brough home to his parents, but he has stopped permitting his daydreams this luxury. Now, driving, the glass-magnified sun hot on the back of his neck, he finds he can't stop the scenes of Lang on the point of death that project themselves in his mind, a death which Albert can forestall if he gets there in five minutes; six will be too late. Albert glances at his speedometer and lets up on his foot.

Approaching the Turnbull exit, the traffic up ahead slows. The steady stream in which Albert has been flowing so smoothly begins to coagulate, then clots. Heavy morning rain has caused a rockslide.

Albert curses and kills the ignition. Immediately he misses the air conditioning, but he's not going to risk overheating his engine. The state police have called in the situation to the road department, who have sent one rubber-tired front end loader. Like ants stealing sugar a crystal at a time, it is methodically clearing away the rocks that block both lanes east. Hours, this will take hours.

Ahead of Albert, a car pulls out of the left-hand lane, splashes across the median, and heads back west, presumably toward the nearest exit and a lesser road east. Albert has been considering the same maneuver. As he is weighing the relative merits of a wait on the Parkway versus no wait and a problematic, greatly inferior substitute, a second car pulls onto the swale. A minute later it is hopelessly bogged down in mud. The driver lays his forehead on his steering wheel. Albert decides to wait. He reaches for the granola bar he is careful always to have in his glove compartment. He isn't hungry, in fact his guts are a knot, but chewing eases his tension. He reminds himself that he is not rushing to snatch Lang Brough dripping out of the currents of death, but to make inquiries about a suspect who may not have set foot in Wolfe County for four years, who may in any case have no connection with Lang Brough whatsoever. His gut seems to think it knows better. The minutes go by.

Dusk comes early to valley towns like Catesby, but Albert beats sundown to the police station. Chief Garvis Winslow is seated at his desk facing the door; his expression tells Albert that whatever Albert wants, Garvis wishes he didn't. At a desk across the room from Garvis's, also facing the door, a young woman is sprinkling a computer keyboard with rapid fingers. The young man lounging against the counter in front of her desk stares at Albert. Albert tells himself that a white stranger in Catesby also would be stared at, and introduces himself to Garvis Winslow. The young woman has never looked up.

On Garvis's desk are a just-opened bottle of Diet Coke and an untorn packet of saltines. "You're lucky you found us here," he tells Albert. "Somebody over to Campton got the idea they needed some more damn paperwork out of us, and Birta and I had to stay late. They don't let you off something else when they give you something new to do."

The desultory whirling of the wooden ceiling fan faintly stirs half a dozen black-studded fly strips; the loose corner of one of the WANTED broadsides flicks against the wall, steady as a dripping faucet. Albert tells Garvis his business.

"There used to be a mess of Ward boys, lived in a cabin not so far from Catesby," Garvis says, "but nobody lives there now. The old man was a moonshiner; don't have many of those, anymore. He died in the pen; got in a fight. Then his wife, she died, and the children, they scattered."

"I'd like to see the cabin," Albert says.

Garvis laughs. "You'll never find it. I'll get one of the boys to take you up there. Haynie'll take you, in the morning." Haynie is the young man waiting for the young woman, who is Garvis's niece and Haynie's wife. Garvis introduces him to Albert.

"I'd like to go tonight," Albert says.

The young woman at last raises her gaze from her keyboard; she and her husband and uncle look at each other. This Bluegrass city man has no conception of what he's suggesting.

"Well, now," Garvis begins. The abrupt, demanding signal of Albert's telephone gives him at least a temporary reprieve. He needs it, to consider how politely but surely to convince this brother lawman that neither laziness nor cowardice is responsible for his unwillingness to try to visit the Wards' cabin after dark, that the idea is downright comically impractical, if not impossible. *Unprofessional:* that's the word he'll use. To attempt such a visit before dawn would be *unprofessional.*

Long habit and firm self-discipline keep Albert's voice neutral as he answers his phone, but he is more than annoyed. There can be no business as important to him at the moment as the business he's about. Whatever his caller wants, Albert is going to refer him to somebody else.

"This is Lorena Snyder, Lt. Blount!" Albert's caller is almost shouting. *Fayette County farm manager's wife,* Albert remembers; *Mrs. Brough's friend.* Birta's fingers are tapping again. Her husband has tactfully turned his back to give Albert at least the illusion of privacy for his call. Garvis has bent his head over his papers with the same courtesy. Actually, Garvis is not reading, but planning the morning. He will go along himself, to make clear to Lt. Blount that his department is cooperative.

Lorena has given Albert's flyer to Tricks and told him who Clint surely must be, but she isn't waiting for Tricks, whose hands for the moment are full. "They've got the man you're looking for in jail here!" she tells Albert.

Clint is refusing to speak a word.

Lorena's excitement shows only in that her answers to Albert's queries are almost painfully loud: these answers are accurate and concise.

Albert asks a last question, thanks Lorena, and hangs up. He can't see that his face has turned the color of blanched liver. His voice, when he turns to Garvis, is perfectly steady. "Apparently my suspect has just been arrested in Cotes," he tells Garvis. "I'd better get over there."

The clicking of the keyboard has stopped. Garvis stands up. "The quickest way is a little bit complicated," he tells Albert. "It's not far, but it can be confusing if you're not from around here. I'll get my car and you can just follow me."

Albert wipes his palms on his pants and takes a first step toward the street door, which has opened while Garvis was speaking. The door bangs shut again behind three boys. Birta glances at the boys and returns her attention to her work. She doesn't expect to deal with them, Albert concludes; he looks anxiously back at Garvis, who apparently does.

Two of the boys are dark, overalled, shirtless. They have stopped just inside the room and remained there, standing with their backs to the wall. The third boy, who is fair, wears a shirt but is barefoot. He has been crying. He limps across the room toward Garvis, ignoring Albert and the couple at the end of the counter.

Garvis has stopped where he is, his head inclined toward the limping boy. Albert has to clench his teeth to stop himself from suggesting that Garvis tend to these children later.

The boy's eyes are dry now; they burn out of a face streaked the colors of parched fields. His lips are cracked, his hair and clothes ragged. When he places both hands on Garvis's desk, Albert sees that they are crisscrossed with dried scratches. Suddenly Albert ceases to blink or swallow or breathe.

Albert has never seen Lang Brough, just a dining room table half covered with pictures of him, neatly trimmed, rosy-cheeked and beaming.

This boy supports his weight on small black-nailed hands as he leans forward, glaring at Garvis. His voice is high and startlingly loud. "My name is Langdon Courtonne Brough," he says, "and I'm supposed to live in Bourbon County. I'm not even supposed to be here!"

Albert's blood seems not to be reaching his elbows, and for a moment his mouth is too dry to speak.

Lang has never heard of Albert Blount. This face that Albert has seen in his dreams for two months looks up at Albert's face with total lack of recognition, with an expression somewhere between disinterest and hostility. Albert swallows at last as he takes that in.

⁓⤸63⤹⁓ {Ruth

Sunset has barely faded when Grove, having cut short his day's work so as to hurry to his lightning-stricken farm, turns into its drive. He is just shutting off his engine in front of his roofless barn when the telephone in the tack room begins to ring, and Ruth beats him to it. Eventually he remembers the instrument in his car, but he can't bear to let go of Ruth, so they continue to crowd over the one receiver, laughing and crying and repeating even the questions whose answers they have both been able to hear, because they cannot hear those answers often enough.

In the months to come, Ruth and the therapist to whom she will take Lang will worry that Lang feels guilt over what they cannot believe didn't happen during his two month stay with Clint. They mistake his denials for shame. Lang will be a father himself before he confesses to his mother that his greatest shame that terrible year was at having burst into tears the moment he heard her voice. The men and woman in the room might have vanished. Not even the presence of the Selden boys stopped him. (Kyle, the one his size, gawked; the big one, Swango, turned tactfully away.) He sobbed "Mother!" and "Mother!" and "Mother!" until his father took the receiver out of her hand and told him that one of the mares he had led to pasture his last morning at home had produced a colt and, "We've been waiting for you to come on home and name him." Lang had just two hours to come up with a name, his father told him, before they would be there and demand it of him.

Then Lang stopped crying and wiped his face with his arm, and realized while doing so that he was remembering both his parents' faces, very clearly.

⟿64⟾   {Postscript, Ruth

"To hell with the seat belt law!" his father growled. So he slept between us, his body heavy as a water-soaked log, very nearly all the way home. Then sight of our smoldering barn sent him into hysterics. "You told me Clint was in jail!" he screamed. We had forgotten to tell him about the lightning. That barn once seen, we could not persuade him that Clint was indeed locked up and the mares and foals safe, until we were able to show him newspaper headlines and photographs.

My parents flew up to see him immediately. Grove's also couldn't wait, so I had them all to cook for, the same three days. Jake says it was good for me. Jake's probably right. Kept me too busy to become the slightest bit annoyed with one single thing said by either grandmother. They all spoiled him (and Tad and Joanna) extravagantly, setting a standard impossible for Grove and me to approach.

I find I don't mind that at all either; indeed, let's face it, I haven't started minding much of anything yet.

The therapist says he is going to be all right.

"Take things a day at a time," Grove says. "The main thing is, we're all together." Surely he must know where that comment instantly directs my thoughts. Yes, he knows; Grove should not be underestimated. He is overlooking no chance to reaffirm his commitment. This is fine, but I don't look at him, won't be caught seeming grateful.

For *him*. For our son, immeasurable gratitude, boundless gratitude. For the smell of his hot hair; for the feel of his bones under my hand that reaches for him every time I walk past him; for the noise he makes eating.

He eats voraciously, as much as Tad. Except for ham, which he won't touch.

The therapist says he is going to be all right.

And what about us?

I took Mother for a drive, just the two of us, when all the grandparents were here in June. "I can't advise you," Mother said. It's a mistake for anybody to advise anyone in a case like this. Nobody who asks for advice tells everything. Things are held back, for lack of time if for no other reason. (Usually, there are other reasons.) Based on what you're told, you can give the best advice in the world and have it be utterly worthless to your listener, because of the things she hasn't told you and isn't going to tell you. No one knows all that's happened to anyone else and no one knows what's going to happen tomorrow or ten years from now. How can I know what course will best serve *you*, honey. And that's what I care about!

"I can tell you what my experience has been and I'm happy if you an make use of it.

"There was a young woman in Copenhagen, that year your father spent the spring and summer at the Royal Academy. She was an architecture student, a graduate student.

"We had decided I shouldn't go with your father to Denmark, because of you children. You were barely five; Langdon was in school.... It was a joint decision. She was very beautiful, and she was there, and she could talk to him, listen to him usefully, not just lovingly like me. They could discuss his work, his ideas....

"It doesn't matter how I found out. Not from him. By the time he realized that I had known, she was married and sending us a birth announcement. He had been over it for years. So far as I know. And I was pretty much over it too.

"I think you grew up believing that your father and I were happy together, and that was true. And when Langdon was killed, I would have died if I hadn't had your father beside me.

"That's all I can tell you."

Mother wouldn't even have had to move out of her house. Her two children were serene, surrounded by cousins and many life-long friends.

Relatively serene. And if my bedwetting reaction to my father's absence was enough to give my mother pause before she told my father where he could go with what Lorena would call his *leftover seed,* what does that say to me now?

Lang is in a fragile state. Joanna seems sturdy, but who knows what she has understood, or misunderstood? Who knows when the bill will come due? These children need a loving home.

Assume a virtue if you have it not was never my favorite of my mother's maxims. In this case, that would mean *Pretend you forgive him, for the children's sake. Pretend you still love him.*

The truth is, I do love him. I can't imagine sex with anyone else. I do forgive him (most of the time; sometimes Lucille boils up, and I must spit or swallow hard, but I'm getting better at swallowing).

But I'm keeping my powder dry. I've bought a computer so I can put my reading lessons on disks. Lang is teaching me how. It's good for us both, the therapist says.

Clint's trial is set for October fourth. We are doing what we can to prepare Lang for that ordeal. The jury convicting Clint will also determine his sentence. They will choose something between thirty years and life, Albert predicts. If thirty years, then Lang will be nineteen before Clint is eligible for parole. Joanna, however, would be only fifteen, and the baby, just the age that Lang is now. And there's always the barn.... But Clint will not get parole in ten years, Albert says. I hope he's right.

The law wouldn't let Albert share any part of the reward from *Crime Stoppers.* Neither may we give him anything, not even a pair of gloves. At my request, he brought Etta Hollamon to dinner, the sharp (in both senses) young woman who wrote the column that he insists broke the case. I didn't sense that they were or would become a couple. I wish Albert would marry; he is an angel with children.

Ours are settling down. School is going to start before Lang's foot is healed enough to go swimming again, I'm afraid. Horseshoe pitching also poses problems, and the pond needs restocking before anyone can fish. I broke down and sought Norma Lee's advice about computer games. Dear Norma Lee is seeing to it that Breck is here almost as much as last summer, which is good of her, because Lang is thin-skinned, moody; not precisely the friend Breck remembers.

He is also quieter. He's taken to telling Joanna that anytime she's talking, it's the other guy who's learning. Joanna's euphoria over his return of course wore off, but she's so happy about the room we're adding to the house, which she will share with the baby, that she's hard to dampen. If I'm as sleepy this time around as I was the last two, I'll benefit from some time off from her, so she is also glorying in the promise of kindergarten. Once her preening might have irritated Lang, but he has more patience with her than before.

With Tad he has less; Tad can't count on him to follow blindly anymore. Can Grove and I? It seems to me that I see him considering what we say, then keeping to himself what he's decided to think about it. "It's normal, Ruth," Grove says. "All boys grow up."

Then I turn my head quickly, feeling that I am about to cry, because this is a boy who almost didn't.

ACKNOWLEDGMENTS

Portions of this work first appeared in *Missouri Review, Southwest Review, TriQuarterly* (a publication of Northwestern University), *In Memory's Field* (Frankfort Arts Foundation, 1998), and *Choice Magazine Listening*.

I am indebted to the Kentucky Arts Council for their 1992 Al Smith Fellowship, which facilitated the writing of this manuscript. I am obliged for the cheerful and marvelously knowledgeable help of Doris Waren and Cathie Schenck of the Keeneland Library and Marilyn Dungan, Susan Eads and Anne Rogers of the Paris-Bourbon County Public Library. I am further obliged to Reginald Gibbons and Ann Hellie for their valuable criticism of Wolfe County portions, and to Carrol Carr, Secretary to the General Manager of Brookside Farm; Dr. Shirley Emerson, Professor of Counseling, University of Nevada, Las Vegas; and my friends Roberta Guthrie, Helen Haukeness, Marcia Hurlow, Cynthia King, Katherine Mears, and Catesby Simpson for their careful reading of early manuscript and for the helpful suggestions each made. I owe particular thanks to Harriet P. McDougal's stern eye for the implausible. Finally, I greatly appreciate the expert counsel of Detective Jeffrey Jett, Kentucky State Police; Dr. John Bizzack, Commissioner, Department of Criminal Justice Training, Justice Cabinet, Commonwealth of Kentucky; J.C.Rankin of the Kentucky Parole Board; James L. Ferrell, M.D.; Sgt. George T. Wells, USAF (Ret.); Pastor Sharon B. Fields, Director, Leadership and Cultural Diversity Office, Midway College; Richard A. Derrickson, Postmaster, Paris, KY; Billy Profitt, of Wolfe and Bourbon Counties; Millard Dryden, late Chief of the Bourbon County Fire Department; David D. O'Neal, D.V.M.; Gordon E. Layton, D.V.M.; Betty Ann Sharp, Bourbon County Deputy Clerk; Charles A. Harris, Manager of the former South Central Bell Paris Office; and my husband, from whom I have learned anything I know about thoroughbreds.

The spiritual quoted is one my late mother used to sing. I have never heard it sung by anyone else, nor have I been able to find it printed anywhere.

M. B. S.

This book has been set in

Stempel Garamond on a Macintosh Quadra 650

using QuarkXPress software. Printing

& binding by Thomson-Shore, Inc.

in an edition of 2,000 copies

on acid-free paper.